He

to the Darkness . . .

LeVar drew in a deep breath and exh
His whole body shook with uncontro
ors. It was the first time he ever was
and he didn't like the feeling. The gu
from his fingers, numb from the recoil.

That mother had been a genuine, absolute psycho,
LeVar thought. "He done scared me white," said
LeVar, trying to laugh away the shakes. And then
the laughter turned to screams.

On the far side of the room, the Dark Man rose to
his feet. The gun blasts had blown away much of
his coat and knocked off his hat, but he seemed
otherwise unharmed. For a bare instant, LeVar
caught a glimpse of a face that was not a face—a
flat, featureless blank, unbroken by nose or mouth,
like a pane of dark frosted glass. Eyes burning like
red coals glared at LeVar with unblinking intensity. In one hand, the giant clutched a meat
cleaver. With his other hand, he reached out and
extinguished the candle.

"My turn," said the Dark Man . . .

THE
BLACK
LODGE

ROBERT
WEINBERG

POCKET BOOKS

New York   London   Toronto   Sydney   Tokyo   Singapore

An *Original* Publication of POCKET BOOKS

POCKET BOOKS, a division of Simon & Schuster Inc.
1230 Avenue of the Americas, New York, NY 10020

ISBN: 0-671-70108-8

First Pocket Books printing November 1991

10 9 8 7 6 5 4 3 2 1

POCKET and colophon are registered trademarks of
of Simon & Schuster Inc.

Cover art by David Fishman

Printed in the U.S.A.

To Peter M. Spizzirri—
"Opener of the Way"

To attain the *sanctum regnum*, in other words, the knowledge and power of the magi, there are four indispensable conditions . . . TO KNOW, TO DARE, TO WILL, *TO KEEP SILENCE* . . .

—Eliphas Levi,
  The Doctrine and Ritual of Magic

THE BLACK LODGE

1

LeVar Bailey felt good—*real* good.

Softly humming a bit of soul music, he slowly stepped out from the doorway of the abandoned barbershop on the corner of Seventeenth and State. Swinging his head from side to side, he carefully checked the area for suspicious characters. No other figure stirred in the dim amber glow cast by the solitary streetlight located only a few feet away. LeVar grunted his approval. He liked empty streets when he visited his "main base."

He set off at a brisk clip, his studded leather boots beating a sharp tattoo on the broken sidewalk. From time to time, he swept the area with quick, sharp glances. He didn't expect any trouble, but years of experience in this deadly business had taught him the value of staying alert.

Fortunately, this part of Chicago's South Side resembled a bombed-out wasteland. Only a few ramshackle buildings broke the stretch of weed infested lots. There wasn't a bus stop within ten blocks. No reason to exit here. Surrounded by major expressways and through streets, this section of the once "great street" saw little traffic after the evening rush hour.

Normally, LeVar made two trips a night to his stash

hidden deep inside the old railroad building. There he
deposited the loot, his "bank," that he collected during
the first part of the evening and broke out a new supply
of crack for his anxious customers. Tonight, he suspected, he might make three visits, maybe even four, to
satisfy the demand on the street. The geeks wanted the
stuff bad and he was their main man.

Up ahead, music bellowed from the jukebox in Christy's tavern. LeVar sucked in several deep breaths, preparing himself for the unlikely chance a violent drunk
might try something stupid.

He prided himself on being ready for anything. These
days, it never hurt to be too careful. Stuffed inside the
front of his shirt, hidden by the heavy folds of the thick
leather jacket he wore even during the hottest days, was
nearly a thousand dollars in small bills.

Not even a bug stirred inside the tavern as he casually
strolled past the open doorway. The regular group of
grizzled old black men sat huddled at the bar, nursing
their beers and shots, impervious to the blaring music
that surrounded them. No one who valued his hearing
drank at Christy's. Crazy Charlie, the latest owner of
the place, was nearly deaf and played the jukebox twice
as loud as necessary. Everyone within a mile radius of
the place knew when the saloon was open for business.

Complaints about the noise did little good. No politi-
cian dared criticize Christy's. Nearly a hundred years
old, the tavern was a Chicago landmark. Al Capone had
been a regular. So had Mayor Anton Cermak. The bar
had survived wars, the Depression, Prohibition and several recessions. A prominent newspaper columnist once
called Christy's the last holdout of Chicago's colorful
past. Most everyone else in Chicago, including LeVar,
considered the dump a major eyesore long overdue for
demolishing.

Breathing a sigh of relief, LeVar walked a little faster.
An early trace of summer weather embraced Chicago
this late April evening, holding temperatures to the low
seventies. Inside his silk shirt, soiled bills clung to his
skin like leeches. Little beads of sweat trickled down

his back, adding to his discomfort. Once he made it inside the warehouse, he could strip off his coat, open his shirt and bundle up the cash. Until then, the money stayed in place, sweat or no sweat.

A thin trace of fog drifted across the street, rolling in from Lake Michigan. Thick clouds covered the moon and stars. Only the glow from the downtown city lights broke up the darkness on the street.

Up ahead, LeVar spotted the Fifteenth Street viaduct. His pace quickened.

"Hey, boy—where you running?"

The question cut the night air like a knife. For an instant, LeVar hovered on the edge of panic. Then reason took over. Stickup boys never asked questions. Only cops.

Calming himself, he turned to a police car at the curb. The blare of the jukebox had covered the approach of the vehicle. Two policemen sat inside the roller, staring at him. The one by the window, a big black man with a scruffy thin mustache and narrow, suspicious eyes, held a flashlight pointed directly at LeVar's face.

The cop kept the bright light in LeVar's eyes, turning everything into a white blur. LeVar suspected the officer held a burner, probably one of those big .357 Specials, pointed right at him just below the window, waiting for any sort of suspicious movement. The "Robocops" played tough in this neighborhood. Time for him to turn innocent, LeVar thought.

At five ten and a hundred and fifty pounds, LeVar cut less than an imposing figure. Slender and thin boned, he looked like a strong wind could blow him away. He was twenty-two, but his youthful features and the Cubs baseball cap he wore took five years off his age. Unlike most of his friends, he wore no earrings, gold chains or wrist bands. LeVar looked the very model of an innocent teenager, an image he worked hard to cultivate.

"Where you goin', kid?" asked the policeman for a second time. Now, having gotten a good look at LeVar, the officer sounded more bored than suspicious.

"I'm meeting my woman downtown, bro," answered

LeVar, his high-pitched voice sounding slightly ridiculous. He recited the lines he'd practiced a hundred times. "I'm late already."

The policeman snorted in disbelief but remained seated in his car. "Walking to the Loop down State Street? Not many people crazy enough to do that anymore. You live around here, boy?"

"Yes, sir. I live at the Temple on Twenty-Second Street." He let just a little of the annoyance he felt creep into his voice. "Don't got no money for the El, sir. Gonna be late for my woman if I don't hurry."

"The Temple? You belong to that Children of Danballah organization that's been on the news so much lately?"

"Yes, sir," said LeVar, proudly, pulling out his Temple ID card. He waved it at the squad car.

The big cop shrugged his shoulders and then shut off the spotlight. "These are mean streets, boy. People 'round here will break your legs for pocket change. No more midnight strolls after this one. You borrow some money from 'your woman' and take the El back to your Temple tonight." The officer chuckled, a deep throaty sound. "Unless, of course, you get lucky and spend the night."

"Yes sir, yes sir," said LeVar with a laugh. He nodded pleasantly to the police as the car rumbled away. "Sure got to be careful around here, sir. Gotta watch out for all those nasty dope dealers makin' the rounds, *sir*."

Sucking in a deep breath, LeVar continued down the street. The encounter with the Rollers left him shaken but equally elated. The fools never once suspected him of being anything more than he claimed. They stayed clear of Danballah's flock. The last time they had hassled one of the Disciples, the story had made the national news. The word was out on the street. Leave the Children alone.

"Religious per-se-cu-tion," said LeVar, letting the words roll slowly off his tongue, trying to sound solemn but not succeeding. The Bocar manipulated the media with a skill born from years of political confrontation.

Clout meant everything in Chicago. And these days, clout depended almost entirely on TV exposure. The local news broadcasts always gave the most air time to the most dramatic political figures. What they said didn't matter—it was *how* they said it.

The cameras loved the Bocar and he knew it. He spoke with a passion and fire. No one dared challenge him publicly—not the mayor, not the district attorney, and definitely not the cops on the beat.

Meanwhile, the Children of Danballah provided a perfect cover for dope dealing. The organization offered a safe base of operations, a steady source of crack and a perfect alibi when necessary. All the Bocar demanded in return was a thousand off the top of every night's take.

Sometimes LeVar barely managed to break even. Crack was cheap and plentiful these days. There was no such thing as customer loyalty among the mainliners. The geeks came to town looking for action. If you missed connections, they found another hustler.

From his office in the doorway of the abandoned barbershop, LeVar ran his operation much like a news vendor selling newspapers in the Loop. The geeks drove up in their big cars, leaning on their horn for some action. A quick dash into the street, an exchange of money for crack, and the deal was made—all in a few seconds.

Like any high-profit business, there were risks involved. Sometimes the geek turned out to be an undercover cop, looking to make a quick bust. Or it could be a hotshot punk, a "stickup boy," looking for an easy mark. The dangers came with the territory.

Tonight, LeVar had scored big with some wealthy teenagers from the 'burbs. They had bought out the store, necessitating this early run for more Rock. Not that LeVar minded. Twenty bucks more and he started flying. With the whole evening ahead of him, he could easily return to the Temple with a pocketful of C-notes.

He ran as fast as he could through the Fifteenth Street

viaduct, crossing the wide street as he did so. The underpass spooked him, especially at night. It was too dark in the center and he disliked the thought of traffic over his head. He never felt safe until he reached the other side.

Suddenly, as he took his first step onto the dirt path leading through the tangled underbrush, LeVar knew he was not alone on the street. Heavy footsteps echoed in the tunnel—sounds coming from the dark underpass.

LeVar stopped moving, waiting cautiously to see who emerged from the blackness. The sounds grew louder and louder, setting his body trembling. The steps were slow and methodical—unhurried and steady even through the absolute blackness of the viaduct. A patch of darkness darker than the night, emerged from the underpass—a giant figure, nearly seven feet tall, striding into the dim light of the city. A black blot of a man with vast shoulders and gorillalike arms. The stranger looked about for a moment, as if getting oriented, and then, spotting LeVar, started toward him.

Running seemed futile. Gripped by a nameless dread, LeVar could only stand and wait as the giant approached. Little by little, as the man drew closer, LeVar realized that the stranger was no supernatural bogey but an ordinary man the size of a professional football lineman. The darkness exaggerated his size and menace. Still, the man's actual appearance did nothing to alleviate LeVar's worst fears.

The Dark Man. The name came unbidden into LeVar's thoughts as he awaited the stranger. The giant wore only black—pitch-black garments that covered him from head to toe. No skin showed. The Dark Man—he belonged to the night, to the darkness.

A heavy black overcoat, buttoned tight across his massive chest, covered the man from neck to ankle. Odd garb for such a warm evening, but LeVar never thought to question. A thick wool scarf snaked around the giant's upturned collar, shielding most of his lower face. An oversize, wide-brimmed cowboy hat sat on his head, pulled down tight to shade his features. Leather gloves covered huge hands with fingers the size of sausages. Old-fashioned work boots, steel tipped and laced up the ankle, completed the picture.

"What's goin' down, bro?" said LeVar, summoning up courage he never knew he possessed.

"I've been looking for you, LeVar," answered the Dark Man, with a voice as smooth as honey. "I've been looking for you all night. You've got what I need, and I'm willing to pay good money for it."

"Yeah," said LeVar, wondering how the Dark Man knew his name. He was suddenly quite conscious of all the money stuffed inside his shirt. "What you talkin' 'bout, dude? Who done told you 'bout me?"

"Friends, LeVar, friends," said the giant, casually reaching into the pocket of his overcoat.

LeVar tensed, expecting the man to pull out a gun or a police badge. Instead, his hand emerged holding a crumpled bill. He offered it to LeVar.

"Go ahead, take it," said the Dark Man, with a laugh. "A gift to you with my compliments. Consider it the first payment in a long and lasting relationship. Go ahead," he urged, "it won't bite."

Tentatively, still fearful of the stranger's huge bulk, LeVar reached for the money. With a lunge, he grabbed the bill and immediately jumped back, out of the Dark Man's reach. The giant remained stationary, chuckling softly. LeVar felt like a fool.

He looked at the bill then looked again. "A *C-note*. You just givin' me this? What kinda jive you handin' out, man?"

"No jive," said the Dark Man. He lowered his voice to a whisper. "Just cold cash for fine coke—for crack."

"I got the best rock around," said LeVar, the juices starting to flow. The Dark Man was talking his language now. "Stuff comes straight from Bolivia to Chicago, with no stops in between. You hear what I'm saying—straight from Bolivia."

"The best cocaine in the world," said the Dark Man, nodding his head in agreement. "I'll buy all the crack you've got. Money's no object."

LeVar couldn't believe what he was hearing. No matter what the price these days, his customers demanded a break. Crack was cheap on the street and competition was tough.

"Twenty bucks a hit?" he said cautiously, ready to drop the price immediately if the Dark Man protested.

"Deal," replied the stranger without hesitation. "On one condition. I need the stuff tonight. *Now.*"

LeVar paused only for a second. He disliked revealing the location of his stash, but this was big money. He fretted that if he let the Dark Man out of his sight, even for a few minutes, the stranger might have a change of heart, or the cops might come cruising back this way and scare him off, or a hundred other disasters might occur.

Besides, LeVar kept a surprise in with his stash in case anyone ever tried any tricks. If the Dark Man planned a sharp move, LeVar would have the last laugh. The comforting thought of his "burner" hidden away with his crack swept away any remaining jitters.

"Follow me," said LeVar, "and stay close. No lights inside but I know the way."

The interior of the old railroad warehouse was a shambles of rotted wood and rusted metal. Parts of the flat roof had collapsed from the weight of snowstorms over the years. Smashed beams and jagged bits of shingles littered the floor. The gaping holes in the ceiling let in enough light for LeVar to make his way through the wreckage.

LeVar knew every nook and cranny of the deserted building. The railroad had gone bankrupt back in the early 1960s. Changing demographics and the urban decay of the inner city made potential buyers wary of the property. The city aggravated the situation by demanding any purchaser pay back taxes on the land and building as well. So for over twenty years, the lot remained unused and the old structures fell into ruin.

Only children were foolish enough to enter the deserted warehouse. Adults knew better. For a decade, the huge old railroad barn served as shelter for teenage runaways from all over Chicago. Then flower power ended and gang warfare hit the ghetto. After several rapes and two murders took place in the isolated depths of the building, the street people abandoned the warehouse. Even the bag ladies and winos avoided the place. It was left free and clear for the pushers and dope dealers.

"Just a little farther, just a little farther," LeVar repeated again and again as they wove their way past mounds of rubble. The Dark Man remained silent.

LeVar's main base was the remains of a small ten-foot square modular office located at the rear of the warehouse.

"Welcome to the candy store," LeVar said proudly, pulling open the door to the room and entering. The Dark Man followed, ducking his head to get through the doorway.

The only piece of furniture in the room was a broken-down old desk, with a huge multicolored candle resting at its center. LeVar lit it with his Zippo. The melting wax sent strange shadows scurrying across the walls. "I found the candle here when I discovered this place," said LeVar. "Probably left over from some honkie orgy. You want the crack?"

Not waiting for an answer, LeVar pulled open the top drawer of the desk. Inside were nearly a hundred plastic Baggies, each containing a white, rocklike ball of pure cocaine—crack. In the rear of the drawer, rested an old .44 automatic—LeVar's "burner." Gently, LeVar placed his right hand on the butt of the gun. "How about some green, man?"

The Dark Man laughed, a low powerful sound like the rumble of distant thunder. "I don't need your poison, little man," he said in his honey-toned voice. "I came here to *slaughter* you."

The candle flickered and sputtered with the sounds of his words. Shadows grouped around the Dark Man, adding to his massive bulk, until he seemed to fill the entire back wall. Still chuckling, the giant reached for something inside his coat.

Not merely kill, but slaughter. The choice of words

frightened LeVar. He decided to put things back on the right track. "Enough bullshit jive," LeVar said, pulling the pistol out from the drawer and aiming it straight at the Dark Man's chest.

"Now the dumb nigger be holding the gun," said LeVar, grinning. The .44 remained steady in his hand. "Looks like the hijacker gets hijacked. Lay out the green. All of it, right now, or I blow you away. No one around to hear you scream."

"You misunderstand," said the Dark Man, in a pleasant, relaxed tone of voice. "I meant what I said. Drug dealers need to be taught a lesson. You're going to serve as my first example. First, I'll chop off your genitals. Next come your arms, then your legs. I'll leave your head till last, though I suspect you'll have died from shock or loss of blood long before I reach that stage."

Out of his coat the Dark Man pulled a huge meat cleaver. He took one slow step forward, lifting the butcher's blade up over his head.

"You crazy sonnafabitch!" screamed LeVar. He squeezed the trigger of the automatic and kept on squeezing. Gripped by fear, he kept on firing until all the chambers were empty. From only a few feet away, he couldn't miss.

The heavy slugs pounded into his assailant. The force of the bullets lifted the Dark Man off his feet and slammed him into the far wall. The small office filled with gunsmoke and the smell of burnt powder.

LeVar drew in a deep breath and exhaled slowly. His whole body shook with uncontrollable tremors. It was the first time he ever wasted anyone and he didn't like the feeling. The gun dropped from his fingers numb from the recoil.

That mother had been a genuine, absolute psycho, LeVar thought. "He done scared me white," said LeVar, trying to laugh away the shakes. And then the laughter turned to screams.

On the far side of the room, the Dark Man rose to his feet. The gun blasts had blown away much of his coat and knocked off his hat but he seemed otherwise unharmed. For a bare instant, LeVar caught a glimpse of a face that was not a face—a flat featureless blank, unbroken by nose or mouth, like a pane of dark frosted glass. Eyes burning like red coals glared at LeVar with unblinking intensity. In one hand, the giant still clutched the meat cleaver. With his other hand, he reached out and extinguished the candle.

"My turn," said the Dark Man.

2

It was a hell of a way to start Tuesday morning. Sid Taine looked down again at the neat stack of hundred dollar bills on his desk and then back up at his prospective client. "Twenty thousand dollars in cash, you said. For four days work?"

"That's right," replied Evangeline Caldwell, flicking an ash from her cigarillo onto the floor. For that kind of money, Sid forgave her lack of manners. "Half now, the rest when you complete the job. All I want you to do is find a man for me before Friday evening." She took a deep drag on the thin cigar. "One *particular* man."

She rested, half-sitting, half-standing, on the wide arm of the old-fashioned high-back chair that faced his desk. Wearing a smartly tailored red knit dress slit up the sides, she burned with a raw, nervous energy that evidenced itself in her every motion.

Taine reached out and picked up the cash. The bills felt cool and crisp. He ruffled the stack with his thumb. It was a lot of money for only a few days' work. "I need a little more information before I make up my mind. Who do you want me to find—husband, father, runaway child . . . lover?"

The young woman laughed, a harsh, cruel sound that

contrasted sharply with her casual beauty. "I keep track of my father by reading the papers. Harmon Sangmeister makes the society page every time he dates another floozy. The same applies to my wayward husband. They both like variety in their women.

"My mother and my older sister died in a boating accident twenty years ago. I barely remember what either of them looked like. Children I consider disgusting little monsters.

"As to lovers, *I leave them,* Mr. Taine. It's never the other way around."

"I'll bet," muttered Taine under his breath. Momentarily at a loss for words, he gazed out the windows that bordered the corner office. His suite, on the twentieth floor of the Acme Building, commanded an unobstructed view of Lake Michigan. Black storm clouds rumbled ominously off shore, darkening the morning sky.

"I merely offered some possibilities," said Taine, turning and looking Evangeline Caldwell directly in the eyes. "Why don't you fill in the blanks."

"Then you'll take the case?"

"I could use the money," said Taine. "But no deals until you give me all the details."

She hesitated for a moment, as if wrestling with some inner turmoil. Taine waited patiently. He knew the value of silence.

In the meantime, he unobtrusively studied his potential client. He rarely entertained such style. She looked like an advertisement from a fashion magazine.

He estimated her age around thirty. She stood a little over five foot five, but her narrow spiked heels added several inches to her height. Her bronze skin and shapely figure proclaimed her a health club regular. The designer dress she wore hugged her trim curves like a second skin. It was cut low across her full breasts, revealing enough to be considered rather daring. Her bright red lipstick and nail polish matched her outfit. Moussed and waxed, her light brunette hair crest in a Mohican-style "punk" haircut that was the rage among the wealthy young socialites of Chicago.

Taine thought it strange that she wore no jewelry—not even a wedding or engagement ring. Then his gaze fixed on a small white medallion pinned directly over her heart. The face of the brooch pictured a long red passion cross, set against a white background. But unlike the Crusader's emblem that it most closely resembled, this cross was reversed, with its long arm pointing upward, its transverse lowered. A green serpent coiled around the base of the cross.

Taine's mouth went very dry. He vaguely remembered that insignia from his studies, but could not place the reference immediately. He knew it symbolized the triumph of darkness over light, of evil over good.

"I assume anything I tell you is in . . . strictest confidence?" asked Evangeline Caldwell, finally coming to a decision.

"Consider it privileged information," said Taine. "No different than what you would tell a lawyer or a doctor."

"No one must know I hired you," she said nervously. "Over the past few years, I managed to save part of my household allowance in a safety deposit box unknown to my husband . . . and my father. This money comes from that source."

Taine again mentally noted the cryptic reference to her father. "I thought you wanted me to find someone? I stay strictly away from marital problems."

"My marriage need not concern you, Mr. Taine," said Evangeline Caldwell sharply. Then the fear crept back in her voice. "I merely want to emphasize that this investigation must be our secret."

"Sure, sure. No offense taken. You have my word of honor not to reveal your secrets. And despite how most people bandy that phrase about these days, when I give my word, I never break it."

She nodded. "So I gather. Your file described you as one of the few honest detectives in the city. That greatly influenced my decision."

Taine let slide her remark about his file. He felt sure she would reveal everything sooner or later. Mrs. Caldwell impressed him as the type that once she got started talking, would not be able to stop. He prompted her in that direction.

"I gather you found other reasons as well?"

"*Several* others," she said.

She reached for her purse resting on the chair. Doing so, she revealed a great deal more of her thighs and breasts. Taine doubted she was wearing any undergarments, and she definitely was not wearing a bra. He gulped and tried to keep his mind on the business at hand.

Mrs. Caldwell straightened, gripping a folded piece of paper in one hand. She waved it at the detective. "I copied this information out of my husband's file on you. He keeps detailed portfolios on people who interest him for one reason or another."

"Sounds perfectly normal to me," said Taine, a trace of sarcasm in his voice. "Your husband a Mafia capo or someone like that?"

"No, of course not. I'm married to Victor Caldwell, the commodities broker. I thought you realized that."

"Oh, that Caldwell," said Taine, not recognizing the name. He hated admitting ignorance about anything so he rarely did. "Why am I in his files? I don't handle cases involving stocks and bonds. And God knows, I can't afford them."

"I don't know. There must be a reason, though. Vincent never does anything without a reason."

She looked down at the sheet of paper. "Sidney Taine," she read, "Thirty-one years old, male, Caucasian. Six feet, two inches tall; weight, two hundred and fourteen pounds. No scars or distinguishing characteristics. Taine runs a private investigation agency from the Acme Building on Chicago's North Side. His one employee, Mary McConnell, serves as both secretary and researcher."

Mrs. Caldwell looked up at him. "Right so far?"

"Two hundred and eight pounds," said Taine quietly. "I've been on a diet."

"Taine only handles missing person cases. In the two years since he arrived in Chicago from San Francisco, he has brought to a satisfactory conclusion nearly ninety percent of his inquiries. Even allowing for some prejudice in his selection of assignments, this record defies statistical analysis. A recent newspaper article called Taine a 'modern psychic detective' because of his use of harmonic frequencies, crystals and other so-called New Age beliefs in his investigations."

Taine pushed himself up and out of his chair. A powerfully muscled man, he moved with the lithe grace of a jungle cat. Walking over to the window that directly faced the lake, he pulled back the curtains to get a better view of the approaching squall. Thunder flickered in the black clouds, which were now much closer to shore.

"Is that true?" said Mrs. Caldwell.

"What? The number of cases I've solved. I believe so. It never occurred to me—"

"No, no," Mrs. Caldwell interrupted, sounding annoyed. "Do you truly believe in psychic phenomena—in Black Magic?"

"By Black Magic, I assume you mean some force opposed to White Magic," said Taine slowly, turning back to face the woman. "Such terms mean nothing. Magic has no orientation. However," he continued, not giving her a chance to speak, "good and evil exist in this imperfect world of ours. Good and evil *men* make their magic black or white."

"You argue semantics," said Evangeline Caldwell, with a wave of a hand. "Now you know why I came to you for help. You never answered my original question. Will you help me or not?"

"Maybe. But not until you give me more details."

"Oh, all right," she said, angrily. "You men are all alike. Always obsessed with facts."

Blowing a smoke ring into the air, Mrs. Caldwell continued in a calmer tone. "I want you to find a man who calls himself Arelim. I know nothing about him other than both my father and my husband fear him. And they are not afraid of many people."

"Arelim," said Taine, repeating the name. "Now I know why you wanted a New Age detective. Not many

15

people would recognize that title. It comes from *The Kabbalah*. If I remember correctly, it's the designation for the Angel of Rigorous Ministry. Or, updating that title, the Avenging Angel."

"I never heard of that Kabbalah thing," said Evangeline Caldwell, looking around the room nervously. "I only heard the name when my husband mentioned it on the phone. But my father called him exactly that—the Angel of Vengeance. I must find him."

"I gather you can't just ask your husband where this gentleman lives?"

She laughed, a little hysterical now. "They don't even know I learned his name. Last week, I arrived home early from an appointment. I heard my husband yelling into the phone. Curious, I picked up an extension and eavesdropped.

"Victor was pleading with my father for assistance. Arelim threatened to interfere with a major business operation being run by my husband. Both men were very cautious about what they said, but I got the impression my father knew all of the details of the enterprise. One thing I can tell you. Victor sounded frightened— very, very frightened."

"Did your father agree to help?"

"Evidently Harmon owed Victor his cooperation. Again, they spoke in vague generalities. They both belonged to the same Lodge and membership required they work together. That convinced me that the old bastard feared this Arelim nearly as much as did my husband.

"You see, my father and Victor maintain cordial relations in public, but privately they despise each other. For them to join forces is incredible. Their hatred runs deeper than mere business rivalry."

Taking a deep breath, she continued. "Years ago, Victor seduced Harmon's mistress. She was living with my father at the time and had access to all of his records and files. For months, she served as a spy at the highest level of father's financial network. Andrea revealed major business secrets to Victor while retaining Harmon's full trust. Harmon lost millions before he finally discovered her treachery.

"Compounding the betrayal, Andrea moved in with Victor immediately after leaving my father. She made no secret which man she regarded as a better lover. The news hit the market like a bomb exploding. His colleagues on the Exchange ridiculed my father for months. The money he lost never bothered him. But he never forgave Victor for the embarrassment he suffered."

"And yet you married the same guy?"

"Victor offered me an escape from a pointless existence. Or so it seemed at the time. And it enraged Harmon to lose another woman to his worst enemy. In those days, it seemed a suitable way to pay back my father for years of neglect."

"I take it that relations are somewhat strained between the two of you?"

"You can put it that way. Harmon goes out of his way to cross Victor in their business dealings. But their battles all take place in the financial markets. Outside that arena, they remain in close contact because of their Lodge affiliation. Two or three times a year we dine together. At such occasions, father is polite but cold. He refuses to speak to me unless absolutely necessary.

"He never forgave his only living relative for marrying his worst enemy. The hatred I see reflected in his eyes frightens me. That is why I must find Arelim before he does."

"You think if you can find him first, that might change your father's opinion of you?"

"I don't give a damn about his opinion," said Evangeline, her face flaring red with suppressed fury. "He deserves every bit of suffering and bad fortune that comes his way. If Harmon fell overboard in shark-infested waters, I wouldn't throw him a life jacket. Instead, I'd laugh myself silly watching the sharks fight over his carcass. *I want to find Arelim for my own reasons.* They need not concern you."

"Sure," said Taine with a short laugh. "I'm just your hired flunky."

Taine dropped back into the swivel chair behind his desk. "Can you tell me anything else about this guy other than his name?"

"No. That was all I heard."

"You want me to find one man in a metropolitan area of six million people, with my only clues his name and the fact he scares your husband and your father? Lady, despite what you saw in that file, I'm not a magician."

"Arelim is."

"Huh. What do you mean?"

"Exactly what I say. Arelim is a black magician. That is what frightens Victor so much. Threats of violence never bother my husband. After years of double crossing, he routinely handles such matters. But the forces of sorcery change everything. That is why he needs my father's aid."

"Extending that chain of logic one step farther, Mrs. Caldwell, that implies—"

"Take it any way you want," she said sharply, rising abruptly from her chair. "Ten thousand in cash for accepting the case. Another ten thousand if you find Arelim before Friday evening."

"Why the Friday deadline?"

She shook her head. "I can't tell you that, either." She shuddered. "Just find him before then. My life depends on it. *My very soul depends on it.*"

"You could go to the police."

"Harmon Sangmeister is above the law," she said, as if stating the obvious. "He lives by his own rules. The police mean nothing to him. They serve as mere annoyances to someone of his wealth and power. You're the only one who can save me, Taine."

Suddenly angry, Taine tightly clenched one hand into a fist. He shook it as he spoke, as if punching out his words. *"No man is above the law.* There always comes a reckoning. I'll take your case. I dislike you depending so much on me, but I'll do my best. How do I reach you if I have something to report?"

She snuffed out her cigar against the bronze paperweight on his desk. "Let me worry about that. I'll keep in touch. Don't ever call me. The servants can't be trusted. They report my every movement to my husband."

"Then he'll know you consulted me this morning."

"I gave my chauffeur the slip. He thinks I'm at a charity bazaar in the Loop. I left by the rear exit and took a cab up here. After I leave, I'll return the same way. At those type of affairs, no one comments if you disappear for an hour or two."

"Sounds very civilized," said Taine, rising.

He circled the desk and helped her with her wrap.

"I make no promises on this job. Miracles usually take more than four days."

"You must not fail," she said, trembling again as she spoke. "My father hosts his Lodge for a mystic ceremony this Friday at midnight. They conduct these meetings once a year, always on the eve of May first. In the past few years, his second wife assisted him. But she died in an auto accident in November. Harmon expects me to take her place. He discussed the necessary preparations with Victor during that same phone conversation."

"Not exactly to your liking, I gather."

"I'm scared, Taine," she said, her face chalk white. "Something terribly wrong takes place at those celebrations. I'm no prude, that's for sure, but whatever goes on that evening is not just immoral. It's *evil*."

"Why not get out of town?"

"Harmon would find me and bring me back. No one crosses my father. You don't know his power. I do. He controls forces beyond belief. Believe me, my only chance is to stay and fight. And I can only do that if you find Arelim."

"I'll do my best," said Taine. He walked with her to the door to the outer office. "Call me tomorrow evening. Hopefully, I'll have something by then."

3

Alone in his office, Taine seated himself behind his desk and flipped on the intercom. "No calls, Mrs. McConnell," he said into the small box. "I want to be alone for the next hour or so."

"Yes sir, Mr. Taine," answered his assistant from the next room.

Taine smiled with satisfaction. Mrs. McConnell was the perfect "woman Friday." She never questioned any of his requests. They had worked together for nearly two years and still called each other by their last names. He knew nothing about her life outside of the office. They never socialized other than sharing a lunch at the restaurant at the foot of the Acme Building when business was slow. Even then, they chatted about the weather, about clients, and the fortunes of the Cubs. Personal life remained off-limits.

He guessed her age to be around forty, give or take a year or two. A slender short woman with jet black hair and green eyes, she dressed simply but well. She was an efficient and highly skilled secretary. More important, she was a talented researcher and investigator. Mrs. McConnell used a telephone like a master swordsman wielded a fine blade. She ferreted out obscure information from uncooperative sources with a surgeon's skill. Taine credited half his success to her expertise.

A wall switch turned on the overhead fan and air freshener. He couldn't concentrate with the strong odor of cigar smoke in his office. He shook his head in disgust, trying to understand why a beautiful woman poisoned herself with tobacco.

Pulling out his key ring, Taine unlocked the bottom drawer of his desk. Reaching in, he pulled out a worn

20

deck of tarot cards kept together by several rubber bands. One massive arm swept all the oddball clutter from the top of his desk onto the floor. Transferring the cards from one hand to the other, he flexed his fingers, getting them loose and supple.

Carefully, he removed the elastics and set the seventy-eight cards at the center of the empty desk. Concentrating now, he broke the deck into two stacks and mixed them thoroughly. He repeated the same routine twelve more times.

Closing his eyes, Taine cleared his mind of all distractions. He inhaled and exhaled slowly and deeply, oxygenating his system. Years of practice enabled him to enter a trancelike state merely through touching the worn edges of his personal tarot deck.

Looking inward, he visualized a great stone pyramid sitting silently in a vast sea of sand. At the top of the pyramid rested a huge blue eye, all-seeing and all-knowing, staring directly at him. To Taine, this mental image symbolized the power of the mysterious cards, the wisdom and secrets of ancient Egyptian sorcerers.

With his eyes open but still filled with the vision, Taine constructed the Kabalistic Tree of Life. In less than a minute he dealt out nine stacks of cards, forming three interweaving triangles. A tenth pack went in the center of the bottom-most figure. The remaining cards he left on the side of the desk, away from the tree.

The first triangle encompassed the spirit, the second stood for reason, and the third symbolized intuition. Taine firmly believed that the cards held incredible secrets of magic for the enlightened. He never started a case without first performing a reading.

The true tarot deck contains seventy-eight cards. There are four suits: cups, wands, coins and swords. Each consists of the numerals from one through ten and the four court cards. Additionally, there are twenty-two major trumps, unusual and obscure picture cards, each one with its own meaning and title.

Taine subscribed to the belief that the cards originated in Egypt. Created by the mystic sorcerers of that ancient land, the tarot deck was the exclusive property of the Priests of Osiris and was used by them to predict the future.

However, during the time of the Roman conquest of Egypt, a pack fell into the hands of a nameless soldier in Caesar's army. Not realizing the deck's true purpose, he instead used them for gambling. Within a few years, the far traveling Legions of the Empire had spread the tarot deck throughout the known world. In that manner, the secrets of Egyptian magic traveled down through the ages.

Working methodically, Taine turned over a card from each deck, following the "Serpent of Wisdom" from the foot of the Tree upward. Each individual tarot card told a story. At the same time, all of the glyphs combined together to form an integrated network of symbols with its own separate meaning. He continued working through the deck, carefully watching the pattern that developed.

After he concluded the first reading, Taine gathered the cards together and repeated the whole procedure. A true divination required three readings.

Each deal yielded the same results. A run of four major trumps occurred in all three passes. First came "The Wheel of Fortune," the card of *destiny*. Following that was "Pope Joan," the trump standing for *a mysterious woman*. Third in the progression was "The Hermit," the symbol of *hidden wisdom*. The final card in all three readings was the thirteen trump, "La Mort," the skeleton—predicting *death*.

Taine banded the cards together, returned them to the drawer and locked it. Pocketing the key, he switched off the lights and exited the room.

"I'm leaving for the rest of the day," he said to Mrs. McConnell. "Mrs. Caldwell made it quite clear she expects results from this investigation by Friday. She's willing to pay for speed, and I can use the cash. Postpone all the other appointments on my calendar till next week. If they can't wait till then, give them Paul Schulz's phone number. He has the necessary manpower and I trust his judgment."

"Whatever you say," replied Mrs. McConnell. "You're the boss."

"After that, I want you to do some checking for me."

"Go ahead," she said, pulling out a pen and memo book.

"I want all the background you can get on Victor Caldwell and his wife, Evangeline Caldwell. I'm especially interested in Victor's recent business dealings. See what your contacts in the business community think of him."

"You want all the dirt and gossip?" asked Mrs. McConnell, tapping her pen against the top of the pad. "You saw how she dresses. Her type always generates the most talk—both true and false."

"Get me everything," said Taine. "I'm not worried about Mrs. Caldwell's reputation." He paused for an instant. "She referred several times this morning to her father, Harmon Sangmeister. Don't turn over any rocks, but learn all you can about the old man as well."

"Sounds nice and juicy. Anything else?"

"Arelim. According to *The Kabbalah,* that's the secret name of Elohim's Avenging Angel."

"You want me to find all other references."

"If you can. Try calling that occult bookstore in New York City. The old man who runs the place is a walking encyclopedia of Hebrew mysticism."

"Still more?"

"Just this," said Taine and took the pen and pad from her hands. Beneath her notes, he sketched a rough drawing of the emblem worn by Mrs. Caldwell. "Track down this design. It's the badge of a medieval occult organization or secret society. I want to know which one."

"With full particulars about the group, I assume," said Mrs. McConnell. She closed her notebook. "This might take some real money. Should I spare no expense?"

Taine nodded. Mrs. McConnell knew the value of a dollar. She only used bribery when nothing else worked. He relied on her judgment in all such matters.

"You took the words right out of my mouth. Our

client is footing the bill. Grease the way if necessary, but maintain a low profile."

"I'll walk on tiptoes."

"That sounds like a good idea," said Taine, pulling a battered hat and coat off the clothes tree by the front door. "Even rich people can be dangerous when threatened."

4

Sullivan Preparatory School on Chicago's north shore promptly dismissed students at three minutes after three o'clock every afternoon of the school year. The principal strictly enforced this rule so that parents knew exactly when to meet their children. In most circumstances, this dogmatic adherence to schedule pleased Janet Packard. Today, stuck in traffic six blocks away and five minutes late, she cursed the day she enrolled her son at the academy. She also cursed the traffic, cursed the weather, and cursed the driver in the car ahead of her.

Muttering a number of very unladylike remarks, she leaned on the horn, venting her rage the only way possible. Under usual conditions, the trip from her jewelry establishment in the Loop to the school took eighteen minutes. She normally left her store at twenty to three, giving herself an additional five-minute cushion.

Today, a wealthy old dowager looking to purchase an expensive diamond bracelet had insisted on dealing with no one but the proprietor. Reluctant to lose a major sale, Janet had handled the negotiations. She pushed the deal through in record time. However, she left the store ten minutes later than usual. Speeding cut that deficit in half, but a broken water main on Sheridan Road ended any chance of arriving on time.

Like many only children raised by a single parent, Timmy was a shy, quiet boy—more at ease with adults than with kids his own age. Despite constant assurances of love and affection from his mother, he exhibited an overwhelming fear of abandonment. The last time Janet arrived more than a few minutes late at school, she found Timmy huddled up against a wall, bawling like a baby. It took a visit to the zoo to calm his fears that time. Janet feared it might be worse today.

As mysteriously as it began, the traffic jam dissolved. Janet slammed down hard on the gas pedal, sending her BMW roaring through the last few blocks to Timmy's school. With a screech of protesting rubber, the car shuddered to a stop in the Academy parking lot at ten minutes after the hour.

Janet jumped out, her eyes anxiously scanning the playground adjacent to the school. Only a few children remained. None of them was Timmy. Feeling the first touch of worry, she hurried over to the building's exit. No one waited inside. Again she checked all the other children in the yard, making sure no one lurked behind a swing or bench. The results proved the same. Timmy was gone.

Her palms sweaty and cold, Janet finally spotted Mrs. Kearny, the playground monitor who regulated afterschool traffic. She rushed over to the elderly teacher. The short, white-haired woman frowned as Janet approached.

"Why are *you* here today?" the teacher asked.

"To pick up Timmy," said Janet, her heart pounding furiously. Had something terrible happened while she was stuck in traffic? Where was her son?

"But your father sent his car for your boy today. The driver assured me you asked them to take Timmy to visit Mr. Packard today." The old woman sounded puzzled. "You did make arrangements, didn't you?"

"Oh, of course," said Janet, trying to keep her anger from showing. "I . . . uh . . . forgot," she said, trying to come up with some plausible excuse. "Business pressures . . ."

"Yes. I'm sure," said Mrs. Kearny, her tone making it perfectly clear she suspected Janet of drinking on the job or worse. The teacher shuddered. "Why does your father insist on employing that spooky chauffeur? That man is positively sinister. What a brute."

Janet laughed. "Bruno? He's as gentle as a puppy."

"Maybe so," replied the teacher, "but he gives me the creeps."

Shaking her head in disbelief, Janet returned to her car. The notion of Bruno, her father's manservant and chauffeur, frightening anyone seemed absolutely incredible. Bruno had served her father since before she was born. To Janet, he was part of the family.

Then she paused, thinking back to her childhood. She vaguely remembered classmates taunting her about "The Asp." The nickname came from the *Little Orphan Annie* comic strip. If Janet remembered correctly, it had been coined not by one of her friends, but by one of her teachers. Bruno's slicked-down black hair, swarthy features and muscular build invited comparisons between him and the cartoon character. Janet knew Bruno as a shy, compassionate man, ill at ease around strangers. She wondered if he dressed the way he did to erect a wall between himself and people like Mrs. Kearny.

Her lips pressed tightly together in annoyance, Janet steered her car into the traffic heading north. Her memory rarely failed at anything and never in regards to her son. Bruno never acted without direct orders from her father. And Leo Packard never did anything without a reason. The uneasy feeling she experienced in the playground returned and she could do nothing to shake it.

Twenty minutes later, she pulled up in front of Brentwood, her father's suburban estate. The huge old house looked unchanged from the days of her youth. With her mother and older brother both long dead and Janet living in a town house, her father spent most of the year at his residence in Florida. Leo opened Brentwood only for his brief stays in Chicago during the spring and fall. He had returned to the city a few weeks ago, but due to conflicting schedules, they had yet to get together. Not that they were very close anyway.

Her father doted on Timmy. He never failed to see her son at least once during his trips north. She wondered if perhaps Leo might be leaving earlier than planned. He could have sent Bruno on his unusual errand because he wanted to spend some time with his only grandchild before he departed. The notion seemed possible but not very probable. Leo was incredibly rich. Money served him, not the other way around. He never allowed time or circumstances to dictate his plans.

Martha Skoup, his father's other full-time employee, answered the door. Martha had served as maid, cook and general secretary for Leo for nearly twenty years. A big, brawny Slavic woman with dark brown hair and matching eyes, Martha had the softest voice imaginable. She never spoke above a whisper. Much of what she said went unheard. Like Bruno, she was absolutely devoted to her boss. Janet knew Leo paid both his servants extravagant salaries, but she suspected that if necessary they would work for nothing. She often wondered what it was about her father that generated such absolute devotion.

"Is Timmy here, Martha?" Janet asked, as she walked into the main hall.

"Yes, Miss Janet. He's upstairs in his room, playing with Bruno."

His room. Actually, it once belonged to her brother, Ralph. For years after his death in a drunk driving accident, the room had remained closed and locked. It was quite clear to Janet that to her father, Timmy represented a small measure of redemption for that tragedy. She still remembered the look on her parent's face that night. Leo had been at a confidential business conference and all efforts to contact him had proven unsuccessful. He had returned home well after midnight, to be greeted by a policeman in the front hall. His wife, Janet's mother, had already collapsed after hearing the news. It was the first of a long series of bouts of depression that inevitably climaxed with her suicide three months later. Only Janet, barely ten years old, waited with the officer.

"Your son must have been drinking heavily for hours," the policeman told her father. "We found several empty whiskey bottles on the floor of his car. We're still not sure where he did his drinking or when.

"The last time any of his friends remembered seeing him was leaving a party around eight. He was sober then. Evidently, in the next four hours, he fell in with another crowd and got smashing drunk. The details usually come out after a while. Sooner or later we'll get all the facts. In any case, we found his car smashed into an oak tree on a deserted stretch of Route Forty-three in the Forest Preserve. According to the coroner, he died around midnight."

"Did he suffer much?" her father managed to ask, his voice crackling with pain.

"The crash killed him," said the policeman, staring at the floor. "The impact sent him flying through the front window. The windshield glass cut him to shreds. It was like he was stabbed by a hundred daggers at the same instant. He probably never knew what hit him."

"A hundred daggers," her father repeated, his face twisted in horror. To Janet, all the anguish in the world seemed wrapped up in those few terrible words.

"Are you all right, Miss Janet?" asked Martha, a note of apprehension in her voice.

"Yes, yes, I'm okay," said Janet. "Just overcome by memories for a moment. Brentwood sometimes does that to me." She paused for an instant. "It was nineteen years ago, almost to a day, that Ralph died."

"Yes, ma'am," said Martha, in her quietest voice. "Dreadful night, that. Killed your mother, too. The shock that is. She never recovered from the news, poor sweet lady. This Friday's the day—April thirtieth."

Janet started up the stairs to Ralph's old room. "Your father is resting on the sun porch, Miss Janet," said Martha. "He asked me to tell you that. He wants to talk to you after you see Timmy."

"I plan on doing exactly that," said Janet.

A heavy burden lifted from her shoulders when she entered the big bedroom and spotted her son. He was bent over a complex mass of plastic and metal in the far corner. Next to him, squatting uncomfortably on his knees, looking quite bemused, was Bruno.

"Mommy, mommy," shouted Timmy as he spotted her, "Grandpa bought me Fortress Maximus. Look, he has three extra Transformers as bodyguards."

Janet grinned. Leave it to her father to find the one toy that Tim really wanted. Her son had been asking for the giant robot for months. It was unavailable at any of the local stores. Transformers were hot and they disappeared the minute they hit the shelves. But such mundane considerations never stopped Leo Packard.

"Where did you find it, Bruno?" she asked as her son excitedly pointed out the huge robot's many features.

"Boss made a few phone calls," said Bruno. As always, his deep, scratchy voice made Janet think of a 45 RPM record being played at 33. "He called in a few favors."

"He made some big men jump through hoops all for a little boy's toy. That sounds like father. Why did you pick up Tim at school, Bruno?"

The chauffeur smiled up at her and shrugged his massive shoulders. "I do what your father tells me, Miss Janet. He says to get the Little Prince and bring him here, so I did it. Never meant no harm."

"No, I'm sure you didn't." As far as Janet knew, Bruno had no family. In a house unequipped for small children, he took care of Timmy during their infrequent visits. With infinite patience and no visible temper, he made a perfect baby-sitter. "The Little Prince," Bruno called Janet's son. And he always treated the boy like royalty.

"Is he an Autobot or Decepticon?" she asked Timmy, bending over to look at the new machine.

"An Autobot, of course," he answered without looking up. "Remember the movie, Mom. Autobots are cars. Decepticons are always jets."

"Of course. I just forgot. How was school today?"

"Good."

Janet nodded. Tim used the same term to describe nearly everything acceptable in life. "How did you do on your spelling test?"

"Good. I got one wrong. That was an A minus."

"How was lunch?"

"Good. Mom, do you mind? I'm trying to concentrate and you're disturbing me."

"Sorry. I'll go talk with your grandfather."

"Okay." He glanced up at her for a second. "Mom, what time is it? *Ghostbusters* is on at four o'clock and I don't want to miss it."

"You've got plenty of time. You can watch it in the study."

"Is Martha gonna make me tacos for dinner?"

"If we stay for dinner, she probably will. She knows your tastes by now."

"I'm sleeping over," said Timmy cheerfully. "Grandpa told me. All week, he said."

"Oh, really," said Janet, her temper rising. "You don't say."

"Your father is waiting for you on the sun porch," said Bruno, avoiding her stare. "Maybe you should talk to him, Miss Janet."

"Thank you for that suggestion, Bruno. I believe I shall do exactly that. Take care of Timmy."

"Of course, miss. He's safe with me."

Wondering exactly what the chauffeur meant by that last remark, Janet left the room. The sooner she spoke with her father, the better.

5

Her father rose from his chair when she entered the sun room. He was dressed casually, in a gray pullover sweater and matching slacks. The colors perfectly complemented his crew-cut gray hair and bushy eyebrows. A dynamic, forceful man, his bearing and posture made him seem inches taller than five foot eight.

"Martha informed me when you arrived." He gestured to a wicker chair facing his. "She made you a Bloody Mary. Sit down, relax, drink."

"You know I never drink during the afternoon," said Janet, as she settled in her chair.

"Bad habit," said her father, sipping from his glass. She knew it contained Scotch straight up. Leo Packard never diluted his liquor. "Best real estate deals I ever landed were over a bottle."

"That's because you got the clients so drunk they didn't know what they were signing," said Janet with a laugh. She took a small gulp of the Bloody Mary. As always, even just a taste left her feeling dizzy. "Martha still mixes them stiff."

"Warms the blood," Leo replied. "You're staying for dinner." He offered the remark not as a question but as a statement of fact.

"So I've been told by my son. Any particular reason?"

"Company. You never visit. I'm a lonely old man."

"Bull," replied Janet. "Don't look for any sympathy from me, you old fraud. At sixty-five, you're in better physical shape than I am. You probably get your kicks from rolling street punks who come begging for change."

"Now, now," her father said, with only a trace of a smile on his lips. "Let's not exaggerate. Though I

31

always did say that age and treachery will always triumph over youth and enthusiasm."

Janet laughed. Her father never changed.

Years ago, while reading a book on World War I, she came across a picture of "Black Jack" Pershing. She found the resemblance between the famous general and her father incredible. Everything matched—their hair, their expression, even the way they both sat stiffly on a couch so that their back never once touched the back cushion. Only much later did she discover her father deliberately copied Pershing's mannerisms for his own ends.

He explained the deception to her in the most simple of terms. "Life—and business reflects life—is a constant struggle for survival. To succeed, you need to use every tool you possess along with inventing new ones along the way. The smart businessman always looks for that extra edge. If my appearance or bearing overwhelms a few clients and makes it easier for me to swing a deal, all the better. Only the strong advance. The weak fall by the wayside. You create your own success."

At twenty, young and idealistic, she thought his words depressingly materialistic. Nine years passed. Life took its toll. She endured a brief, terrible marriage; gave birth to a son; divorced. Black and white merged into a thousand subtle shades of gray. Now, struggling to establish her presence in the cutthroat jewelry market, she considered his early advice the bedrock of her career.

"You sent Bruno to pick up Timmy from school. Why?"

"I told you. I felt lonely."

With a snort of annoyance, Janet rose to her feet. "Time for us to leave. You're treating me like a child. I won't stand for that. Call me when you want to tell me the truth."

"Enough foolishness," said her father, in the flat, neutral tone he used when angry. "Sit down. You can leave if you really want to. But Timmy stays here."

"Leo, *what is going on?* What are you hiding from me?"

32

"No reason to get all worked up," he said, taking a deep swallow from his glass. "You know me well enough. I prefer not to take any chances in life. Recently, your ex-husband has been seen in the company of several notorious criminals. Today, certain facts came to my attention that disturbed me. I thought it better to be cautious than sorry."

"Roger threatening Timmy? Harm his own son? I don't believe it."

"Think again," said Leo, again in that cold, emotionless manner that sent chills through her. "Consider . . . ransom."

"You think he plans to kidnap Tim?" Janet asked, anger twisting inside her like a poisonous snake. "He wouldn't dare."

"You know better. Roger would dare anything if it suited his purpose. He never worried before about the morality of his actions. I assure you that in the years since your divorce, he has not changed a bit."

Janet shook her head. "There's a big difference between sex in public places and kidnaping."

"Not to Roger. He is totally self-centered. Whatever furthers his ambitions is good. Anything that thwarts his plans is bad.

"He hungers for the fame and fortune he thought marrying you would provide. He still hates you for divorcing him. Roger sees Tim as his ticket to those riches."

"Holding his own son for ransom? That's crazy."

Leo Packard sighed deeply. "You betray your naive faith in human nature when you say things like that, Janet. Roger is an obnoxious bastard, but he is nobody's fool."

"The police . . ."

". . . would see it as two wealthy parents squabbling over their only child. A smart lawyer could keep the case tangled in court for years."

"Meanwhile, Roger would have Tim. But why?"

"I believe the word ransom came up in our conversation. Though I'm positive that term would never actually be mentioned. Pay up and get your son back. Otherwise, fight your ex-husband in court for custody.''

"No. I don't believe it," she said, her cheeks flushed with anger. "I know Roger too well. He despises lawyers. He could never work that closely with one. More important, he fears you. The power of your fortune scares him.''

"I think you underestimate his ambition.''

"Not true. Remember, I lived with that son-of-a-bitch for over a year." She paused, her thoughts speeding far ahead of the conversation. "Anyway, what do you want us to do? Timmy can't stay in hiding for the rest of his life.''

"He need only remain here till Saturday," said her father, a bit too quickly. "By then, I'll have this whole mess straightened out. I'm working on it right now. Give me till then, won't you?''

He rushed on, not waiting for her answer. "No need to get Timmy all upset. Bruno can drive him to school each day and pick him up afterward. Let him invite some of his friends over to play if you like. There are plenty of toys in the house, and Tim enjoys staying here. Martha loves when he visits.''

"But my plans for the week . . ." said Janet, growing more suspicious of the whole story by the minute.

"Change them. Cancel what you can't postpone." Leo's voice grew deathly calm. "I cannot guarantee Tim's safety unless he remains here, Janet.''

Leaning forward, her father stared directly at her, his dark eyes hard as stone. "I never liked Roger. He struck me as a dangerously unstable individual, not a suitable husband for my only child. When you realized the error of your ways and divorced him, I secretly rejoiced. Old enough to know when to keep my mouth shut, I did exactly that.

"Meanwhile, I hired a team of investigators to keep close tabs on your ex-husband. An incredibly self-centered individual, Roger never adjusted to your leaving him. That denial struck at the very core of his being. Instead of trying to understand the reasons for the breakup, he shifted all of the blame on you."

"No surprise there," said Janet. "He always found some convenient excuse for his failures. He never admitted he might be in the wrong."

"Such individuals never accept responsibility for their own actions," said her father, pausing only for an instant to emphasize his point. "Roger hated you with an all-consuming rage. Every setback he suffered since then became linked with your departure. Resentment grew inside him like a cancer. He wanted to strike back at you, but no opportunity presented itself."

"You seem to know quite a bit about him."

"I pay for the best, Janet, and I get what I pay for. Over the past few years, one of my men has become close friends with Roger. He confides nearly everything to him. And thus, to me."

Leo paused, as if gathering his thoughts. "In recent days, that agent reported a disturbing change in Roger. In the past few weeks, he stopped frequenting his usual haunts. His actions, never the most stable, became more and more erratic. And he suffered a tremendous loss of weight. It all pointed to one inescapable conclusion.

"This morning, Roger didn't show up for work. My detective, playing the concerned friend, checked his apartment. He checked out last night, leaving no forwarding address. I dared not wait till my men found him. I acted immediately, instructing Bruno to pick Tim up after school."

"Hold on a minute," said Janet, incredulously. "This entire paranoid scenario took place because Roger went on a diet?"

Her father sighed again. He shook his head slowly from side to side. "My poor, innocent daughter. Roger lost twenty pounds in two weeks. Only one diet works that fast—the crack diet. Once you get hooked on the drug, you don't eat, you don't drink, you don't sleep. All you want is crack."

For once, she was struck speechless. Her ex-husband hooked on the most addictive drug known, still hating her for leaving him years before. Seeking revenge, he plotted to kidnap the one person she loved more than life itself. It sounded too incredible to be true. But the newspapers were filled with accounts of grisly murders based on similar circumstances.

"Now you understand why I fear for Timmy's safety," said Leo. "People smoking crack commit the most violent crimes imaginable. The 'rush' they receive from the purified cocaine is a hundred times the high from any other drug. It reacts directly with the brain, destroying their ability to think clearly. They cease to act rationally.

"You read about the drug wars in Washington and New York. Dealers shot down their rivals in broad daylight. Madmen turn their guns on innocent bystanders. Two-bit hustlers battle with machine guns, killing anyone in their path."

Leo's hands clenched into fists. "I dare not take the chance with Tim's life. Will you?"

"No. Of course not."

"Good." Leo relaxed a little, leaning back in his chair. "After dinner, you can make a quick trip home to gather some clothes for your visit. It should only last a few days. My men are working on the problem as we speak."

6

Lisa Ray softly hummed her favorite Aretha Franklin song as she scrubbed the last traces of dirt from the stack of tiny glass bottles floating in the kitchen sink. With a satisfied chuckle, she surveyed the hundreds of clear containers drying on the nearby counter. Every day the line of bottles grew longer. Every day her bank got fatter. And every day, she drew a little closer to her dream car.

She still remembered the laughter of her so-called friends when, late one hot summer night last year, she told them her plans. "My ride is a pink Cadillac," she told Delores and Tasha and Neise. "I saw Aretha driving one in a music video. It got big fins and chrome and white-walled tires. That car called loud to me. If the Queen of Soul rides one, I want it, too."

To the others, it was all a big joke. They all knew she worshiped Aretha and taunted her unmercifully about her own lack of talent. Now the three of them had something new to tease her about.

"Where you gonna get that big money?" Tasha wanted to know. "Only flashy whores or soul sisters make that change. We all know you ain't got the voice." Then Tasha laughed that deep down dirty laugh of hers. "And you sure can't sell that stick-pole body of yours for nothin'."

"You should know all 'bout selling for cheap," Lisa had shot back, her eyes filling with tears. "You hump anybody that got five bucks and a zipper."

"Who you callin' a cheap ho'," said Tasha angrily. She swung a fist wildly at Lisa, catching her with a glancing blow to the forehead.

"Yeah," said Neise, giggling, "Tasha ain't no cheap lay. She charges ten bucks, not five. She's high-class."

The conversation had degenerated from there, but Lisa learned her lesson. She never again mentioned her secret dream to anyone else. Instead, she stored the image of the shiny new car with big fins deep within herself, waiting for the time and opportunity to make it all come true.

Now, bending over a sink full of steaming hot soapy water, she was making her dream reality. She worked hard but the money was good and the risks minimal.

Deciding to take a short break, Lisa pulled the plug from the drain and let the soapy water empty out of the sink. Turning on the cold tap for an instant, she rinsed her calloused fingers under the freezing water. This constant washing painfully dried out the skin of her hands. The flesh was thin as paper, splitting into a network of fine red lines around her knuckles and joints. Skin cream provided no relief. Only ice water lessened the burning sensation. Still, she considered the minor pain a small price to pay for the money she was earning.

Lisa glanced around the small kitchen. A long narrow box of a room, it was five feet wide and twelve feet long. An open doorway, covered by a curtain of glass beads running from floor to ceiling, bisected the inner wall and led to the living room. Almost directly opposite that passage was a heavy wood door that opened outdoors onto a rickety old wooden stairway that doubled as a fire escape. A heavy steel chain and three sturdy dead bolt locks, each spaced a foot apart from the next, held the door closed in an unbreakable grip.

The keys for the locks hung on a wood bar off to the side of the door. The back entrance provided an emergency exit only for the most extreme disasters. Oliver worried more about someone breaking in than their ever needing to get out.

The refrigerator was a relic from the fifties, with an icebox the size of a toaster. The oven didn't work, but that didn't matter. One burner still functioned on the stove and that was all they needed. They rarely ate anything other than canned food or boxed cereal. Oliver mistrusted frozen foods and refused to eat anything fresh. He was a little bit crazy, Lisa knew. But he was her man and she could put up with his weird ideas. Unlike Neise's lover, he never beat her. And he shared with her the money they earned working like slaves, keeping alive her dream.

The place was a dump, she concluded for the hundredth time, but it was home. At least, for now, until they made enough money to blow this town. She and Oliver had lived and worked in this rat-hole for the past five months. Twenty-three weeks of sixteen-hour days making crack for the Children of Danballah.

She did most of the busy work—cleaning the tubes, buying the supplies, measuring out the rock into each container. Oliver functioned as the brains of the operation. He handled the actual manufacturing, wielding a portable blowtorch with the experienced hand of a prison school graduate.

"You got them vials ready yet?" Oliver called from the front room. "Them Hernandez Brothers done be here soon and they ain't the patient sort."

"Sure, sure," said Lisa, gathering up the glass vials in a breadbasket lined with cloth napkins stolen from uptown restaurants.

They prided themselves in the purity of their crack. Nobody made better rock. No impurities tainted their product. It was pure coke in hard rock form, stored in clean glass containers kept airtight with oversize rubber caps. Nobody died from their crack, Lisa told herself every time she heard about another drug death on the street. No one died from good crack.

Meanwhile, just to be on the safe side, she never smoked the stuff. She kept clean. Crack heads screwed up too often, had their heads too high in the clouds to manufacture the best stuff. She didn't even smoke those "fry daddys," hand rolled cigarettes laced with crack, preferred by most of her friends. Deep within herself, she knew if she ever started crack, she would never get that pink Cadillac.

Pushing aside the glass bead curtain, Lisa brought the basket full of tubes into the living room. Oliver waited impatiently by the heavy old workbench in the center of the room. In one hand, he held a portable propane torch, fueled from the squat metal tank in the corner. Sitting on the table were two big bottles, each half filled with water; several small boxes of baking soda; and a half-dozen long metal spoons.

A large clean sheet of brown wrapping paper covered the far end of the workbench. Lying on top of the paper rested the two miniature hammers they used to break the crack into small chunks. Lisa set down the basket of vials next to the hammers.

"Hurry up, woman," said Oliver, glancing down at the cheap plastic watch he always wore. "It almost seven. You know those dumb Spics ain't gonna do no waitin'."

Lisa nodded without saying anything. Oliver was right. The two swarthy Columbians they had dubbed the Hernandez Brothers for lack of any real names never deviated from their schedule. They made a pickup every night at ten after seven. If the crack wasn't ready, they left without it. A few missed deliveries, Lisa knew, and the Big Bosses closed their factory down for good. Say good-bye to that pink Cadillac.

Hastily, she walked over to the only other piece of furniture in the room, an old sofa they had found in the apartment when they first moved in. From beneath the worn cushions, she yanked out the plastic bag full of cocaine delivered by another set of messengers an hour before.

Meanwhile, with a snap of his fingers, Oliver lit a kitchen match and fired up his torch. A low chuckle crossed his lips as he stared into the pure blue flame. His eyes widened like a child fascinated by a new toy.

Lisa repressed a shudder. This obsession with burning things was another one of Oliver's little quirks. The fire called to him like a drug. Arson had put him in Joliet for three to five, with time off for good behavior. Lisa secretly worried that next time the charge might be a lot worse. Every time he stared so happily at the blow-torch flame, she wanted to scream. His madness frightened her badly. As if reaffirming a pledge, she silently swore that as soon as they made enough bank to buy that Cadillac, she was gone, leaving Oliver and his torch to fend for themselves.

Blissfully unaware of anything but the steady blue blaze of the flame, Oliver pulled on a pair of asbestos oven mitts to protect his hands from blistering. It was time to make crack.

Into one of the glass bottles half filled with water, Lisa dumped the package of cocaine and most of a box of baking soda. With a laugh of sheer pleasure, Oliver hit the jug with the blowtorch flame. Inside the container, the mixture bubbled and steamed, boiling in seconds. The hot liquid crackled loudly, like the sound of breaking plasterboard.

"That's why they call it crack," Oliver had told Lisa the first time she helped him. He knew everything there was to know about the drug. "Pure cocaine, with no distractions."

Within minutes the cocaine powder boiled down to an oily base, with the baking soda soaking up all the impurities in the drug. Oliver popped off the torch and grabbed the other bottle of water. He poured an equal amount of cold water into the still seething mixture. Seconds later, the oily cocaine base hardened into little white balls, resembling small rocks.

"Now we're cookin'," said Oliver, his tone more relaxed. "I'll spoon it out. You do the hammering."

They worked well as a team. Oliver employed a steady hand, untroubled by the steam inside the bottle, to dish out the small crack pellets onto the brown paper. But his calloused fingers couldn't manage the delicate job of breaking down the crack into fingernail-size chunks to fill the glass vials. Lisa enjoyed that part of the job. Each container completed was another dollar in her bank, another step closer to her pink Cadillac.

The shrill ringing of the downstairs alarm caught them both by surprise. They were on the fourth floor of the otherwise abandoned tenement building. According to their boss, this was a safe location. Voodoo cult signs filled the hallway and the outside walls of the building. Nobody ever messed with the Children of Danballah. But Oliver, obsessively cautious from his time in prison, had rigged up warning bells that sounded whenever someone stepped on each of the lower floor landings of their home. He liked to know when anyone, expected or not, entered the building, and where they were.

"Hernandez Brothers done be early tonight," said Lisa, trying to fill the glass bottles faster. "Ain't due for twenty minutes yet."

"The Hernandez Brothers ain't *never* early," said Oliver, a strange glitch in his voice.

Hurriedly, he scooted over to the one window overlooking the street. "No car out there," he said as he

41

peered into the thickening twilight. His voice trembled with excitement. "No car at all."

He turned around and faced Lisa, his face flushed. "Must be some stickup boys looking for a quick score. Figure to hit us right before the pickup time when we got most the rock ready for shipment. Smart dudes, looking to catch us by surprise."

He chuckled, that insane quiet giggle that frightened Lisa more than she dared admit. "They be smart. But not as smart as me." He reached for his blowtorch. "Not as smart, no way."

Lisa backed away from the table, the crack momentarily forgotten. "What you planning to do, Oliver?" she asked, already knowing the answer.

"Gonna make things hot for those stickup boys," he said, giggling wildly now. With a flourish, he lit the propane torch. He swung the pencil-thin, foot-long finger of flame around like a sword. "I knew in my dreams this would happen someday. I knew it. Fixed my torch a special way, just waiting for the time. Got me a nice long flame to do some cuttin'."

A cold feeling of uneasiness swept over Lisa. The warning bell on the second floor landing rang shrilly, as she tried to stay calm. She realized now that Oliver was more than a little crazy.

"No need for us to fight," she said, slowly backing up toward the kitchen as she spoke. "We ain't paid to fight."

"They don't need pay me nothing," said Oliver, laughing and waving his torch. "I fight for free."

"What if they carryin' burners," said Lisa, desperately trying to penetrate the madness that was engulfing her boyfriend. "Maybe one of them sporting an Uzi like Willis. Whatcha gonna do then?"

"No Uzis for stickup boys," said Oliver, his voice wavering just a bit. Evidently, he never considered the possibility of heavily armed opponents. "Anyway, up close my torch is all I need."

The alarm from the third floor landing made them both jump. "Coming up fast now," said Oliver, swinging around to face the front door of the apartment. "No time to turn chicken now."

"But . . ." began Lisa.

Knock, knock, knock. The door to their apartment rattled as a heavy fist pounded on the thin boards. "Anybody home?" asked a voice smooth as silk. "Anybody in there?"

"Po-lite stickup boy is all," said Oliver softly, his confidence returning. "Ain't foolin' no one."

"Nobody home but us dumb suckers," said Oliver. He wrenched open the apartment door with one hand, swinging round his blowtorch with the other.

Lisa screamed. A giant in black filled the doorway. He wore a long slick raincoat, buttoned tight across his massive chest, stretching from knee to collar. A wide brimmed cowboy hat angled down across his face, completely shadowing his features. Black shiny gloves, stretching all the way up to the sleeves of his coat, encased his massive hands.

"Good evening, Oliver," said the Dark Man, raising a huge butcher's cleaver in the air. The blue flame of the blowtorch reflected against the cold steel. "Good evening, Lisa."

Oliver, shouting something incomprehensible about tasting fire, shoved the propane torch right into the giant's face. Lisa gagged as the smell of burning rubber and cloth filled the apartment. The Dark Man staggered back, stumbling into the hallway. Laughing wildly, Oliver started to follow.

"Come back, you fool," Lisa shrieked, a sense of disaster gripping her tightly. "He ain't burnin'—he ain't burnin'."

"What you sayin'," said Oliver in a puzzled voice, as he squinted over the edge of the flame into the hallway.

"She's right, you know," said the Dark Man, stepping forward again. His raincoat was smoldering and charred at the collar. A thin ring of flame burned steadily across his hat, revealing a glimpse of the face beneath. Two bright red coals of eyes glared at them out of a featureless mask of black glass. "Fire can't harm me."

With incredible speed, the Dark Man swung his knife at Oliver's head. Instinctively, the young man ducked and raised the hand holding the blowtorch to block the attack. Steel met steel, sending sparks flying. Oliver gasped in pain as the force of the blow knocked him to his knees. The blowtorch went flying across the room.

Oliver scrambled after his weapon. Almost casually, the Dark Man reached down and grabbed Oliver by the ankle. With a powerful wrench, he spun the young man around, flat on his back.

"No, no!" Oliver shrieked in panic. "Take the crack, take it, take it. Take my woman, anything. Just let me live!"

"Sorry, Oliver," said the Dark Man with a shake of his huge head, "but no deals today."

Without another word, the giant swung the butcher's cleaver at Oliver's neck. The heavy blade bit deep into muscle and bone, sending bits of gore flying up in the air. Oliver gurgled horribly.

Ignoring the gruesome sounds, the Dark Man wrenched the blade out of the body, sending a fountain of blood to the ceiling. Almost instantly, he followed the first blow with another, so powerful that it almost severed Oliver's head from his torso. Then another, and still another. Methodically, the Dark Man worked at dismembering the black man, spraying blood and guts across the room.

Lisa closed her eyes tight, as if hoping the whole scene would disappear. But she couldn't block out the grisly sound of each blow of the butcher's cleaver. And when she opened her eyes for an instant, the Dark Man looked over at her, as if sensing her gaze, and said, "You're next, Lisa," in the most pleasant of tones.

Madness overwhelmed her. She turned and fled into the kitchen, mouthing incoherent sounds of absolute horror. Then the realization of her own peril broke through the fear. Lisa realized that if she didn't act immediately, she faced the same fate as Oliver. "Out the back door," she muttered wildly to herself. "Out the back door."

Frantically she yanked off the steel bar that held the

door shut and threw it to the floor. Her heart pumping furiously, Lisa wrenched on the doorknob with all her strength. The door refused to move. The three heavy-duty security locks held it rigid against the frame.

In the other room, the grisly sounds of chopping ceased. In a panic, Lisa grabbed the three keys off the wood bar. In seconds, she forced the first key into the top lock. A quick wrench of the bolt opened it.

The second key slid in equally smooth. Another turn and that lock slid open. Now only the third dead bolt, at the level of her knees, remained.

"Leaving so soon?" asked the Dark Man pleasantly, ripping aside the beaded curtain with one huge hand.

Features twisted in terror, Lisa sank down to the floor next to the door, her eyes fixed on the bloody butcher's cleaver held in the giant's other hand. The Dark Man's coat dripped blood and gore. His cowboy hat was gone, revealing a face that was not a face at all. A featureless mask of blackness, unbroken except for two burning red eyes, looked down at her. Without tongue or mouth, he spoke.

"Now it's your turn."

She screamed as the monster raised the blade over his head. Then the giant paused, as if suddenly aware of something taking place behind him. He started to turn when the thundering roar of gunfire filled the room.

To Lisa, it seemed like a giant hand lifted the Dark Man up off the floor and flung him face-first into the outside wall. He smashed so hard into the plasterboard that the whole apartment shuddered with the impact. Without a sound, he collapsed into a massive heap, only a few feet beyond her.

Cursing loudly in Spanish, the Hernandez Brothers stood just outside the door to the kitchen, pointing at the fallen giant and the ruins of the living room. Each man gripped a smoking heavy-duty automatic in one hand. Gesturing wildly, they turned and started searching the blood-soaked parlor. Lisa knew without asking that they were looking for the shipment of crack.

Beside her, the Dark Man stirred and shifted in place.

Busy in the other room, the two Columbians didn't notice the giant's movements. Relentlessly, the giant pulled himself up against the wall. Without making a sound, he rose to his feet, still gripping his butcher's cleaver. Noiselessly, he swung around to face his two new enemies. Lisa huddled into a small ball close to the door, praying that the monster wouldn't look down.

"Madre dios!" shouted one of the Hernandez Brothers, suddenly catching a glimpse of the Dark Man. The two men, their faces white with fright, backed away from the crack table, fumbling with new clips for their pistols.

"Two more fools," said the Dark Man, in the same relaxed tone as before. The back of his coat was ripped to shreds where he had been hit by bullets. Yet his body, the color and texture of shiny black glass, showed no signs of damage. Ignoring the two guns pointed at him, the giant stepped back into the front room, butcher's cleaver raised high in the air.

Still crouched on the floor, Lisa fumbled with the last key, as behind her, the air filled with the sounds of gunfire and screams. "Gotta hurry, gotta hurry," she whispered to herself as she fitted the key into the third dead bolt lock. "Nobody stoppin' that dude. He be Death."

A quick twist and the lock opened. Cautiously, afraid of attracting attention, Lisa reached up and turned the doorknob. With the merest whisper of protest, the porch door opened.

Behind her a man shrieked in terrible pain. Then silence engulfed the room. Swiftly rising to her feet, Lisa slid out the back exit and onto the porch, closing the door behind her.

She stood on a wood landing only a few feet square. Leading down from the platform was a rickety flight of wood steps to the next floor. The railing was gone, and several of the steps had caved in, leaving dangerous gaps in the path.

In the alley far below her was an old garbage Dumpster, filled with refuse. Nothing moved. The only other inhabitants of this forgotten part of the city were nocturnal beings who spent nights like this out on the street pumping and hustling. Lisa was alone.

Pressing her body close to the building, Lisa started down. Her arms gripped the decaying walls with all the strength she could muster. Without any outer railing, one false move would send her tumbling to the street. With her eyes fixed on the broken wooden slats, Lisa took a tentative step forward. Then another, and another.

Like an exploding cannon, the rear door slammed open. The Dark Man strode onto the outside landing, his butcher's cleaver dripping fresh blood. Almost instantly his huge red eyes caught sight of Lisa only a few yards away.

Turning toward her, the giant took a step down.

Crack! The decayed board snapped in two, causing the whole walkway to tremble and rocking the Dark Man back. Lisa pressed tight against the building and kept on edging forward.

"Too shaky for me," said the Dark Man as if making casual conversation. Without another word, he reentered the apartment.

Lisa sucked in a deep breath of relief and worked her way down another few steps. The third floor landing was only a few feet away. She knew that all of the other outer doors to the building were boarded shut. She and Oliver had checked them out long ago. The only way down was by the fire escape to the alley. Once there, she was safe.

"Here, Lisa, catch," called the Dark Man. He moved so silently that she hadn't realized he had returned to the platform. With a gentle throw, he tossed something small and wet at her.

The object, soft and damp like an old cloth, landed on her shoulder. Instinctively, she glanced sideways to see what it was. Horror engulfed her when she saw the Dark Man's gift. Lisa's shrieks echoed through the lonely alleyway. Again and again she screamed, unable to stop.

Resting on her shoulder was a human hand. Broken

and smashed to near putty, it resembled a piece of raw meat. One finger was missing, and another had been chopped off at the second knuckle. Bits of flesh and bone dangled like obscene strings where the hand had been chopped away from the wrist. Drops of warm blood soaked through her thin dress, onto her skin.

Desperately, Lisa clawed at the crumbling shingles of the wall while she battled to hold her sanity. For an instant, madness reached for her. And then drew back, as it encountered a solid bedrock of resistance beneath the fear.

Cautiously, she shook her upper body until her movement sent the grisly souvenir tumbling to the street below. Lisa knew that her survival depended on not giving up, no matter what. The dismembered hand only served as a reminder of her fate if she didn't keep moving. Not daring to look back at her tormentor, she inched her way forward.

Lisa paused only a second on the third floor landing. No time even to catch her breath. The Dark Man had disappeared into the apartment. She felt sure he had not given up.

The fire escape descending to the second floor was in much better condition. A remnant of railing still existed and while the steps still shook and groaned as she hurried down, they held firm. Her feet just touched the next landing when Lisa smelled smoke.

She looked up to the fourth floor. The landing was ablaze, with jagged gouts of flame licking at the side of the building. The old wood structure burned like parchment. Tongues of red flame leapt down the steps as if chasing after her.

The Dark Man stood undisturbed in the midst of the inferno, a figure of absolute blackness surrounded by fire. He leaned over the railing and stared down at her with unblinking red eyes. One huge hand gripped Oliver's propane torch, a jet of blue flame crowning the nozzle.

The wood only a few feet above Lisa's head exploded into a shower of burning fragments. They dropped around her feet like a thousand hungry insects searching for food. In seconds, the wood slats beneath her feet caught fire. Burning fingers of flame grabbed at her. Eyes stinging from the acrid smoke, she stumbled about in pain, seeking escape. Hot ash nipped her exposed skin in a hundred places.

With a roar, the fire escape below her caught fire, blocking her only avenue down. Desperately, she banged on the doorway into the second floor apartment. It didn't budge. The roar of the flames grew louder, making it impossible to concentrate.

Driven by the fury of the fire, she crashed into the landing rail. Her eyes caught sight of the half-filled garbage Dumpster twenty feet below. With a lunge of sheer desperation, Lisa launched herself over the railing into the air.

She hit the refuse and dirt in the rusted metal Dumpster with a thump. Her legs and arms ached, but otherwise she seemed unharmed by her fall. She rolled around in the waste, reaching for the edge of the bin.

A small object thumped down on the garbage, only inches away from her. The propane torch, thrown there by the Dark Man in one last desperate attempt to destroy her. With a groan, Lisa flopped over the side into the alley just as the refuse caught fire.

Forcing herself to keep moving, Lisa staggered across the alley, staying far away from the furiously burning building. In the distance, the shrill sound of fire engines filled the night air.

"You escaped me for now, Lisa," called the Dark Man, his form invisible in the midst of the raging holocaust. *"Just for now."*

Then, as if by afterthought, he added, "Remember me to your friends. Tell them I'll be coming for them as well. Soon. Real soon."

7

Taine pulled into the parking lot at Gallagher's Pub a little before seven that night. A popular Yuppie hangout on Chicago's Near North Side, it was almost deserted this early in the evening. The social drinkers and cruisers didn't make the scene until well after dark, which suited Taine just fine.

Entering the lounge, Taine walked over to the huge horseshoe bar that dominated the front of the establishment. "I'll have whatever's on tap," he told the lone bartender.

With a casual eye that missed no detail, he turned and surveyed the few patrons close by. Not spotting a familiar face, Taine waved the bartender over.

"Jack Korshak anywhere?" he asked. "He told me to meet him here at seven."

"Sure. He came in around twenty minutes ago." The bartender waved to the rear of the pub. "He always takes a booth in the back. You Taine?"

"That's my name."

"He said for you to join him when you arrived. Last table before you get to the kitchen. We hold it for him special. He comes in here so often, we kinda think of it as his table. You know, just like in the movies."

"Yeah, I hear you loud and clear," said Taine with a laugh. He picked up his drink and headed in the indicated direction. "Like *Citizen Kane* or *All the President's Men*."

Jack Korshak raised his drink in greeting when Taine approached. A short, totally bald man with a thick black beard that covered his face from ear to ear, he resembled some mad Russian poet much more than a financial

50

reporter. Korshak covered the stock market and related areas of interest for the *Chicago Post*.

Taine met Korshak a year earlier while investigating a commodities swindle. Mutual respect and a shared sense of the absurd forged a casual but lasting friendship.

"Ah, my favorite occult detective in Chicago," said Korshak, holding out his hand for a quick shake. "Or maybe I should qualify that a little bit. The only *occult* detective in Chicago. No matter. Sit down and relax. You eat dinner yet?"

"No," answered Taine, "but—"

"But nothing," said the other man. "I'm like Nero Wolfe. Can't talk business until after a meal. Besides, they make great Italian beef sandwiches here. I already ordered them for the two of us. Got you the special; sweet peppers, cheese, and red sauce on the side. Large order of fries as well—greasy things but incredible. Should be ready in just a few minutes."

"You're gonna die of a heart attack before you reach forty, Jack," said Taine, laughing. "If your liver doesn't go first from all the beer you drink."

"Nah," said Korshak, raising his glass for another quick gulp. "I know better. It's all propaganda from the Milk Board. Beer never hurt anybody. It's that dairy stuff that kills you. Remember that Woody Allen movie? The one where he woke up in the future and everyone was eating chocolate bars because they were good for you.

"Sleeper," said Taine, with a sigh. Jack loved movies but rarely remembered their titles. And his memory of certain scenes proved often to be extremely subjective. He conveniently forgot the parts he didn't like or that contradicted his opinion.

An attractive young woman in an abbreviated cocktail waitress outfit brought their sandwiches and another round of beer. Despite his protests, Taine was hungry. The two friends devoured the sandwiches and fries in silence, devoting all of their energy to their meal.

"What did I tell you?" said Korshak ten minutes later

as their waitress cleared the plates and brought another round. "Best beef sandwiches in the city."

"I can't argue," said Taine. "In any case, you're the expert. I rarely eat out. It costs too much."

"I write it all off as a business expense," said Korshak. "The paper picks up my tab for lunch and my dinners get deducted as business expenses. I'm the ultimate capitalist. Remember the trickle down theory the Republicans championed? I'm living proof of it. All the money I make goes to my favorite restaurants. If I stopped eating out, a hundred busboys would get fired."

"I can't argue with logic like that," said Taine, smiling. "But don't you ever miss a good home-cooked meal?"

"Ha," said Korshak. He took a long swig of beer before continuing. "Never. Give me pizza, ribs, tacos, and fried chicken any day. You still living by yourself in that apartment on the Near North Side?"

"Yes," answered Taine, wondering what oddball line of reasoning his friend was pursuing.

"Still single, no female attachments or such."

"Or such," repeated Taine. "I'm still on my own."

"Do your own cooking, then?" said Jack, with a satisfied expression on his face.

"When the mood strikes me," said Taine. "I rarely make anything fancy, though. Most nights I'll broil a few hamburgers or fix a steak. Once in a while, I'll cook some chicken."

"Ugh," said Korshak, wrinkling his face in disgust, his whole body trembling. "I close my case. You touch *raw* meat."

"Sure. You can't cook without it."

"Which explains why I eat out all the time," said Korshak. "I could never touch the stuff. The very thought of handling uncooked meat gives me the shivers. When I was a kid, my mother koshered our meat at home, on a board over the sink. She put the salt on to draw out the blood, the whole works. What a mess it made. Ever since, I never could face a piece of raw meat without getting a queasy feeling in the pit of my stomach.''

"Lucky you didn't become a crime reporter."

"Tell me about it. But enough about my phobias. What's new with you? Your cryptic call whetted my appetite. I gather you're working on a case involving the Chicago financial community?"

"Correct," said Taine. "However, I would appreciate it if the whole bar didn't know all the details. Lower your voice a little. I'm handling a rather delicate case and need some information about one of the principals. I thought you might be able to help. What can you tell me about Harmon Sangmeister?"

"Harmon Sangmeister?" asked Korshak, all the color draining from his face. *"The* Harmon Sangmeister?"

"Is there more than one?"

"Not funny, my friend," said Korshak, his tone much subdued. "There ain't much funny about Sangmeister."

"I've heard that already. Can you fill me in on his background—how he made his fortune, who he associates with, what he does for fun? You know what I want—the usual dirt."

Jack Korshak shook his head. "You don't know what you're asking for." Taking a long, deep swig of beer, as if for courage, he then continued. "Let me explain in my own roundabout way.

"Tom Joshko, the guy I started with at the *Post*, handled the financial section of the paper for twenty years. His stringers covered the financial district like a blanket. Tom knew the ins and outs of every major deal consummated in this city and revealed more than a few of them in his column.

"Yet, for all of his smarts, Tom Joshko never once wrote an original story about Harmon Sangmeister or his financial empire. I repeat, not once. The only news Tom ever ran about Sangmeister in his column came from the wire services.

"He never told me the reason, but I guessed early on. Joshko valued only one thing more than the truth—his health.''

"Exactly what are you implying? Do you think Sangmeister threatened your boss? I thought occurrences like that went out with Al Capone."

"You tell me," said Korshak, signaling the waitress for another beer. "Tom Joshko was a crusty old bird. Nothing frightened him. But he steered clear of Harmon Sangmeister."

The reporter held up one hand, forestalling any questions by Taine. "Let me finish. I've got another story for you. This one is a little more to the point.

"Phil Barkley used to write a terrific column for *Chicago Business Monthly*. He uncovered more embarrassing facts and figures than *The National Enquirer*. And he backed up all his claims with solid, well-researched data. More than one financial empire collapsed due to his probing.

"In his last piece, Barkley hinted that he had uncovered some deep, dark secrets behind the Sangmeister fortune. He never came right out and said exactly what he meant, but the mere suggestion of impropriety sent HS stock plummeting twenty points on the New York Exchange.

"That article never appeared. It was scheduled for the January 'eighty-four issue of *CBM*. In November, Phil Barkley came down with bronchial pneumonia. He died the day the magazine hit the stands—without his column. The editor claimed that Phil never submitted final copy.

"No one had a clue to the contents of the piece. Barkley never shared his sources with anyone. Whatever he uncovered about Sangmeister died with him.

"One or two brokers screamed foul play, but after a few weeks, the hubbub died down and the story drifted out of the news. Sangmeister stock rose to previous levels."

"Coincidence?" asked Taine.

"Maybe," said Jack Korshak, "but I'm still not finished.

"We keep a running morgue file on all the big shots in the city. Every newspaper maintains one. Information comes from all the news stories featuring the celebrity throughout his career. When that person dies unexpectedly, you use the info in the file to write his obituary. It provides the basic facts and history, while interviews with family and friends fill in the human element.

"I'm responsible for keeping the financial biographies current. Every time Donald Trump does something spectacular, I dutifully record it in his file. And so it goes for most of the major figures in the business world. After a while, the files get pretty thick, filled with all sorts of meaningless trivia. You want to know the brand of cereal the chairman of General Motors eats for breakfast? I can tell you. Or how much money, to the dollar, Howard Hughes was worth when he died? Ask me anything about anyone—except one man—Harmon Sangmeister."

"He never makes the news," said Taine cautiously.

"You guessed it. The guy controls one of the largest business empires in the United States, second perhaps only to the Pritzker family. No one knows for sure, since no one knows the full extent of his holdings. He works through so many holding companies and secondary trusts that you can't pin down all of his assets. Only a few people outside of the financial field realize the power and influence this guy wields.

"He never grants interviews. He rarely speaks in public. Unlike a lot of millionaires, he exhibits no desire to give away a penny of his fortune. The only time he earns a mention in the paper is in the gossip columns. His only human failing seems to be blond bombshells. Every picture I've ever seen of him features some buxom blond bimbo hanging on his arm. According to the reports, Sangmeister believes in liberal doses of sex and is willing to pay for his pleasure."

"Sounds like your typical sweet, wholesome millionaire," said Taine. "I guess I'll survive without that background check. Don't worry about it. Sangmeister's involvement touches only the fringes of this case."

"Yeah?" said Korshak, straightening up in his seat a little. "How is that?"

"I'm checking into rumors concerning a secret investors' group," said Taine, watching his friend's expression carefully. "I thought Sangmeister might belong."

"Groups like that are strictly illegal, you know," said Korshak suspiciously. "Last winter, the FBI broke up a huge network operating at the Commodities Exchange. Sangmeister's name never came up in the investigation."

"Does that surprise you?" said Taine, still treading cautiously. "You already told me how secretive he is. These federal dragnets rarely snare all of the guilty parties."

"You could be right," said Korshak. "It sure would explain a lot of mysterious deals that take place for no apparent reason. An insiders' club, composed of millionaires, manipulating the market. It sounds too good to be true."

His eyes narrowed in thought. Taine waited, wondering if his friend needed a bit more prodding. One more hint might tip the scales.

"It doesn't add up," said Korshak slowly, rubbing his beard with one hand. "Why hasn't anyone ever heard of this mysterious group before? After all, there's always jealous outsiders, and disgruntled ex-members. Franklin said it best. 'Two can keep a secret if one of them is dead.' These days, nothing stays confidential very long."

"Except, according to you, Harmon Sangmeister's business dealings," said Taine, knowing he had hooked his friend. Now he just had to reel him in. "Perhaps Sangmeister controls any mention of this club in the very same manner."

"This sounds a bit dramatic," said Korshak. "But one thing I've learned when dealing with millions and millions—nothing is too outrageous when that much money is involved. Let me see what I can turn up on this. You in a hurry for information?"

"Does immediately sound too soon?"

"Give me a day," said Korshak, signaling for another round of beers. "Even a master technician needs time. Phil Barkley still worries me. Let me do a little networking so I don't leave a paper trail for anyone to follow. Not that I suspect anything, but . . ."

"Agreed," said Taine. "Let me handle all the rough stuff. You get me the info, I'll supply the story when it breaks. I can use anything you get, but don't do anything foolish on my account."

"Nah," said Korshak. "I only do the dumb stuff on my own."

8

Tim happily babbled his way through dinner, keeping up a running conversation with everyone at the table. He was in all his glory with a room full of adults to entertain. Janet often wondered how her son managed to remain quiet at school. All of his teachers remarked on what a polite, shy boy he was in class. He enjoyed playing in the various team games in math and spelling and reading, but he rarely volunteered information unless asked. At home, he voiced an opinion on everything.

While Janet listened half-heartedly to his conversation, her son found a ready audience in his grandfather. Her father never spoke down to Tim, and he accorded him the same respect he gave to any adult. He further delighted the boy by addressing him as "sir," or "young Mr. Packard."

Leo never rushed Tim. He always gave the boy plenty of time to verbalize his thoughts, and always answered Tim's questions thoroughly and methodically. Leo Packard was an even-tempered, *patient* man.

Ruefully, Janet admitted she had no patience. She was always in a hurry.

On the wall of her tiny office in the jewelry store hung a small sign that summed up her own philosophy in two Latin words. *Carpe Diem.* "Seize the day." Janet tried to remain true to that maxim. Still, sitting here at the dinner table with her father, the most successful businessman she knew, Janet wondered if perhaps his way might be better.

"Mom," said Tim, loudly, effectively breaking through her inner reflections. "Mom, you didn't answer me."

"Sorry, son," she said, shaking her head to clear the cobwebs from her brain. "What did you say?"

"When are you going home? I need my other Transformers."

"I'll leave in just a few minutes. Did you have any homework tonight?"

"Nope."

"Are you sure? What about math?"

"Mo-o-om," said Tim, with an exasperated tone to his voice that drew that one word out into three syllables. "I did my math in study time. I finished all my homework in school."

"Okay, then. Make up a list of which toys you want me to bring back with me. Don't overdo it. You know how much those metal marvels weigh. Your poor mom isn't a weight lifter. No more than ten Transformers."

Tim frowned, faced with making hard choices. "Fifteen?"

"Ten," said Janet, firmly. "And not all the big ones, either. Your mother wasn't born yesterday."

"Just bring back all the ones on the shelf over my dresser," said Tim. "I put all the best ones there for protection."

Then, as if remembering something important, her son turned to her father. "Good gosh. What time is it, Grandpa?"

"Five minutes till seven," said Leo, with only the slightest hint of a smile on his face. Like most young precocious children of the television generation, Tim often used words and phrases not in normal everyday usage. He possessed a huge vocabulary and believed in using it.

"Something important happening at seven o'clock?" asked Leo.

"*Back to the Beach* is on channel nine tonight," said Tim. "The kid who tells the story is really Dudical. I want to watch it. Did you ever see it, Grandpa?"

"I rarely watch TV other than the baseball games, sir," answered Leo, the look on his face passing judgment on modern programming. "But I will join you if I am permitted to read my book while we peruse this classic."

"Sounds like a good deal to me, Tim," said Janet, rising from her chair. "Grandpa never watched TV with me when I was a kid."

"I drew the line at soap operas," said Leo, grimacing. "You refused to watch the Cubs."

"Nothing ever happens in baseball games," said Janet. "And what little action takes place, they show on replay so you don't even have to pay attention."

"Which is exactly why I like them," said her father. Then, changing the subject without a pause, "Bruno will drive you to your condo."

"Father," said Janet, sounding very much like her son a minute before. "I'm a big girl."

"Agreed." He glanced at Tim before continuing. "This is neither the time nor place to argue. Do it to humor a worried old man. Please?"

Janet could scarcely believe her ears. Her father never asked for favors. More than anything else, this latest request brought home the danger of the situation. "All right," she said. "But Bruno can wait in the car while I pack. You know I hate anyone hovering over me while I work."

"That sounds fine," said her father, rising from his chair. "Come, sir. Let us retire to the television room and feast our eyes on Ms. Funicello's ample charms."

"I'll take care of the dishes, Miss Janet," said Martha, stacking up the dirty plates. "Why don't you get going. Bruno is waiting in front with the Rolls. You can make it back before Master Tim goes to sleep."

"Thanks, Martha," said Janet, heading for the door. "I always seem to be in a rush these days."

"You should try to slow down a little, miss," came Martha's last bit of advice. "Patience *is* a virtue."

A virtue she sorely lacked, concluded Janet, a few minutes later, as Bruno steered the huge touring car out into traffic. Moments like this were too few and far between. With a sigh of satisfaction, she kicked off her heels, stretched her arms in a huge yawn, arching her back against the rich leather of the Rolls Royce interior.

The quiet ride soothed her jangled nerves. The soothing hum of the huge automobile's engine made her sleepy. She felt incredibly tired. This constant running from place to place, day after day, wore her out. She needed a little time for herself. If only the day lasted for a few extra hours.

What she really needed, Janet ruefully added mentally, was a man. Much as she disliked admitting it, she was lonely. And pretty horny as well.

The tragic death of her mother proved to be the breaking point for her father. He buried himself in his work, as if trying to blot out all memory of his losses. His efforts paid off handsomely. The Packard empire thrived. What matter if the dreams and hopes of one small child were forgotten.

Janet was shuttled from one boarding school to another. She only returned home for holidays, and even then, her father was rarely around. A lonely, self-contained child, she grew up feeling not so much unloved as ignored.

She experimented with sex as a teenager. A few casual encounters with various boyfriends left her unsatisfied and uninspired. She quickly concluded that like many experiences in life, the actual event rarely lived up to the expectations.

By the time she entered college, Janet was a sophisticated young woman of the world. Or so she thought. She was completely in control of her emotions and sure of her place in the world. With her goals firmly in place, she was determined to let nothing stand in her way. Looking back across the years, Janet often laughed at the certainty of her beliefs. She had been pretty stupid.

She had met Roger at a fraternity party during her junior year at college. Smart, sophisticated, a bit jaded, Janet considered herself much too worldly to be swept off her feet by mere physical attraction. She was waiting for the right man—perfect in every respect. At least that was what she thought until that fateful encounter one hot spring evening.

He was tall and handsome and quite daring. Despite all the trappings, beneath the sophisticated shell she wrapped around herself, she was still incredibly naive. None of her previous romantic liaisons prepared her for someone like Roger.

Her girlfriends had talked her into attending the mixer. Needless to say, the other girls disappeared in minutes after arriving, leaving Janet on her own. Exactly how she met Roger she couldn't remember. It was one of those chance conversations that began with other people and ended up with the two of them wandering off looking for a quieter place where they could be heard above the noise. They settled in a quiet alcove in the rear of the building, with a bottle of inexpensive champagne.

Roger seduced her with an ease born of years of experience. He instinctively knew how to proceed without upsetting her. For a long time, all he did was gently massage the back of her neck as he entertained her with funny stories and supplied her with drink after drink. His attention, without any strong advances, put her at ease. At the same time, the warm night air and the bubbly wine made her giddy.

After a while, his caresses traveled a little farther down her back and arms. Then his hands shifted to across her neck and behind her ears. It all seemed perfectly harmless.

As did his first gentle kiss. And the next, and the next after that. By then, one hand held her close to his chest while his other lightly brushed back and forth across her breasts. The giddy feeling melted into a tingling that spread from his fingers throughout her body. She never felt so excited in all her life.

Sensing her excitement, his lips traveled down across her neck. Both his hands were busy now, firmly stroking her breasts through the thin material of her blouse. She was not wearing a bra and her nipples stood rigid and hard with excitement. When he suddenly unfastened several buttons so he could reach inside her top, she protested weakly for an instant. But only for an instant.

Overwhelmed by passion, she found herself powerless to resist his advances. At his urging, they exited the party by a rear door. In a secluded glade only a few minutes away from the frat house, they made passionate love in the moonlight. First with his fingers, then his tongue, and finally with the hardness of his body he brought her to climax after sexual climax. By the time he finished, she was his.

The next night, they made love for hours in her apartment, trying every sexual position imaginable. During a break, she found herself confessing her innermost sexual fantasies to her new lover.

"I think everyone in the world harbors a little bit of exhibitionism. I know I've always had this wild dream of revealing my body in public. Just the thought of being naked, surrounded by a crowd of strangers, gets me excited. I've never done it, of course. Once or twice, I pulled my skirt up to my thighs while driving. And I've gone to class with nothing under my skirt. But that's about as far as I ever dared."

The conversation died as passion engulfed them again. However, the thought evidently intrigued Roger. Enough so, that the next night, he insisted they go to a drive-in movie and investigate the possible opportunities offered.

At first Janet balked at the idea. It was one thing to imagine such ideas, but completely different to be faced with the actual situation. She finally agreed to go as long as they remained very discreet.

Roger kept his hands to himself in the twilight. However, that soon changed once the sun went down and the movie started. As the night grew darker, her lover grew bolder. "No one can see us," he whispered in her ear as he rubbed her inner thighs. "And no one cares what we're doing here. Everyone knows you don't go to drive-ins to watch the movie."

Despite her misgivings, she yielded. After all, it was her fantasy. And, secretly, the thought of being nude in the car excited her. "Just my panties," she said. "No one can see into the car anyway."

He needed no further invitation. Both his hands slid under her skirt and helped raise her buttocks off the seat. In seconds, her silk undergarments were on the floor of the car. His sensual touch had her moaning with pleasure in seconds. Janet quickly forgot her worries about being discovered.

When his tongue replaced his probing fingers, the wave of sexual pleasure that swept through her body destroyed what little resistance she still possessed. The rest of her clothes followed her undergarments to the floor of the car. Her wildest dreams turned into Technicolor reality as Roger brought her to one sexual peak after another. That night, all of her inhibitions collapsed in ruin as they engaged in an orgy of incredible lust.

From then on, whatever Roger suggested, she tried. The more daring the location, the greater the thrill. They had quick sex in elevators; long intense sex in the back rows of movie theaters. Cars and boats and planes all served their purpose. At one of the finest restaurants in town, she brought him to a shuddering climax, using her hands, while an unsuspecting waiter described the menu. He returned the favor a few nights later while riding the Ferris wheel at a local carnival.

Bruno's voice brought her back to the present with a jolt. "We're here, Miss Janet." Then, when she didn't answer after a few seconds, asked with a bit of concern in his voice, "Are you all right back there?"

"I'm fine," she replied, drawing in a deep breath. "I kinda dozed off. It's been a long day."

And I need to get screwed, she mentally added to herself. Sliding across the seat to the door made her acutely aware of the dampness between her legs. Merely thinking about sex got her wet. Since her divorce, she had remained celibate except for a few very unsatisfactory one-night stands. Time for Tim to spend a few nights with relatives, she decided with a grin as she exited the car.

"Wait for me here, Bruno," she said, pulling out the keys to her town house. "I should only be a few minutes."

"Whatever you say, miss."

Bruno leaned back up against the side of the Rolls, his arms folded across his chest. In the dim twilight, his face took on a dark, almost sinister appearance. Suddenly in a rush to get moving, Janet turned and hurried up the walk to her condo.

9

Janet took one step inside her town house and then stopped, slightly confused. It was after seven. A light should be on in the living room. The parlor lamp worked by a timer so that she never entered the building in total darkness. Tonight, the town house was pitch-black.

She hesitated, wondering if she should get Bruno. Then she made a face and entered the main hallway of the apartment. No reason to make a fuss over a burnedout light bulb. Leo's story had her seeing ghosts around every corner.

Moving a bit faster than usual, she went over to the switch for the upstairs light. That worked fine, sending a bright beam of light tumbling down the stairs. Feeling a bit more confident, she hurried up the steps to the second floor.

It only took a few minutes to pack Tim's clothes. At his age, fashion meant nothing. Several pairs of jeans, underwear and socks, and a half-dozen T-shirts decorated with every imaginable picture from Thundercats to He-Man. For kids, shirts with buttons had gone the way of the dinosaurs. Now every child looked like a walking advertisement for a toy company. Even boy's underwear featured pictures of their favorite heroes.

The clothing all fit in a small suitcase Janet kept for just such visits. Toys were another matter altogether. Surveying the cluttered floor of Tim's room, she let out a heavy sigh. Only a few patches of the bright blue carpet were visible from beneath the stacks of go-bots, thundertanks, Dragonlance heroes, and most of all, Transformers. Her son took very good care of his toys. They rarely broke. Instead, they grew old in his room.

Searching under Tim's bed, Janet found a Transformer carrying case. The plastic covered box held twelve normal-size robots. They had agreed on ten.

Carefully, she picked ten of the machines off the shelf behind his bed. Though the toys were sturdily constructed out of steel and plastic, Janet knew in her heart that someday she would accidentally crush one and Tim would never forgive her. The only child to turn to a life of crime because his mother broke his favorite Transformer. She handled the robots like fresh eggs, gently placing each one in a space in the carrying case.

By now, after two years of constant watching and rewatching the entire cartoon series on TV and then on videotape, she knew all of the major characters from the series. Brave and noble Optimus Prime definitely was a must, as was the evil Megatron. Bumblebee, the Yellow Volkswagen autobot; Grimlock, the leader of the Dino-Bots; and Starscream, the most vicious of the Decepticons; all fit snugly in the box.

Finally finished, Janet hauled the suitcase and the toy box onto the landing. The clothes hardly weighed anything but the container of Transformers felt like it held bricks. Her muscles groaned in protest. *One of the joys of modern motherhood*, she thought, as she rushed into her bedroom.

Looking around the room confirmed the notion that her son inherited his messiness from her. There were clothes scattered everywhere. Her dressing table was filled to overflowing with makeup and cosmetics. Her ironing board, not used in many months, stood in one corner with stacks of skirts and dresses resting on top of it. It made an extremely convenient shelf.

On the floor were a half-dozen boxes, some with covers on, others without. Inside were her winter clothes, packed away with no place to go. Janet often joked she needed another town house just for her possessions. Tonight, in a rush to get going, it seemed like a perfectly logical answer to her problem. Like her son, she couldn't bear throwing anything away. When a garment went out of style, she bought something new and hung up the old outfit in the closet.

With a determined look on her face, she dragged out her own suitcase and began filling it up with necessities. She worked on the "clean" principle—anything clean went in the suitcase. Fortunately, a maid came once a week and among other things, did the laundry. Otherwise, life would be unbearable.

Next she packed a small handbag with cosmetics. While she believed in the natural look, a little help never hurt. Some extra cash, hidden in the drawer with her panty hose, completed her preparations.

Janet glanced down at her watch and cursed. She had spent nearly a half hour packing. So much for taking a few minutes. If she didn't get going, she wouldn't be back in time for Tim's bedtime. Tonight, more than most evenings, she wanted a little time alone with her son.

Huffing and puffing, she dragged her suitcase to the landing. Two trips to get the stuff outside, she decided. Bruno would help if she asked, but she rejected that thought immediately. Knowing her house was a mess was one thing. Letting other people see it was another. She could manage on her own.

Moaning and groaning and spitting out a few choice words, she stumbled down the stairs carrying Tim's suitcase, his toy box and her handbag. Reaching the bottom, she dropped the luggage haphazardly on the floor and started back up the steps. Better to finish the job right away before her muscles betrayed her.

She fought the bulky suitcase down the stairway, one step at a time. It took a few minutes and a lot of sweat, but finally all of the luggage was together in the hallway. Bruno, she decided, could haul the bags out to the car.

Resting on top of the suitcase, she realized the light was now on in the parlor. That fact alone she might have rationalized as the timer kicking in late. But nothing could explain the soft sound of the radio coming from the room.

More curious than afraid, she walked over to the threshold of the living room. A brief look confirmed her suspicions. Sitting on the sofa, obviously waiting for her, was her ex-husband.

He was still tall and dark, but no longer handsome. The muscle and blood had melted away, leaving only skin and bone. Roger had always been slender. Now he looked emaciated. His shirt hung loose and limp across his shoulders and chest. A belt, tightened to the last loop, held up blue jeans otherwise much too big for his waist.

Bright blue veins stood out in bold blue relief in his hands and neck. The skin stretched like white parchment across his narrow cheeks. Bloodshot red eyes hid deep in his face, surrounded by black lines from lack of sleep.

His hair bothered her the most. Roger had always been obsessive about his hair. Oftentimes, she felt he spent more time combing and brushing it than he did with her. Now it dropped dirty and tangled in an unkempt mass down to his shoulders. He looked like hell.

"Hiya, babe," he said softly. "Long time no see."

"Roger," she managed to reply. "How long have you been sitting there?"

"I got here around an hour ago. The door was unlocked so I let myself in. When I found nobody home, I decided to wait. That's when I shut the light. Bright lights bother my eyes lately. Saw you come in, but figured I would wait awhile before saying anything. Going someplace?"

He was lying about the door. She always checked it before she left the house each day. It automatically locked when closed. Still, she decided to play it cool.

"I'm staying with my father for a few days. His driver is waiting for me outside. You remember Bruno, don't you?"

"Sure, sure," said Roger, a brief smile flickering across his lips. "Big, strong, tough Bruno. Not a nice guy to have angry at you."

There was only a hint of mockery in his voice. Just enough to show he understood her veiled threat and it didn't bother him a bit. She edged back a little from the sofa.

"Hey," he said, raising both hands as if in a peace offering. "Don't get all riled. I came to make peace, not start any trouble."

His voice gained strength as he talked. "Times change and so do people. I realize that now. We both made a big mistake getting married. We mistook lust for love. It didn't work—couldn't work. Neither of us were ready for the responsibilities. When you got pregnant, it freaked me out. I was a heel. I admit it. But that was a long time ago."

Janet couldn't believe what she was hearing. This confession didn't jive with what her father had told her earlier. Sincerity echoed in every word he spoke.

"We've both changed a lot," he continued, his expression serious. "You've matured, grown older. Same with me. I've settled down now. Got a good job, making a nice living. It seemed like a good time to put an end to the bitterness between us."

Little by little, the tension drained out of Janet as she listened to Roger. Everything he said made sense. To her, he sounded a lot more rational than her father's warnings of this afternoon. Cautiously, she stepped back into the parlor and slid into the big armchair facing the couch. She wanted to believe him.

"Okay. I agree with most of what you say. But the past is long dead. There's no starting over."

"I understand," he answered, his eyes avoiding her

gaze. "What existed between you and me died a long time ago. But why should Tim suffer?"

He rushed on, blurting out the words as fast as he could speak. "I want to see my son. I *need* to see him. You owe me that much. He's as much mine as yours. I want to be the father he never had. I need him and he needs me."

It suddenly no longer rang so true. The line about the open door bothered her. As did his appearance. Silently, she noted how tightly clenched together he held his hands. His whole body trembled with the effort, as if ready to explode.

"Well," she said, temporizing. "Maybe we could work out some sort of visitation arrangement."

"I've got a better idea," he said, his voice a little more hurried, a little more anxious. "Like I said, I've nailed down a good job. I work for an import-export line. Main office is located in Chicago. Good central location for our type of work, but we deal with firms throughout the country. We're expanding at an incredible rate."

"Go ahead," she said, not knowing where this was leading.

"Big business makes demands on you. I've been working real hard. You know the story—day and night, seven days a week, driving myself into the ground. No need to tell me how terrible I look. I see it every time I walk by a mirror."

"Maybe you should get more sleep," she said, as if compelled to make some remark.

He laughed. It wasn't the hearty sound she remembered but a high-pitched whine that broke off as quickly as it began. "You sound like a mother now. I don't need much sleep. Two, three hours a night keeps me going."

He leaned forward, hunching his shoulders together, lowering his voice to a whisper. "Sleep," he said in a whisper barely audible, "is the next closest thing to being dead. I don't want to spend part of my life pretending to be dead. I want to live." His eyes widened as his voice grew louder. "Live."

His hands were visibly shaking now as he continued. "Sorry. I didn't mean to get distracted. My mind wanders a bit these days. You're right, of course. I've got to get away before I collapse. That's where Tim comes in."

"Tim?" Cold fear gripped her. Beads of sweat dotted Roger's forehead and his eyes glared wildly at her.

"My boss is sending me on vacation. We do a lot of business in Florida. I told you we're involved in import-export, right? We've lots of contacts down south. Anyway, I leave day after tomorrow. Thought it would be the perfect chance for me and Tim to get to know each other a little better. I'd take him to Disney World. We could see all the sights, maybe spend some time at the beach. What better way to reacquaint myself with my son?"

Janet laughed. She couldn't help it. It burst out of her like an explosion. "You want to take Timmy with you on a trip to Florida? Just like that, after ignoring him for eight years, you've suddenly decided to make amends by taking him to Disney World. Give me a break, Roger."

"Don't laugh," he said slowly, traces of anger in his voice. "Don't you dare laugh at me."

His hands clenched and unclenched constantly as he spoke. "I'm finally making my mark in the world. All the breaks are turning in my favor. No more two-bit crapola jobs for me. Important people are noticing my work. They even invited me to join their Lodge."

His body shook with every word he spoke. Abruptly, he thrust out his left hand, almost punching her in the face. A heavy gold ring encircled his middle finger. Janet caught a brief glimpse of an inverted cross with a serpent twined about it. Then he pulled his fist back, as if having second thoughts about showing her the emblem.

"Only a select few belong to this organization. They're the smartest, most powerful businessmen in the city." His voice trembled as if in awe of the group. "And they want me to become a member."

"Wonderful," she said, rising from her chair. Roger's

behavior frightened her. More than a trace of madness echoed in his voice. "But I still can't let you take Tim with you. He's in school this week."

"He can miss a few days," said Roger, also rising to his feet. "Kids always take time off for vacations. By the way," and his tone grew suspicious, "where is Tim tonight?"

"I told you already. He's spending the night with my father."

"No. You said nothing of the sort." Roger's features twisted in rage. "You never mentioned that old geezer. He's why you won't let Tim go with me, isn't he. The old man always hated me. Thought his daughter was too damned good for me. That's the real reason, isn't it? Isn't it!"

Roger's voice grew wilder and wilder. Angrily, he reached out and grabbed her with clawlike hands. Thin fingers dug sharply into the skin of her shoulders, causing her to scream in shock. Despite his wasted appearance, his body blazed with maniacal strength.

"Enough of this nice guy crap," he barked out and flung her back into the armchair. Instantly he was straddling her, his legs pressed hard against her thighs.

Brutally, he reached down and grabbed her blouse. With a savage rip, he tore the garment down across her breasts, revealing her naked flesh.

"Still not wearing a bra." He laughed. In seconds, he had passed from normalcy to madness. "How about a quick feel?"

His hands grabbed her breasts and squeezed hard. Jagged flashes of pain coursed through her body. Screaming, she lashed out with both hands, trying to push him away.

Snarling like a mad dog, he grabbed both her hands with one of his. He squeezed hard, laughing as the bones of her wrists grated against each other. Sneering in her face, he reached down with his other hand for the waistband of her skirt. She could feel the hardness of his erection pressing against her through the coarse material of his jeans. Hurting her like this excited him.

Summoning all of her remaining strength, Janet jerked her knees up hard. But Roger was too high up on her body for the thrust to be very effective. He grunted in shock but held on tight.

"Bitch!" he shouted and slapped her hard in the face. The taste of blood filled her mouth.

"You'll beg for me to do it by the time I'm finished with you," he said, and slapped her again. And then again.

Janet could feel her grip of consciousness slipping. Everything grew black. Panic-stricken, she was dimly aware of Roger struggling to pull off her skirt. *He's going to kill me after he's finished,* the thought flashed through her head. *The crazy bastard is going to kill me.*

Then, miraculously, his weight was no longer on her body. As if from another world, she heard furniture crash on the other side of the room. Trying to gather a deep breath into her lungs, she forced open her eyes.

Her ex-husband lay sprawled against the TV, moaning softly, barely conscious. Standing close by him was Bruno, face red with anger, his huge hands clenched in massive fists.

Glancing around, the chauffeur saw her struggling to rise and rushed over. Still gasping for air, Janet tried pulling the remnants of her clothing over her body.

"After so long, I started to worry, Miss Janet. Even with the light on, it seemed like you were taking an awfully long time. I got more and more worried. So I finally decided to investigate. Are you okay, miss?"

"The cavalry arrived just in the nick of time," whispered Janet, still feeling a bit groggy. Her face hurt like hell. She didn't even want to think what it looked like.

"He just went nuts all of a sudden," she said, trying to explain to herself as much as Bruno. "One minute, we were talking. The next, he was trying to rape me."

"It's the dope, Miss Janet," said Bruno, trying to avert his eyes from her near naked body. "That stuff drives them out of their mind. Once it takes control, they don't know when to stop. They lose all sense of what they're doing. He would have killed you without even realizing it."

"Bruno!" Janet screamed, catching a sudden motion out of the corner of her eye.

The big chauffeur whirled just as Roger swung a heavy brass table decoration at his head. The blow caught Bruno on the shoulder instead. He crashed to the floor, but not badly injured as his attacker intended.

Roger made the most of a few seconds. He dashed for the front door. Without a word, he disappeared into the darkness of the night.

Groaning, Bruno rose to his feet. "He's a bad one, Miss Janet. A real bad one."

Mutely, Janet nodded in agreement. And she thought, he wanted her son.

10

The smell of blood filled Papa Benjamin's dreams. A mystic circle surrounded him and one other, while outside howled a bit of the dark world.

With a shudder that shook his whole body, Papa Benjamin opened his eyes and looked around his small bedroom. The clock on the nightstand said five-fifteen. Drawing in a deep breath, he forced himself to sit up in bed. No more sleep this morning. Not after a nightmare like that.

His old bones creaked and groaned in protest as he swung his legs off the mattress and onto the threadbare carpeting. Dressed only in a pair of white undershorts, he wobbled across the room to the bathroom. It mattered little that it was two hours before he normally started his day. For nearly thirty years, his routine never varied. He saw no reason to change it just because of a vision from the voodoo Mysteres.

After the bathroom, he wandered into the kitchen. A bowl of raisin bran and milk, topped with a banana, served as his breakfast. He ate mechanically, hardly tasting the food. Normally he listened to the morning news on the portable TV perched on the kitchen counter. Today he decided to leave the set off. He wanted his mind clear of distractions for what was to come.

He returned to his bedroom to change. From the bottom drawer of his dresser he pulled out a pair of white cotton pants, a white cotton shirt, and matching white socks and shoes. All were spotlessly clean and pressed, though he had not worn the outfit in more than ten years. Almost reverently, he dressed, carefully pulling on his finest clothes. With a shake of his head, he remembered his wonderful straw hat, gone more than three decades. In those bygone days, it gave him a look of stern dignity that few houn'gans in Haiti could match.

Standing, Papa Benjamin looked at himself in the full-length mirror hidden behind the door of his bedroom. Even without a hat, he decided with a small flicker of a smile, he cut an impressive figure for a man born nearly eighty years ago.

Papa Benjamin stood five foot six inches tall and weighed one hundred and thirty pounds. His skin was the color of dark chocolate and appeared even darker against the pure white of his outfit. He was entirely bald, the result of a childhood illness. Not a trace of beard or mustache graced his slender, dignified countenance.

High cheekbones, with a sharp nose and thin lips, gave his face a quiet dignity emphasized by his great age. All of his features combined to draw attention to his dark brown eyes—eyes that seemed to reflect a depth and wisdom beyond mortal man.

Satisfied with his appearance, Papa Benjamin decided it was time to go downstairs to his oum'phor. Swiftly, he descended the steps from his apartment to the temple below. He often joked with the members of his society that the exercise going up and down the long flight of stairs kept him fit. He secretly half-believed the tale himself.

THE BLACK LODGE

He had bought this building thirty years ago, soon after his escape from Haiti. An abandoned warehouse, he had acquired it for a price little more than back taxes. Located in one of the worst slums in Chicago's South Side, the huge building perfectly suited his purpose. With the help of several other houn'gans in the midwest, he had converted the old storage barn into an oum'phor on the first floor and living quarters for himself on the second.

In the three decades since his arrival, other buildings in the neighborhood had been bought and sold many times. Vandalism and gang warfare had decimated much of the surrounding area. Few landlords were willing to take a chance in such locations. Only Papa Benjamin's temple had remained undisturbed and untouched through the years. To him, the oum'phor stood as a living symbol of the power of the voodoo Mysteres. He refused to consider that its survival also owed a great deal to the continual presence of one of the most feared voodoo doctors alive.

At this hour, the temple was dark and deserted. No services were scheduled for today. He suspected that there would be no celebrations for several days. His dreams of blood foretold of terrible things in the hours ahead. As houn'gan of this society, he made all the rules, set all the dates of worship. Until this trouble passed, there would be no gatherings.

Papa Benjamin needed no light to make his way across the peristyle, the large room where most of the ceremonies took place. He had designed the entire first floor and knew every inch of it by heart. By necessity, he had taken liberties with the layout of the voodoo temple. The weather in Haiti was a great deal different than Chicago. Instead of a compound consisting of several partly enclosed buildings, one large room served as his peristyle, while an old office in the rear functioned as the Holy of Holies.

Still, tradition reigned when possible. A thin layer of earth covered the wood floor. A model of a small ship hung from one of the beams of the ceiling—the ritual

75

symbol of Erzulie, the most important goddess of voodoo. A color portrait of President Bush was thumbtacked to the back wall of the room. Standing next to the picture was an American flag.

At the exact center of the peristyle stood the center post, the *poteau-mitan*. The square-cut post, set in a circular pedestal of masonry known as the socle, stretched from floor to ceiling. It was here that all voodoo ceremonies took place. According to tradition, the top of the post touched the sky, while the bottom was anchored in the center of hell.

From base to top, the pole was covered with a complex spiral design representing the two serpent gods of voodoo—Danballah Wedo and Aida Wedo. The beam itself represented the chief god of voodoo—Legba Ati-Bon, the Wood of Justice.

On the far side of the room was the door to the office that functioned as the actual oum'phor, the Holy of Holies. It was there that Papa Benjamin conversed in private with the Great Invisibles. Though basically a trusting man, he kept the only key to the chamber on a gold chain around his neck. Trust extended only so far. Unlocking the door, Papa Benjamin entered the small room and turned on the overhead light.

As always, a flicker of emotion passed through his body as he looked about the room. This room was the center of his life. Here, he communed with the gods of voodoo. Though the Mysteres were often raised during ceremonies in the peristyle, they normally only spoke with Papa Benjamin when he was alone in the oum'phor, seeking instruction or wisdom.

Unlike most religions, a voodoo priest served as much more than a mere religious leader. Not only did he direct his followers in worship, but he also functioned as spiritual adviser, doctor, magician, and sometimes prophet. He was the center of the voodoo community.

Every voodoo society worked independent of all others. No higher authority governed individual houn'gans. Each priest served the gods directly. His word was law.

Papa Benjamin took his responsibilities quite seriously. For more than sixty years, he had served the Mysteres. They were not the most important thing in his life. They *were* his life.

Dominating the square cubicle was a rectangular platform, the height of a man's chest, known as the *pe*. It was here, leaning on the pe that he spoke with the gods. Resting on the platform were Papa Benjamin's most powerful voodoo charms.

Instinctively, he picked up his *asson*, the calabash rattle that was the symbol of his office. For six decades that *asson* had summoned the Mysteres from the astral planes of the Invisibles. It vibrated with all the mystical powers of voodoo. Just holding it filled him with the glory of his beliefs.

"The bones" whispered a voice from within one of the covered jars, the *govis*, that lined the altar. "Take the bones, houn'gan."

Shocked, Papa Benjamin took a small leather bag from the rear of the pe. He recognized the voice of Ogou Fer, the god of logic and wisdom. Normally the Mysteres spoke to him only when summoned by the secret words and rituals. For them to bridge the gap from the world of the spirit on their own indicated vast and terrible powers at work.

Visions of blood from the night before filled his thoughts and set his body shaking. Drawing in a deep breath, Papa Benjamin gathered his things together, shut the light and departed the chamber. Carefully he locked the door and hung the key around his neck.

No longer feeling quite so confident in the dark, Papa Benjamin hurried over to the light switches on the outer wall of the peristyle. With the touch of his hand, light flooded the meeting room. The overhead clock, another touch of reality dictated by the modern world, read seventen.

Gently rattling the leather bag in his hand, Papa Benjamin slowly made his way back to the center post of the peristyle. He suspected it would be hours before his visitors arrived. The scum of the night rarely stirred in the early brightness of the morning.

11

When they finally came, they arrived in spectacular style. Loud fists pounded on the doors of the temple. The room shook from the force of the blows.

Papa Benjamin calmly gathered together the bones spread out on the socle and returned them to the leather bag. He carefully rested the small sack next to his asson on the masonry.

"Only fools knock at the doors of a church," he called, in a voice surprisingly strong for one so old. "All are welcome here. Even the Children of Danballah."

There were four of them, as he knew there would be. First came the bodyguards. Two huge black men, each well over six feet tall, they pushed open the doors cautiously, as if expecting a trap. They could have been twins, with their shaven heads and wraparound metallic sunglasses. Their open-weave muscle T-shirts proudly displayed every inch of their massive chests and arms. Anger surged through Papa Benjamin's mind as he stared at their arrogant expressions.

Thirty years ago, in Haiti, two similar men killed his son during an argument over a delinquent tax bill. The pair belonged to the Tonton Macoute, the dreaded secret police of "Papa Doc" Duvalier, the island's absolute ruler. Only afterward had the murderers learned the identity of their victim. By then it was too late. Even they were not safe from the wrath of the most powerful houn'gan in all of Haiti.

The power of the Great Serpent claimed each of them. Friends found the first man dead in bed, his face a mask of terrible agony, his body swollen to twice its size. "Death by snakebite," the doctors ruled, even though no snake was ever found and it would have taken the poison of a dozen vipers to cause such a reaction.

The second killer died while eating lunch. Halfway through a meal at a local restaurant, he started complaining of pains in his stomach. Rushed to the hospital, he died soon after, shrieking in anguish. An autopsy indicated he also died from multiple viper bites, all inflicted *inside* his body.

Duvalier, no stranger to the dark forces of voodoo, reacted predictably. Justice meant nothing to him. His Tontons demanded Papa Benjamin's head. He offered them exactly that. The dictator posted a reward of ten thousand American dollars for the houn'gan's decapitated body. In Haiti, where the dead sometimes walked, only a headless corpse meant absolute safety.

Papa Benjamin fled to the United States, one step ahead of his supposed executioners. Several unexplained deaths later, he arrived in Chicago, ten thousand dollars in his pocket and no one on his trail. Duvalier later passed into history, as did the Tonton Macoute. Papa Benjamin remained.

Obviously satisfied no hidden assassins lurked in the shadows, one of the bodyguards signaled to the others waiting outside. Willis Royce, Bocar of the Children of Danballah, entered, followed by his personal protector, "Ape" Largo.

A notorious gambler before his miraculous conversion five years earlier, Royce still dressed like a pimp. Almost as tall as his bodyguards but tending to fat instead of muscle, he wore a full-length black fox fur coat that nearly dragged on the floor. His face was an advertisement for every sin of the flesh and spirit. Only his eyes were hard—black and suspicious and very, very cold.

Papa Benjamin had never met the cult leader though he had seen the man a number of times on television. He was not impressed. Royce called himself Bocar, the title given to a master of the darkest secrets of voodoo. He claimed all sorts of mystical powers. Perhaps he knew a few of the secret words. But seeing the man in person, Papa Benjamin felt sure that Royce never "went under the water."

Mentally dismissing the false Bocar, Papa Benjamin found himself instead staring at the man's infamous bodyguard and confidant, "Ape" Largo. In all of his nearly eight decades, he had never seen a human being so ugly.

Standing a little over five feet tall, Largo resembled nothing less than a cross between man and gorilla. Huge arms, banded with muscle and covered with curly black hair, dangled from incredibly vast shoulders. His limbs stretched so long that his fingers almost touched the ground. A huge barrel chest rested on short bowed legs. His neck, little more than a thick band of flesh, connected his freakish torso to a misshapen bullet head.

His features consisted primarily of a mouthful of teeth, a flat nose and piggish eyes almost hidden in wrinkled folds of skin. Two massive eyebrows met directly above his nose and curled back to meet his closely cropped black hair. There was no questioning how "Ape" Largo earned his nickname.

Local rumor had it that Royce's assistant served as the Bocar's personal death squad. Five, perhaps six, unsolved murders were directly attributed to his brute strength and animal nature. However, no one dared accuse the monster in public and the police seemed unaware of his gruesome activities. The other two bodyguards intimidated most people. Largo scared them.

"I've come to make peace," said Royce suddenly, breaking the silence. His voice echoed and reechoed in the vastness of the peristyle. "This bloodshed must end."

Papa Benjamin, sitting in a folding chair right next to the center post, nodded sagely. He had no idea what Royce was talking about, but there was one sure way to learn. He motioned to one of the long wooden benches that hugged the walls of the room. "Sit," he said, politely, "and we will talk."

Royce gestured to Largo. Without a word, the massive bodyguard walked over to the nearest bench, grabbed it in the middle with one hand and raised it into the air. Effortlessly, he brought the long wooden seat over to within a few feet of Papa Benjamin. He lowered it carefully so not to disturb the earthen floor. Royce nodded in wordless thanks and sat down. Largo took his place, standing directly behind his boss, his huge arms folded across his chest.

The other two bodyguards remained at the doors. With their metallic sunglasses hiding their eyes, they could have been asleep on their feet with no one the wiser.

"I'm not a greedy man," said Royce nervously. "I'm willing to share and share alike. There's more than enough loot for everyone. No need for violence. After all, we both worship the same gods."

"Tell me what you want," said Papa Benjamin, trying to keep his temper under control. Every word this liar spoke rubbed salt into open wounds.

"For years, people in-the-know warned me of your power," Royce continued, his voice shaking now. "Foolishly, I laughed at them. I considered voodoo just another scam like all the other religions. Promise the suckers a better future and in the meantime rob them blind."

"And now?" asked Papa Benjamin, curious in spite of himself.

"I know the truth," said Royce, in a whisper barely heard. "The Great Serpent lives. Forgive me. I beg you. Remove the curse."

For a moment, Papa Benjamin sat silently, trying to make sense out of nonsense. Finally he spoke.

"The curse?" he said, with a cruel laugh. "I placed no curse on you. Whatever horrors assail you, they are not of my calling. I would not dirty my hands with your blood."

"You're lying," said Royce, his voice rising a notch. "You're lying. You want it all."

"All of what?" asked Papa Benjamin, angrily. "For thirty years, I have struggled to guide the faithful of this city in the true worship of the voodoo Mysteres. At most, my followers number a few hundred. How many flock to your ministry, oh mighty Bocar of Danballah? Ten thousand, twenty thousand? More than that? How many dishonest politicians take your money and curry your favor? How many crooked policemen look the other way when you pass among them? How many children have drifted into drugs and prostitution in the name of the voodoo gods? I want nothing of yours. I spit on your money! I spit on you!''

"Wait," said Ape Largo, unexpectedly. The bodyguard's voice sounded like sandpaper being dragged over a steel pipe. "Angry words never solved anything. At least listen to what we have to say. Whether or not you had anything to do with them, these murders affect you as well as us. So far, the killer has only attacked our followers. Yours could be next.''

"Speak, then," said Papa Benjamin, already regretting his outburst. He noticed that Largo kept one huge hand on Royce's shoulder, preventing the cult leader from rising. The bodyguard intended this conversation to continue whether his boss liked it or not. Perhaps the servant possessed more brains than the master.

"Someone—no, make that some *thing* is murdering my people," said Royce dramatically. "At least five died on Monday. He slaughtered another dozen or more last night. He strikes fast, and then disappears into the night.''

"Or more?" asked Papa Benjamin.

"After he kills them, he chops up their bodies and scatters the pieces," answered Largo. "We've found that many heads so far. But matching up arms and legs and torsos takes time. Our count might be off by a few.''

"He devours their souls," said Papa Benjamin slowly, searching old memories for the right words. He suddenly felt very cold. "As a child, I heard of such killings. My father, himself a powerful houn'gan, told me of the 'Red Sects' who lived in the mountains and practiced human sacrifice. Followers of the Pethro Mysteres, they called themselves *Cochons sans poils*.

"Tell me," he continued, directing his remarks more

to Ape Largo than Willis Royce, "did this killer leave a mark on the floor? Perhaps he drew some symbol on the walls?"

Wordlessly, Ape Largo circled the bench and knelt on the earth floor between the two older men. With one finger he traced five designs in the dirt.

"At every location, we discovered the same design. The Dark Man painted these in the blood of his victims," said the bodyguard. "In each case, he used a decapitated hand of a dead man as his brush."

Papa Benjamin bent over to stare at the tracings. "He draws power from their blood. For blood is life. Each death makes him stronger."

Papa Benjamin shook his head in bewilderment. "I do not recognize any of these *veves*. They represent no astral force I ever encountered." Then he hesitated for a second, thinking about what had been said. "You called him 'the Dark Man.' Why?"

"One girl escaped this monster," said Largo. "Out of all the people attacked, she was the only survivor."

Tersely, the bodyguard described Lisa Ray's adventure of the night before. "She constantly referred to her attacker as the Dark Man. That name seemed as good as any."

"A giant dressed entirely in black; invulnerable, unstoppable," repeated Papa Benjamin. Fragments of dream rushed through his head as he spoke. The Mysteres often worked in strange and terrible fashion. "You suspect . . . ?"

"Baron Samedi," answered Royce, drawing in a deep breath. "The Rada gods want their revenge. The Lord of the Cemetery seeks to destroy me and all my followers."

"What about the police?"

Royce laughed, a short bark of derision, signifying his thoughts of the Chicago law enforcement authorities. "Are you jiving me? You think the police care about me? They're looking the other way. Dumb honkies can't wait to spit on my grave."

"My patron exaggerates a little," said Largo, showing

a mouthful of teeth. His face twisted into so frightful a sight that it took Papa Benjamin a few seconds to realize that the bodyguard was attempting a smile. "However, the police offer little in the way of hope. This monster strikes at random, leaves no fingerprints, and disappears without a trace. Personally, I think he scares the shit out of them. I know he affects me that way."

"And Ape don't scare easy," said Royce, with a shiver.

"I will try to help you," said Papa Benjamin, somberly, "but for a price."

"Name it," said Royce.

"I want twenty-five thousand dollars in cash," said Papa Benjamin calmly, with only the barest trace of a smile on his lips. "Not a penny less. In small, unmarked bills, as they say in the detective movies."

Royce turned to one of the two goons stationed at the doors. "Get it," he said. "Just the way he wants."

The cult leader faced Papa Benjamin. "It'll take a little time. Even I don't keep that kind of loose cash lying around." Then his tone grew cold. "For this money, you will remove the curse from me?"

"I offer no guarantees," said Papa Benjamin, his voice equally frigid. "If I had my way, you would suffer the same fate as your disciples. But my oum'phor badly needs repair. My congregation wants to start a preschool for their children but there is no money. The food pantry for those too poor to fend for themselves is empty. Your 'contribution' will help pay for these things. I am a man of my word. What I can do, I will do."

Willis Royce lapsed into a sullen silence. Papa Benjamin glared at the cult leader, his heart heavy with anger. The voodoo gods had answered his prayer for aid. This money solved many of the problems faced by his congregation. But helping garbage like Royce went against all of his principles.

Unexpectedly, Ape Largo broke the silence.

"Extrapolating a little from your remarks, I take it you suspect this assassin comes directly from the spirit world?" he asked in his gravelly voice. "Are we dealing with a man 'mounted' by a god or an actual supernatural manifestation?''

Again Papa Benjamin was impressed by the body-guard's obvious intelligence. His harsh voice could not disguise his choice of words. He was well educated, a trait not shared by most of his comrades. The man intrigued Papa Benjamin.

"You know, then, what it means to be 'mounted' by one of the Mysteres?''

"Only from the descriptions that I've read,'' said Largo. "I never actually witnessed such an event. I gather the event corresponds with the Christian concept of possession. A god literally takes control of a worship-er's body—speaking through him, directing his every action.''

"And more,'' said Papa Benjamin. "The Mysteres can impart that follower, the 'cheval' incredible pow-ers—''

"Including superhuman strength and immunity from bullets?'' broke in an angry Willis Royce. "It ain't possible.''

"Anything is possible,'' replied Papa Benjamin, firmly. "However, I understand your doubts. I find that part of the girl's story hard to believe myself. We shall soon know the truth.''

He raised up the small leather bag from the socle. "The bones will reveal all. They never lie.''

"You read the bones?'' asked Ape Largo, his eyes fixed on the pouch.

"You are dealing with a true houn'gan, child,'' said Papa Benjamin, the sarcasm thick in his voice. "Not a self-proclaimed prophet of a makeshift cult formed only to line his pockets.''

He gently shook the sack, setting the contents rat-tling. "My father gave me these bones. His father gave them to him. And so it always was, back to Africa. By the word passed down to me from my sacred ancestors, these bones came from the holy city, Ife', where voodoo began. They are powerful charms. With them we can learn the nature of your enemy. And once that is known, we will know how to placate the god who controls him."

"Well, let's get started," said Royce, spotting his other bodyguard reentering the room. "Here's your money."

"First we count, then we work," said Papa Benjamin firmly.

"What's wrong?" asked Royce. "You don't trust me?"

"My trust is earned, not bought," replied the voodoo doctor. "Your word means nothing to me. Count."

12

Twenty minutes later they were ready to begin. "Remain quiet unless I give you permission to speak," said Papa Benjamin, his gaze taking in the other four men in the room. "I need complete silence to read the bones."

Gesturing Royce and Largo back, Papa Benjamin knelt down in front of the center post. Resting his elbows on the socle, he carefully opened the leather bag containing the bones. Gently, he shook the contents into his right hand.

Incredibly ancient, the bones glistened white in the artificial light. Though he had handled them a thousand times, a sense of awe still gripped Papa Benjamin at the touch of the skeletal remains.

Beneath his breath, he spoke the words of power. Most voodoo ceremonies were performed aloud, with the congregation joining in as both participants and chorus. However, reading the bones was one of the secret rites, known only to a select few.

With a flick of the wrist, Papa Benjamin flung the bones onto the brickwork. Waiting a few seconds after they came to rest, he peered intently at the patterns they formed on the socle.

"I see shadows," he said almost immediately. "Powerful forces move in the background. They stand behind you, Willis Royce, these dark shadows. Is my vision correct?"

"Well, certain wealthy men help finance some of my operations," said Willis Royce cautiously. "They put up a lot of the cash involved in the project threatened by the Dark Man."

Swiftly gathering up the bones, Papa Benjamin tossed them down for a second time. "There is blood here, much blood. And I sense an evil not of our world. One man controls this force."

"But which god works against me?" asked Royce, forgetting the caution for silence.

"None of the gods," answered Papa Benjamin, a thin trickle of sweat running down his forehead even in the coolness of the building. "The bones speak of ancient sorcery, magic from a time before Ife'. This Dark Man belongs to the night. Death walks hand in hand with him. My magic can do little to stop him. If he finds you, nothing on earth can save you."

Papa Benjamin gathered up the bones and cast them for a third time. For a long time he stared at the pattern they made. Then he turned and looked directly at Royce.

"Treachery and betrayal surround you. Trust no one. Your enemies know your every secret. One who calls you friend controls the Dark Man."

"One of my own men?" said Royce. He glanced around suspiciously at Ape Largo, then at the two bodyguards by the door. "I don't believe it. Nobody dares double-cross me."

"Believe what you want," said Papa Benjamin. Carefully, he collected the bones off the socle and dropped them back in their sack. "I only read what the bones revealed. Now leave me alone. I've wasted too much time on this matter."

"What the hell," said Royce angrily, rising from the

bench. "You mean that's it. I get five minutes worth of fortune-telling for twenty-five big ones. Not much of a deal to me."

With a snap of his fingers, the cult leader waved forward the two goons in the doorway. As they shuffled forward, Ape Largo dropped back off to the side, away from the action. His gaze darted back from his boss to Papa Benjamin, but he made no move to interfere.

"Show grandpa here your toy, Morris," said Royce, with a harsh laugh. "Maybe that will start him talkin' again."

With a grin, the slightly taller of the two bodyguards pulled a long switchblade from his boot. With a flick of the wrist, he flipped the knife open, revealing a six-inch blade of polished steel.

"You cannot threaten me," said Papa Benjamin, with only the slightest tremor in his voice. "Remember our bargain."

"Bargain?" said Royce. "I don't remember making any bargain. You boys remember any bargain?"

No one said a word. The two goons edged a bit closer to Papa Benjamin. Ape Largo remained where he was, his huge arms folded across his chest.

"Time for us to take our money and leave," said Royce, gesturing to his men.

"I forgive you for your lack of knowledge, mighty Bocar," said Papa Benjamin, his voice loud and quite steady. If anything, he sounded amused.

"Only a voodoo adept trained in Haiti knows that you never renege on a contract made on sacred ground. The Mysteres forbid such conduct in their presence."

Papa Benjamin's voice sank down to a whisper, but one that could be heard throughout the peristyle. "They take special offense when you try cheating one of their servants. Because they are so sensitive, the voodoo gods grant their houn'gans certain extraordinary powers.

"For example," he continued, "a powerful papa-loa possesses an invisible grip."

Papa Benjamin stretched his left arm straight out, palm up, fingers spread open. "In this fashion, acting

88

through the invisible world, I can grab hold of your testicles . . . and squeeze."

And with a harsh laugh of triumph, he clenched his hand tightly into a fist.

Willis Royce shrieked in agony and clutched his groin with both hands. Moaning horribly, he dropped to the floor. Muttering incomprehensible obscenities, the cult leader rolled back and forth in the dirt, oblivious to anything else.

"Leave now," said Papa Benjamin, aiming a finger at the two goons trying to help Royce to his feet. "Take your mighty Bocar with you. And tell him, when he recovers, that he is no longer welcome in my oum'phor. The next time, I will not let go so quickly."

In a mad shuffle, the two bodyguards were out the door, dragging Royce, still moaning in pain, between them. In the peristyle, only Papa Benjamin and Ape Largo remained.

"A very nice example of using the power of suggestion to its maximum effect," said the bodyguard, flashing his grotesque smile. His laughter sounded like a cement truck in action. Strangely enough, Papa Benjamin found himself warming to this incredibly ugly character.

"You doubt my power?" he asked, only half in jest.

"I never said that," replied Largo, his hands dropping in a defensive position between his legs. "I always considered voodoo a perfect amalgam of the practical and the supernatural. As a man looking for his roots, the religion always fascinated me. I joined Royce's group hoping to learn more. It didn't take me long to realize my mistake."

"I could teach you many things," said Papa Benjamin, his mind working at a furious pace. "A true houn'gan is always willing to instruct those seeking the truth."

"Sounds fascinating," said Largo, "but no way I can accept. Royce depends on me. I doubt if he would take kindly to my unexpected departure. But"—and the disappointment was apparent in his every word—"thanks again for the offer."

"Perhaps events will change," said Papa Benjamin.

"Yeah, sure," said Largo, turning to the door. "I better get going. The others will start wondering what happened to me."

"Go in peace," said Papa Benjamin, with a shrug of dismissal.

Then, just as the giant reached the doorway, Papa Benjamin had a sudden change of heart. Anxiously, he called out to the other man.

"Largo. Wait. One more thing I saw revealed in the bones. Death knocks three times. Do not forget. Death knocks three times."

"In these crazy times, I don't forget anything," said Largo. "Thanks for the tip. I hope I can figure out what it means."

Largo disappeared out into the street. Now only Papa Benjamin sat in the peristyle. Visions of blood and slaughter filled his eyes. Royce was a walking dead man. He had seen that the minute the cult leader walked into the room. But with luck, Ape Largo might escape the doom that pursued his boss. Good fortune aided by certain entreaties to the gods of voodoo, Papa Benjamin decided. The Mysteres worked in strange and devious paths. This time he suspected their plans and his coincided. Finally his nightmares of hours past made sense.

13

The smell of freshly brewed coffee greeted Taine as he walked into his office a little before nine. Mrs. McConnell poured him a cup as he hung up his raincoat. Outside, a light but steady drizzle soaked the city.

Sitting across from his secretary, Taine listened attentively as she reported her findings. Mrs. McConnell used large yellow legal pads to record her notes. At least a dozen pages were covered with scribbled facts.

"I'll start with Evangeline Caldwell," she began, a slight note of disapproval in her tone. "Finding information on her proved no challenge. Her exploits filled the scandal sheets. An enterprising filmmaker could produce a spectacular X-rated movie of her life. She might even play herself, if the mood struck her."

"I gather our client leads the wild life?" asked Taine.

"Wild hardly describes her activities. Evidently she and her husband have a very open marriage. Both regularly make the gossip columns with their sexual shenanigans. But the possibility of divorce never comes up."

"Yet," said Taine, "when she came here, she wanted the visit kept secret from her husband. Illicit sex is okay but seeing a detective is not. Sounds like she has a wonderful home life."

"You know her father is Harmon Sangmeister, reputedly the richest man in Chicago, perhaps the entire country. I'll come back to him later. Angel, the nickname she prefers,"—and Mrs. McConnell could not suppress a snort of derision as she spoke—"and her papa have never gotten along very well.

"She attended a half-dozen private schools as a teenager. No one was willing to comment on her expulsions. However, I gathered all of them involved breaking the rules regarding proper behavior for young ladies. Our Angel started swinging early and never stopped."

Mrs. McConnell turned over the first page of her legal pad. "I compiled a list of her more outstanding conquests."

Mrs. McConnell held up her notebook. The page was covered from top to bottom. Taine recognized a number of well-connected businessmen, several movie actors, a TV newscaster and three baseball players.

"She's no angel," he said, with a shake of his head.

"You'll even notice several women on the list. Ms. Caldwell obviously believes in equality among the sexes."

Turning the page, Mrs. McConnell continued. "Her

husband provides her with a very generous allowance. She makes the most of it. Though they might whisper behind her back, the owners of the most expensive stores on the Magnificent Mile welcome her with open arms when she comes calling. Our little Angel is notorious for dropping big bucks when she goes on a shopping binge.

"Her tastes run to the latest in the neodecadent punk rock fashion. She sticks to the basics—customized black leather jeans, spandex tops; or tight knit dresses in primary colors. According to one of her more outrageous interviews, she dislikes undergarments and rarely wears any."

"Enough lurid details," said Taine, raising one hand in protest. "Did you find anything about her that might tie into our investigation?"

"Not much. As I mentioned, the bitterness between her and her father actually exists. They hate each other. The old man didn't even attend her wedding. Though it's quite possible she didn't invite him.

"I can't imagine anyone blackmailing Angel. She enjoys flaunting her excesses. Nothing shames her. Meanwhile, Victor obviously knows and tacitly approves of her indiscretions. It frees him for his own lustful activities."

"Which leads us to the big question," said Taine. "What sort of bizarre ritual or ceremony frightens a woman like Angel?"

Taine expected no answer nor did Mrs. McConnell offer one. "What did you learn about her charming husband?"

Another shuffle of yellow pages. "Victor Caldwell defies ordinary descriptions. Physically, he stands five-eight, weighs three-fifty—"

"Three hundred and fifty?" interrupted Taine, not believing his ears.

"That's correct," said Mrs. McConnell. "He blames glandular troubles for his weight. Most people I interviewed thought his habit of eating a pound box of chocolates every day might contribute to his problems. And he routinely goes on incredible eating jags where he devours a half-dozen hamburgers, a carton of soda pop and a half-gallon of ice cream. Victor firmly believes in 'Everything to excess.' "

"He sounds charming," Taine said. "Yet both you and his wife referred to his numerous amorous encounters. Am I missing something here?"

Mrs. McConnell gave Taine an odd look. "Victor doesn't rely on his good looks to attract women. Instead, he attracts them the old-fashioned way, with money. His seventy-five million supplies him with all the bimbos he desires."

"He's older than Angel?"

"Ten years. She's thirty. He's forty, pushing a hundred. Between his lifestyle and weight, he should have died years ago."

"I think that's plenty on his personal life. What about his business dealings?"

Another shuffling of notes. "Mr. Caldwell's name came up a number of times in the recent FBI probe of the Commodities and Futures Exchange. According to stories leaked to the papers, Victor masterminded a secret network of traders who swapped information on major buy-and-sell transactions. Advance tips can make brokers millions if they coattail their purchases with big corporations. It enables them to plunder the market without risking a dollar in real money. They skim off huge profits just by making a few phone calls.

"Needless to say, such insider trading is strictly illegal. However, when the charges finally came down, Victor's name was notable only by its absence. In fact, not one of the brokers linked with him in the scam was accused of wrongdoing. For all of the sound and fury, the FBI had no hard evidence proving any of the allegations."

"What happened?" asked Taine.

"Absolute and total silence defeated them. In these types of investigations, the FBI depends on their moles for inside information.

"That worked fine with the one large group of traders.

Those idiots convicted themselves. Remember the stories in the newspapers detailing their weekend orgies and lavish trips to the West Indies. Sooner or later that sort of behavior catches up with you."

"I gather Caldwell's friends kept a low profile."

"Correct. Despite a paper trail that indicated a networking scheme of colossal proportions, the FBI couldn't do a thing. All of the suspects belonged to a certain club, but no law prevented that. Plenty of other people, not in the Commodities and Futures Market, belonged to the same organization.

"All of the government's circumstantial evidence meant nothing unless someone cracked. They tried infiltrating the private club but their agents were routinely denied membership. Bribes met open hostility and were immediately reported to the proper authorities. Veiled threats were ignored. The FBI was stumped. They never ran into a wall of silence like this before.

"Caldwell's attorneys immediately claimed the FBI was engaged in a political vendetta, based on sheer coincidence, against their client. They wanted an apology issued and the agents in charge of the investigation fired. The whole mess ended up in court where it will be buried for the next ten years."

"What's the name of this wholesome organization defamed by our federal investigators?" asked Taine.

"I thought you would never ask. They call themselves *The Mystic Order of the Knights of Antioch*."

Taine closed his eyes for a moment, marshaling his thoughts. He had suspected the worse. Now he knew for sure.

"No connection I assume with the Knights of Columbus, the Masons, or other well-known fraternal groups?" he asked, already knowing the answer to the question.

"None of them ever heard of the Knights of Antioch."

"That emblem I asked you to check on . . ."

"Their insignia," said Mrs. McConnell, sounding smug and satisfied with herself.

"Surprise, surprise," said Taine. "What else did you learn about this secret society?"

94

"According to what little information is available to the public, the Lodge is a private fraternal order of men and women from the business community. Membership is by invitation only. They hold quarterly meetings, usually a dinner at a fancy restaurant in the Loop. No business takes place at these meetings, nor are any dues collected."

"How do you join?" asked Taine.

"They contact you. I gather that only the wealthiest, most powerful men and women in the city are invited. The order is quite secretive about its membership rolls."

"Victor Caldwell and Harmon Sangmeister both belong."

"Of course. I greased more than a few palms at certain downtown dining establishments. Amazing how much information a hundred dollar bill can buy these days. Here's a list of some of the more prominent people in the organization."

Mrs. McConnell handed Taine a yellow sheet filled with names. He nodded in satisfaction. His assistant handled bribes much better than he did. He lacked the necessary patience and finesse to realize exactly when to make the right offer. Mrs. McConnell suffered from no such inhibitions.

Taine scanned the list she handed him. He felt somewhat chagrined to admit he recognized fewer names than on Evangeline Caldwell's roll call. So much for his familiarity with the movers and shakers of Chicago business.

"I take it this club represents a lot of money."

"Billions," said Mrs. McConnell, forming each syllable into a separate word.

"A lot of power rides with that kind of cash," said Taine. "Hard to believe they don't use it somehow."

"Very hard to believe," repeated his assistant. "Why do I get the impression, Mr. Taine, that I'm telling you things you already know?"

He ignored her question. Instead, he asked another of his own. "Who runs the show—Caldwell or Sangmeister?"

"Definitely Angel's big bad daddy. According to my

restaurant friends, he's ruled the Lodge for over twenty years.''

"Tell me a little about the mysterious Mr. Sangmeister," said Taine, changing subjects.

"He likes bleached blondes with big tits," said Mrs. McConnell.

Taine shook his head as if trying to get his ears working correctly. Mrs. McConnell never talked like that. "Would you care to repeat that?"

Smiling at his reaction, she did exactly that. "I said he likes bleached blondes with big tits."

"And . . ." prompted Taine.

"And nothing," she said, making a face. "Thus my expression of displeasure. Except for his taste in women, I discovered absolutely nothing of importance about Mr. Sangmeister. All I learned was that nobody knows a thing about him. After hours of work, I ended up with a big fat zero.

"His obsession with privacy rivals the late Howard Hughes. For all I know, he is Howard Hughes, living under an assumed name.''

Taine left it at that.

"Anything else to report?"

"That book dealer in New York sends his regards. He says you should settle down and get married."

"That means his weird daughter is still single," said Taine, laughing. "He introduced me to her on my last trip to the Big Apple. She dressed only in black and devotedly believed in astrology. Fortunately our signs didn't coincide. You asked him about Arelim?"

"Of course. I got a rather cryptic reply. He said you would understand. He called the Angel 'The Finger of Elohim.' That make any sense to you?"

Taine frowned. "I think so. But so what? It doesn't *mean* anything. I need some solid facts. It's time for me to do some talking to the members of the Knights of Antioch. I'll start with Victor Caldwell."

"One last thing," said Mrs. McConnell as he prepared to leave. "I asked your friend in New York about the society. He suggested we consult *The History of Occult*

Societies by Russell Arrigo. I called the main library and they have a copy in their reference section. If you want, I could go down there before lunch and duplicate any reference to the Knights."

"It sounds like a longshot to me," said Taine. "But a little background on the organization might be useful. Don't forget your umbrella, though. The weatherman predicts rain all day and night. We'll both probably need something hot to drink before the day is over."

14

Maturity, Janet decided as she rolled over in bed and buried her face in the pillow, was knowing when to say enough. In the last four years, she had only missed a half-dozen days of work. All of those were the result of Timmy's illness, from chicken pox to the flu. Her own health was perfect. Natural disasters, from snowstorms to floods, never fazed her. Depression and other personal problems always took a backseat to the business. Until today.

She couldn't face her employees with her face battered and bruised from Roger's beating the night before. Fortunately his slaps had not done any major damage. But they had left her black-and-blue. She looked like the loser in a rough-and-tumble boxing match.

When she arrived back at the estate last night, Timmy was already asleep. With him safe in bed, Janet felt immeasurably relieved.

Real violence frightened her son. At this age, he handled TV shows pretty well. Like most normal children, he understood the difference between acting and actuality. Watching a thousand robots destroy each other in cartoons never upset him. The wild antics of professional wrestling thrilled him. But catching a glimpse of the news showing soldiers armed with nightsticks breaking up a student demonstration in China terrified him for days. Janet shuddered as she imagined his reaction to her condition last night.

Planning ahead for the morning, she arranged for Martha to wake Tim in the morning, feed him breakfast and get him off to school with Bruno. Janet often slept late when they stayed at Brentwood, so her absence wouldn't worry her son. By the time he returned from school, her features should be pretty much back to normal. Any bruises could be explained away by a bad fall.

With a groan, she rolled over and stared at the clock on the nightstand. It was nearly nine-thirty. By now the girls at her store were probably wondering what happened to her. For an instant she considered driving downtown. But the mere motion of sitting up sent ripples of pain shooting through her body. Her breasts ached. Her neck creaked in protest. And her face felt like a hundred toothpicks were stuck in her cheeks. She dropped back down to the pillow. The business would have to survive without her meddling.

Janet got out of bed a half hour later. A quick call downtown reassured her that her assistants were managing fine. Leah, the girl who answered the phone, sounded positively chipper when Janet admitted she might not come into work tomorrow either.

A leisurely breakfast served in her room by Martha helped raise Janet's spirits. Over the last bite of bacon and eggs, and hash browns and toast, she meditated thoughtfully on Roger's weird behavior.

Deadly drugs obviously motived most of his actions, along with his hatred of her. He was always intense in all of his actions. A number of times during their stormy relationship she felt he was borderline psychotic. Smoking crack had evidently destroyed his last shreds of self-control. The drug unleashed the mad beast lurking within his mind. Whatever fate her father planned for her ex-husband, he deserved it in full.

Still, Leo's story about a kidnaping sounded awfully suspicious. In his present state, Roger seemed incapable of planning such an elaborate scheme. Nor could she believe anyone would be stupid enough to help him. The more she thought about it, the more she was convinced her father had juggled the facts for his own ends.

Leo often manipulated information to come up with unusual variations on the truth. He never lied. The need never arose. Instead, he took one or two unconnected facts, and with a wall of lies and half-truths, constructed an elaborate charade to further his ambitions. After listening to Roger's ranting last night, Janet believed the part about kidnaping Tim. However, she suspected that the reasons behind the crime dealt with something other than blackmail.

Riding back to Brentwood last night, she came to the conclusion that Leo was hiding something from her. She needed to do some investigating on her own. Thus, on her return to the mansion, she told Leo all the details of Roger's attack except one. She never mentioned her ex-husband's lodge pin. It was her secret. Today she planned to learn the meaning of that bizarre charm.

The design looked familiar. Her memory rarely failed her. She was sure she had encountered that emblem before. As a history major, she had studied unusual societies and religions throughout the world. One of her old textbooks probably contained the information she needed.

Unfortunately, she had deposited all of her college books into the trash bin after finals her senior year. She decided the main library in the Loop would be the best place to find a copy of the textbook she had used in college.

After getting dressed, she wandered over to Tim's room. A quick search turned up a box of crayons and a sheet of blank paper. She drew a rough sketch of the design engraved on Roger's ring. It wasn't great, but it served its purpose.

Studying the picture, she detected a strong note of sexual symbolism in the basic structure. A vague memory tugged at her subconscious mind. She grasped at a fleeting recollection of ancient fertility rites discussed in anthropology classes years ago. In pagan rituals, serpents and knives usually meant blood and sacrifice.

Suddenly in a hurry to learn more, she folded the sketch and put it in her purse. A quick word to Martha and she was off. Leo had left early in the morning on a series of business meetings and was not expected back until late that afternoon. Bruno was picking up Tim from school. For one of the few times in the last few years, she had the day entirely to herself.

An hour later Janet was waiting impatiently at the reference desk of the main library. It was pouring outside and the water dripping off her umbrella was forming a huge puddle on the marble floor. The librarian, an elderly gray-haired lady, was explaining how to use the microfilm system to an anxious college student. Janet tapped one foot anxiously against the hard floor. She hated delays.

"Sorry to keep you waiting," said the librarian, coming over to her. "How can I help you?"

"I need information on secret societies," said Janet. "I've already gone through the encyclopedias and standard reference volumes on the open shelves but didn't find anything. One of the books listed a title in the bibliography that sounded promising. I checked the card catalog and it lists the volume as being in the noncirculating section."

Janet handed over a small sheet of paper. "I copied down the reference code. The name of the book is *The History of Occult Societies* by Russell Arrigo."

"How very, very odd," said the librarian. She smiled at Janet's confusion. "You're the second person today who requested that book. Two in the same day, and before that, not a nibble for years. There must be something in the air."

The librarian shuffled off to the noncirculating section. Desperately, Janet bit the inside of her lip and tried to come up with a believable story. Finally, as the elderly woman returned carrying a thick, dictionary-size volume, Janet settled on her course of action.

"You said another person requested this book this

morning?" she asked, letting her voice tremble a bit. "Did he say why?"

"Actually it was a woman. Nice, personable sort," the librarian added. "She needed information on a group called The Mystic Order of the Knights of Antioch. I remember because it was such an odd name for a secret society."

Swiftly Janet turned to the correct page. "It can't be," she gasped in surprise as she found herself staring at a picture of the emblem from Roger's ring. "It can't be true."

"Is something wrong?" asked the librarian.

"I've been working on my doctoral thesis for two years," said Janet, improvising as she went along. "It's a study of primitive and modern secret societies. It links the various groups by beliefs, traditions and customs. This Order is very obscure. If someone else is researching them as well, they might be working on the same topic. It would mean I've wasted two years of my life!"

Janet poured every bit of emotion possible into her short and passionate speech. Several patrons in the reading room turned to stare at the tears running down her cheeks. Janet didn't care. She had to discover the identity of the other woman.

"Now, now," said the librarian, patting Janet on the hand in a motherly fashion. "The other patron called first to see if the book was available. She left a phone number. I still have it here. If you like, I can give it to you. Here it is. Her name is Mary McConnell."

"Oh, could you," said Janet, trying not to overdo it. "I'll give her a call later in the day and just make sure we aren't working on similar projects. I appreciate it so much."

Janet managed to duplicate the article without attracting too much more attention. She tucked the phone number safely away in her purse. She left the library a few minutes before noon.

Janet ate lunch in the main dining room at Marshall Field's. Waiting for the waitress to bring her sandwich, she studied the short article on the Knights of Antioch.

Nothing in the piece awakened any forgotten memories. Still, Janet felt certain she had seen that distinctive emblem before.

More important, she had the phone number of this other person also researching the same group. The librarian was right. Chance stretched only so far. Janet meant to find out this afternoon why this Mary McConnell was investigating the Mystic Knights. With Roger and her father both mentioning a weekend deadline, there was no time to waste.

15

The man who thought of himself as Arelim frowned at the cards on his desk. Like all great magicians, he implicitly believed in the power of the tarot deck. Today his reading left him puzzled. And a little worried.

All three passes yielded the same run of four major trumps. First came "The Hermit," the symbol of hidden wisdom. Next came "The Wheel of Fortune," the symbol of destiny. Third in the sequence was "Pope Joan," the card signifying a mysterious woman. The final card in every run was "La Mort," the trump of death.

Normally, he experienced little trouble interpreting the divination. The meaning of three of the cards he understood perfectly. Death walked in the Dark Man, "La Mort" brought to unholy life by his dark magic. Hidden wisdom gave him the power to control that unstoppable killer. Each murder committed by his agent advanced his destiny. It progressed with a certainty almost without question. Except the recurring image of Pope Joan troubled his vision.

With a curse of annoyance, he gathered the cards together and flung them into the top drawer of his desk. Perhaps he worried too much about nothing. A new woman served as priestess in the ceremony Friday night. She could be the mysterious figure indicated by the tarot deck. The explanation left him unsatisfied and annoyed.

Arelim disliked uncertainty. The element of chance added unforeseen elements to the dangerous game he played. His enemies already knew about the Dark Man. The black girl's escape had been an unfortunate slip. Yet, in a way, it had actually worked in his favor.

He played with that thought for a moment. The first few killings had been attributed to a new gang trying to expand into the Chicago marketplace. Up to last night, the Children of Danballah had been preparing for war. Such battles were a fact of life in the drug trade. The dealers recognized them as an inevitable result of their occupation. That much easy money always attracted casual violence.

However, the girl's description of the Dark Man and his attack changed all that. Suddenly, the Children found themselves faced with an enemy they couldn't comprehend. Death beckoned with a butcher's cleaver. Street punks understood a maniac armed with a machine gun. But they panicked when faced by an unstoppable killer who chopped them to pieces and then painted the walls with their blood.

Arelim smiled. Perhaps the black girl served as Pope Joan in his tarot reading. Her unexpected survival had changed the complexion of the game. Sometimes, he planned too carefully. The Dark Man operated too efficiently. One terrified living witness spread the panic much better than a dozen unconfirmed rumors.

The coming violence today and tomorrow would squash what little resistance still remained. The drug lords' empire was already crumbling. With a few well-defined slashes, it should be in ruins by Friday night. The rise of the Dark Man signaled an end to the Children of Danballah.

Shaking his head, Arelim rose from his chair and circled his desk. All of his plans culminated Friday evening. Over a year of scheming and plotting climaxed in only two days. If anything, he regretted the game was coming to an end so quickly. He enjoyed such exercises.

Even though he always won, he still enjoyed the challenge of manipulating his enemies. Nothing gave him greater pleasure than pulling the right strings at the right times.

To Arelim, life itself was a game. The greatest of all challenges, it gave meaning to an otherwise meaningless world. Great men played, with other men as their pieces. It was a game without rules, without judges.

He secretly sneered at the fools who proclaimed that the extent of their possessions crowned them the winners. He knew the real truth. In the great game, those who wielded the most power were the true victors.

That was why rich men entered politics. They spoke of public duty and civic obligations. But deep beneath all the rhetoric lurked that overwhelming passion for power.

Keeping that thought firmly in mind, he spoke the four words of domination. He needed no other spell. The ancient words reverberated through the room like living things. The very walls seemed to shiver with their passing.

In front of Arelim, the air twisted in upon itself. Darkness swirled out of nothingness, coalesced into the stuff of nightmares. Where there was nothing, was something. Before the magician, radiating cold evil, stood the Angel of Death.

A product of Arelim's innermost passions and hatreds, the creature fashioned its image from the worst fears of its victims. Throughout history, it had worn a thousand shapes, each time reflecting the greatest horrors of the time. The one who summoned it gave it purpose, gave it life. In modern Chicago, it was the Dark Man.

"You are ready to proceed with the next stage of our program?" Arelim asked his creation.

"Of course," answered the creature, his voice smooth and confident. "You know that. Are your thoughts not my thoughts? I know exactly where to look. Their blood calls to me."

"The ones you seek are old and weak."

"It doesn't matter," said the Dark Man. "My strength comes from their death. Young or old, healthy or sick, they all quench my thirst. My power increases with each killing. The actual act provides me with their life energy. Only the runes matter. Can't you feel the power surge through you each time I inscribe those letters in their blood?"

Arelim nodded. They were linked together, the two of them, with bonds closer than any mortal ties. As the Dark Man grew stronger, so did Arelim. It was an unholy symbiosis. His creation obeyed his every command without hesitation. But what if the servant turned on its master?

Arelim pushed the thought out of his mind. Without him, the Dark Man had no life. It was anchored to this plane of existence only through him. For all of its monstrous powers, the creature needed him to survive. His worries were groundless. Or at least he told himself that.

Originally, Arelim planned using this supernatural being only to destroy the Children of Danballah. That plan continued without a flaw. Now, new ideas crowded his dreams at night. Why banish the creature back into endless night so quickly? There were many others who deserved to die.

The sensation of each death, flowing through him from the Dark Man, filled him with an unholy joy. It satisfied him like no other pleasure. Like some sort of psychic vampire, he fed on their life energy. And with each killing, his own command of magic increased.

"You enjoy murdering these cretins?" Arelim asked, curious about his creation.

"Of course," said the Dark Man, chuckling. "I find great pleasure in their screams. Unfortunately, most of them die too quickly. The ones who struggle provide me with the greatest entertainment."

"Tonight, we will both feast on the life forces of strong young bodies," said Arelim, a bizarre tremor of pleasure rushing through his body as he spoke those words. "All things come to those who wait. I learned that long ago in business. The others will not be home until nightfall. These 'seniors' "—and he sneered at that term—"gather during the day. One stroke and you will have them all. Crush them until the blood drips out from between your fingers."

With a jerk of his hand, Arelim dismissed the Dark Man. "Go now. Find them and kill them all."

"Your wish is my command," said the Dark Man, laughing again.

He turned and was out the far door of the room in an instant. He moved so silently, so gracefully, his exit took a second to register on Arelim's mind. Somehow, the giant walked the streets of the city without being seen. Only his victims noticed him.

Arelim returned to his chair. Gone were his earlier fears about the tarot reading. Summoning forth the Dark Man always banished his worries. The giant killer was unstoppable.

Arelim's plans were entering their final stage. Even if his enemies suspected the worst, it was too late for them to escape. Faced with the Dark Man, death was inevitable. Nothing living could stop him. *Nothing*.

16

Charlene Jackson looked sixty, acted fifty, but was actually seventy-seven years old. She was a heavyset black woman, with big hips and a perpetual frown. That look of dismay masked a gentle nature and sweet disposition. For over fifty years she had served as the secretary of her church, donating her time and effort, weekends and evenings, for the benefit of her community. Everyone in her neighborhood referred to her as "Saint Charlene." The pastor of her congregation considered her one of the pillars of his congregation. No one knew about her other job.

Nine o'clock every Sunday night, a certain pizza delivery truck pulled up to the widow Jackson's modest bungalow on the Near South Side. The same two men always emerged from the small van. No one ever questioned why it was necessary for *two* men to handle the delivery. Or why they spent several minutes checking out the neighborhood before hurrying up to Charlene's house with her order. On the South Side, you kept your questions to yourself.

Anyway, it was inconceivable that Charlene would be involved in anything the slightest bit illegal. She always spoke out against the gangs at church meetings. Though all of her grandchildren were long out of school, she still contributed to the "Say No to Drugs" program. When a paramedic had been shot entering the nearby housing projects last year, "Saint Charlene" had organized the fund-raising drive to pay for his hospital bills. She hated crime.

However, no one questioned that she also needed money to pay the bills. The social security check she received each month barely covered her necessities. And the retirement money from her deceased husband's pension plan didn't go very far. In years gone by, during the ice-cold winter, her gas and electric bills alone nearly overwhelmed her. She had lived in constant fear of one or the other utility being shut off.

Then last year, during a particularly bitter cold snap, a guardian angel arrived at her door. In clear, concise terms, he explained how he needed help that only she could provide. While her mission bent and twisted a few laws, it served a good purpose. Working for the Lord absolved her of all guilt. And the small cut she earned made life a good deal easier.

Charlene avoided thinking about the source of that money. Like most people, she found the easiest way to evade the truth was never to confront it. She pointedly skipped all the articles in the paper about drug money and switched off the TV whenever a story concerning crack or cocaine was broadcast.

As if seeking pardon for her imagined sins, Charlene donated part of the money she earned each week to charity. Her favorite organization was the local halfway house for addicts. It made her feel a little better that if the money did come from drugs, it was being used to combat their influence.

Today, staring at a table full of cashier's checks and postal money orders, she felt a lot more confident than usual. The newspapers and TV were filled with the latest scandal regarding an evangelical TV ministry. According to all the reports, the preacher involved took in nearly a hundred thousand dollars every week through pledges and cash donations. That sum dwarfed the amounts she handled. The comparison put all of her fears to rest.

Every week, the two pizza men brought her several sacks of money. The cash came from the thousands of donations received every day by the Church of Danballah. The Reverend Royce needed funds to carry out his good work. His followers throughout Chicago and the nation provided the money.

Unfortunately, according to the preacher, most of the funds came to the church in small cash donations. The little people supported his ministry. But the government wanted to see checks. The income tax people cast a suspicious eye on large cash deposits. Despite the church being a nonprofit organization, they insisted on taxing the cash.

Charlene didn't exactly understand the situation but it sounded right to her. The politicians always treated the black folks like second-class citizens. Nobody stood up for their rights. When a strong leader like Reverend Royce came along, "The Man" tried to knock him down hard. Only Willis Royce didn't fall easy. He came from the streets and knew all of the tricks.

So the politicians tried to trick him with taxes. They allowed him to deduct all of his donations paid by check. But the IRS counted all of the cash money he received as income. The bosses wanted to cut him off from the little people who formed the backbone of his church. And they would have done it, except for Charlene.

The money came to her in secret, so as to keep it hidden from The Man. There were dozens of thick stacks of bills, held together by heavy rubber bands. According to Royce, other women removed the donations from envelopes received at the church. A small portion of the funds went into the bank to confound the tax agents. The rest ended up with Charlene.

She followed the same routine every week. Late Sunday night, she sorted out the currency by denomination, forming huge stacks on her dining room table. Most of the money was in singles, fives and tens, but there were occasional twenties and fifties, and even a rare hundred.

For all of her poverty, Charlene never once felt the desire to steal a penny of the loose cash. If what the Reverend told her was true, these donations represented the dreams of thousands of her brothers and sisters throughout the country. She would sooner cut off her fingers and toes than rob from her fellow sufferers.

After all the piles were neatly arranged, she counted and totaled the entire sum. She worked with a small, hand-held calculator and checked her work three times. Most weeks, the amount hovered around thirty thousand dollars.

Monday morning, she divided up the cash into amounts ranging from one to three hundred dollars each. Each small stack she put in a brown manila envelope, labeling it on the outside in pencil.

In the early afternoon, she made her rounds. Taking the El to the North Side, she visited several dozen currency exchanges. She carried the money in a big paper sack, her old sweater concealing the envelopes underneath. Nobody took notice of a big old black woman on a shopping trip. Charlene blended right in with the Chicago scenery.

At each currency exchange, she converted a package of bills into a cashier's check. The small amount rarely interested the clerks working the windows there. They routinely handled much larger sums without question.

In all cases, Charlene had the checks made payable to herself. Again, this was a common practice. Such transactions took place every day.

Over the course of several hours, more than half the cash turned into paper. The rest of the money she converted with the help of the government.

Most post offices required that postal money orders be paid for in cash. Charlene spent the rest of the afternoon going to several dozen substations buying postal money orders. Again, she kept the amount as small as possible to attract little notice.

Printing carefully, she filled in the necessary information. Instead of putting in her own name, she used a dozen fictitious aliases as the buyers. In all cases, however, she was named as the recipient.

Tuesday was bank day. Instead of traveling by El to currency exchanges or post offices, she rode the subway downtown to the Loop to visit a dozen different banks. She maintained an account in all of them.

In each institution, she deposited several of the money orders and cashier's checks. Again, the amounts were small enough to pass by bored clerks without notice. No one cared about an elderly black woman depositing a few thousand dollars in checks every week.

"Good investments by my late husband," she confided to anyone willing to listen. Only one or two of the tellers even knew her name.

Today, Wednesday, was when she wrote checks. The efficiently laundered cash now returned to the Church of Danballah in the form of checks, written from a dozen different accounts in major Loop banks. None of the donations were large enough to raise any eyebrows. Despite all of the attention paid Royce, none of the investigators bothered checking the identities of all of his supporters. The IRS knew little old ladies provided the Church with much of its operating capital. No one suspected that the funds actually resulted from the efforts of a few dedicated women.

For her efforts, Charlene kept 5 percent of the cash involved. Part of the sum she used for her expenses.

The rest of the money, amounting to nearly one thousand dollars, she kept in a metal box hidden beneath her bed. Despite all of the numerous bank accounts she had opened at the orders of Willis Royce, she mistrusted the financial institutions. She preferred to have her money safe at home where she could keep an eye on it.

Charlene was counting her bankroll that Wednesday afternoon around two o'clock. There was nearly twenty thousand dollars in the box. For weeks now, she had been debating buying an automobile. It had been years since she had owned a car.

At her age, it was more of a hassle than it was worth. Parking was a problem; there was insurance to be paid; and car thieves routinely patrolled her neighborhood. Finding a service station where an attendant pumped the gas for you was another problem. Too many places only offered self-service. There was no way, at her age she was going to fill the gas tank.

Still, she did a lot of traveling every week. Riding the El in the winter was no fun, and she often had to walk for blocks making her trips to the currency exchanges. A car provided instant mobility for her aching feet. The argument raged on in her mind, with neither side emerging as the clear winner.

Thump, thump, thump. The whole bungalow shook from the hard knocking at her front door. Hastily, she shoved the iron box filled with money back under her bed.

"Hold your horses," she called rushing to the living room. "I ain't so fast no more."

The door resounded again with three powerful knocks before she reached it. Her visitor's lack of patience riled Charlene. Nobody had any patience these days. It was always hurry hurry hurry. "What the hell's the matter with you?" she demanded angrily, flinging open the wooden portal.

"Not a thing, Charlene," said the Dark Man.

"May I come in?" he asked, crossing the threshold into her house before she answered. He gently closed the door behind him.

"Who—who are you?" she asked, backing away from the giant dressed entirely in black. "You a friend of the Reverend?"

"Not exactly," said the Dark Man, with a chuckle that sent tremors running up and down her spine. "Actually, I've come to tell you how your friend Mr. Royce is playing you for a fool."

"Whatchoo talking about, boy?" said Charlene in her sternest voice, trying to make it clear to this giant that his appearance didn't frighten her. But her brave words rang hollow in her ears.

"It was a sweet scheme," said the Dark Man. "The Reverend used a half-dozen women just like you to launder his drug money. He told them all the same sad story. He knew none of you would suspect him of deceiving you."

"But The Man . . . the taxes . . ." said Charlene, trying to find the lies in the Dark Man's story.

"All bullshit," said her tormentor. "He took advantage of your good nature and unquestioning trust. And he greased the way with a little greed."

Charlene shook her head in despair, recognizing the truth. She had willingly cooperated with the Reverend for a small cut of the profits. "You here to take the money? You from the police?"

"No," said the Dark Man, reaching with one hand beneath his coat. Smoothly, he drew out a bloody red butcher's cleaver. "My authority comes from this."

Before Charlene could react, one of his huge gloved hands had her by the neck. Up went the cleaver. Her terrified eyes followed its terrible arc.

"Final audit, Charlene," said the Dark Man. Down came the cleaver.

17

Victor Caldwell resembled a giant white slug. Tiny black eyes hidden by thick folds of flesh peered out at Taine in open hostility. Reluctantly, the obese financier shifted forward in his chair and offered a hand in greeting.

"Pleased to meet you, Mr. Taine." His grip felt like the kiss of a dead fish. Caldwell withdrew his hand instantly, as if contaminated by the touch of another human being. "What can I do for you?"

"I appreciate you seeing me on such short notice. I know how busy you are."

"You told my secretary it was urgent we speak. Obviously, you impressed Vanessa with your sincerity." Caldwell stirred uneasily in his huge chair. "My time *is* precious."

"Then I'll be brief." Taine leaned forward and stared the commodities broker directly in the eyes. "My business here concerns a man named Arelim. I was led to believe you might know his present whereabouts."

The only sign of distress Victor Caldwell exhibited was a slight tightening of the skin around his piglike eyes. His tone remained neutral, uninterested. "Arelim, Arelim? An odd name, that. I meet so many people in this business. Most of them I forget rather quickly. Vanessa remembers for me. Maybe we should ask her. Is it his first name or last?"

"Both," said Taine. "You're positive on this?"

"I never heard of him," said Caldwell testily. "Sorry. I can't help you."

As if dismissing Taine from his thoughts, the fat businessman started shuffling through some papers on his

113

desk. Then, as if in afterthought, without even looking up he asked, "Who gave you my name?"

"He said he was a friend of yours," said Taine carefully. He suspected their conversation was anything but finished. "He mentioned something about a Lodge—the Knights of Antioch."

That remark caught the fat man's attention. The muscles in his neck involuntarily tightened, jerking his head up like a puppet on a string. His pale white flesh took on a distinct reddish hue.

"How interesting," he said, licking his lips between sentences. "I take it you can't reveal this friend's name?"

"Correct," said Taine. "I promised him confidentiality. I doubt if he would have talked otherwise."

"Not very surprising," said Caldwell. "The Order strictly enforces certain rules. Chief among them is a promise never to discuss Lodge business with outsiders. The penalties are quite severe."

"Am I right in assuming then, that you do know Arelim?" asked Taine, following up quickly on Caldwell's remarks. "But that your Lodge vows forbid you to speak about him."

"Nonsense," said Caldwell. "I already told you. I never met the man."

"But he has threatened you," said Taine, sensing the fat man changing his tune. If Caldwell didn't want to talk, he would have never agreed to see him in the first place.

"Well, yes," said Caldwell. He glanced around the office as if checking for eavesdroppers. "What's your role in this madness, Taine? Don't give me that innocent detective bit. I wasn't born yesterday. Where do you fit in?"

"I know that you aren't very happy with the help you've been getting from Harmon Sangmeister," said Taine. "And you don't trust the old boy for a second."

"Damn right," said Caldwell, leaning forward on his desk. There was a whining edge in his voice when he spoke. "Harmon's done a lot of talking lately but that's about all. It's been that way for the last six months. He's through and everybody knows it. This Arelim crap is the last straw."

"You would handle things differently," said Taine, trying to keep the other man talking.

"You bet your ass I would," said Caldwell. Pig-eyes narrowed and his whining voice suddenly grew suspicious. "You seem to know quite a bit about the Black Lodge. Who gave you the key to the mint?"

"Check your own files," said Taine, with a nasty twist to his voice. He picked his words very carefully. "I moved here from the West Coast a few years back. Or should I say, *I was sent.*"

The force of those words rocked Caldwell back in his chair. "I always suspected there were groups like ours all over the country," he whispered.

"Throughout the world," said Taine. "I was sent by concerned parties to put your house in order.

"Now cut the crap," he continued in the same harsh tones, "and tell me what gives on this Arelim business."

"You know most of it," said Caldwell, his voice subdued. "The threats started a few months ago. They came in the mail. All of the masters received them. They were short and to the point. Disband the Lodge or die."

"Everyone ignored them of course?"

"Of course."

"And then."

"Nothing much. Only Sangmeister seemed genuinely worried. He's had this pet theory for years. According to the old man, since a Black Lodge existed, then perhaps so did a White Lodge."

"A White Lodge?" asked Taine, trying not to appear too ignorant.

"Yeah. Imagine that," said Caldwell with a laugh. "A band of White Magicians who have gathered together to oppose the powers of darkness. As if it really mattered. Black or white or medium pink, the words mean nothing to most of us. Nobody in our Order cares about color schemes. A few fanatics like Sangmeister uphold the old ways. The rest of us are in it only for the money—and the power."

"So Sangmeister thinks that Arelim is a member of this so-called White Lodge?"

"Yeah. He claims this White Lodge has sent an Avenging Angel to destroy us for our sins. I thought the old fool had gone over the edge until the threats started getting a bit more personal."

"Mentioning you by name?"

"Right as rain," said Caldwell. "As if killing one Master would damage the Lodge in any way. The Order cannot be destroyed that easily. One death, or even several, would merely open up a place for another novice or two to move up into the ranks of the Masters."

The fat man hesitated, as if struck by the meaning of his own words. "Which sounds like a definite motive to me."

"You suspect someone?" asked Taine.

"Dozens of them," said Caldwell. "They all know the only way to advance in the Lodge is through treachery and deceit. Few Masters ever die of old age. I never considered one of our novices as the source of the threats." He laughed loudly. "It all makes sense."

"Why threaten you in particular?" said Taine, trying to keep one step ahead of Caldwell. "Why mention anyone by name? Wouldn't a general threat raise less suspicion?"

"I do stand out in a crowd," said the fat man, waving one bloated arm as if dismissing any doubts. "Everyone knows that I covet Sangmeister's position as Grand Master. Perhaps Arelim thought that by threatening me he would gain the favor of the old man. How should I know? You're the detective."

Caldwell paused again. "Which raises an interesting point. If you came here two years ago, why did you wait till now before identifying yourself?"

Taine rose from his chair. It was time for him to get going, before Victor Caldwell started asking too many questions.

"There was no time limit placed on my mission," he

answered, heading for the door. "I watched and waited for the right time. I'll see you again, soon, Caldwell. Thanks for the information."

"The right time," repeated Caldwell slowly. "What do you mean by that? Why for all I know, you could be Arelim."

"Now isn't that an interesting thought," said Taine and exited.

18

Two detectives came to see Papa Benjamin around three o'clock that afternoon. He had been expecting their visit ever since Willis Royce told him about the murders and their seeming connection with voodoo. The police might be slow, but they were not stupid.

He knew both of the officers quite well. One of them, Calvin Lane, had grown up only a few blocks from his church. A large, innocuous-looking man, his bland features concealed a sharp, probing mind. Calvin had worked his way up through the ranks to Homicide Investigations.

Equally intelligent was his partner, Moe Kaufman. Papa Benjamin had met the detective several years ago at De Paul University night school. Kaufman had been a student in the Comparative Religions course. He was finishing his degree at night while working days on the police force.

Papa Benjamin had attended several sessions of the class as a guest lecturer. Kaufman went out of his way to introduce himself. Even then, he understood the importance of religious leaders in the black community. He accorded the same respect to a voodoo priest as he did to a Catholic priest or a Baptist minister. Kaufman had ambitious plans in the department. He worked hard maintaining his friendships all through the city.

"Sorry to bother you, Papa," said Calvin Lane, shrugging his shoulders as if lifting a heavy burden. "But we have to follow up every possible lead in these killings. If you'll pardon the expression, the shit has hit the fan."

"What killings are you talking about?" asked Papa Benjamin. If the police knew nothing about Willis Royce's visit, he didn't plan on telling them about it. "I saw nothing on the news about any murders in the city."

"They haven't made the news yet," answered Kaufman, with a heavy sigh. "But the lid's about to pop. Someone leaked the story to the papers. It's gonna be hell tonight."

"Some maniac is loose in the streets," said Lane, continuing as soon as his partner stopped speaking. "We assume it's only one man, but considering the slaughter that's taken place, it could be a whole army of lunatics."

"Words can't describe the carnage," said Kaufman, keeping the singsong description going. "In the last few nights, this guy has chopped a dozen people into little bitty pieces. I mean, we are talking maniacal here. This killer has to be a real looney tune. I never saw anything like it."

"You're telling me," said Lane, talking as much to his partner as to Papa Benjamin. Describing the killings to a third person gave the two men a chance to air their own fears and frustrations to each other without menacing their relationship. "Damned coroner complained the whole time he was at the last place. Said a regular body bag wasn't good enough for cases like this. There are too many unidentified parts floating around."

Calvin Lane's black features had a distinctly green tinge to them as he continued. "The worst part of all was the blood. What a mess."

"Blood everywhere," agreed Kaufman. "And the damned symbols painted on the walls."

"Symbols," said Papa Benjamin, knowing it was time for him to interrupt. "What kind of symbols?"

"That was why we came down to see you, Papa," said Lane. "Several of the guys in the department feel sure the whole thing revolves around some crazy cult thing. You know, like those killings that took place in Mexico a few months ago."

"Yeah, especially since we've found large amounts of crack at every site," said Kaufman. "The whole case stinks of drugs."

"Top brass think it's a war between rival gangs over territory," said Lane. "But nobody can explain why the killer never takes the rock or the cash when he leaves. He ignores the stuff in plain sight. This guy ain't a regular stickup boy."

"Perhaps a vengeful parent?" said Papa Benjamin.

"Nah. That stuff only happens in the movies. You watch too much TV, Papa," said Kaufman.

"Anyway," continued the Jewish detective, pulling several large black-and-white photos out of a briefcase, "the chief insisted we come down to the oum'phor and talk to you."

"I told them it was a waste of time," said Lane defensively. "But the boss insisted."

"I understand, Calvin," said Papa Benjamin. "Whenever things like this take place, the uninformed always blame voodoo. What they do not comprehend, they fear."

"They've watched too many reruns of *I Walked With a Zombie*," said Kaufman. "To most people, voodoo consists of zombies, drums and biting chickens in the neck."

"You have a way with words, my friend," said Papa Benjamin with a smile. "Now show me these pictures."

Moe Kaufman handed over the photos.

The pictures were close-ups of a blood-splattered apartment wall. Filling most of the bare space were five unusual symbols, crudely etched in blood.

"I do not recognize any of these markings," said Papa Benjamin after a moment. "They are not true voodoo *veves*. Yet, they do look vaguely familiar."

"Maybe from that religion course," said Moe Kaufman, sounding slightly guilty. "We already know what they are, Papa Benjamin. The chief insisted we show the photos to you just on the off chance we might stumble onto a lead."

"What are you saying?" said Papa Benjamin, sounding properly indignant. The two officers looked stricken. Then, before they had a chance to apologize, he chuckled with amusement.

"So your chief thinks that I am strong enough to cause such destruction? How did I get so powerful? Perhaps by wrenching the necks of chickens?"

"It was a crazy idea," said Calvin Lane. "But they're grasping at straws downtown. It's the Gacy mess but lots worse. I mean, this guy is still on the loose, and he's armed with an axe or something."

"So, satisfy the curiosity of an old man," said Papa Benjamin, fishing for a little more information. "Tell me about the meaning of those symbols."

"They're Hebrew letters," said Moe Kaufman. "Five Hebrew letters. Don't ask me what *that* means. The chief himself is handling that aspect of the investigation. He's talking to some expert from the university right now. The boss needs something to tell the reporters other than the usual crap. Otherwise, the whole city is going to go apeshit."

"I have this terrible feeling," said Calvin Lane, as the two detectives prepared to leave. "Things are gonna get a whole lot worse before they get better."

"Tell me about it," said Kaufman. "You get any sleep last night? I didn't. Every time I closed my eyes, I kept seeing those blood-stained walls."

Kaufman turned to Papa Benjamin. "Sorry to have troubled you, Papa. Calvin and I knew better. But you can't argue with the chief."

"I understand," said Papa Benjamin as he walked the two detectives to the door. "I am not offended. Go in peace."

Alone again, Papa Benjamin pondered over what the two officers had revealed. The sight of the actual symbols painted in blood had shaken him more than he cared to admit. This was not the act of some homicidal maniac. The markings had been done too exact, too careful to be the work of a madman. The five letters served as a focus point of unholy magic.

In voodoo the *veves* obligated the Mysteres to descend to Earth. They acted as astral forces and personified the Loas. When called, the symbols forced the Mysteres to attend the voodoo ceremonies. Usually the symbols were traced in flour or cornmeal. For important rituals, facial powder or gunpowder was used to draw the pictures. Only the *Cochons sans poils* painted their *veves* in blood. And the Red Cults never killed so savagely and so often.

Those tracings spoke of a darker, older magic than voodoo. The decapitations and use of the victim's blood hinted at rituals older than civilization.

"For the Blood is the Life," whispered Papa Benjamin, reciting the ancient chant of human sacrifice.

For the first time in many years, he felt afraid. His was the power of the voodoo Mysteres. All of his life, he had fought for those beliefs, confident in his own strength. The Loas gave him courage no matter what the odds.

Now he faced a magic stronger than his own. This vampiric monster, the Dark Man, drew his life from the death of others. Even in voodoo, nothing was stronger than death.

The easiest thing for him to do would be to ignore the killings. The killings did not involve any of his congregation. He owed nothing to Willis Royce. If that charlatan dealt in drugs, he richly deserved his fate. Why tempt fate? His duty to his own followers demanded he remain neutral in this battle.

Still, deep within himself, Papa Benjamin felt troubled. By passively accepting the murders, he was in effect condoning them. No matter how good the cause, indiscriminate killing was wrong. The death of innocents must be punished. No amount of mental gymnastics could change that basic fact.

His path was clear. Despite all of his fears, all of his doubts, Papa Benjamin knew what he had to do. He had always stood unwavering against the forces of darkness. He was too old to change now. Besides, Ape Largo needed his help to survive. To save the soul of an innocent man, he must defeat the Dark Man.

19

The metal sign on the office door was reassuring in its understatement: SIDNEY TAINE: INVESTIGATIONS. Janet read then checked the slip of paper she clutched in one hand. Not that she needed to compare the two. They were the same and had been the same since she had approached the door five minutes earlier.

The reverse phone directory had provided her the name and address of the agency. Faced with the likely prospect that the mysterious Mrs. McConnell had been at the library researching a case, Janet had decided on the direct approach. A phone call might clear up the mystery. But on the other hand, it might create more problems than it solved. Personal contact was the only sure way of learning the truth. Timmy's safety demanded she make the effort.

Gathering together her courage, she gripped the doorknob and pushed open the office door. Inside was a small reception room, furnished with a few chairs, an end table and the usual magazines. Directly across from the door loomed a large desk. Behind it sat a middle-aged woman Janet guessed to be Mary McConnell. At least, she looked like an Irishwoman, with her well-defined features, dark hair and hint of freckles. To the right side of the desk was a further door, obviously leading to Sidney Taine's office.

"Can I help you?" asked the woman.

"Uhh, I hope so," said Janet, momentarily at a loss for words. She was treading in completely unknown water here. A half-dozen alibis and deceptions flashed through her mind. Rejecting them all as too transparent, she settled on the one approach that might yield some results—the truth.

"Are you Mary McConnell?" When the woman nodded in reply, Janet rushed on. "I'm Janet Packard. The librarian downtown gave me your name. We both went to the main library today searching for information on the Mystic Order of the Knights of Antioch. I want to know why you were there?"

"That's confidential, of course," answered Mrs. McConnell. Her friendly smile took most of the bite out of the words. The secretary acted as if she fielded questions like this all the time. "I can't tell you anything without Mr. Taine's permission. Even though I did the research, it's his case. He's not in the office right now, but I expect him back shortly. Why not wait around and talk to him?

"Besides," continued Mrs. McConnell, "he's a pushover for women in distress. Especially good-looking blondes like you. The boss called in from the Loop around twenty minutes ago. He was on the way back here after a late lunch. Give him five or ten minutes more.

Janet didn't have long to wait. Two minutes after she had settled in a chair at the far side of the office, a big, burly man rushed into the office, slamming the door behind him. "Hurry up," he said to Mrs. McConnell, "turn on WBBM-AM. My whole drive back, they've been promising news of a late-breaking story of a rash of murders on the South Side. The anchor keeps on referring to them as 'Cult related.' I want to know what's going on."

"There's someone here to see you, Mr. Taine," said Mrs. McConnell, gesturing with her head as she twirled the station selector of the radio on her desk. "Her name is Janet Packard. I think you ought to talk to her."

The big detective turned to face Janet. She rose from

her chair, bringing her eyes almost level with his. For an instant, they just stood there, as if evaluating each other. Then, holding out a hand, Taine stepped forward.

"Please excuse my rudeness," he said, in a surprisingly mellow voice. "When I get excited, I tend to block out any distractions. It's a bad habit."

They shook hands briefly. His grip was firm but restrained. Janet got the impression that this was a man who knew his own strength and kept it tightly under control.

"They're on with that story," said Mrs. McConnell.

With a quick "Excuse me for a minute," Taine hurried back to the radio. As the detective bent close over the desk to listen, Janet took the opportunity to study him closer.

She guessed the detective to be about her age. Dark eyes and wavy brown hair blended well with his pleasant, even features. Not exactly handsome, he fit under the general heading of "good-looking." Tall and athletic in build, he was well muscled but definitely not fat.

He moved with the lithe grace of a trained athlete. Astonishing for a man his size, Taine made not a sound as he walked. His feet hardly seemed to touch the ground. Janet liked what she saw. But she also knew the dangers of making snap judgments based solely on pleasant features. A multitude of deadly sins often lurked behind nice eyes.

With a whistle of surprise, Taine rose to his feet. "Five Hebrew letters drawn in the victim's blood," he muttered, as if thinking out loud. "Now I know what that old codger in New York meant."

His expression troubled, the detective again faced her. "I apologize again for my lack of manners. But things are boiling over here and I expect they'll only get worse."

"Ms. Packard came here looking for information on the Knights of Antioch," interrupted Mary McConnell. "She found us through the library. I thought it best if you talked to her. We were the only people to use that book in years."

"Coincidence only stretches so far," said Taine, an odd note in his voice. "We definitely should hear your story, Ms. Packard. Why not step into my office? We can talk in there.

"Meanwhile," he said to his assistant, taking one of his business cards from the desk and scribbling something on the back of it. "See that this note gets delivered to that loudmouth leader of the Children of Danballah. I don't care how you do it. If necessary, take a cab downtown to their church and hand it to the gatekeeper. Just make sure he understands Willis Royce has to see the message."

Taine smiled. "We might have a little business to conduct, Mr. Royce and I. Friday is still two days away. Time for us to earn some of that ten thousand bucks. Don't worry about the phone here. I'll handle any calls from my office. Get going."

Entering his office, the detective beckoned Janet to an old-fashioned high-back chair. It faced a huge desk, a twin to the one in the outer room. After she sat, he paced over to a wall of windows looking out on the lake.

"Now," he asked, turning back so that he faced her, "why are you interested in the Black Lodge?"

"You mean the Order of the Knights of Antioch?" said Janet, slightly confused. "It's a long story."

"I'm a good listener," said Taine, smiling at her. "It comes with the occupation. Let's compare notes. Why not tell me all about it."

Janet hesitated, wondering if it was wise trusting the detective. Considering her options, she decided to gamble and take him at face value.

"It all started yesterday," she began, "when I went to pick up my son, Tim, from school."

For the next twenty minutes, Janet recited the events and conversations of the past twenty-four hours. Here and there, she cut the story a little. Transformers made little difference to the final outcome. Nor did Mrs. Kearny's fear of Bruno. Otherwise, she let the facts speak for themselves.

Taine listened attentively. He remained standing during her entire story, his arms folded across his chest, lines of concentration etched in his brow. He interrupted only a few times, seeking to clarify one point or another. By the time Janet finished, all of the good humor had vanished from his face.

"I don't like it," he said, biting his lower lip as if pondering her story. "I don't like it one bit."

He dropped into the swivel chair behind his desk. For a moment, he closed his eyes as if in deep concentration. Opening them, he stared at her with an attentiveness that she found unusually refreshing. "Your ex-husband sounds extremely dangerous. Are you sure your son is adequately protected?"

"Bruno drove him to school this morning and will meet him afterward," replied Janet. "Tim is safe with him. Roger is terrified of Bruno—always has been. I'm not worried."

"If you say so," said Taine, frowning. Then, abruptly, as if changing the subject, "Did you read about the Mystic Order of the Knights of Antioch?"

"Just a quick skim at lunch," said Janet. "The article implied that the group no longer existed."

"I'm not surprised," said Taine. "Like most cults, the Black Lodge survives best in secret."

"That's the second time you referred to them by that name," said Janet. "What do you mean by the Black Lodge?"

"The Knights of the Temple, or as they were soon renamed, the Templars, were a military order founded in the twelfth century to battle the Saracens in the Holy Land. Consisting of a dedicated band of toughened knights, the Order quickly gained fame for their heroic acts. They became the standing host of the Church in the Middle East. Their official garb was a white cloak, symbolizing purity, supplemented with a red cross.

"The Templars thrived under papal favor and soon became a rich and powerful league of nobles. They divided the East into five provinces, each with its own 'Temple Court.' There were also strong branches of the organization in France, Spain, Portugal and England. At the head of the society was a Grand Master, elected to his post by thirteen knights.''

"The king of France outlawed them," said Janet, remembering a fragment of history from her college days. She wondered about the purpose of this story.

"Philip the Fourth saw the powerful organization as a direct threat to his rule. With the aid of Pope Clement, in 1307 he charged the Templars with heresy. Little evidence was offered to warrant the accusations, but no one dared disagree with the pope.

"Over fifty Templars were burned at the stake, and hundreds of others perished under torture. The order was disbanded, their wealth divided by the king and pope.

"However, not all of the knights died at the hands of the Inquisitors. The few who escaped formed a new Lodge, the Order of Antioch. Betrayed by their Church, they abandoned all pretense of piety. Their only goal was the pursuit of material pleasures. They became a society of black magicians.

"Ever aware of the pope's avarice, this new Order operated in total secrecy. In mockery of the Church, they adopted a new standard—a white mantle with an inverted red cross, the symbol of the Antichrist. At the base crawled a serpent, signifying the triumph of evil over good."

"They were Satanists?" asked Janet, not liking the turn of conversation.

"They worshiped only greed," said Taine firmly. "Whatever the cost, they paid the price willingly.

"The Order soon disappeared into the mist of history. From time to time, some reference to the group appeared in Church records. By and large, they were forgotten. Just as they wished.

"Reports of their activities still surfaced, but few people recognized them as such. Over the years, the society evolved into a much more insidious organization. Avarice remained their only goal. However, most wars were no longer fought on battlefields. Empires were won and lost in executive boardrooms. Swords and shields gave way to stocks and bonds. The right word or casual nod could make a man rich.

"In late nineteenth-century England, the Order accidentally emerged from the shadows. The leading members achieved a certain notoriety as the Black Lodge. That name came from *The London Times* which broke the story."

Taine spoke with a force and conviction that captivated Janet. He reminded her of several of her college professors. Those men had lectured with such passion they made their subject come alive. The detective expressed himself with that same intensity.

"Evidently a major schism had developed in the Order a few years earlier. Fortunes were lost and not recovered. One of the losers grew so bitter he turned to the papers for his revenge. Over the course of six months, numerous anonymous articles appeared in *The Times* by this ex-member of the Order. The pieces detailed the widespread use of dark sorcery and influence peddling on the London financial markets. The tales of black magic were politely ignored. Not so the reports of manipulating the market. No formal charges were ever filed, but a number of important brokers suddenly disappeared from sight."

"Black magic?" repeated Janet doubtfully. "Surely you don't mean ghosts and vampires and stuff like that."

"What you and I believe doesn't matter," said Taine. His expression was deadly serious. "The only ones who count are the members of the Black Lodge. All of the mystical trappings contribute to the strength of their fellowship. Every Lodge functions in that fashion. Don't scoff at their beliefs. The members of the Order take them very seriously."

"And you think a branch of this Order of devil worshipers exists now in Chicago?" said Janet.

"I know it," said Taine. "I just returned from interviewing one of the members. The Black Lodge wields incredible power in the Windy City."

"And my ex-husband, my *psychopathic* ex-husband

wants to join their ranks?" Janet shuddered. "This is all too incredible to believe."

"Which is exactly how the Order manages to avoid detection," said Taine. "Nobody is willing to believe stories involving stock brokers and black magic. I can't blame them, and I know the truth."

Janet said nothing in return. Taine's revelations frightened her. It took no great leap of faith to convince her he spoke the truth. Crazier stories filled the newspapers every day. It just took a few seconds for the shock to fade.

"So what am I supposed to do?" asked Janet. "I can't go to the police with a story like this. What do you suggest?"

"Actually, I don't think you have too much to worry about," replied Taine. "As long as you keep a close watch on your son, I can't see how your ex-husband can do anything much. Maybe your father and his men can deal with him."

The detective seemed genuinely concerned about her worries. He sighed, as if making a major decision. "I've got to stick around the office for the rest of the afternoon. A million things need my personal attention. However, if you like, I can stop by your father's place early this evening. I'd be glad to check out the security system there if it would make you feel any safer."

"Would you, really?" said Janet, anxiously. "I'd be willing to pay any fee . . ."

"No charge for this visit," said Taine, with a wave of one big hand. "Didn't Mrs. McConnell tell you I'm a sucker for blondes in trouble?"

She blinked twice, wondering if her thoughts were that obvious.

"She enjoys revealing my secrets," said Taine, laughing at her discomfort. "It's my one weakness."

"You're a very special person," said Janet, meaning every word.

Taine actually blushed at her praise. He opened his mouth as if to say something, but then thought better of it.

"Why not come for dinner?" she continued, suddenly wanting her father to meet this very unusual detective. "Dad enjoys company and you could meet Tim as well."

"I don't see why not," said Taine, grinning. "I try not to socialize during a case, but you're not a client. I eat alone much too often. Despite what you see on TV, most detectives don't know a lot of beautiful women."

"I'll take that as a compliment," said Janet rising from her chair, her smile matching his.

"I meant it," said Taine, also getting to his feet. "Beauty comes from the spirit as well as from the flesh. I meet too many self-centered people filled with hate in this line of work. Despite outward appearances, they are truly the ugly ones. Your concern about your son reflects in your every word. To me, that really makes you beautiful."

"Wow," said Janet, swallowing hard. She giggled, feeling slightly giddy. "Wow again."

"Not that you look so bad from a purely physical point of view, either," said Taine, with a slight shake of his head. "Whatever. No more compliments till dinner."

"See you at six," said Janet.

Walking to the elevator, she couldn't help smiling like a fool. The world suddenly seemed a lot brighter. She had almost forgotten the thrill a compliment brought. Once her father dealt with Roger and Tim was safe, maybe she would take life a little easier. Success beckoned, but she needed a personal life, too.

Taine fascinated her. Janet couldn't deny the strong attraction she felt for the rugged detective. And he seemed equally interested in her. It wasn't until she was standing outside in the rain, waving for a taxi, that she realized Taine had never once mentioned the reason he was investigating the Black Lodge.

20

A minute after Janet Packard left his office, Taine's phone rang. The harsh jangling rudely brought his mind back to the real world. She was a very good-looking woman, and her mental abilities obviously matched her physical assets. Not many people could have tracked him down so quickly. She combined beauty and brains, a rare combination in any person. Her ex-husband, Taine decided, had to be one of the biggest jerks of all time to walk out on her.

"Taine, here," he said, picking up the receiver from his desk.

"It's me," said Jack Korshak on the other end of the line. "The boy reporter."

"I was hoping you would call," said Taine. "You find anything juicy about our buddy—"

"No names," interrupted Korshak before Taine could finish the sentence. "People tap phones these days."

"Getting a bit paranoid, Jack?" asked Taine. Korshak normally scoffed at such possibilities. He didn't rattle easily.

"It never hurts to be careful," said the reporter, his voice serious.

"I spent most of the morning digging through our files. After that, I made a few phone calls. All the puzzle pieces fit together in a very nasty fashion. Our mutual friend plays quite rough when it comes to his personal life. Wait till you hear the statistics. You make any plans yet for dinner? Max Walker told me about this hamburger place on the Near North Side that serves the best onion rings in the city."

"Sounds like heaven," said Taine, "but, believe it or not, I'm having dinner with a beautiful blonde."

"Sid Taine, the legendary lone wolf, on a date?" asked Jack Korshak, his voice rising a note in amazement. "She wouldn't happen to be a client by any chance?"

"Not at all," replied Taine, trying to sound insulted. "Actually, she's a blonde, with blue eyes, around one hundred fifteen pounds, five foot four or five, with a terrific figure."

"Spare me the details," said Korshak, with a groan. "You detectives are all alike. You give everyone you meet the once-over while you're talking to them. You count the number of teeth she has?"

"She's also quite bright," said Taine, cheerfully ignoring the question. "And she thinks I'm quite special."

"Well, that kills the bright part right there," said Korshak. "Need I ask if she's richer than Croesus?"

"From what I gather, she is rather well-off," said Taine.

"You see that movie, *Fatal Attraction?*" asked Korshak.

"No," said Taine. "Why do you ask?"

"You wouldn't understand," said the reporter. "Anyway, take my advice. If she's single, marry her. If not, kill her husband, then marry her. A good lawyer will get you off easy."

"We're only talking dinner here, Jack," said Taine, laughing. "I just met her this afternoon."

"Big deal," said Korshak. "My brother dated his wife for three years before they finally got married. He's been miserable ever since. Give me love at first sight any time."

"Thanks for the advice. I'll keep it in mind.

"Meanwhile, where'll you be later tonight? I want to learn what you found out."

"Try Gibbons Lounge," said Korshak. "I like staring at all the young things who come there looking for action. Wednesday night is ladies night. Girls wearing miniskirts and high heels drink for free. Talk about bimbo city."

"Delightful," said Taine. "I'll see you there."

Still smiling, Taine hung up the phone. Korshak had a unique way with words.

Taine checked the outer office. Mrs. McConnell had still not returned from her errand. Which suited him just fine. He returned to his office, locked the door, and got out his tarot deck. Time for another try at fortune-telling.

Not surprisingly, the cards fell in the exact same pattern. Three passes yielded identical results. Four trumps predicted his fate, if he could only grasp their meaning.

Destiny seemed self-explanatory. Originally, he assumed Evangeline Caldwell was the mysterious woman. Now Janet clouded the picture. A handful of secrets lurked behind the screen of hidden wisdom. Of all the trumps, death promised an end. But only the cards knew who was scheduled to encounter "La Mort."

His phone rang again. Swiftly, he bundled the cards together and dropped the deck into his desk. Only then did he grab the receiver.

"Taine here."

"Why did you visit my husband this afternoon?" demanded an angry Evangeline Caldwell. "I told you to stay away from him."

"I thought you were going to call tonight," said Taine, his voice cool and calm.

"The hell with tonight," said Evangeline, venom dripping from her every word. "I want an explanation of your conduct right now."

"According to my recollection of our conversation, you never once told me not to interview your spouse. Besides, your name wasn't mentioned during the entire conversation." Then, as an afterthought, he added, "Is it true your nickname is Angel?"

"He's suspicious all the same," Evangeline answered, still angry. "He warned me not to leave the house alone. The fat fool mumbled something about a mad killer on the loose, with both of us on his list. And what does my nickname have to do with this case?"

"Maybe your husband cares for you more than you

realize," said Taine. "Have you listened to the news this afternoon?"

"Victor cares only for himself," said Angel, without a tremor of doubt in her voice. "To him, I'm just a trophy who walks and talks."

"I'm working on your case right now," said Taine. "By tonight I should know pretty much where we stand. Do you want to call me then?"

"I'll try," she replied. "If I can break away for a few minutes. Victor told me he plans to stay at home with all the doors and windows locked and a bunch of security guards stationed everywhere. It sounds so cozy."

"Sarcasm gives you ulcers," said Taine as the line clicked dead.

Idly, he wondered about Victor Caldwell's sudden concern for his wife's safety. Was the millionaire really worried? Or was he setting up an alibi for Angel's disappearance? The truth in this case remained elusive as ever.

Despite Caldwell's insistence to the contrary, Taine doubted that Arelim was one of the Lodge novices. Killing one of the masters of the Order usually took a lot more skill than any initiate possessed. The inner circle achieved their position through both skill and ruthlessness. They kept close tabs on anyone moving up through the ranks. If Taine's hunch proved correct, this Avenging Angel controlled forces far beyond a novice's ambitions. He would know more once he talked to Willis Royce.

21

The doorbell sounded at exactly six o'clock.

"He's punctual at least," said Leo Packard, smiling at his daughter. "Roger was always late."

"Father," said Janet, hurrying to answer the door, "please don't mention my ex tonight. The less said about him the better."

"Amen," said Leo. "Well, open it already. The poor man is standing out in the rain while you chatter."

"I look okay?" asked Janet for the dozenth time, as she turned the knob.

"Stunning. After all, you did change outfits three times."

Taine stood on the front porch, waiting patiently under a huge black umbrella. He was conservatively dressed in a dark brown corduroy suit that emphasized his broad shoulders and powerful chest. An intricately designed tie offset the somber cast of his jacket. Freshly shaved, he was the soul of respectability.

In the hand not clutching the umbrella, the detective held a bouquet of red roses. "Red roses to chase the blues away," he said, handing her the flowers.

For a second, their eyes met and sparks flashed. "Please come in," said Janet, holding the roses tightly as if they might suddenly vanish.

"Terrible weather," said Taine, shaking off his umbrella in the front hall. "April showers bring May flowers but this is ridiculous."

Behind Janet, Leo loudly cleared his throat.

"I heard you, Father," said Janet. Half-turning, she made the introductions. "Sidney Taine, my father, Leo Packard."

"Pleased to meet you," said Taine, offering his hand. "I've heard a lot about you."

"All lies, I assure you," said Leo with a laugh. "You impressed Janet. I can see why. How about something to drink before dinner?"

"Beer would be fine," said Taine. "Preferably a light." All three of them walked into the front parlor.

"I'll be back in a minute," said Janet. "Let me get a vase for these roses. Dad, I'll have my usual."

When she returned a few minutes later, Taine and her father were discussing the Cubs chances in the upcoming baseball season. "Dinner will be ready in fifteen minutes," she said, taking a sip from her drink.

"Perhaps a brief inspection of the house," said Leo.

"That sounds fine with me," replied Taine. "I took the liberty of arriving a little early and checked the grounds on my own. Those three men watching the house," he said to Leo, "I assume are working for you?"

"Three men?" said Janet. "What three men?"

"Employees of mine," said Leo, sounding rather annoyed. "It seemed like a wise move at the time. Now, I wonder."

"By concentrating solely on the house, they ignored their surroundings," said Taine. "Your men appeared edgy, probably due to this incessant rain. They needed a break."

"I'll cut down on their shifts," said Leo. "And make sure they keep a better perimeter watch."

"One highly motivated individual," said Taine seriously, "could eliminate that trio in seconds, leaving you helpless. A psychopath won't hesitate killing anyone who stands in his way. From what Janet told me of her ex-husband, he fills the bill. You can never be too careful with a lunatic like that on the prowl."

"Mommy, mommy," cried Tim from the second floor landing, breaking the thread of conversation, "is the company here yet? I'm getting hungry."

"Yes, the company is here," answered Janet. "Why

not come down and meet him. Dinner will be ready soon.

A nervous twinge tugged the muscles in her neck as Tim came flying down the stairs. Her son meant more than anyone in the world to her. The fears of the everyday world melted before his innocence and unquestioning devotion. She silently prayed that he would like Taine.

Half-running, half-sliding across the high-polished floor, Tim came to rest only a few feet from the detective. He stared up at the big man with inquisitive eyes. Under one arm, he carried Optimus Prime.

"Hey, who's this?" asked Taine, sounding puzzled. "You told me Tim was a little kid. This mug looks pretty dangerous to me. You sure he isn't a secret agent in disguise."

"Sometimes I wonder," said Janet, smiling. "Tim, shake hands with Mr. Taine."

"Sure," said Tim, grabbing one of Taine's huge hands with both of his. He pumped the detective's arm up and down enthusiastically. "Do you really think I look like a secret agent?"

"No question about it," said Taine. "And I should know. I've met some pretty dangerous characters in my day."

"My mom says you're a detective," said Tim, releasing Taine's hand. "Do you carry a gun?"

"Not unless I need one," said Taine. "Guns create more problems than they solve. I only use one in emergencies."

"Detectives on TV always carry them," said Tim.

"They fight more dangerous criminals than I do," answered Taine. "Your mom is going to show me around the house. Want to keep us company?"

"Sure." Then, holding out Optimus Prime, "Do you like Transformers?"

Taine hesitated, his face puzzled. For the first time, Janet saw him at a loss for words. He pondered the question for a moment, then answered tentatively. "I haven't played with trains since . . ."

"Not trains," said Tim, laughing, "Transformers. You know, like Optimus Prime and Starscream and Bumblebee."

"Robots that transform into cars or planes," said Janet, coming to the confused detective's rescue.

Reaching past him, she took the metal figure from her son's hands and swiftly folded it together in the correct manner. In seconds, she changed the big red semi into a heroic robotic figure, armed with a powerful laser cannon. Fortunately, Optimus Prime was one of the few Transformers she knew how to manipulate.

Taine stared at her, astonished. "Incredible. I never saw anything like that."

He turned to Tim. "Anybody who owns toys like this one *must* be a spy. Do you have more of these Transformers? I thought so. How about it? Can you bring some others down?"

"If Mom says okay," said Tim. "She says they belong in my room."

"Mom's are like that," said Taine, shaking his head in dismay. He smiled at Janet and took one of her hands in his. "What do you say, boss? Can your son break the rules this one time?" He squeezed her hand gently. "Please."

"Just this one time," said Janet, trying not to laugh.

With a whoop of delight, Tim went running up the stairs two at a time. Still holding hands, Janet and Taine watched him disappear into his room. The detective grinned and tried to explain. "They didn't have toys like this when I was a kid."

"You made a conquest," said Leo, forgotten in the exchange about toys. He headed for the kitchen. "Two of them, I suspect. Excuse me if I make a quick phone call."

They played with Transformers until dinner. At the meal, Tim kept up a running commentary on the history of the robots from their creation millions of years ago on the planet, Cybertron, to their adventures set in the near future. Janet tried to quiet him down for a few minutes, then gave up, recognizing a battle lost before it started.

Martha outdid herself on the food. They feasted on gulf shrimp sauteed in butter and garlic, wild rice and fresh green beans. Between bites, Taine entertained them with stories of some of his more unusual cases. Janet suspected the detective exaggerated the ineptness of the criminals to lessen her fears. He spoke with the calm assurance of a man confident of his own abilities. By the end of dinner, Janet found herself wondering why he was unattached in a city full of predatory females. She made a resolution to herself to discover the answer to that riddle—once they were alone.

After dessert, her father and Taine carefully checked all the doors and windows of the house. The old mansion passed every inspection Taine suggested. A private agency maintained Brentwood when Leo was not in residence. Most visits home, he updated the security system and alarms. He believed in leaving as little to chance as possible. Too many lunatics preyed on the rich for Leo to leave his safety to chance.

It was Bruno's night off, but her father came to the rescue. "Come on, Mr. Packard. Martha rented *Ghostbusters* on videotape. We can watch it in the TV room and give your mother a break from your chatter."

"Only if we make popcorn," said Tim.

"Popcorn it is."

Leo shook hands again with Taine. "Nice meeting you, young man," he said warmly. "Stop by again soon."

Then, finally, they were completely alone. Together, they sat down on the big sofa facing the empty fireplace. "How about a mint?" said Janet, sliding closer to the detective.

"No thanks," said Taine. "I've eaten enough for a week. So much for my diet. You don't eat like this every night do you? You can't with a figure like yours?"

"Martha went wild tonight," said Janet, smiling. "We don't have many guests for dinner. You gave her a chance to show off."

"Well, she impressed me," said Taine chuckling. Somewhat nervously, he glanced around the room. "This place is incredible. I thought mansions this big only existed in the movies."

Janet laughed and moved even closer. Taine looked distinctly uncomfortable. With a sudden flash of insight, she realized that the detective was intimidated by her looks and her money. For a change, she was the aggressor in a relationship. Sidney Taine was afraid of her.

"Tim really likes you," said Janet, trying to put Taine more at ease.

"And I like him," said Taine, genuine affection in his voice. "A lot of parents want their kids to grow up too fast. They don't give their children a chance to enjoy their childhood. I see the results of that all the time. Unhappy kids turn into unhappy adults. Those are the people who keep me working. It's pretty depressing stuff. It's nice to meet someone who really loves her son."

"You're incredible," said Janet, shaking her head in disbelief. Taine's eyes widened as she playfully rubbed his lapel with her thumb. "How is it that a sensitive, intelligent man like you is still single?"

"Lots of reasons," said Taine, his voice shaking just a little. "I'm a loner, always working on my own. Nor do you meet very many unattached women working as a detective. The ones I encounter usually leave me cold. You're the exception," he added, his voice sinking almost to a whisper.

"Besides, this job keeps me pretty busy. And I've been told that I talk too much."

"Definitely," murmured Janet, her face very close to his. She expected to be kissed. She wasn't disappointed.

Fifteen minutes later, Taine gently unwrapped her arms from around his neck. "Much as I want to stay, I've got to leave."

"Can't it wait?" asked Janet, trying to sound seductive.

"Don't tempt me," said Taine, shaking his head. "I've got to see a man tonight about the case I'm involved with. What he knows might save my client's life." He hesitated for a moment then continued. "It might save Tim's."

That last remark put an end to her protests. Straightening her clothes, she walked the detective to the front door.

"When will I see you again?" she asked.

"How about tomorrow evening? Let me take you out for dinner." He grinned. "Even a great mom needs a break from her son once in a while."

"Sounds terrific to me. Call me."

One last kiss and he was gone. Janet stood in the doorway watching his car until it was out of sight.

Sighing deeply, she closed the door. Her body still trembled with desire. The depth of that passion worried her. For all of Taine's fine words, she really knew nothing about him. The detective needed to answer some important questions before she trusted him completely. Until then, she vowed to keep a tighter grip on her emotions.

22

Taine stifled a groan when he walked into Gibbons Lounge an hour later. He had spent nearly twenty minutes driving around the neighborhood looking for a parking space. The eight-block walk in the steady drizzle had not improved his temper. Now he found himself in a loud-volume, low-mentality, singles' bar. These places drove him crazy after a few minutes.

Scanning the room, he caught a glimpse of Jack Korshak on the far side of the bar frantically waving his hands in the air. With a constant string of "Excuse me's" and "Pardon me's" Taine forced his way through the crowd.

Korshak waited at a table the size of a postage stamp. "Grab a chair from somewhere," he shouted over the roar of conversation. "You want a beer?"

Taine nodded. Checking the area, he spotted an empty chair at a table a few feet away. Struggling against traffic, he pushed his way over and grabbed it. Shaking his head in annoyance, Taine forced his way back through the crowd, dragging the chair after him.

"I hate singles' bars, Jack," said Taine, sitting down. He bent his head close to his friend to be heard. "The people are all loud, rude and obnoxious. Plus the noise gives me a headache."

"What better place to discuss secrets?" asked Korshak. "Nobody can eavesdrop on us here. These lounges confound the experts. Even directional mikes strike out because of the background noise. And," the reporter added, eying an attractive brunette in a black leather miniskirt, walking past their table, "the sights make up for any lack of atmosphere."

"You're nuts," said Taine, slowly shaking his head. "What did you learn about Harmon?"

"It's not what I learned that scared me," said Korshak. He bent close to Taine, keeping his voice so low that only the detective could hear him. "It's what I found out about all the investigations concerning our dear friend."

"Quashed?" said Taine.

"*Killed* better describes the situation," said the reporter. "I dug back eleven years. All I turned up were zeros—each one standing for a dead reporter. Nine good men died in a little more than ten years. The only thing linking them together was an interest in Harmon Sangmeister.

"Can you blame me for acting paranoid?" continued Korshak, taking a swallow of beer. "This guy plays rough."

"No chance of coincidence?" asked Taine.

"Not unless you believe in the tooth fairy," said Korshak. "The reason no one ever noticed the pattern is that most of these men died from natural causes. One got hit by a car, but the police actually caught the driver soon after. He was the typical drunk, out on a suspended license. No hint of conspiracy in that death or any of the others.''

The reporter looked around the bar suspiciously. ''Care to explain how this mysterious millionaire murders people by lung cancer, pneumonia or heart attacks? It can't be true, but the facts speak for themselves.''

''Stick to the financial section,'' said Taine, ''and leave the police blotter to the professionals. With enough money, you can set up just about anyone for a one-way trip to the morgue.''

Smiling, Taine pointed at Korshak's drink. ''For example, suppose one of Sangmeister's goons followed you to the bar. A slick operator, he manages to slip some knockout drops in your beer. The expensive stuff is odorless, tasteless and doesn't show up in an autopsy unless you look for it. When you collapse in agony, he rushes over and proclaims himself a doctor. After a quick examination, he proclaims you've just suffered a stroke and summons an ambulance.

''No one ever notices how quickly it arrives. By the time you arrive at the hospital, your brain is mashed potatoes. Slick and quick and, as you so aptly stated, no hint of conspiracy.''

''How wonderful,'' said Korshak. He gently pushed his drink to the middle of the table. ''From now on, I only drink beer from bottles. Still, things could be worse. I could be Sangmeister.''

''What do you mean?'' said Taine.

''Nobody on the street has seen the gentleman in question for months,'' answered the reporter. ''The old man always worked through proxies, but lately he's been nearly invisible. During the Commodities Exchange probe, the FBI sent a special agent out to his country estate to interview him. They only do that in very special circumstances.''

''What are you leading up to, Jack?''

''I called in a bunch of favors today, Taine. It cost me, but I got to see the report from the field agent who interviewed Harmon. According to the G-man, Sangmeister looked like he had one foot in the grave. The old man played around with the wrong doxie once upon a time. He's dying—dying from AIDS."

"You sure?" asked Taine.

"The agent quoted a doctor's records no less. All of Sangmeister's millions can't buy him a second more of life. The report gave him two months or less. That was five weeks ago. Let me tell you, this will be one obituary I'll enjoy typing."

"Don't start working yet," said Taine, testily. "Remember what I told you about the corrupting power of money. Even government agents can be bought or fooled. I'll believe Sangmeister dead when I see him buried."

"Not to change the subject," said Korshak, looking down at the table and lowering his voice to a whisper, "but are you involved with some sort of feud with a black street gang?"

"No," said Taine, with a frown. "Why do you ask?"

"Sneak a peek at the two dudes in the doorway," said Korshak, with a slight nod of his head in the general direction of the entrance. "They've been giving you the eye for the past few minutes."

"Don't worry about me having any trouble spotting them," said Taine. "Here they come now. I believe I know what they want."

Two black men, both in their early twenties, clad in blue jeans and muscle T's, walked over to the table. Around them, the crowd melted away as if by magic.

"You Taine?" asked one of the pair, politely.

"That's me," he answered, his voice equally polite.

"We got a car outside," said the other. "The Bocar wants to talk to you. He wants to talk to you real bad."

Taine rose from his chair. "And I want to talk to him."

He dropped a twenty on the table. "The beer's on me tonight, Jack. Make sure they only bring you ones with the caps still on tight. Thanks for all the neat info. It helps."

"Right," said Korshak. "Stay cool, Taine."

"Don't you worry 'bout your friend," said the taller of the two black men. He laughed at the strained expression on Korshak's face. "We just be his escort. Bocar would have our balls if we let him get hurt."

Then, to his companion and Taine, "C'mon. They don't like our kind in here. Time to move."

With a shrug of his shoulders, Taine headed for the door, his escort bringing up the rear.

23

Ape Largo picked up the phone on the first ring.

"Yeah?" He waited a few seconds for an answer, then growled, "Well, bring him right up as soon as they arrive."

He turned to his boss and grinned. "That was Jo-Jo downstairs. Two of the boys found Taine at a bar on the North Side. They're on their way back now."

Royce licked his lips for the hundredth time that night. Ape knew what that meant. "I need a drink," said the Bocar of Danballah. "Get me that fifth of gin."

"You had enough, boss," said Ape, unhappily reaching for the bottle. Royce stopped using a glass hours ago. The gin bottle was nearly empty but the Bocar was still stone cold sober. He sweated out the liquor as fast as he poured it in.

"Keep your advice to yourself, you dumb shit," said Royce angrily. "Give me that damned bottle."

Silently, Ape handed over the fifth. With a snarl of satisfaction, the Bocar tilted the bottle up in the air and swigged down the rest of its contents. Staggering back a step, Royce flung the empty decanter across the room.

"Damn stuff tastes like piss."

Ape refrained from asking Royce how he arrived at the comparison. No use making a bad situation worse.

Maybe when that detective arrived, things would improve. They couldn't get much worse.

The murders this afternoon had sent the Bocar into hysterics. He had personally recruited the six old women who laundered drug money for the Children. Only a few members of his inner circle knew of their existence. Now all six were dead, victims of the Dark Man. There was no mistaking the killer's grisly work.

The third floor of the main Temple, where Royce normally lived in luxury, resembled an armed camp. A half-dozen heavily armed men patrolled the corridor outside the main suite. Inside, Ape, Morris and his brother, Boris, all carried sawed-off shotguns tucked in their belts. At the moment, the two big men were in the other bedroom playing cards. Ape was stuck baby-sitting Royce.

Muttering something incomprehensible under his breath, the Bocar wandered over to the TV. Ape breathed a sigh of relief as his boss dropped onto the couch and turned the set back on. Royce was hooked on soap operas. He owned several VCRs and faithfully recorded every daytime serial on the air. When the phone rang, he had been only halfway through today's episodes. Hopefully, the detective would arrive before the end of the tape.

Ape tracked down the empty gin bottle and tossed it in the garbage. Along with protecting Royce, he reluctantly served as chief adviser, confidant and personal manservant. That last job drove him crazy.

Lately, he found himself exercising his self-control depressingly often. It hadn't always been that way. When he first started working for Royce, the man had treated him like a valuable aide and ally. The Bocar recognized those heavy brows concealed a brilliant mind. He understood that beneath incredible slabs of muscle beat a man's heart.

More than anything else, Ape yearned for the respect his brutish body denied him. He wanted to be treated as a person, not a freak of nature. Only recently had he finally realized that he would never achieve his goal while working for Royce. It was time for him to move on.

A sharp rapping at the door shook him out of his reverie. As if shot from a cannon, the Bennett brothers came barreling out of the other room. They might be dumb, but they didn't lack for courage. Carefully, Ape counted the knocks. Five sounded by the time Morris reached the door and flung it open. Three shotguns pointed into the hall.

"Hey, shove the burner." It was Jo-Jo from downstairs. Behind him stood a powerfully built Caucasian that Ape knew must be Sidney Taine. "You'll scare our guest."

Jo-Jo waved the detective into the room. "Make yourself at home, bro'," he said, laughing.

"You boys seems a bit edgy," said Taine, stepping forward. "Expecting a little trouble?"

"Excuse our weapons, Mr. Taine," said Willis Royce, coming across the room, offering an outstretched hand in greeting. "But as you know, we live under siege."

Ape marveled as always at the Bocar's ability to pull himself together whenever necessary. Royce had an incredible tolerance to alcohol. He drank like a fish, yet never seemed to get drunk. It was an uncanny talent and one that frightened Ape. There were secrets Royce kept even from him.

"Have a seat," said the Bocar, gesturing to a card table and chairs. "Can I offer you something to drink?"

"A beer would be fine," said Taine. "A light if you've got it."

Morris headed off for the kitchen. Royce and Taine sat down at the table, facing each other. Ape stayed in the background. No reason to call attention to himself. He wanted to hear this conversation.

With a certain grim satisfaction, Ape noted that Royce appeared uncertain about the man he faced. Taine represented an unknown element in this gruesome battle with the Dark Man. Usually Royce tried to overwhelm anyone he met. Taine didn't look like the type who bullied easily.

"You sent me a card today," said Royce, watching the detective sip his beer. "On the back was scribbled *'The five symbols represent four words.'* Needless to say, the message caught my attention. I instructed the Children of Danballah to bring you here. My apologies if it caused you any inconvenience."

"No problem," said Taine, putting down his beer. "You want information. I have it. The only thing we need to settle is the price."

Royce made a face. Ape smiled, remembering a similar deal from earlier in the day.

"How much?"

"I don't want money," said Taine, leaning across the table, his gaze fixed on Royce. "I'll trade information for information. You talk. I talk. We both come out ahead."

"Not the way I see it," said Royce. "The Dark Man ain't after your butt. Why should I trust you?"

Ape sensed that his boss did not like the terms one bit. However, he had little choice in the matter. And Taine knew it as well.

"Take it or leave it," said the detective quietly.

"All right, all right," said Royce, his voice hollow with fear. "You first, though."

"Fine with me," said Taine. "Once you provide me with the details of these murders."

"Ape," said Royce, not even turning, "get our guest another beer. Morris, Boris; you two keep a close watch on the doors."

"Tell me about this Dark Man," said Taine, as Ape headed for the kitchen. "I want to hear everything you know about him."

24

Carefully, Felice counted the soggy currency in her purse. Deducting the money needed to cover her few bills, she still came up five bucks short. Cursing, she shoved the purse back beneath the front seat of her car. On a night like this, it might take hours to make that necessary five spot.

For a second, she considered driving back to her apartment and forgetting the crack party at Annie's tonight. A thin, cold drizzle soaked the streets. The dreary weather kept most people off the street. And it cut down her chances of finding a stud looking for some quick action to almost nothing.

With a shrug of disgust, Felice pulled out the last fry daddy from her blouse pocket. She rolled the cigarette herself, liberally lacing the tobacco with powdered crack. The rush it provided hardly matched the incredible jolt provided by the pure stuff. Still, smoking a daddy kept her jiving when life looked especially bleak.

Inhaling deeply, she pulled the smoke deep into her lungs. The familiar surge of pleasure hit her hard between the eyes. A tingle of excitement coursed through her body, arousing her senses. Her nipples swelled into hard points, while deep down between her legs, a raging fire flared. Even the smallest amount of crack set her off. She needed a man real bad. Especially one willing to pay five bucks for her uncontrollable lust.

Before leaving her car, Felice gently extinguished the fry daddy with her fingers. The unsmoked half went into a half-finished pack of gum in her glove compartment. The location and smell kept it safe from prying eyes. Using a roach clip, she always smoked the cigarette down to the bare paper. Nobody wasted good crack.

Getting out, she locked the car then hid the keys in a hollow space behind the rear license plate. She never carried her car keys when she walked the street. Some things were better kept secret from the cops and her johns. A smart hooker trusted no one.

Stretching, she smoothed down the tight black leather miniskirt that barely covered her thighs. A thin red windbreaker shielded her head and upper body from the rain. Beneath it, she wore a bright green tube top that hugged her large breasts like a second skin.

Only her shoes were practical. Felice wore sneakers instead of the usual six-inch spike heels favored by most whores in the city. Cops rarely bothered chasing hookers during a sweep. Good shoes meant the difference between a night in jail or safety at home. Selling her body since she was nineteen, Felice knew all the angles.

A small, fold-up umbrella completed her outfit. On a night like this, it served a multitude of purposes other than keeping her dry. Used properly, the stick made a dangerous weapon. Equally important, when held at the right angle, the dark canvas shielded a variety of sins from casual bystanders.

Felice set off at a brisk pace down the block. She was parked only a few minutes away from a local community college. Eight o'clock classes ended in four minutes. With luck, she could score a few tricks and be on her way to Annie's before ten.

She worked colleges as frequently as possible. Only a few other hookers bothered. Most of the girls preferred the downtown crowd or the swingers on the North Side. They were always looking for the big score, hoping to pull in a quick fifty or C-note. Felice thrived on turnover.

Some nights, she screwed a dozen or more different men in the course of a few hours. When she was high on crack, nothing mattered. Totally amoral, she was willing to do anything for a price. Oftentimes, she took on two johns at a time. She did it on her back or on her knees; standing up or bent over. Whatever the customer wanted, she provided. Place and position never mattered. Only the price counted.

Just as she reached the edge of the four-square-block campus, the rain stopped. Surprised but pleased, Felice walked a little faster. Keeping her eyes open for college security guards, she headed for the Math and Science Building.

The eight o'clock bell sounded a few seconds after her arrival. Running up the concrete stairs leading to the hall, she quickly climbed onto the far shoulder of the entranceway. Folding her legs beneath her, she sat down on the cold stone. For all purposes, with her windbreaker drawn closed at her neck, she could easily pass as a typical coed.

To her intense disappointment, only a few students came pushing their way through the doors. No time to scout out another building. With a practiced eye, she scanned the possible marks. In seconds, she fixed her attention on a mismatched pair of young white men dressed in business suits. Black girls always fascinated white boys. Felice considered the possibilities and smiled wickedly.

Jumping off the wide ledge, she walked swiftly after the two students. Buried deep in conversation, they didn't even notice her until she came up beside them.

"Interesting class, gents?" she asked, her voice low and sultry. Neither man was particularly handsome, but neither looked that bad either. In her present state of mind, she would screw a statue if it possessed the right equipment.

"I thought so," said the shorter of the two. Dark brown eyes peered out at her through thick, horn-rimmed lenses. "Do we know you?"

"I'm Felice," she said, dragging her feet. As she expected, both men also slowed down to stay even with her.

"Pleased to meet you," said the one wearing glasses. "I'm Cliff Kowalski." He gestured with his head at his taller companion. "This is my friend, Mark Finkel."

"You boys looking for some action?" asked Felice unzipping her windbreaker.

"You—you must be kidding," stuttered out Finkel, his face turning a bright red. "We're students."

Felice laughed. Reaching up, she hooked both thumbs over the edge of her tube top. With a well-practiced move, she pulled the material down and across her body, exposing her large breasts. Her swollen nipples glistened in the dim lights from the nearby classrooms. "Come and get educated," she said.

"But it's on campus," said Cliff, looking around for signs of life. They stood alone in a dark patch between two old brick buildings.

His friend didn't seem to care. As if hypnotized by Felice's massive breasts, Finkel tentatively reached out and touched her with one hand. Gentle fingers massaged one rock hard nipple. Felice swayed forward in excitement, a low moan escaping her lips. Finkel needed no further encouragement. In seconds, his hands were eagerly exploring her exposed body. Bending over, he lowered his mouth onto her left breast. She gasped with pleasure as his teeth nipped her flesh.

Really hot now, Felice grabbed Cliff by the arm and pulled him close. "Feel me," she said, passion thick in her voice. "You know where. Right down there."

Still clutching his right arm, she thrust his hand beneath her short skirt and between her legs. She never wore panties. His probing fingers sent spasms of excitement pounding through her body. She felt like an animal in heat. Unconsciously, she thrust her body forward, already locking into a sexual rhythm with her two new lovers.

"Back by the bushes," she gasped out after a few seconds. "We can do it there. I'll take you both at once."

No worries about campus security now. In the near total darkness, they ripped off their clothes. Hurriedly, Felice positioned herself between the two men. "Give it to me hard and fast," she said to Cliff, bending over and spreading her legs wide apart. "None of those slow, gentle strokes. I want it rough."

"I've got something special for you," she continued, peering up at Mark. Grasping his erection firmly with one hand, she smiled broadly and licked her lips. "You keep on pumping and let me do the rest."

Then, knowing she was completely in command of the situation, she added, "Twenty bucks, each, okay with you boys? Maybe, if you're good, real good, we can try a few special tricks. Cost a little more, but you gotta pay for an education."

The two young men were in no position to argue. Felice literally had them exactly where she wanted. Wordlessly, they nodded in agreement.

Abandoning herself totally to lust, Felice started humping and pumping. Hot sex now, crack party later. Life was sweet, real sweet.

25

Show me those photos," said Taine, when Willis Royce finally finished his story.

The pug-ugly everyone called Ape brought over the prints. Taine had heard stories about the infamous Ape Largo but never encountered him before tonight. The grotesque bodyguard measured up to his advance billing. He was the ugliest man imaginable. However, Taine knew better than to judge by appearances. More than once, he caught Largo smirking at some remark made by Royce. Taine suspected that the bodyguard might be a lot smarter than he looked.

One glance at the pictures confirmed Taine's suspicions about the brutal murders. Vague theories hardened into fact. The five sigils answered a number of pressing questions. But those disclosures only raised new and troubling mysteries.

Willis Royce impatiently drummed his fingers on the card table, waiting for answers. Taine didn't like the Bocar. More important, he trusted him even less.

He knew just enough about the cult leader to keep him on his guard. Years ago, "Smooth" Royce ran one of the largest numbers games on Chicago's South Side. Though he claimed all of his money came from sharp business deals, everyone knew he made his money operating an illegal lottery. Though never arrested, Royce topped the police lists of crime bosses in the city.

Despite or because of his reputation, Royce was one of the most popular black men on the South Side. To the poor residents of the inner-city slums, Royce was a man to be admired, not shunned. They loved the way he lived in style, spending money in wild orgies of self-indulgence. "Smooth" loved fast women and fast cars, and he kept himself well supplied in both.

His only son, Ernie "Rolls" Royce, earned his nickname from his taste in cars. He drove around the toughest sections of the city in a Rolls Royce Silver Phantom. Like his father, Ernie claimed he worked as an "investment counselor."

It surprised no one when Ernie and his fine automobile vanished one crisp spring morning. Nor was anyone particularly shocked when his bullet-riddled body was found a few weeks later, stuffed in the trunk of his otherwise pristine mint Rolls Royce. Gangland killings rarely made the front page of the papers in Chicago.

His funeral attracted plenty of media attention, though. They buried Ernie sitting up, carefully propped up behind the steering wheel of his beloved automobile. The wake lasted four days, and when the liquor finally stopped flowing, they lowered the Silver Phantom and its driver into the ground using a derrick and hoist.

Shortly after the funeral, Smooth Royce made the headlines again. Renouncing his earlier lifestyle, the numbers kingpin turned to religion. The death of his son had opened his eyes. With much fanfare, Royce embraced voodoo. According to his press releases, it was the only true religion for Afro-Americans. He immediately launched a one-man crusade to save other young men and women from the evils of crime. Royce called his new cult the Children of Danballah and took for himself the title Bocar.

The mayor, anxious to take advantage of any positive news from the inner city, immediately praised Royce's "miraculous" conversion. Federal officials, accused for years of ignoring blacks, seized the opportunity to make themselves look good. A very generous amount of government community development funds made its way to the Children's treasury.

Almost overnight, Royce became a leading spokesman for black youth. His conservative message of self-help and financial independence played well with the rich and powerful. While other groups struggled to make ends meet, the Children of Danballah continued to thrive. Only a few doubters expressed concern about the growing influence of the organization. They were ignored by a press more interested in style than substance. The media counted on the fast-talking Bocar for controversial quotes on otherwise slow news days. He never disappointed them.

Taine suspected that Royce's tumble from grace would be equally swift. These brutal killings by the Dark Man had exposed disturbing ties linking the Children to the crack trade. The future of the voodoo cult appeared extremely uncertain. Meanwhile, the Dark Man posed a more immediate threat for the Bocar and his followers.

"In Hebrew, the language of these five letters, you read from right to left," said Taine. "Mem, men, shin, pe, pe," he pronounced solemnly, progressively pointing to each symbol in the photo.

"Taken together, they represent four Hebrew words. Each mem stands for *mene*. Shin becomes *shekel*, or as it was originally called, *tekel*. The two pe's taken together form a plural version of the word *peres*, which translates as *upharsin*."

"So what?" said Royce, obviously unimpressed.

"I know those words," said Ape Largo unexpectedly from the corner. "When I was a kid, my mother read me stories from the Bible." His face crinkled into what Taine guessed to be a smile. "I loved the real dramatic ones. That's why I still remember the Handwriting on the Wall."

Taine nodded. His opinion of the bodyguard went up several notches. Not many people remembered the Book of Daniel. "Mene, Mene, Tekel, Upharsin," he continued. "The Handwriting on the Wall revealed God's judgment of Belshazzar, king of Babylon."

"Go on, go on," Royce demanded impatiently.

"In a minute," said Taine. "I've demonstrated my good faith. Now it's time for you to do a little talking."

"Ape, you take Morris and Boris in the other room and wait till I call," said Royce, grimly.

The Bocar watched his three bodyguards leave before saying another word. "What they don't know won't hurt me. Especially that freak, Ape. I'm having second thoughts about him." Royce's fingers beat a nervous tattoo on the tabletop. "Ask your damn questions. You seem to know an awful lot already."

"What's your relationship with the Knights of Antioch?"

Royce's eyes narrowed into tiny slits, focused only on Taine. "I belong to the Order."

"I thought so," said Taine, hard pressed to keep the satisfaction from his voice. "Did they supply you with the capital to start the Children of Danballah?"

"Most of it," said Royce, clipping his words short. "The idea came from me but the Black Lodge put up the necessary cash. And they skim twenty-five percent off the top of each month's take."

"How does Victor Caldwell fit in?"

"He deals directly with the Bogota Syndicate. Fat Boy pays for the stuff through stock transfers arranged by his company."

"What about Sangmeister?"

"That old snake?" Royce spit on the floor. "He

doesn't do nothing, but he still gets his cut as Grand Master."

The Bocar's hands knotted into fists. "Caldwell phoned me earlier tonight. He told me all about your visit. It sounded awfully strange to me."

"Too bad," said Taine, a ruthless edge to his voice. "See my tears. I don't give a damn what you think, Royce. Not a damn."

"Enough small talk," said the Bocar, licking dry lips nervously. "I told you what you wanted. Finish your story.

"Ape—get back in here with the boys," he called loudly, as if suddenly afraid of being alone. "And bring me another bottle of gin."

"The original words referred to ancient measures of weight," continued Taine a few minutes later. "Taken together, they signified a deadly progression. The prophet Daniel interpreted their message as 'God hath numbered thy kingdom and finished it. Thou are weighed in the balances and found wanting.' Late that same night, Babylon fell to the Persians. The king and all his court died in bloody carnage."

"That sounds an awful lot like a death sentence to me," said Ape Largo.

"I don't care what you think," said Royce, angrily. "Keep talking, Taine. What does this mumbo jumbo have to do with the Dark Man?"

"I'm getting to that," said Taine, a note of annoyance in his voice. "Give me a minute to explain." He paused, as if searching for the right words.

"In the vast netherworld of humanity's shared subconscious exist powerful creatures of absolute darkness. Students of the Kabbalah refer to them as the Sheddim, chaotic beings created by Elohim before mankind. Most people think of them as demons and boogeymen. Elemental, nameless horrors, they normally touch our world only through dreams.

"However, an extremely powerful sorcerer can summon one of these monsters from the outermost dark with certain words of power. Once here, he anchors the being to our world by the use of a True Name. Evidently, one of your enemies has done exactly that. The thing you call the Dark Man is the living embodiment of modern society's worst fears and nightmares. It exists only to destroy.

"There are hundreds of different types of Sheddim. Together, they constitute the entire catalog of the supernatural horrors of legend. All of them draw their strength from human flesh and blood. However, only a few, such as vampires and werewolves, actually feed on physical sustenance. The rest feast on the vital force, the souls if you prefer, of their victims. Killing gives them life. Those symbols, drawn in human blood, channel the psychic energy of his prey to the Dark Man. With each death, he grows more powerful."

Royce took a long, hard swallow from the gin bottle. "You ain't telling me a whole lot of useful information," he said, slurring his words together. "I need to know how to stop this thing. Do we shoot him with silver bullets or what?"

"I doubt if that would work," said Taine. "The Dark Man himself is probably unkillable. Remember, he is a direct physical manifestation of the evil within us all. The best you can hope is to send him back to the outermost darkness."

"Yeah," said Royce, morosely. "How do we manage that?"

"An exorcism," said Ape Largo, his voice cold and grim.

"My thought, too," said Taine. The ugly man continued to surprise him. "If we somehow cornered the Dark Man, an exorcism might banish him from our world."

"I know a little about those ceremonies," said Royce unexpectedly. "After all, I am a Bocar. Two things I remember concerning these rituals. You need to know what type of demon you battle before you can imprison it. And you must name a demon before it will depart."

"Quite correct," said Taine. "Unfortunately I have no clue as to what type of Sheddim the Dark Man actually is. We must learn that before he can be defeated. But I do know his name.''

"What the hell," said Royce, spilling some of his precious gin on the carpet. ''What bullshit you pulling now, you smartass white boy?''

''Now, now,'' said Taine, smoothly. ''No racial slurs. Remember, we're trading information. I'll reveal what you want to know once you tell me how Roger Fremont fits into the plans of the Black Lodge.''

"Fremont," said Royce, his brow furled in thought. "I don't remember any novice named Fremont. What does this dude look like?''

Taine described Janet's ex-husband the best he could, relying on her sketchy account of his features.

''Nobody matching those specs belongs to the Order,'' said Royce. ''Besides which, you said he's a crack head. We don't admit geeks into the Lodge.''

''He wore a ring with the seal,'' said Taine.

''Jewelry can be stolen. Crack addicts rip off anything they can lay their hands on.''

Royce's tone grew desperate. "Listen, Taine. The secrets of the Black Lodge cannot be revealed to outsiders. No matter what the price, I can't talk about the inner workings of the Order. However, I'm not violating my oath when I swear to you that this Roger Fremont never attended any of our meetings. No matter what he claims, he doesn't belong to the Knights of Antioch.''

Taine recognized the truth when he heard it. He shook his head in annoyance. So much for easy answers.

''To summon a Sheddim, a magician must give the creature a name of power. We already know the Dark Man uses the Handwriting on the Wall as a focus for its dark hunger. Logically, those same symbols are the ones that first summoned it to our world.

''Continuing with that thought, in the Book of Daniel the text states 'The fingers of a man's hand came forth and wrote upon the wall.' It seems quite unlikely that the Dark Man, by coincidence alone, uses a human hand for his bloody paintbrush.''

''What are you leading up to?'' asked Royce.

"According to the great Kabbalistic scholars, the Lord God, Elohim, never directly interferes with mankind. Instead, he works through agents, the Angelic Host. Thus, when the Bible refers to 'the finger of God,' it actually means a messenger of the Lord."

"So what you're saying," continued Ape Largo, picking up the complex idea, "is that when Daniel wrote that a ghostly finger inscribed the Handwriting on the Wall, it was actually done by one of the Heavenly Host. And when summoning the Dark Man, the magician empowered this demon through use of the name of that powerful angel. It almost seems sacriligious."

"Exactly why a black magician would do such a thing. Every clue ties the two supernatural beings together," said Taine.

"So the Dark Man shares his name with the messenger of Elohim in the Book of Daniel," said Royce. "Which is . . . ?"

"Can't you guess?" answered Taine somberly. "It's Arelim—the Angel of Rigorous Ministry. The Avenging Angel."

26

Around the same time Taine walked into the Temple of Danballah, Felice arrived at the crack party at Annie's place. She got there a little later than she originally planned, but she had no complaints. Nothing ever happened at a crack party anyway. And the seventy bucks tucked in the hidden pocket of her skirt would keep her high for a week.

Seven other girls sat on the battered chairs and sofa that filled up most of Annie's small living room. Light came from an old red hurricane lamp on the floor. The dim glow of a portable black-and-white TV set cast weird shadows on the walls. Annie left the television going day and night. Not that she watched anything. She just liked the constant noise.

Crack Annie herself unlocked the door to the apartment and let Felice in. Normally during a crack party, Annie was flat on her back on the living room floor, screwing her man, Leon. The combination of crack and a roomful of young women kept her stud hard for hours. Leon loved performing in front of an audience. No one ever objected. Crack had destroyed their few remaining sexual inhibitions long ago.

Most of the time, the crack heads just watched. Annie never allowed any other men at her parties. She worried about possible violence. Crack and sex made a volatile combination. Put a jealous man at an orgy and blood would flow.

Annie believed in sharing with her friends. If they wanted to join the fun, she never objected. Leon liked variety. During the course of a long evening, they indulged in every sexual position imaginable between two adults. Another girl only widened the possibilities. Once or twice, when the crack was really good, all of the other girls joined in, turning the party into an hours-long marathon sex session.

That was the way it was until two weeks ago Friday. During the day, Leon worked as a cook at the local hamburger joint. It didn't take much brains and paid just enough to keep him and Annie in crack. However little he earned, it must have seemed like a lot to the five teenagers who waylaid him after work.

Attacking Leon in the alleyway behind the restaurant, his assailants savagely beat him with rusted pipes and chains. Though he screamed and screamed for help, no one came to his aid. Getting involved too often meant getting killed.

It only took a few minutes for the gang to break both his arms and most of his ribs. When they only found twenty dollars in his pockets, one of the boys stuck a gun in Leon's mouth and blew away half his head.

When she learned the news, Crack Annie locked herself in her apartment and didn't come out for three days. She spent the entire time smoking rock, burning Leon out of her system. When she emerged, there was no sorrow left in her. After two weeks, her lover's body still remained unclaimed at the morgue. Leon no longer meant anything to Annie. Only crack mattered. The parties continued as before, but without the sex on the floor.

"Where you been, girl?" Crack Annie asked Felice. "Party started a long time ago."

"I had my own party," said Felice, grinning. "Got me some hot white boys with real money." She handed Annie two twenties. "Here's my share. Keep the rest on credit."

She inhaled deeply, filling her lungs with drifting whiffs of smoke. Felice looked around the room. All the usual girls were here, sitting in their usual places. No one bothered greeting her. Crack heads never spoke when they smoked crack. They devoted all of their attention to their pipes. The only noise in the room was the crackling sound emitted by the beads that gave the drug its name.

"What's with Rebeeka?" she asked, shrugging her shoulders at the motionless figure hunched over in one corner, her head wedged between her knees.

"She's been on a permanent mission all day," said Annie, unconcerned. "Beeka got here before everybody and started smoking right away. She quit 'bout an hour ago. Don't you worry none. She just needs some rest. It takes a long time to come down from a deep case."

"Guess so," said Felice, vaguely troubled by Beeka's appearance. Nobody slept in such an uncomfortable position. Still, it was none of her business.

"I got us some real fine rock today," said Annie, unusually talkative. "The Children been making deals lately. This stuff is real pure. You go flying on these rocks."

"Yeah," said Felice, dropping onto the couch and grabbing a crack pipe. "Time to take off."

All ready to light up, she hesitated for a second.

"What you say about getting this rock from the Children. I heard some talk a stickup boy killing them left and right. They called the dude the Dark Man."

"Who cares?" said Annie. "Dumb rollers shoot each other all the time. They never touch the crack heads. We be the ones that pays the bills."

Felice nodded and touched a match to the rock. Two quick puffs and she went zooming off into the stratosphere. All of her worries and troubles evaporated in a cloud of instant gratification. It was like someone turned a switch in her brain to maximum ecstasy and then left it there. The pleasure blotted out all other sensations. For ten minutes, she hardly thought at all.

Smoking crack satisfied her more than sex and without any of the bother. Given an unlimited supply, she would do nothing else. Or so she felt when she was flying.

Other times, that same thought gave her the chills. A close friend of hers starved to death last month. The police found her, a crack pipe in her hand, bags of unopened food in the kitchen. Crack killed if you let it take complete control of your life. Felice knew she was too smart to ever let that happen.

Ten minutes and she came tumbling down from the clouds. The same size rock once sent her soaring for twice that time, but that was six months ago. The more hits you took, the more you needed to get high.

As usual depression set in, hitting her hard and fast. It was the drug's one side effect that always strung Felice out to dry. Only one thing eased the shakes. She needed another rock. First, though, she needed a drink to calm her nerves. Then she would head back into the clouds.

Rising to her feet, Felice stumbled past her silent friends into the kitchen. Only the TV made noise. The set served to block out the sounds of the street. The neighbors never complained. People who lived in a crack house learned to mind their own business. Geeks made dangerous enemies.

Annie always left a pitcher of gin and fruit drink,

"swamp juice," by the sink. The powerful mixture always chased the blues away. Carefully tilting the container, Felice filled a plastic cup to the rim. Sipping her drink, she headed back to the living room.

"Tap, tap, tap." Someone was at the door, gently knocking to be let in.

"I got it," said Annie, reaching for the knob. Nobody worried about The Man in this building. The police knew better than to enter this neighborhood on foot. Only crack heads came to see Annie.

Untroubled and unsuspecting, Crack Annie opened the apartment door. For a second, she froze, her body blocking the entrance. Then, with a shriek of fear, she tried slamming the door shut.

A huge fist smashed through the paneling, sending Annie tumbling back onto the sofa. Cursing loudly, several of the girls pushed her violently away. Annie crashed to the floor, half dazed from the fall.

Meanwhile, the Dark Man forced his way through the door and into the apartment. Most of the women never even saw him arrive. For an instant, he stood unmoving in the ruins of the doorway, as if deciding on a plan of action. Then, before anyone could react, the intruder attacked.

Standing at the far side of the room, Felice saw it all happen. Reaching out with one immense hand, the gigantic stranger grabbed LuAnn Coye by the hair. Brutally, he yanked her out of her seat and up into the air. She never had a chance to scream. Timing the blow perfectly, the Dark Man swept his other arm forward, aiming it straight at LuAnn's face. In his hand he clutched a gigantic butcher's cleaver. With a grisly *thunk* the blade bit deep into her flesh.

The girl's features erupted in an explosion of blood and gore. Fragments of bone and cartilage splattered against the killer's topcoat as he wrenched his weapon free. Calmly, the Dark Man raised his blade high into the air and chopped again. His second cut severed LuAnn's head from her body, sending her torso spinning to the floor. Her still-beating heart sent a fountain of hot blood splashing across the room and all of its occupants.

Dazed and horrified, the crack heads struggled up from the couch. A few of them still clung possessively to their crack pipes. None of them seemed sure of what was taking place.

Laughing, the Dark Man grabbed Wanda Hanson by an arm. Her screams echoed through the small room. Desperately, she tried to pull away. There was no escape. Like a flash of lightning, the bloody cleaver slammed into her stomach. Bright red blood gushed from her lips. Ruthlessly, the Dark Man twisted his blade and ripped it up and across. With a violent shudder, Wanda's body collapsed in ruin as her steaming insides spilled in a gory mess onto the floor.

"Let's have some fun," said the Dark Man, chuckling. Waving his cleaver in the air, he stepped forward, intent on his next victim. Beneath his feet, the blood-soaked carpet unexpectedly shifted, sending him toppling to the floor.

"Get that mother!" screamed Crack Annie, rising up from behind the sofa. In one hand she clutched a six-inch switchblade. Madness filled her eyes. "We gotta kill the son-of-a-bitch while he's down!"

Shrieking like harpies, the women attacked. The crack in their system gave them courage they otherwise lacked. It was kill or be killed. Only Felice hung back, frozen by fear. Her legs refused to move. She could only watch and hope.

Two girls, one on each side, trapped the Dark Man's arms between their arms and legs. A third girl hung on tightly to his feet, not letting him rise. Hovering over his chest, Crack Annie jabbed away with her knife. "Die, damn you, die!" she screamed as she stabbed him repeatedly in the chest.

Felice's eyes bulged in horror. Each time Annie pulled the knife free, the blade emerged clean. No blood stained the metal. The killer didn't bleed. It took Crack Annie a few seconds to realize her folly. By then, it was much too late.

"Party's over," said the Dark Man, his voice filled with good cheer.

Wrenching his body around, the giant sent one girl flying across the room. She smashed into the wall and lay very still.

One hand free, he reached around and grabbed the girl holding his other arm by the face. He squeezed tight. Bones crunched like candy beneath his fingers. Blood jetted high in the air as he continued to apply pressure. Her body only twitched for an instant.

The third girl died with her skull smashed in. She never saw death coming. Rising to his feet between the corpses, the giant faced Crack Annie.

The girl stared at her bloodless knife and then back up at the Dark Man. "They never touch the crack heads," said Annie, a note of annoyance in her voice. Then, before the Dark Man could attack, she rammed the switchblade deep into her stomach. Her eyes blinked rapidly and then closed. She collapsed and died without another word.

"She cheated me," said the Dark Man, turning to face Felice. "I hate when they do that." He held up his cleaver. "I'll have to take my time with you. I always do with the last one."

"No, no, no," said Felice, stepping back. A terrible coldness gripped her body. Death stood five feet away. "Take Rebeeka, not me. You forgot Rebeeka."

"Sorry, dear. She's been dead for hours," said the Dark Man. "Her heart gave out right after the party started. That final rush popped all the blood vessels in her lungs. Crack does that to a lot of people. You're the only one left, Felice."

Up went the cleaver. Then, the giant paused, as if hearing voices in the distance. Tilting his head, he stood perfectly still. "They know my name," he muttered. Then, louder, "They know my name."

Felice reacted the only way possible. She flung her drink at the Dark Man's face and ran for the door. She dashed into the hallway before the giant realized she was gone.

Jumping an entire flight of stairs with each leap, Felice went flying down three floors in an instant. Momentum carried her across the hall and out the front door. Grabbing the porch railing, she leapt down concrete steps to the sidewalk. Behind her, she could hear the Dark Man laughing. He sounded amused by her escape.

"Your body belongs to me, Felice," he called from inside the building. "I'll get you in the end."

Dazed but unharmed, she bolted across the deserted street. The fall of soft rain on her skin never felt so sweet. She made it out alive with everyone else dead. Breathing hard, she forced herself to keep moving. The farther she got from the scene of the crime the better. She had no desire to be here when the police finally arrived.

A puzzled look crossed Felice's face as she stumbled along the street. She had escaped the Dark Man but his last words implied otherwise. She wondered what he meant. Shaking her head, she continued walking. Too bad all that crack was gone. She was dying for a hit.

27

Mommy's got a boyfriend, mommy's got a boyfriend," chanted Timmy as Janet tried to put on her makeup.

"Quiet down, you babbling brook," she said, laughing. Her hands shook too much to apply her eyeshadow. "You want your mom to look like an Indian?"

"A red Indian or one from India?" asked Tim curiously.

"A Sioux Indian," said Janet, smiling at her boy. "That means I'll sue you if you don't let me get ready. Mr. Taine should be here in a few minutes. Let me finish getting dressed. Go bother Bruno or your grandfather."

"Grandpa told me to pester you," said Tim. "He said you needed the company."

Which meant her father wanted some peace and quiet. She understood his feelings perfectly. No adult alive could ever keep up with a typical eight-year-old.

"Mom," said Tim in his most-serious sounding voice, "are you going to marry Mr. Taine?"

"Timmy!" said Janet, caught off guard. "I only met him the other day."

"I know," replied her son, "but you like him a lot. I can tell."

"I like a number of people," she said, with a shake of her head, "but that doesn't mean I plan to marry all of them."

"He likes you, too," said Tim, completely ignoring her words. "Kids sense feelings better than adults."

"He hasn't asked me," said Janet, trying to recapture the conversation.

"He will," answered Tim. "I bet you ten dollars."

Downstairs, the doorbell rang. "That's him right now," said Tim, flying out of the room. "Maybe he brought me a toy."

"Don't bother Mr. Taine too much," she called after her son. "Tell him I'll be ready in just a few minutes."

Anxiously, she turned back to the mirror and made a few final adjustments to her lip gloss. Satisfied, she stepped back and contemplated the whole picture. She still looked awfully good for thirty. A new dress and a pearl necklace didn't hurt either.

She had stopped into her shop early Thursday morning. To the surprise of the staff, she stayed for less than fifteen minutes. A few necessary checks got written, a few problems that required her attention got answered, and then she was gone. Along with her went one of the nicer pearl necklaces from the safe. Janet smiled as she remembered the incredulous looks on the faces of her girls. At least she gave them something to talk about for the rest of the day.

Bruno brought the necklace back to Brentwood while Janet went shopping for a dress. After much looking, she settled on a basic black cocktail dress with a high choker neck that left her shoulders and back bare. Coupled with a finely knit white shawl, it accented all of her curves and none of her faults.

The entire day she refused to question her motives or desires. Forgotten were her doubts from the previous night. In the daytime, her questions about Taine's past seemed unimportant. Instead of logic, she let her emotions guide her actions. By the time she arrived back at Brentwood, Janet felt positively giddy.

Taine called just before five. He had made reservations at one of the nicer Italian restaurants on the North Side and would pick her up around seven. As before, the detective was a few minutes early. That suited her just fine. She hated being late, but she also knew the value of a good entrance.

As she descended the stairs, Janet caught a fragment of conversation between her father and Taine.

"Then you believe that even dangerous criminals deserve a second chance?" asked Leo, a note of disbelief in his voice.

"It all hinges, of course, on their desire to reform," said Taine. "I'm not advocating letting mass murderers go free to kill again. However, we must temper justice with mercy. Every man deserves the opportunity to change his ways."

"Nicely put," said her father, "though I suspect few people today would agree with your position."

"If sin exists," said Taine somberly, "then so must redemption. Otherwise only evil triumphs."

"These days, that happens all too often," said Leo. "Enough gloom and doom. Here is Janet now."

The look on Taine's face made all of her shopping worthwhile. Even Leo looked impressed.

"Mom's all dressed up," said Tim proudly. "She looks like a movie star."

"She surely does," said Taine, walking over to meet her at the bottom of the stairway. "I believe *stunning* is the appropriate term." He took her hands in his. "I'm properly dazzled. You're beautiful."

169

The sincerity in his voice set her pulse racing. For the first time in years, she found herself blushing. "I'm glad you think so," she said, struggling to find the right words. As she spoke, she gently squeezed his hands. "I wanted to wear something special for you."

"We better get going," said Taine, struggling to maintain his composure. "We don't want to be late."

"Taine brought me a micromaster Transformer," said Tim from the corner of the room. "Neat, huh, Mom?"

"Very neat," she agreed. "Mr. Taine and your grandfather must share the same contacts."

"You'll need an umbrella," said Leo, peering out the front doorway. "It started drizzling again."

"Monotonous, isn't it," said Taine. "Fortunately, after nearly a week of rain, I've taken to carrying an umbrella with me wherever I go."

"Don't let Tim stay up too late," said Janet, as the detective helped her put on her topcoat. "I probably won't be home till after his bedtime."

"Have a good time," said Leo, waving them out the door. "Tim will be fine with me. Enjoy your evening."

28

Chuckling, the man who considered himself Arelim shut off his television. "The police expect a break in the case momentarily," he said in a high-pitched voice, mimicking the female newscaster. "Stay tuned for further details."

The futile efforts of the police amused him. They labored in vain, hampered by their beliefs in rational explanations. The possibility that a supernatural entity might be committing the murders never once entered their minds. The occult baffled them and because of that, they ignored it. Instead, they concentrated on purely physical solutions.

Meanwhile, the newspapers shared the same prejudice. The media blamed a major rift between the Columbian and Bolivian drug cartels. It made good copy and tied in with recent events in South America.

As of yet, no one offered an explanation of the Hebrew symbols scrawled in the victim's blood, but Arelim expected some incredible theory would surface sooner or later. He loved it all.

The Dark Man fed on the death energies of his victims. Through use of sympathetic magic, he devoured that force from their vital fluids. The mystic symbols the Dark Man drew served as a visual conduit in the ceremony.

However, there was no reason for him to dismember his prey. That tactic came directly from Arelim. He knew the ghoulish bent of the press. The more grisly the crime, the more news it generated. He wanted as much publicity as he could get. The butchery assured him of that.

By now, even the most illiterate crack head knew the dangers of dealing with the Children of Danballah. The organization tottered on the brink of ruin. Tonight he would finish them for good. His plans progressed smoothly. Only a few minor annoyances stood in his way.

"Mene, mene, tekel, upharsin," he recited as he sat down behind his desk. When he looked up, the Dark Man stood where there had been nothing. The giant in black nodded a greeting to the sorcerer; not as a servant to his master, but as his equal. Knowing the nature of his creation, Arelim expected no less.

"You let four escape last night?" he asked.

"As you commanded," said the Dark Man. "One girl eluded me on her own. The others I pretended to miss in the confusion. I made sure all of them caught a good glimpse of me. None of them will ever forget what took place. Nearly fifty of their friends fed my hunger."

"All of the crack came from the Children?"

"Of course. I searched the streets until I found a few fearless hustlers still peddling their wares. In the privacy

of an abandoned warehouse, they proved most coopera-
tive in revealing the locations of several nearby crack
houses.''

''You killed them anyway?''

''What else did you expect? In the end they begged
me for that release. I spent several hours amusing
myself.'' The Dark Man laughed. ''It made up for the
boredom of the afternoon.''

''Play all the games you want,'' said Arelim, chuckling. ''Nothing can save the Children of Danballah. Your
killings have broken their grip on the drug market in this
city.''

''Perhaps,'' said the Dark Man, catching the sorcerer
off guard with his remark. It was the first time the giant
had ever expressed an opposing view. ''But I think
not.''

''What do you mean?''

''Remember Lisa Ray? She was the first one to elude
me.''

''Yes, yes,'' said Arelim, impatiently. ''The girl who
worked making crack. What of her?''

''She's back at work, running a crack factory for the
Black Guardians street gang. It only took a couple of
days until the shock wore off. My threat obviously
didn't stop her. Her ambition far outweighed her fears.

''Despite all of the murders, most of these dealers
continue to sell their drugs. They are too stupid to recognize their peril. They coexist with death already. I
merely represent another obstacle in their path to riches.
Nothing you or I do will rid the streets of such people.''

''So I realize,'' answered Arelim, somewhat testily.
He disliked being contradicted. ''You know my plans
down to the last detail. My immediate goal is to merely
destroy the main organization. Unchecked and uncon-
trolled by Royce, the small gangs throughout the city
will soon be at each other's throats. Then we shall witness wholesale slaughter that will dwarf your solitary
efforts. It is all so predictable that it almost bores me.''

''Boredom leads to mistakes.''

"I never make mistakes," said Arelim angrily. "You know what I expect from you?"

"It all comes together this night," said the Dark Man. Reaching beneath his coat, he pulled out his butcher's cleaver. Casually, he waved the deadly tool back and forth through the air. "Royce is surrounded by a dozen armed bodyguards."

"None of whom can stop you," said Arelim.

"I know," said the giant, with a laugh. "But they'll try. Oh, yes, they'll try."

"No mistakes this time," said Arelim, sternly. "I want *no survivors* to tell the tale. When the police finally arrive, I want them to find a Temple filled with death. In the meantime, I will make sure the news media learns of the carnage. A few TV and newspaper reporters at the scene should suffice."

"You treat this all as a game," said the Dark Man, shaking his huge head in bewilderment. He sounded almost human. "Life and death mean nothing to you. All of these people serve only as pawns in your elaborate schemes."

"The only life that matters to me is my own," said Arelim. "Everything else is secondary. I obey my own rules. And I crush anyone who stands in my way."

"*You* crush them?" said the Dark Man, with a laugh.

"With your help, of course," said Arelim hurriedly. By his very nature, the monster considered himself a totally independent entity. Arelim had no desire to inform him otherwise.

"I want you to kill one other tonight as well," he continued, rushing on to another subject. "This private investigator, Sidney Taine, knows much too much about the Black Lodge. He even claims to belong to a similar Order on the West Coast. I cannot see him causing any major problems, but why should we take chances. He might prove troublesome later. Eliminate him."

Yawning, the man who considered himself Arelim rose up out of his chair. "Remember my orders. Kill everyone in the Temple with Royce. I want no survivors. If any escape, track them down and kill them afterward. They all must die."

Reaching down, he picked up a small framed photo of a young woman off his desk. "Taine promised to help her," he said smiling.

Gently opening his hands, Arelim let the picture drop to the floor. With a loud crack, the glass shattered, sending bright little shards flying across the carpet.

"No one interferes with my plans," he said, his face twisting with rage. "No one. Kill him. Kill him tonight."

29

They wined and dined in style. Taine had reserved a small private room at a very exclusive restaurant and they ate alone by candlelight. The food was superb, complemented with several fine bottles of wine. By the end of the meal, Janet was at peace with the world and very much enamored with her escort. Which made it all the harder to face him with her doubts.

"Taine," she said cautiously, as they lingered over the last bites of dessert. "Is something the matter? You look worried." She laughed, trying to ease the tension. "The bill more than you expected?"

He smiled as she hoped he would. "No. Even a poor detective can afford to go out to a place like this once or twice a year. Not that I could make a habit of it, but you deserve it. And so do I."

"Was it something I said?" she asked, getting a little nervous. "Or something I did?"

"No, no, no," said the detective raising his voice a fraction. "You're perfect. Beyond perfect if such a category exists. My worries have nothing to do with you. This case I'm working on is driving me crazy. I have a little more than twenty-four hours to come up with a miracle. And I don't see one materializing out of thin air."

"Want to talk about it," she asked, secretly rejoicing. "Another person can often spot obvious things you miss." Impulsively, she reached across the table and squeezed one of his hands. "I want to help you. Please let me."

"I can't see that it would do any harm," said Taine. "After all, in a way, the case concerns you as well.

"Excuse me if I leave out a few names. I promised my client to keep her identity hidden, and my word is my bond. The same with a few of the other players in this complicated drama. Otherwise, here's everything I know."

For the next half hour, Taine related the details of his search for the mysterious Arelim. Janet listened intently, trying to absorb everything he told her. Despite all of his assurances to the contrary, she felt sure the detective deliberately left out some important information. He glossed over a number of conversations. Still, a pattern emerged. A pattern that frightened Janet.

"Today I wasted my time interviewing six other businessmen on Mrs. McConnell's list," concluded Taine. "I ran smack into a wall of silence. All of them denied any knowledge of the organization. They refused to budge an inch, even after I threatened to reveal their membership in the group to the FBI."

"I still don't see the connection between the Lodge and Roger. You even said Royce never heard of my Roger. What reason does he have for kidnaping Tim?"

"The connection exists," said Taine. "I'm convinced that the Black Lodge forms a link between your troubles and those of my client. I just can't make that final connection."

"So Angel Caldwell is afraid of her father?" said Janet, thoughtfully. "I can't say I blame her. The old man always gave me the creeps when he visited Leo."

"He sounds—" Taine stopped in the middle of the

sentence. "How did you know Evangeline Caldwell is my client?"

"You forget we circulate in the same circles. Angel and I are only a year apart in age. She hangs out with a fast crowd but I see her from time to time at important social functions."

"Leo and Sangmeister?"

"Years ago, they pooled their resources on several business deals. Harmon visited Brentwood several times. The old buzzard reminded me of an undertaker. I was always waiting for him to say 'Room for one more.'

"Even in those days, everyone knew that Angel hated him. No one blamed her. He was a cold fish. Though her marriage to Victor Caldwell seemed like a step in the wrong direction."

"They make an odd couple," said Taine.

"Definitely. But their lifestyles mesh perfectly. As you probably know, Angel is anything but an angel."

"I gathered as much," said Taine dryly.

"What about this White Lodge? Do you think that Arelim belongs to this mysterious counterforce to the Order?"

Taine shook his head. "Impossible. His tactics betray him. Good cannot use evil to fight evil. As I told Angel, magic has no orientation. It is neither black nor white. Only the user gives it character. A white magician using killing magic descends to the level of the Black Lodge. The secret of Arelim's identity lies with the Order he claims to oppose."

"Claims?" she asked, quick to pick up on the remark.

"The Black Lodge cannot be destroyed so easily. Caldwell made that quite clear. Murder a member and another takes his place.

"The only way an outsider can wipe out a pyramid organization is to kill all of the members and potential members. Remember, the masters of the Lodge achieved their positions by climbing over the bodies of their predecessors. Even Arelim would find himself hard pressed to defeat them all. Nor do I think he plans such an undertaking."

"You lost me."

"These murders revolve around a power struggle in the Lodge. Willis Royce controls the lucrative drug trade for the Order. He has grown incredibly rich and powerful the last few years with the boom in the crack market. Enough so that another Master wants it all.

"Using the Dark Man, he is smashing Royce's network which he will then replace with one of his own. He's breaking all of the laws of the Lodge, but only the Grand Master of the Lodge can settle disputes among the members. With Sangmeister ill, perhaps dying, Arelim must figure he can get away with anything. And he's right. If he defeats Royce, no one will dispute his claim to the drug trade. Only money and power matter to the members of the Black Lodge."

Janet sat quiet for a moment, trying to frame her next question in the best of terms. "What I don't understand is why Victor talked so freely with you? He revealed a lot more about the Lodge than anyone else. Why didn't he clam up like the rest of the members?"

"I asked the right questions," said Taine, slowly. "He hated Sangmeister and feared Arelim. When I mentioned both in the same conversation, it set him off. I was lucky."

Luck, she suspected, had nothing to do with it. Taine spun an intricate web, but he was not telling her the entire story. He had said something important to Caldwell that he did not want her to know. Instantly, all of her fears came rushing back, stronger than before.

"Royce trusted you, too," she said, feeling her way along. "How come? Why does everyone trust Sidney Taine?"

Taine shrugged his shoulders and smiled. "I never thought about it much before. Maybe I just have the right kind of features. People naturally trust me."

"Wait a minute," said Janet, starting to get annoyed. "You're evading the issue. I want a straight answer. The more you tell about this case, the more one thing becomes clear. The common element in all of these weird happenings is not Arelim or the Dark Man, but

177

a character named Sidney Taine. This whole mystery revolves around you. A man, who I have come to realize, I know nothing about."

An odd look passed across Taine's face. "I'm basically a loner. Detectives are like that. I never talk about myself."

Janet shook her head. "You're trying to treat me like a child, Taine. I'm not that dumb. Things just don't add up."

She paused, gathering in a deep breath. "You're too well informed about things. I remember when I met you in your office the other day. You never had a chance to scan that article on the Knights of Antioch. Yet, you knew all about them. In fact, you kept on calling them the Black Lodge. That's what confused me for a few minutes. The author of the book never referred to them as that. Only you knew that name and the history behind it."

Taine didn't say a word, so she continued. "I can sense you're hiding things from me. How is Roger connected with the Black Lodge? Who is behind these killings? What is going to take place tomorrow night? There are too many questions and not enough answers."

The detective shook his head regretfully. "You want to know things I can't tell you, Janet. I'm a private investigator. No matter how much I care for you, I can't violate my client's trust."

"Don't give me that line," said Janet, bitterly. "I wasn't born yesterday. We aren't in court. You can tell me anything you want. But you won't. You just don't trust me."

"That's not true," said Taine.

"Yes, it is," said Janet, her voice steady. "Remember, Taine, I've been through it all before. I refuse to be a sucker again."

A solitary tear trickled down her cheek. Angrily, she brushed it away. "I trusted you. I really did. I was dumb enough to think you cared for me. I fell for you like a love-struck teenager. Don't you realize that trust works two ways? How can I believe you if you won't tell me the truth?''

Taine looked miserable. He started to speak, then stopped, then started again. "You're making too much of a fuss over nothing," he said softly. "At least, give me the benefit of a doubt.''

Reaching out, he took one of her hands in his. "I do care for you. More than I probably dare admit, even to myself. But there's more to this case than you realize. Give me one more day, Janet. It all ends tomorrow night. Trust me—trust me until then.''

Taine sounded sincere, but sincerity wasn't enough. She wanted to believe him. She needed to trust him. But memories of Roger haunted her. She couldn't stand being hurt again.

"I'll think about it," she said, fighting to keep her emotions in check. She was resolved not to let her physical desires overwhelm her common sense. "Give me the night to think things over.''

"I'll settle for that," said Taine, a downcast look on his face. Yet, for all of his solemn airs, the detective sounded quite pleased with her decision.

A faint smile crossed his lips. "Not much of a wild evening on the town. Still, the world continues to turn. Maybe things will work out better than you imagine. How about if I get the check and take you home?''

Janet forced back a sigh. So much for Timmy's marriage plans, she thought. "Sounds like a good idea to me.''

30

As Ape reached for a cold can of ginger ale, the lights went out. Cursing, he lowered the soda pop back onto the refrigerator shelf, gently closed the appliance door and pulled out his shotgun. Silently, he slid through the door to the parlor.

Once in the other room, he quickly dropped to his hands and knees. Close to the ground he presented less of a target. Ape feared his own companions as much as the Dark Man. Nervous men often acted without thinking. And all of them were armed with sawed-off shotguns.

"That you, Ape?" whispered Boris Bennett from across the room.

"Yeah. What's going on?"

"I don't know. Morris hustled the boss in the bedroom right away. I told him to barricade the door. You wanna check the hall?"

Beads of sweat popped out on Ape's forehead. He might be brave, but he wasn't crazy. "Not me. How about you?"

Boris chuckled. "Count me out. I'm nice and comfortable here, with my head attached to my shoulders. Maybe give Jo-Jo a call downstairs."

Ape crawled over to the phone. Picking up the receiver, he dialed the extension for the first floor phone.

"Lights went out in the whole damned Temple," answered Jo-Jo on the first ring. "I sent two of the boys to check the fuses in the basement. You want me to call Com-Ed?"

"Do that," said Ape, feeling slightly relieved. "You staying cool?"

"No problem. That spook don't worry me. We got a

180

dozen boys roaming the halls with Uzis. He be a fool to come here."

Ape shook his head in the darkness. He didn't share Jo-Jo's confidence. The power failure worried him. "Call me back in five minutes. Even if you get the lights fixed."

"Will do," said Jo-Jo and hung up.

Still tense, Ape put the receiver back on the hook. Other than the sound of his own breathing, the room was silent. "Jo-Jo says not to worry."

"Good for him," answered Boris, from close to the front door of the suite. "You tell him to send some dudes with flashlights?"

"Never thought of that," said Ape, feeling awfully stupid. "We got some candles in the kitchen."

"Better than nothing," said Boris with a snort of annoyance. "Get them while I push the sofa in front of the door."

Ape did as he was told. He felt like a complete idiot. The absolute blackness of the room had him off balance. He wasn't thinking straight.

It took a few minutes of feeling around the bottom of cabinets till he found the package of candles. Royce used them in some of his more esoteric ceremonies. Flicking on the gas range, Ape lit three of the wax sticks. Dim light filtered through the kitchen. Dark shadows leapt onto the walls. Quickly, Ape started four more candles burning.

Using some of the dripping wax as a base, he sealed several of the lights to plates. Carrying two of them, he stepped back into the living room.

"You done made my day," said Boris, his face breaking out in a big grin. With a sigh of relief, the bodyguard rose from the heavy couch wedged up against the front door. "I told the boss everything was okay."

Ape glanced over at the phone. Five minutes had come and gone. "Jo-Jo didn't call back."

Boris frowned. "That ain't like him. He always follows orders. You wanna call him?"

"Not yet," said Ape. The muscles in his neck tightened. "Maybe he's talking with the power company."

"Yeah, maybe," said Boris, not sounding convinced. Neither was Ape.

The minutes ticked by slowly. Anxiously, both men paced the room, gazes fixed on the phone. But it remained silent. Finally Ape picked up the receiver and dialed the first floor.

It rang twenty times before Ape gave up. Licking his lips, he tried calling the police emergency number. Nothing happened.

"Outside line is dead," he told a grim Boris Bennett. "We're trapped up here on our own."

"She-it," said Boris loudly. "We got a dozen men in the halls. Where they all be at?"

Ape's throat felt as dry as the desert. "I need a drink. You tell Royce the bad news."

When Ape returned from the kitchen, Morris was in the living room whispering with his brother. Royce remained in the inner bedroom. The Bocar had been drinking all day and evening. But all the liquor in the world couldn't provide him with enough courage to face the Dark Man.

"Morris will go downstairs and see what gives," said Boris.

"That sounds dangerous," said Ape.

"You got any better ideas?" asked Boris. "He's the quickest of us three. Maybe things ain't as bad as we think."

"Or maybe they're a lot worse," said Ape.

Morris shrugged his shoulders. "Only way we find out for sure is go look." He turned to his brother. "You got a signal?"

The other Bennett nodded. "Two long knocks, then one short. Don't forget. That be the only way you get back in here. You try anything else, Ape and me blast you away."

"Two long, one short," repeated Morris carefully. "No sweat."

Cradling the sawed-off shotgun in one hand, he pulled

the sofa away from the door with the other. Cautiously, he opened the bolts holding the suite door shut. With a quick jerk, he pulled the door open and peered into the pitch-black hallway.

"Nobody here," he whispered. "Give me some of those candles. I'll be back before you know it."

Morris disappeared into the darkness. Boris closed the door and locked it. "Twelve bad dudes out there," he said, his voice strained with worry. "What happened to them?"

The flickering light from the candles barely illuminated the suite. Fingers of darkness crept in from all corners of the room. Ape kept a tight grip on his shotgun. Boris stayed close to the door, his head turned as he listened for movement outside.

Five long minutes passed. Then, without warning, the lights came back on. Ape sucked in a deep breath, as the tension drained from his body.

"Hot damn," said Boris, relief etched in his drawn features. "Now we're cookin'. Things be back under control. All we need is Morris back with the news."

As if in answer to his wish, two long knocks rattled the suite door. A pause, then a third.

"That's him," said Boris, fumbling with the lock. "He even remembered the code."

Ape frowned. The timing seemed a little too perfect. The three knocks on the door echoed in his mind. Instantly, he recalled Papa Benjamin's warning.

"Don't open it!" he yelled, hoisting up his shotgun. But Boris was already swinging the portal open.

"Bad move," said the Dark Man from out in the hall. With a vicious overhand chop, he swung his butcher's cleaver. The steel blade caught Boris square in the forehead. Incredible force drove it deep down through bone and brain, crushing the man's features like putty.

The big bodyguard died instantly. His body dropped to the floor like a sack of wet cement. For a second, the Dark Man stood in the bright lights of the hallway. Weaponless, he was never more vulnerable.

Panic-stricken, Ape opened fire. He was so close to

the Dark Man he hardly needed to aim. One blast, then a second shook the room. The killer shuddered as the shotgun shells tore into his body. The twin explosions ripped the monster's overcoat to shreds and sent his cowboy hat flying back into the hall. The Dark Man staggered but refused to go down.

For a second, Ape's breath froze in his lungs. No description truly captured the horror of the Dark Man. He had no face. Two red eyes glared out from a sheet of absolute darkness. The monster personified the night.

The giant lunged forward, intent on the cleaver still wedged in Boris's forehead. With a growl of despair, Ape hurtled across the room for the same target. Perhaps the Dark Man's own weapon could bring him down.

A gloved hand reached the wood handle an instant before Ape's grasping fingers. With a laugh, the Dark Man wrenched the cleaver up and free from its prison of flesh.

Unable to stop, Ape tumbled hard into the giant's legs. The two of them crashed to the floor, a tangle of arms and legs.

Desperately, Ape grabbed the hand holding the butcher's cleaver. Exerting his full strength, he wrenched hard, trying to break bones. The Dark Man only laughed.

With incredible power, the killer ripped his arm free of Ape's grip. Effortlessly, he rose to his feet. Still chuckling, he reached down for his next sacrifice. Steel fingers wrapped around Ape's jaw and pulled him upright.

"This is it," said the Dark Man, still gripping Ape by the chin. Smoothly, he raised the cleaver up into the air.

Others had made the mistake of holding Ape in similar fashion. Instinctively, he leapt off the floor. Drawing his legs in close to his body, he thrust out hard, catching the Dark Man full in the chest. Completely unprepared for the wrestling maneuver, the giant toppled back, releasing his intended victim.

Ape dropped to the floor in a roll and came up running. He went flying through the door and into the hallway. Behind him, bellowing in anger, came the Dark Man.

Legs pumping like pistons, Ape charged for the stairs at the end of the corridor. With his short legs and barrel chest, he wasn't built for speed. Any second he expected to feel the bite of the Dark Man's cleaver.

Ahead of him was the open stairwell. Ape saw a crumpled form at the top of the steps. It was Morris. He never even made it off this level. A pool of red marked the spot where he encountered the Dark Man.

Unable to slow down, Ape went barreling across the bloody floor. Skidding wildly, he slammed into the corpse blocking the stairs. Momentum carried him up and out. Arms outstretched, he went flying down the stairs. Unable to protect himself, he crashed headfirst into the railing on the lower landing.

Terribly dizzy, he rolled over on his back. Death stood ten feet away. Casually, in no hurry to finish his task, the Dark Man kicked at an indistinct object by his feet. It landed with a soft plop only a few inches away from Ape's face. Shocked eyes stared blankly into his from Morris's bloody and battered features.

"I heard that two heads are better than one," said the Dark Man, chuckling at his ghoulish joke. He started to descend the steps. The blade of his cleaver gleamed brightly in the hall lights.

Ape struggled to his knees. Still reeling in pain, he grabbed hold of the railing and inched his way upright. His fingers clutched the wood bannister tightly as he forced his body to respond. His only hope depended on catching the Dark Man by surprise. Ape refused to die without a struggle.

"Fighting to the end," said the Dark Man approvingly. "How pleasant. I always enjoy killing a good loser."

He took a step down. Then another. Then, unexpectedly, he stopped. "Royce opened the hidden passage in his room," he said, sounding slightly annoyed. "If I waste too much time with you, he will escape."

The giant hesitated, as if torn between two choices. For a second his attention wavered. Realizing there would be no second chance, Ape seized that moment to act. Calling on all of his remaining strength, he raised himself up and over the railing.

He dropped the two stories to the main floor in a second. The ground rushed up to meet him but he knew exactly what to do. Perfect timing made the difference. Grabbing hold of the lowest bannister, Ape swung his body up and over into a flying somersault. He landed lightly on the balls of his feet, ready to run.

"I'll deal with you later, Ape Largo," called the Dark Man from the hallway above. "Royce dies first, then I'm coming after you. No one escapes me tonight. No one."

Groaning in pain, Ape headed for the front door. Willis Royce no longer needed him. Only an undertaker could help the Bocar. His death signaled the end of the Children of Danballah.

Bloody sigils covered the walls of the Temple. Ape fixed his eyes on the front door. He dared not look in the corners of the room. Too many of his friends perished here tonight. The very air stank of death.

Gasping for breath, he burst out of the building into the damp night air. Inside, a solitary scream echoed through the halls. Willis Royce had met the Dark Man. Soon the killer would be after him.

Ape knew that without supernatural aid he was doomed. For the first time in his life, his massive strength meant nothing. That detective, Taine, spoke the truth. The Dark Man embodied all the power of night.

Grimly, Ape started running. One slim hope beckoned in the darkness. His only chance for salvation lived eight long blocks away.

31

Papa Benjamin loved Johnny Carson. He particularly liked Johnny's opening monologue. The talk show host expressed the complex frustrations of daily life in the funniest way imaginable. It was the one show on television that the voodoo priest never missed.

Johnny just walked out on stage when someone started pounding away on the door to the oum'phor. Since the police visit, Papa Benjamin had locked the front entrance of his church each night. Grumbling, he flicked on his VCR to record. As he made his way downstairs, he gave thanks to the voodoo Loas for the magic of videotapes.

The houn'gan stared out the peephole into the darkness. A very frightened and disheveled Ape Largo stood outside. Papa Benjamin sighed in disappointment. No Johnny Carson for him tonight. He might never see another monologue. It all seemed quite unfair. Making a face, the voodoo priest opened the door.

Ape stumbled into the oum'phor, his clothes soaking wet from the light drizzle outside. His breath came in short, quick gasps as he sucked in air. Papa Benjamin silently noted the man's ripped clothes and numerous bruises. Ape looked like the loser of a vicious assault.

"I ran all the way here," said the bodyguard, spitting out the words between gulps. "He killed all the others. I'm the only one left. And he's on my trail."

Papa Benjamin knew without asking who Ape meant. A deep sense of self-pity filled his soul. The voodoo gods asked too much of an old man. But he knew the choice was his to make.

He either accepted his role or rejected it. The Loas

believed in free will, even for their priests. The final decision rested entirely with him.

"We don't have much time," said Ape urgently. "Can you stop him?"

"Perhaps," answered Papa Benjamin. "But the question is, why should I?"

"Huh." Terror returned to Ape Largo's features. "What do you mean?"

"You do not belong to my congregation," said Papa Benjamin, measuring his words carefully. He needed to make one final test. A houn'gan without spirit served only himself, not his followers. Did Ape Largo possess the necessary courage?

"I owe you nothing," he continued. "You work for a fraud and a corrupter of children. His organization mocks every true worshiper of the Invisibles. What reason can you give me to save your worthless soul?"

Ape stood there, stunned, his face ashen. "If you won't help fight him, I'm dead meat. I saw how the Dark Man operates. He's unstoppable."

Papa Benjamin shrugged his thin shoulders. "He wants only you. This fight does not concern me."

Carefully, the voodoo priest watched for Ape's reaction. For a moment, the big man said nothing. Eyes closed tightly, as if glimpsing his fate, he shook his huge head in despair. Then, as if gathering together his nerve, the massive bodyguard straightened. Hands the size of shovels curled into fists. Turning away, he faced the door.

"I can't say I blame you," he said calmly. "No reason for you to suffer because of my mistakes. I brought this on myself by joining Royce's operation. Time for me to get going. Maybe I can shake him in the Loop."

Satisfied with his choice, Papa Benjamin raised a frail hand in protest. "A man faced with death should always try a little bargaining," he said with a smile. "Consider the alternative."

"What can I offer?" said Ape, desperately. "Like you said, I don't even belong to your church."

"That can be arranged quite easily," said Papa Benjamin. "Are you willing to pay for your life with your life?"

"I don't understand," answered Ape, his glance flickering back and forth between Papa Benjamin and the outside door.

"I can save you," said the priest. "Or at least, I can try. But if I do, you must dedicate your life to the voodoo Mysteres."

Seeing the astonished look on Ape's face, the priest hurried on. "If we survive this night, you must stay with me and study to become a houn'gan. After I die, you will become the leader of this congregation for the rest of your life."

The gnarled old priest smiled gently at the bewildered bodyguard. "Make your decision. Do you 'pass through the water' or die beneath the knife?"

"I accept," said Ape without hesitation. "I give you my word."

"We will seal the agreement in blood another time," said Papa Benjamin. "I sense your enemy—our enemy—approaching. Quickly, clear away all the chairs around the center post. I need my supplies from the pe."

Ape rushed to obey. Meanwhile, the voodoo priest hurried over to the Holy of Holies and filled his pockets with a variety of small objects.

"Faster, faster," he commanded, running back from the oum'phor. "I need time to prepare our defenses."

"What else do you want me to do?" asked Ape, as he moved the last of the chairs to the rear of the peristyle, leaving a clear space some fifteen feet across at the center.

"You learned more about this Dark Man since your visit? Good. Tell me everything you found out while I work."

Papa Benjamin dumped out all of the items in his pockets onto the socle. Grabbing a thick piece of white chalk, he carefully drew a large circle some nine feet in diameter around the center post.

Next, he drew a second circle, a foot less in measure,

inside the first. As he worked, he listened closely to Ape's description of the Dark Man's mystic origins.

"This man, Taine, knows a great deal about the Invisibles," said Papa Benjamin cryptically. "I would like to meet him."

Finishing the second ring, Papa Benjamin rose to his feet. He pointed to the two circles. "No matter what you see, no matter what you hear," he said, in a tone not to be disobeyed, "do not cross this inner circle."

Ape nodded, warily, his eyes filled with apprehension. "Those chalk markings are going to stop the Dark Man?"

"Your methods worked so well?" asked Papa Benjamin sarcastically. He handed Ape a small box pulled from his pile of charms. "Put these carefully between the two circles. Make sure to rest them so that no part touches either chalk mark."

The massive bodyguard shook his head in disbelief. The container held a pile of tiny silver crucifixes. "How will these help us?"

"You understand little of the true nature of the Mysteres," said Papa Benjamin. "Voodoo comes from the Church in Rome, though they hate us for that. If we survive this night, I will teach you the great secrets of your heritage."

As he spoke, the houn'gan inscribed a large X in the circles. He centered it at the base of the socle, with its arms touching the outer line.

In flowing hand, he drew an elaborate ritualistic picture of two snakes, separated by three stars and followed by a cross, in each quarter of the circle. The voodoo priest worked astonishingly fast, drawing the complex picture with bold, sure strokes.

"I learned this *veve* in Haiti," he said, when he finished the last picture. "It is the sign of Danballah Wedo and Aida Wedo, the great serpents of voodoo. Only they can protect us against the evil in the night."

"You told Royce your magic was useless against the Dark Man," said Ape.

"I cannot defeat this monster," said Papa Benjamin.

"That much is certain. I pray that this magic circle will protect us from his fury."

Reaching down, he picked up his asson. Standing where one arm of the cross touched the inner circle, he shook the dried gourd in the air and said loudly three times, "I call upon the powers of Legba Atibon CataRoulo."

At the second line he summoned "the powers of Kevi-ozo Dan Leh." In the third position, "the powers of Maitre Agoueh Ro Io." And at the fourth line, "the powers of Ai-zan A Veleh Ketheh."

Finally, standing next to the center post, he shook his asson for the last time. "By the powers of all the Vou-doun; by the powers of Faith, Hope and Charity; make this circle our sanctuary. Let none who wish us harm stand in the shadow of our *poteau-mitan*."

He turned to Ape and shrugged his shoulders. His old eyes gleamed with excitement. "My father taught me that ritual sixty years ago. In all of my days, I never once used it. Until tonight."

"What now?" asked Ape.

"We sit and wait," said Papa Benjamin. "Not for very long, I suspect. In the meantime, tell me about yourself, my student. The more I know about your past, the better I can plan your future. How did a man of your education come to work for Willis Royce?"

"You want to hear my life story with the Dark Man due here any minute?" said Ape, incredulously.

"Why not?" replied Papa Benjamin. "Remember this as your first lesson, Ape Largo. Fear makes you weak. It strengthens our enemy. He lives on such emotions. Better to laugh at death than to cower before it."

Folding his legs beneath him, Ape squatted on the dirt floor next to Papa Benjamin. In a voice like the rasp of an old record, he began his story.

32

Leo met her at the door.

"Tim fell asleep a few minutes ago. I heard the car in the driveway and came down to investigate." His brow wrinkled with concern. "You're home rather early. I didn't expect you back for hours. Is something the matter?"

Janet nodded, not knowing what to say. She had never discussed her personal life with her father.

"Take off your coat," said Leo, "and come with me to the sun porch. The sight of all those lush green plants always relaxes me. They'll do wonders for you. Once your nerves settle down, we can talk."

As usual, Leo was right. The peace and serenity of the arboretum acted like a powerful tranquilizer. The two of them sat in silence for nearly twenty minutes. Gradually, Janet felt the tension draining out of her body. Taking a few deep breaths to brace herself, she told her father the whole sad story.

"So you think you lost him already?" he asked when she finished speaking. He shook his head in disagreement. "I believe you underestimate Taine's persistence. He struck me as a very determined man who usually got his way, no matter how long it took."

A bittersweet smile crossed Janet's face. "You project your own personal characteristics on other people, Father," she said, wistfully. "He asked me to trust him, to take him at his word, and I couldn't do it. I wasn't ready to make that kind of commitment to a stranger. I refused to blindly trust a man I hardly knew. That thought terrified me."

A stray tear trickled down her cheek. "He brought it

on himself,'' she said, feeling sorry for herself. "What's he hiding? Why can't he tell me the truth?"

"You raise a good point," said Leo, folding his fingers together across his chest. "Perhaps you already know the answer. Sometimes the solution to a question is obvious if we just look in the right place."

He leaned forward, his expression benign. "Assuming Taine truly cares for you, why wouldn't he tell you everything you want to know? Try to think of a motive for his actions."

"I don't know," said Janet, feeling as dejected as ever. She had no idea what her father was talking about. "I just don't know."

Leo made a face. "If you would use your brain for a minute, the answer is obvious. At least, it is to me. Your hero wants to protect you from harm. According to what you told me, he knows quite a bit about this Black Lodge. How much is too much? The Masters of the Order obviously consider Mr. Taine a threat to their secrecy. Remember the fate of those reporters investigating Harmon Sangmeister. These men play very rough."

"But—but—but," stuttered Janet, sensing the truth in Leo's words. "Do you really think he's worried about my safety?"

"It makes perfect sense to me," said Leo. "Taine strikes me as the noble martyr type. He suffers from a mental disease too common among dedicated young men—an overactive sense of responsibility. To keep you from suffering, he sacrifices his own chance for happiness."

"I think you tend to exaggerate a bit," said Janet, her spirits lifting a little. "I agree that Taine does sound rather formal at times. I know why. Like lots of single men, he's really very shy. I can manage that. You make Taine sound foolish."

"Of course I do. You know my opinion of self-sacrifice," said Leo, smiling. "To yourself be true—and let everyone else look out for themselves.

"I look at things from a practical standpoint. Taine is risking his life for his client and a girl he met a day ago.

That seems like a pretty bad bargain to me. The odds are all with the Black Lodge. Still, I can't help but admire his courage."

"And I turned my back on him," said Janet, bitter with herself. She felt like a heel.

"Grow up, Janet," said Leo, snorting in derision. He looked at her for a minute without saying anything. Finally he shook his head in annoyance.

"I see now how Roger manipulated you with such skill. To think I raised a child so easily deceived." He beat his fingers together as he spoke, a sure sign of his annoyance. "Taine *wanted* you to reject him. He planned that whole scene in the restaurant. It was the one way he could get you out of the picture. Think about it for a minute. Who initiated the discussion in the first place? There was no reason for him to discuss the case tonight. If he wanted to keep everything confidential as he claimed, he never would have mentioned his investigation at all.

"Give Taine a little credit. He deliberately distorted everything he told you so as to make you suspicious. If that ploy hadn't worked, he would have tried another. Face the facts. He threw you a line and you grabbed it."

"But why couldn't he have told me the truth and let me make my decisions based on that?" said Janet.

"I already told you. He wanted you safely out of the way before taking any more risks. Taine obviously felt that if he told you the truth, you might have insisted on helping him despite the danger."

"Goddamn it," said Janet, her expression furious. Finally, she understood what had taken place. "I hate it when other people make up my mind for me. Taine treated me like a child. That rotten son-of-a-bitch. I'm going to set things straight with him right now."

Her face burning bright red, she stood up and headed for the door.

"Where are you going?" asked Leo. "You can call him from the phone here."

"Call him?" she answered. "Call him? I'm looking

up Mr. Taine's address in the phone book. Then I'm going right over there to tell him what I think of his lousy scheme."

"Calm down, Janet," said her father. "Remember, he acted this way because he wanted to protect you."

At the door to the arboretum, she turned and flashed Leo a quick grin. "I know that, too, Father. That's the other reason I plan to visit Mr. Taine. Don't wait up for me."

And with a laugh at his incredulous expression, she departed.

33

It beat the hell out of fighting a bear," said Ape, shaking his head ruefully. Seeing the confused expression on Papa Benjamin's face, he laughed.

"Circus sawdust runs in my veins instead of blood. At least it feels that way at times. Until I met Willis Royce, I spent most of my life in the sideshow.

"I was born and raised in a traveling circus. My father worked as the strongman for the show. He made his living bending nails and ripping phone books for the rubes on the midway. The show billed him as "Tongo, the Ape-Man from the Congo," though he was born and raised in Jersey City. Obviously, I inherited my strength and good looks from him.

"My mother was employed as a cook for the show. No beauty queen, she married in desperation and lived to regret it. Dad drank too much and too often. A cold, distant man, he turned into a loudmouth, aggressive drunk after a few beers."

Ape's face twisted into a cold mask of anger. He spoke as if a disinterested observer, but pain filled his every word. "Like many alcoholics, he refused to recognize his problem. Instead, he took out his frustrations and anger on his wife and child. I grew up terrified of his weekly beatings."

"Why didn't your mother leave him?" asked Papa Benjamin.

"She wanted to," said Ape, "but he swore that if she ever did, he would track her down and kill her. She believed him, and so did I. He made her life a living hell.

"An ugly, misshapen child, I grew up with few acquaintances and no close friends. The older I got, the worse I looked. When I was six, I got tagged with the nickname, 'Ape.' It fit me like a glove. After a while, even my parents called me that. Don't ask me my real name. I don't remember it.

"None of the other circus people allowed any of their children to come play because of my father's reputation. The only joy in my life came from the circus school.

"All of the performers' children attended the classes. They were conducted by the show's manager, John Huff. A bright, articulate man, he changed my life. He taught me the beauty of the printed word. Through him, I discovered the wonderful world of books. Reading offered me the only escape from my father's brutality."

He sighed deeply. "Mother never got away. They both died just before my fourteenth birthday, in a fiery automobile accident. Drunk driving, the police ruled it. I was free from my father, but I lost the only person who ever loved me.

"I stayed on with the circus, working first as a roustabout and then, later, in my father's old job as the strongman."

"What about the authorities?" asked Papa Benjamin. "You were only a teenager."

"Things worked different in a traveling show," said Ape, chuckling. "Two days after the accident, we were three states away at our next booking. Nobody ever came searching for me. Not that it mattered. Circus people looked after their own.

"Besides, at fourteen, I stood five feet tall and

weighed nearly two hundred and thirty pounds. I could bend tenpenny spikes with my fingers and crush bricks in my hands. No one doubted me when I claimed to be eighteen.''

"You learned how to fight in the circus?" asked Papa Benjamin.

"Nah. That part of my education came later. I did spend a lot of time working out with the high-wire people though. With my strong arms, they figured I could become a tremendous aerial performer. I picked up a lot of tricks, but never could master the more difficult maneuvers. For all of my size and strength, I lacked the proper coordination.

"The circus disbanded when I was twenty-two. TV and movies and other forms of entertainment killed the traveling shows. Only a few big outfits could afford to keep going. Ours wasn't one of them.

"I went to night school for a while, trying to complete my education. Trouble was that nobody believed I had a brain in my head. The teachers took one look and classified me as hopeless before I said a word. After a short time, I gave up on regular schools. Between public libraries and correspondence schools, I learned on my own.

"Without any family or friends, I spent those years drifting from place to place. Most of the time, I worked as a bouncer in bars. It was easy work and paid pretty well. My ugly features proved to be an asset. One look at me, and the most unruly drunks usually settled down quick.

"I tried working as a pro wrestler after that. The job paid great. Most of the guys involved in the racket were a pretty good bunch. They accepted me with no questions. For the first time in my life, I was surrounded by men my size. And being so ugly actually worked to my advantage. I made a wonderful villain. Unfortunately, my lack of muscular control tripped me up again.

"No matter how hard I tried, I couldn't control my own strength. During rehearsals, I constantly sent men flying out of the ring by accident. Once or twice, I tore off a turnbuckle without realizing it. Not surprisingly, the other wrestlers refused to fight me. Even though it was all faked, they dared not climb into a ring with me. One wrong move on my part, and they could be permanently maimed or even killed.

"My life reached an all-time low after that. Jake LaBruski, another ex-wrestler convinced me to work with him on a bar hustle.

"Jake owned a trained bear named Otto. He bought it from some carny owner years before. A big, fat Asian black bear, Otto had been taught to box. Bears are a lot smarter than you think. Actually, all he did was swing his huge paws at anyone foolish enough to get close to him. Which, as you might guess, was me, night after night."

Papa Benjamin frowned. "You fought with this beast?"

"The term *fighting* exaggerates what actually took place. It was more like a sparring match. The bear outweighed me by five hundred pounds. I wasn't crazy enough to get him angry. He considered the whole thing a big game.

"The three of us, Jake, Otto and me, drove from small town to small town, on a tour of all the cheap bars and sleazy dives in the South and the lower Midwest. Jake did all the arranging. Otto and I provided the entertainment."

Ape shook his head. "What thrill people got from watching a man battling a bear never ceased to puzzle me. But they flocked to the show. Otto and I fought to standing room only crowds wherever we went. We were as popular as Jell-O wrestling or dwarf throwing. The law gave us trouble from time to time, as did the animal rights people, but Jake always managed to keep the show on the road."

"This bear, Otto," asked Papa Benjamin, "he never hurt you?"

"Not intentionally," said Ape. "I managed to dodge around the ring pretty well. Once in a while, though, he swatted me pretty good. That always got the crowd cheering. You should have heard them yell the night he cracked two of my ribs."

"You met Willis Royce at one of these matches?"

"Yeah. Say what you want about the Bocar, but you got to admit the man had style. He wanted a bodyguard whose very appearance would scare off any potential troublemakers. I fit the bill. Not many men wanted to tangle with a guy who resembled a gorilla. A few well-placed rumors, and my reputation grew to match my looks."

"All of those killings attributed to you?"

"Pure BS," said Ape. "Royce linked my name with every unsolved murder in the Midwest. Nobody other than the cops ever bothered checking the truth behind the stories. After a while, the police stopped wasting their time. They realized I'm no killer."

"I suspected as—" began Papa Benjamin but never finished.

A loud hammering jarred the door to the oum'phor, effectively silencing him in midsentence.

"Like all evil spirits, he knocks before entering an inhabited room. Remember," he added sharply, "do not disturb the markings of the circle."

Ape drew in a deep breath as Papa Benjamin called out in a shrill voice, "Enter, in the name of peace and the Mysteres of voodoo."

34

The locked door swung open silently, as if guided by ghostly hands. A few seconds passed and then the Dark Man walked into the room. Ape immediately noted that the giant wore his long coat and cowboy hat. In his gloved right hand, he openly carried his blood-stained butcher's cleaver. Ape felt sure the outfit was another manifestation of the creature's physical form. The dark clothes and weapon were as much a part of the thing as were its hands and legs.

"That detective, Taine, spoke the truth," whispered Papa Benjamin. "This creature belongs to the night itself. He is a creation of nightmares, of absolute darkness."

Ape licked his lips and glanced about the room. The lights seemed dimmer. Long, menacing shadows stretched from the Dark Man to the walls. Ape suddenly was very conscious of the fact that the only thing separating him from his nemesis was a thin line of white chalk.

He looked back at Papa Benjamin for reassurance. As if sensing his fears, the little old man smiled at him and nodded briefly. His face reflected a confidence that Ape only wished he shared.

"Royce took a long time to die," said the Dark Man, his voice deep with menace. Each step he took brought him closer and closer to the magic circle. "I tried to keep him alive as long as possible. A little cut here, a little cut there, until his body was spread all over the room."

The monster's loud laughter filled the oum'phor. The walls shook with his terrible humor. "What an enjoyable time I had. If only all of my victims struggled so hard to stay alive. You can't imagine the pleasure he provided. Unfortunately, he died before I could express my thanks. So it goes."

The giant shook his fist holding the butcher's cleaver. "Enough talk about him. I still have another meddler to eliminate tonight after I'm done here. You escaped me earlier by a trick, Ape Largo. I dislike being fooled. I'm here to collect my debt. You owe me one life—yours."

With two quick steps, the Dark Man reached the edge of the *veve*. Caught unawares, Ape instinctively ducked down and threw his arms up over his head. Beads of sweat exploded across his forehead. He fully expected to die in the next few seconds.

Up into the air went the bloody cleaver. Gracefully, almost like a ballerina, the Dark Man pivoted on one huge leg, directing all of his thrust into one devastating strike.

Like a bolt of lightning, the cleaver hurtled downward, aimed directly at Ape's head. The air trembled with the force of the blow. There was nothing Ape could do to stop it, nor did he have to. With a screech of shrieking metal, the weapon slammed to a dead stop halfway through its arc.

Ape glanced down to the ground. Try as he might, the Dark Man could not move the cleaver an inch past the outer line of the *veve*. It was as if the magic circle created an invisible shield extending up and around the chalk lines.

Papa Benjamin laughed, a short barking sound that mocked the Dark Man. "I thought as much. Your magic cannot harm us. Go away and leave us alone," he commanded, with a wave of one hand. "Your filth desecrates the grounds of my oum'phor."

The Dark Man hesitated for a second, as if considering the request. Then, with incredible speed, he slashed down again with his cleaver. This time, Ape didn't even blink as the blade froze when it encountered the invisible barrier.

For the next ten minutes, the Dark Man chopped furiously at the magic shield. Ape watched in horrified fascination as the monster struck one futile blow after another. Untiring, he tested every inch of the circle. The magic held firm against his attack.

Finally the giant gave up. Tucking the cleaver inside his coat, he stepped back. His red coal eyes burned angrily in the darkness beneath his cowboy hat.

"You can't stay inside that circle forever, little man," he said in a harsh voice, not even remotely human. "How long will you make me wait?"

Swinging his head from side to side, the Dark Man looked around the oum'phor. "The light in here bothers me. Would you mind if I turn it out? Let's get real cozy."

With a laugh, he waved one giant hand in a casual

gesture. Instantly, all of the lights in the building went out. The room plunged into total darkness.

"Do not move an inch," said Papa Benjamin, his voice calm. "A few steps in the wrong direction would kill us both."

Ape could hear his companion fumbling with the items on the socle. "After your story, I expected as much," said the priest, striking a match against the socle. He grinned at Ape in the flickering light. "Thus I brought with me a good supply of candles."

Carefully, Papa Benjamin placed a burning white wax candle at the end of each of the four lines of his cross. Meanwhile, Ape scrambled the short distance to the center post.

Outside the circle, the Dark Man paced back and forth just beyond the chalk lines. His red eyes glared at them in unblinking rage.

"When the time comes, I'll make sure you last a long, long time," said the Dark Man. The sound of his voice made Ape shiver. "I'll start with your toes. First I'll break the bones, then I'll cut them off one at a time. Then, when you think the pain can't get any worse . . ."

In clear, pure tones that rang through the darkness, Papa Benjamin began to pray.

"Our Father . . .
    Hail Mary . . .
    Glory Be to the Father . . ."

At the end of each invocation, Papa Benjamin shook his asson in the direction of his enemy. Bathed in the white light of the candles, the little priest stood firm and unyielding against the threatening darkness. He was no charlatan like Willis Royce. For the first time in his entire life, Ape knew he stood in the presence of a true holy man, a priest of the voodoo Mysteres, houn'gan of the Invisibles.

"Hail Jesus . . .
    Glory Be to the Son . . .
    Holy Angels, we are on our knees at the feet of Mary . . .
    Saint Anthony, hear us . . .

Jesus, hear us . . .

Saint Patrick, Danballah Wedo, hear us . . .''

The Dark Man howled in pain. Shaking his massive head, he fell back and away from the magic circle. Unseen winds tugged at his overcoat and hat, ripping at his sleeves. Papa Benjamin's prayer and *veves* had summoned the Great Serpent of Ife'.

Roaring with incredible agony, the Dark Man stumbled into the shadows of the oum'phor. A creature of the night, he sought escape in the darkness. But there was no hiding from the power of Danballah, the most ancient god of voodoo.

"Saint Luke, hear us . . .

Hail the Master Creator of Heaven and the Earth . . .

Come, my God, come . . .

Saint Peter, give us the key which opens the gate . . . ''

With that entreaty, the lights above quivered, and then flashed back on. The Dark Man screamed as the full force of the beams struck his body. In the brightness, he seemed smaller, less threatening.

The rattle of the asson filled the room. Papa Benjamin continued to chant, each verse of his prayer slashing into the Dark Man like the cut of a knife.

"Great God, intercede for us . . .

Saint Joseph, intercede with Jesus our Redeemer, for us . . .

All saints, all saints, all saints, hear us . . .''

"Enough!" shrieked the Dark Man at the invocation of all saints. "You've won this round, old man. But I'll be back. I'll be back soon enough!"

Ape blinked in astonishment. The Dark Man moved faster than humanly possible. Whirling around and about, he was out the door of the oum'phor in a second. His departure was in some ways the most frightening aspect of the entire incident. Nothing even vaguely human moved that fast. It emphasized the Dark Man's supernormal aspects. For all of his human shape, he was definitely not mortal.

"You frightened him off," said Ape cautiously, turning to Papa Benjamin. "You defeated the Dark Man."

"I won a small victory," answered the houn'gan, with a heavy sigh, "but it will take much more than a few prayers to destroy this monster."

Thoughtfully, he pointed to a serrated machete hanging on the rear wall of the oum'phor. "Take the Sword of La Place. It defends the righteous against the forces of evil. Perhaps we can use it against our enemy."

"Use it?" asked Ape. "What do you mean?"

"We cannot rest until we destroy the Dark Man," said Papa Benjamin wearily. "Otherwise we will live in constant fear of his return. The magic circle protected us from his attack this time. However, I do not plan to live at the center of a *veve* for the rest of my life."

"You're calling the shots," said Ape, not very happily. "I gave you my word. What next?"

"We try phoning that detective, Taine," said Papa Benjamin, heading for the stairs to his apartment. "The Dark Man mentioned another victim for tonight. He obviously meant Taine. We must warn him."

"What if we can't reach him in time?" said Ape, knowing the answer even as he asked the question.

"Then," said Papa Benjamin somberly, "Mr. Taine, and anyone with him, is a dead man."

35

The rickety old elevator wheezed and creaked its way up to the top floor of the eight-story building. Janet carefully read the inspection notice posted next to the door. According to the card, this rickety box could hold six people safely. The mere thought of sharing the lift with five other hapless souls gave her claustrophobia. Slowly, ever so slowly, the elevator continued to rise.

THE BLACK LODGE

Taine lived in a time-worn apartment house on the Near North Side, only a few blocks from the lake and not far from Wrigley Field. By the time she found a parking space, the rain that had been falling all evening dissipated into a light mist. Still, she took her umbrella when she left the car. In Chicago the weather changed every hour.

With a prayer of thanks, Janet got off the elevator. There were eight units on each floor. According to the listing in the lobby, Taine lived in apartment 805. Quietly, she walked halfway down the hall to the correct apartment. Purse and umbrella held in one hand, she gently rapped on the door with the other. She couldn't repress a grin, envisioning Taine's surprised look when he answered her knock.

After a few seconds, the smile faded into a frown of annoyance. No sound of movement came from inside the apartment. She had never given any thought to the possibility Taine might not be home.

She knocked again, a little harder this time. Still no answer. Shrugging her shoulders, she reached down with her free hand and tried turning the doorknob. Maybe he was listening to a stereo with headphones. Or he could be so lost in a book he completely blotted out the rest of the world. Taine struck her as just the type.

To her surprise, the door was open. Janet hesitated for a minute, wondering if she was doing the right thing. What if she found Taine entertaining another guest. Immediately her mind flashed a picture of her lover clutched in the embrace of a very naked Angel Caldwell.

Janet fought back a giggle. Angel devoured innocents like Taine for breakfast. And for other snacks as well. There seemed little chance of facing that surprise. Much likelier to find Taine curled up in bed with a good book than a cheap slut like Angel. Confidently Janet entered the apartment.

None of the lights were on, but all the curtains were open. This high up, the bright orange glow of the city's sodium vapor streetlights cast an eerie pall over the dimly seen furniture.

"Taine," called Janet, softly, sensing something wrong. Nobody went to sleep with the door unlocked and all the lights off. "Taine?"

No one answered. Cautiously she moved forward to the center of the room. A freestanding giant goose-necked lamp hovered over a comfortable-looking dark sofa. Janet turned the switch back and forth. Nothing happened.

"Must have blown a fuse in the apartment," she said aloud, trying to build up her courage. "The circuit breakers must be in the basement."

She debated returning to the hall. The empty apartment gave her the creeps. Still, she wanted to surprise Taine with her presence. What better way than to be here when he returned from fixing the power?

Feeling a bit edgy, Janet sat down on the sofa. Nervously she fumbled with the latch of her purse. She always carried a package of mints in the bag. She needed one now.

Sucking on the candy helped calm her down. The familiar sweet taste of sugar always provided her with a quick lift. Relaxing, she eased herself back on the couch. From what she could make out in the darkness, the place struck her as a typical bachelor's apartment. Pleasant enough, but static, she decided. Except for a big wood bookcase stuck in one corner, crammed with hardcovers and paperbacks, the room lacked character.

Behind her, she sensed rather than heard, someone moving. Her eyes widened in shock. She scrambled to her feet, turning as she did so. There was no question as to the identity of the monstrous figure that had emerged from the bedroom and now stood between her and the apartment door.

"Surprise, surprise," said the Dark Man, with a voice filled with good cheer. "I come looking for an inquisitive detective, and who do I find instead? A beautiful lady in distress. I consider that a pretty fair trade."

"What do you want from me?" said Janet, backing away from the giant.

"Not much," answered the Dark Man. Reaching

beneath the folds of his overcoat, he pulled out his butcher's cleaver. "I don't want much at all. Just some of your blood to clean my blade."

Janet screamed. And screamed again.

The Dark Man laughed, shaking his huge head. "Make all the noise you want. No one ever responds in apartment buildings. The neighbors don't like getting involved. They refuse to meddle in things that don't directly concern them. What a wonderful attitude. It helps make my work so much easier."

Moving deliberately, the Dark Man circled the couch, closing in on her. Dropping her purse to the floor, Janet retreated around the other arm of the sofa, trying to keep the furniture between them. The door of the apartment beckoned, but she feared exposing her back to her pursuer. She needed a few seconds grace.

For an instant, they faced each other again across the width of the couch. This time, her back was to the door while the Dark Man fronted the sofa.

"We could play like this for hours," he said with a chuckle, "but I get dizzy easy." Stepping forward, he put one huge foot onto the cushions. "Shortcut time."

Fate gave Janet one chance, and she took it. Desperately, she thrust her umbrella straight at the Dark Man's chest. Shoving with all her strength, she jammed the central rod hard into her unbalanced attacker. Using it like a spear, she pushed him back across the room. At the same time, she slammed her palm on the button that automatically unfurled the umbrella's canopy. Wide leaves popped open, tangling with the folds of the Dark Man's overcoat.

Momentarily confused, the killer bellowed in annoyance. He slashed haphazardly at the cloth and metal spokes with his cleaver.

Ripping open the front door, Janet dashed into the hall. "Help, help!" she screamed. "Murder, murder, murder!"

Not a door opened, not a person replied. There was no time to start banging on individual doors, and Janet doubted it would do much good. Already, she could hear the Dark Man coming.

She sprinted down the hall to the elevator. Furiously she pounded on the button summoning the lift. With a whir of gears clanking into motion, the cables started to turn. Glancing up at the floor indicator, Janet groaned in despair. The car was rising from the first floor. It would never get there in time.

The stairs offered her the only possible alternative. A heavy fire door marked EMERGENCY EXIT ONLY was located in a small alcove to the side of the elevator. But she was eight long flights of steps up from the street.

"No more chances!" shouted the Dark Man, from the entrance to Taine's apartment. Waving his cleaver high in the air, the monster spilled out of the door into the hall.

Janet leapt for the fire exit. Slamming down hard on the crossbar, she butted her shoulder into the heavy steel barrier. The door remained closed. Unused for years, it was warped shut.

Frantically Janet smashed her body against the metal panels. She hit it with all her strength. Nothing happened. Backing up, she slammed into it again. The barrier creaked a little but refused to give. A third time she flung herself full force into the metal. With a groan of rusted steel, the exit swung free.

Darting through, she found herself in a dusty, poorly lit stairway. Up or down? Her clothes made the decision for her. She had changed from heels to flats for driving. Otherwise she still wore the black cocktail dress and silk stockings from her date earlier. She would never outrun the Dark Man in that outfit. The roof offered a slim chance of escape, but the stairs promised none.

Quickly she climbed the dozen steps leading to the roof. She never felt more out of shape than during those few seconds spent scrambling upward. Huffing and puffing, she just reached the trapdoor leading out when the emergency exit crashed open. "I'm going to get you, Janet!" shouted the Dark Man, spotting her almost instantly.

If a deadbolt lock held the trap closed, she was dead. Grimly Janet pushed up with both hands. Surprisingly the door rose smoothly. Moving as fast as humanly possible, she climbed out through the opening onto the roof.

She slammed the trap shut behind her. In seconds the Dark Man would be up the stairs. Somehow she had to prevent him from opening the door.

Scrambling to her knees, Janet grunted in sudden pain as a sharp object tore at her leg. Astonished, she found herself staring at a slide-bolt screwed into the heavy wood door. Another one matched the first on the other side of the hatch. Evidently other people used the roof for privacy. That explained the greased hinges and the outside locks. Sliding the bolts shut effectively sealed off the roof from the world below.

Crash! The hatch shuddered from the impact as her pursuer smashed at it from below. He hit it again and again, unceasingly, untiringly. Biting her lower lip, Janet backed away from the door. The bolts held firm, but the wood paneling could only stand so much. It would only be a few minutes before the Dark Man broke through.

The rain had stopped, and the moon and stars winked at Janet through small breaks in the cloud covering. Together they provided her with enough light to survey her haven. There wasn't much to be seen. Except for a few slabs of rotting wood, the roof was bare. Anxiously she looked for some sort of ladder attached to the wall.

A minute's searching confirmed her worst suspicions. There was nothing. Despite city ordinances, no fire escape descended to the street below. The stairs were the only way down. She had made the wrong choice. Now she was trapped on the roof of the tallest building in the neighborhood.

"Help me, help me," she shouted to the empty streets, realizing the futility of her cries. Even if someone summoned the police, they could never make it to the top of this building on time. Behind her, she could hear the wood cracking before the Dark Man's relentless hammering. This time there was nowhere to run.

36

Taine heard the screams nearly a block away from his apartment. Faint, desperate cries for help rode the night winds. Instinctively he started running, trying to pinpoint the scene of the crime. Unlike most city dwellers, he felt a moral obligation to get involved.

Within seconds he realized the yelling came from the roof of his building. An imminent sense of dread sent him sprinting at top speed along the sidewalk. He might be imagining things, but that voice sounded like Janet's. Fear turned into shock as he spotted her car parked on the street. How and why she was here didn't matter. She was up on the roof. And her terrified shrieks signaled the presence of one other—the Dark Man.

Taine barreled through the front lobby of the apartment building without slowing down. Screeching to a stop, he anxiously hit the call button for the elevator. Gears whirred as the cables started turning. The car was up on the eighth floor. It would take minutes before it reached ground level. There was nothing he could do but wait and pray.

He had gone for a stroll twenty minutes before. The events at dinner still weighed heavily on his conscience. Even though he acted in Janet's best interests, he felt pretty bad about the whole scene. Deliberately hurting anyone, even with good cause, never appealed to him. And Janet meant much more to him than most people. In just two days, she had become someone very special.

He still wondered if he had revealed too much to her about the Black Lodge. Earlier it seemed like the best course. If Janet didn't know the truth, she might underestimate the measures Roger would risk to join the order. Now he questioned the wisdom of his actions.

The long walk in the night air had strengthened his resolve. He hated deceiving Janet, but he had no choice in the matter. Unknown to her, sinister undercurrents swirled about her young son. Timmy meant much more to this case than she realized. Her misguided interference could easily result in the boy's death. Arelim plotted on many levels. Taine felt like a blindfolded chess player, trying to guess his opponent's next move in advance. He had no room for error.

With a shudder of protesting steel, the elevator door ground open. Taine rushed in and pressed the button for his floor. With painstaking slowness, the door slid closed and the lift started to rise. His throat dry, his body drenched in cold sweat, Taine watched the levels tick by. An eternity passed in little more than a minute.

With a jolt, the car finally came to rest. Precious seconds ticked by until the door opened again. Taine dashed into the hallway. His incredulous eyes spotted the fire door ripped off its hinges. From above, from the roof, he could hear faint screams. Janet was still alive. But for how long?

A sharp damp wind howled in the stairwell. Taine stumbled up the steps, his fear making him clumsy. The trapdoor leading outside had been smashed to splinters. Another indication of the inhuman strength of his enemy. How could any mortal man defeat this monster? It seemed impossible. But he had to try.

Grabbing hold of the remains of the hatch, Taine pulled himself up onto the roof. It only took an instant to locate Janet and her attacker. The Dark Man had maneuvered her into the far west corner of the building. She was backed up to the juncture of the two intersecting walls. In her hands, she held a long narrow wood post. A dozen feet away stood her tormentor.

Taine crept closer not making a sound. He could hear the Dark Man talking. With Janet trapped, the monster seemed in no hurry to finish the job. Instead, he was describing his plans to torture her to death.

It matched perfectly all of the eyewitness accounts of the Dark Man's butchery. Whenever possible, the killer tortured his victims first, both mentally and physically. According to the few people who escaped the monster's wrath, he seemed to enjoy taunting his prey. Several newspaper and TV reports described in ghastly detail the mutilated condition of the corpses found at the scenes of his attacks. In many cases he cut them to pieces, one joint at a time. In others he literally skinned his victims alive.

To Taine, the grotesque acts of sadism indicated a human mind at work. Only men tortured their victims. Supernatural beings killed with ruthless speed. Yet the Dark Man reveled in such opportunities. He combined the worst traits of man and monster. Taine knew that meant something. But what?

Mentally struggling to link all of the clues in some logical manner, Taine crawled closer and closer to the creature. Physical attacks failed to stop the killer. He was invulnerable to ordinary weapons. Yet Taine felt sure the Dark Man could be defeated. An unconquerable evil contradicted all the laws of the universe. He just couldn't quite perceive the creature's weakness.

He had no time left for mental gymnastics. Now was the time for action. Eyes intent on his enemy, Taine rose to his feet. Legs pounding, he charged across the roof at full speed. Less than five feet away from the Dark Man, he leapt into the air in a flying tackle aimed at the creature's waist.

"I particularly enjoy slicing up women," Taine heard the Dark Man saying. The creature's concentration focused entirely on its helpless victim. The attack from the rear caught him completely by surprise.

Taine slammed into the Dark Man with a solid thunk. Janet screamed, in shock, surprise and relief. The force of the tackle sent both man and monster tumbling to the shingled floor. Momentum carried them a half-dozen feet farther across the roof. The butcher's cleaver went flying off into the darkness.

"Run, Janet!" shouted Taine, jumping to his feet. He didn't have time to see if she obeyed. In a fight, you only worried about your opponent.

Already the Dark Man was sitting up. Years of training came to Taine's defense. Reflex action guided his every move. Whirling around for additional force, he kicked the monster at the juncture of head and body. His heel struck the creature right in the neck. Again the Dark Man sprawled onto its back.

Hastily Taine limped away. Normally a blow like that crippled or killed. The Dark Man hardly seemed shaken. Meanwhile, half the bones in Taine's foot felt broken. Fighting the monster was like attacking a brick wall.

"Well, well, well," said the Dark Man, rising slowly to its feet. "You surprised me, Mr. Taine. No fair, hitting from behind. Care to try that again? I'm ready for you now."

Reaching into its coat, the monster pulled out another cleaver. Janet screamed, but Taine felt no surprise. It was all part of the Dark Man's image. Those words echoed in Taine's mind as he retreated swiftly. He headed for the trapdoor where Janet waited.

He clenched his fists in frustration. The Dark Man's secret continued to elude him. He felt sure he possessed all the pieces of the puzzle. But he couldn't assemble them properly.

"You can't get away," said the Dark Man. "No one ever does. In the end, I always win."

A sudden, violent gust of wind slashed across the roof. It caught all of them by surprise. Sharp talons of air snatched the Dark Man's cowboy hat and sent it flying over the side of the building. Burning red eyes glared out at Taine from a featureless face.

Suddenly it all made sense. Everything the Dark Man did, everything he said, combined into one astonishing revelation. Taine knew the truth.

"Find me a mirror," Taine whispered to Janet. "Go downstairs and find me a mirror." For an instant, their eyes met and held. "And hurry!"

Unquestioning, she slipped through the smashed hatchway and descended into the stairwell. Taine hoped she knew where to look.

Grabbing a rotting two-by-four, he backed away from

the trapdoor. Now all he had to do was stay alive until Janet returned.

"How noble," said the Dark Man, with a chuckle. "I can't object to your heroism. After all I came searching for you, Mr. Taine, not her. Your detecting days are over. Permanently. The girl hardly matters. She hardly matters at all."

37

Janet flew down the hall to Taine's apartment. A few curious neighbors, having summoned their courage, peered out at her from behind chained doors. No one said a word. She was totally on her own.

Gasping for breath, she paused for a second, leaning on the wrecked sofa for support. Without a few seconds rest, she would never be able to continue. The apartment blazed with light. Evidently the Dark Man had been responsible for the blackout. With him gone, the electricity flowed once again.

Panting, Janet tried to calm down. Taine acted like he knew the Dark Man's secret weakness. He was counting on her to find a mirror. She dared not fail. Not even the burly detective could match the Dark Man's strength. If she took too long, Taine died.

That last thought got her moving, though her body still ached in a hundred places. No more time to waste recovering. Anxiously she scanned the living room walls. No luck there. Taine didn't believe in decorating with glass.

Ignoring the pains in her legs and chest, Janet headed for the bathroom. It seemed the logical location for a mirror. Hopefully Taine used one for shaving. Somewhere in this apartment there had to be a looking glass.

Unfortunately the only mirror in the bathroom fronted

the medicine cabinet. She doubted it would come loose without a hammer and screwdriver. And even if she had the tools, she didn't have the time. Starting to grow anxious, she headed for Taine's bedroom.

"Yo—anybody here?" said someone from the front room. The caller's voice sounded like a comb being pulled over a metal pipe. Shifting direction, Janet staggered back to the parlor. Peering through the door into the apartment were two oddly matched black men.

She immediately recognized Ape Largo. The bodyguard lived up to Taine's description as the ugliest man alive. Almost as wide as tall, he nearly filled the doorway himself. In one hand, he held a silver machete. Next to him stood an elderly wisp of a man, wearing a starched white shirt and matching pants. His gaze darted quickly from the wrecked couch to the smashed door and finally settled on her. Nodding his head in greeting, he waved one slender hand at the destruction.

"I am Papa Benjamin," he said crisply. "This man is Ape Largo. We came looking for Mr. Taine. We hoped to warn him of his peril. Obviously we arrived too late. What happened here?"

"The Dark Man," said Janet, the words pouring out of her in one gulp. "He's on the roof. Taine, too, fighting him. He needs help."

"Which way?" asked Ape, his head swinging from side to side like some wild beast scenting a kill.

"Up the stairs by the elevator," said Janet. "But don't go yet. He sent me after a mirror, any mirror. The only one here is attached to the medicine cabinet. I can't pull it free."

Papa Benjamin turned to Ape. "Give me the Sword of La Place," he said, without a second's hesitation. "I will aid Mr. Taine. You help this young woman. And hurry. I doubt that even the Sword can actually hurt the Dark Man."

Grasping the sword tightly to his chest, the old man went running down the hall. Janet shook her head in astonishment.

"He's a pistol, ain't he?" said Ape, as if reading her mind. "Come on. Show me that cabinet."

Seconds later they stood in the small bathroom. Ape stared at the mirror and then shrugged. "He really needs this?"

"Yes," said Janet, not sure of the reason herself. "Yes, yes, yes."

"Okay," said Ape. "I got the message. Move back out of my way."

Opening the cabinet, Ape ran his fingers along the long row of metal hinges that held the mirror in place. "This shouldn't be too hard to break off," he said, pushing the frame all the way to the wall.

For the next thirty seconds, Ape swung the door back and forth, trying to snap the hinges. The metal clamps bent slightly but refused to give. Janet fidgeted, counting the seconds. She could see Ape getting annoyed.

"Enough of this crap," he said, finally, his voice thick with anger. Bracing one foot up against the wall, he grabbed the top and bottom of the mirror in his hands. Huge muscles swelled in his arms and chest as he applied pressure, twisting the frame like putty. For a second, nothing happened. Then metal shrieked in agony as the mirror shifted in his grip.

Grunting, he continued turning. The entire cabinet shook beneath his assault. Tiny chips of wood and plaster went flying into the air. Sucking in, Ape jerked both arms diagonally at the same time.

With a snap like a whip, the mirror came free. "Cheaply made," said Ape, tucking the metal frame beneath one arm. Seeing the look of stunned disbelief on Janet's face, he grinned. "I usta fight bears."

They made it up the stairs to the roof in less than a minute. In the far distance, Janet could hear the wail of sirens. Finally someone in the building had summoned the police.

An incredible sight greeted them as they crawled through the hatch into the open air. Bright moonlight, breaking through a gap in the clouds, cast an eerie glow across the top of the building. An obviously shaken

Taine rested with his back to the chimney. Coat slashed to ribbons, he dripped blood from a dozen gashes across his chest and arms. A few feet away loomed the Dark Man, the butcher's cleaver glistening red in one hand. Holding the monster at bay stood Papa Benjamin. The old man wielded the Sword of La Place like a surgeon. He flicked the machete to and fro, weaving a barrier of cold steel that the Dark Man could not pass. The monster's black overcoat, cut to shreds, bore mute testimony to Papa Benjamin's skill as a swordsman. Every time the giant tried to attack, the little priest met him head-on. The sword danced in his hands like a living thing.

As if sensing their approach, the Dark Man suddenly backed away from his intended victims. Still hatless, the monster turned its smooth, featureless face toward them. Red coals flickered in surprise when he spotted the mirror Ape carried.

"Welcome to my parlor," he said, in the sweet mellow tones that Janet found particularly frightening. "I feel like a spider welcoming the flies to dinner. Especially you, Mr. Largo. You escaped me twice tonight. You should have left it at that. No one gets away from me three times."

The Dark Man's head swung around to take them all in beneath the glare of its burning eyes. "Too much talking and not enough action. I've played this game long enough. Unlike the movies, this time the bad guy wins."

"The bad guy?" said Taine, with a laugh. Hobbling over to Ape, he grabbed hold of the mirror. "Who do you think you're kidding? You know better."

"What do you mean?" said the Dark Man, a note of fear in his voice.

"Who are you?" said Taine, shuffling closer to the creature. "Tell me the truth. What's your name—your real name?"

"I'm Arelim, the Avenging Angel," said the Dark Man, sounding confused. "You guessed my secret the other night. I'm the greatest sorcerer in all the world."

"Arelim? Sorcerer?" said Taine, laughing harshly. "You poor deluded fool. You're not even a man. You're just a shadow, a monstrous reflection of the true Arelim's soul."

"No," said the Dark Man sharply, backpedaling from Taine. "You're lying, trying to deceive me."

"Am I?" said Taine, raising the mirror up to eye level. *"Prove it.* Take a look at yourself in the mirror."

The Dark Man hesitated and then stepped forward. Reaching out, he took the mirror from Taine. Gloved hands raised it directly in front of his face.

Janet held her breath, not knowing what to expect. Papa Benjamin muttered something in a low voice, probably a prayer. Ape Largo shuffled his feet back and forth.

"Who are you?" asked Taine, his voice ringing in the clear night air. *"What* are you?"

"I—I—I am Arelim," said the Dark Man. There was an emptiness in his voice not there a minute before.

"Who are you?" demanded Taine.

"I . . . am . . . Arelim's . . . shadow," replied the Dark Man. Each word came out softer than the one before. The last blended into the wind, almost impossible to hear.

The mirror crashed to the roof, breaking into a thousand pieces. Janet gasped. Before her very eyes, the Dark Man *wavered.* He looked like a TV picture losing its resolution. The monster flickered, seemed to shrink back in on itself. His red coal eyes faded orange, then pink, as all the color drained out of them.

"A . . . shadow." The words floated across the rooftop, merging into the night air. And with those final words, the Dark Man disappeared.

Drawing in the first breath of air in several minutes, Janet rushed over to Taine. He looked ready to collapse. She grabbed him around the waist, steadying him. He draped one arm over her shoulders, shifting some of his weight onto her.

Bright eyes looked down into hers, and he smiled faintly. "What happened to 'wait till tomorrow'?"

"I changed my mind," she said, taking in one deep breath after another. "That's a woman's prerogative."

She took in a deep breath and then another. Raw emotion swept through her body, almost overwhelming her senses. The events of the past hour had numbed her feelings. The threat of terrible, violent death, made her appreciate the gift of life so much more.

Clutching Taine tightly to her, she stared into his eyes and let her heart speak. "I love you," she said, simply and honestly. "I love you very much."

"I love you," said Taine, holding her close.

And, for a moment, the horrors of the night paled to insignificance.

38

Behind them, Ape Largo coughed discreetly.

"I don't want to break up this touching scene," he said, in his gravel-pit voice, "but the cops will be here any minute. We better come up with a story, fast. They don't take kindly to getting called for no reason."

Taine frowned, and regretfully let go of Janet. The last thing he needed in his business was trouble with the authorities. Mentally, he reviewed his options. After rejecting several improbable stories, he decided to keep it simple.

"A thief caught in the act," he said, knowing how stupid it sounded. "Janet and I returned from dinner to discover him in my apartment. We chased him to the roof, but he managed to elude us in the darkness. You and Papa Benjamin arrived on the scene after he already escaped."

"You're kidding," said Ape, shaking his head in disbelief. "The cops ain't that dumb. You can drive a truck through the holes in that pack of lies."

"They can believe whatever they want," said Taine. "Other than a few smashed doors, show me evidence a crime took place. Let them get a statement from one of my neighbors. I'd love to hear that conversation. I'll cover the cost of the repairs. Beyond that, nothing in the apartment was taken. If I don't file a complaint, the whole case gets filed and forgotten."

"Yeah?" said Ape, gently nudging the shattered mirror with one foot. "How you gonna explain this?"

"I'm not," said Taine. "You want to try?"

"Not me," said Ape.

"Well, hopefully, maybe they'll ignore it as well. What else can they do?"

"What about those other cleavers?" asked Janet, staring at the dark corners of the roof. "One went flying over there."

"It's gone," said Taine. "When the Dark Man vanished, all traces of his presence disappeared with him. The cops won't find anything linking him to us."

Leaning on Janet for support, he motioned the others to follow. "Better to meet the police in my apartment than up here. Besides, I need some first aid. Not to mention a cold beer."

It took less than an hour to placate the police. As expected, none of the residents on the eighth floor admitted hearing or seeing anything unusual. Taine had not summoned the patrol car and he refused to file a complaint. The officers were left with no choice other than to write off the entire incident as a foiled burglary attempt. Grumbling, they departed after a cursory search of the premises turned up nothing suspicious.

In the meantime, Ape repaired the broken doors using several large pieces of plywood he found in the basement. While not professionally done, the patches worked better than nothing.

"All right," said Ape, eyeing Taine thoughtfully. Taking another sip from his can of ginger ale, he asked the question in everyone's thoughts. "How did you do it?"

They sat clustered around a small table in Taine's kitchen. Though it was well past midnight, none of them appeared ready for sleep. They had spent the last forty minutes comparing stories. The facts pinpointed the Dark Man's activities throughout the long evening. But nothing anyone said explained his destruction. Only Taine knew the truth.

"After my conversation with Willis Royce," he began, "I felt certain the Dark Man was one of the Sheddim, summoned to our world by a member of the Black Lodge. However, like demons, the Sheddim take on many different forms. Each one requires a different ritual or exorcism to banish it from our world. Without the knowledge of what type of monster I faced, there was little chance to defeat it. If you remember, Ape, I explained that problem to Royce. He ignored me and my warnings."

Taine frowned, trying to sort out his reasoning as he spoke. "The sadistic cruelty of the Dark Man bothered me. The creature didn't merely kill its victims, but whenever possible, tortured them as well. Beyond that, he seemed to actually enjoy what he was doing. Brutally murdering people didn't satisfy him. Instead, he needed to describe to them in great detail exactly how he planned to do it. It made no sense.

"Another aspect of the case troubled me. The Dark Man knew too many of the secrets of the Black Lodge. He exhibited knowledge of every aspect of the crack trade, including secrets known to only the innermost circle of the Order. For all of his powers, he could not read minds. Yet somehow he knew many of the names of its victims. To me, that signaled a human operator behind his actions.

"More surprising, the Dark Man continually underestimated his opponents. We all know that. Each of us managed to escape him in one fashion or another. Ape eluded him three times. Yet the monster possessed incredible supernatural strength and cunning. He just rarely bothered concentrating his full power against any particular opponent. He displayed the typical misplaced self-confidence of an indulgent megalomaniac. The Dark Man exhibited all too familiar weaknesses."

"He acted like someone who always gets his own way," said Janet. "I know plenty of people like that. Harmon Sangmeister and Victor Caldwell both fit that description. Why, even my own father acts that way sometimes."

"The rich are different," said Taine, flashing her a brief smile. "In any circumstances, the Dark Man paraded all the traits of a deviant personality instead of some supernatural entity. That type of behavior narrowed down my search quite a bit. Still, I needed one final clue before I finally realized his true nature."

"But you knew what he looked like," said Ape. "Didn't that matter at all?"

"Not enough for me to guess his basic character. You see, the Sheddim always adapt to their surroundings. When summoned to our world, they draw on the subconscious fears of modern mankind for their shape.

"In the Middle Ages, they appeared as hooded brigands and outlaws. In the seventeenth and eighteenth century, the Sheddim took on the guise of Inquisitors and Masked Headsmen. More than likely, Jack the Ripper was a Sheddim called forth by a Victorian sorcerer. He embodied all the repressed fears and violence of that age.

"When raised from the netherworld, the Dark Man assumed the appearance of a man most likely to frighten modern city dwellers. Thus he roamed the streets in the person of a maniacal killer armed with a butcher's cleaver. He merely fleshed out our worst urban nightmares."

"You're telling me," said Ape. "So now we know the why and the how. What's the punchline?"

"His features gave him away. Or, should I say, his lack of features. When the wind blew off his hat and revealed his glasslike countenance, I immediately recognized the Dark Man as a doppleganger."

"A what?" asked Ape. "Sounds German to me."

"Right you are," said Taine. "The name comes from the German and roughly translates as 'double-goer.' However, the concept predates civilized history. Ancient folklore is filled with tales of witches and warlocks sending out their shadows on missions of evil. And everyone is familiar with stories about the good and evil parts of a man's personality battling for control of his body. All of these legends share a common background—a ghostly duplicate of a living man existing separate from the host body."

"So that's what you meant when you called the Dark Man a shadow of Arelim," said Ape, shaking his head. "He seemed pretty deadly for a shadow."

"When the sorcerer we know only as Arelim raised a Sheddim from the outer darkness, he anchored the creature in our reality by the use of a Name of Power. He called the creature by his own name, Arelim, forging an unholy psychic bond between himself and the demon. In creating a doppleganger, the true Arelim impressed his own personality onto the Sheddim. The creature thus gained all of the sorcerer's knowledge and character. In return, whenever the Dark Man took a life, it shared the resulting psychic energy with its master."

"So the double inherited both Arelim's strengths and faults," said Papa Benjamin, slowly, as if weighing each word. "That explains many of his actions. The Dark Man's sadism reflected the twisted mind of his master."

"You ever gonna tell me how a mirror destroyed him?" asked Ape, impatiently tapping his fingers on the table.

"Can't you guess?" said Taine. "All dopplegangers suffer from one fatal weakness. They think of themselves as a real person. Their very existence depends on maintaining that illusion.

"Despite all of the obvious contradictions and anomalies, the Dark Man thought he was the real Arelim. He refused to consider any other possibility. Oftentimes, according to legend, psychic doubles tried to replace their masters. By their very nature, dopplegangers always believed they were the originals, not the copies. So it was with the Dark Man."

"Aha," said Ape. "The light finally dawns. I think I finally understand.

"A creature of absolute night, the Dark Man had no true features. His face was blank, like a slab of glass. So he cast no reflection in the mirror. When he saw that, it made him realize the truth about himself."

"The knowledge that he was nothing more than a copy of a real human being destroyed him," said Taine. "He could no longer exist in our universe. Instead, the Dark Man returned to the eternal darkness of Kelippot, the shells of those worlds created before ours."

Janet yawned. Taine looked over to the clock. It was nearly 3:00 A.M. He needed rest. They all did.

"What happens next?" asked Ape. Both he and Papa Benjamin rose from their chairs, getting ready to leave.

"I don't know," said Taine. "Arelim still lives. I have no idea how the destruction of his doppleganger affects his plans. My main concerns remain unchanged. I want to help Evangeline Caldwell escape the evil taking place this coming night. And keep Timmy safe from his father."

"In either or both situations," said Papa Benjamin, "you can count on our aid. Even with the Dark Man gone, this Arelim threatens us all. I cannot believe he will abandon his evil schemes despite this major setback. Only one thing will stop him. Death."

39

A mind-shattering pain woke Arelim from a deep sleep. A thousand invisible needles stabbed at his flesh. It felt as if he were being skinned alive. Unseen claws tore at his insides. Fire raced through his veins, causing him to shrink in sudden agony. His blood boiled and steamed within him.

Every muscle and joint in his body screamed in agony. His eyeballs seemed ready to pop out of their sockets. He never before experienced such intense pain. It felt as if his entire body were being ripped apart.

He instantly guessed the source of this torture. The psychic bond between him and his doppleganger linked their senses. However, only the strongest sensations passed between them.

Normally he only experienced the surges of energy each time the Dark Man sacrificed another victim. Tonight someone had discovered the secret of his creation. The Sheddim no longer believed in itself. It was returning to Kelippot. But the link between them still remained. Like a gigantic psychic anchor, the Dark Man was dragging him along to the outer dark.

For a second, Arelim panicked. Kelippot housed horrors beyond human imagining. It was a realm of madness of the mind and the spirit. Outside the universe, it existed in a timeless state of ever enduring. A man trapped there would suffer eternal, unceasing mental and physical torment.

Discipline saved him. Unable to banish the pain from his body, he used it. Channeling the hurt like a raging river, he forced the current to bend to his will. Ignoring the anguish caused by every movement, he spoke the words of power.

"Mene, mene, tekel, upharsin."

Nothing happened. Grimly, he repeated the line. It offered the only chance of salvation.

"Mene, mene, tekel, upharsin."

The grip of pain slackened just a bit. Enough though to strengthen his resolve to continue. He knew the phrase would save him. Words of power defined existence. Even the chaos of Kelippot could not stand against them.

"Mene, mene, tekel, upharsin."

Each time he recited the four words, the pain lessened. Little by little, his strength returned. And, with that strength, came a new sensation—an awareness of a dark, violent power within.

Feeling slightly dizzy, he sat up in bed. A snifter of brandy sat on the nightstand. A quick drink gave him a needed lift. He staggered on wobbly legs across the room to his desk. It took less than a minute to construct the Tree of Life. As he suspected, the same run of four cards appeared in every deal.

The Wheel of Fortune

Pope Joan

The Hermit

La Mort

Arelim stared at the major trumps. The message remained unchanged from the previous day. He smiled in satisfaction. Despite the unexpected setback, nothing had changed. All of his schemes proceeded as planned.

Let his enemies celebrate their small victory. They would soon learn the truth. The doppleganger never figured in his final victory. The Dark Man merely represented his own lusts and desires. Those remained unchanged. If anything, this minor setback actually strengthened his resolve. Nothing could stop him.

After all, it was his magic that summoned the Dark Man from the realms of eternal night. He had spoken the words of power that drew it from the gulf. His wishes, his dreams had given the doppleganger form and purpose. Together with his creation, he had planned each killing, feasted on each death. And with each sacrifice, he had grown stronger through the unholy bond that joined them together.

The Dark Man no longer existed in this world. But his legacy lived on. Arelim raised his hands. They looked . . . bigger. His gnarled fingers no longer ached from arthritis. Powerful muscles rippled beneath the flesh.

He laughed. The sound echoed in the bedroom. Darkness coursed through his body. He never felt so alive, so aware, so hungry for life—human life.

Taine and his friends thought they had destroyed the Dark Man. Not so. Instead they had merely accelerated a process that started with the first killing. Each death had drawn Arelim and his doppleganger closer and closer together. Blood forged unbreakable ties that even death could not sever.

Still chuckling, Arelim looked down again at the four tarot cards. Their symbols clearly indicated his triumph to come.

The Wheel of Fortune spoke of his destiny. No power on Earth could stop him now. Tomorrow night he would smash those who stood against him. It was his destiny.

Pope Joan represented a mysterious woman. He knew for sure this card meant Janet Packard. Her young son played an important role in his plans. The boy's death would be a fitting climax for the evening's activities.

The Hermit signified hidden wisdom. In his hands, he held the secrets of the ages. No magician alive could match his powers. He stood alone, invincible from physical harm.

La Mort, the skeleton, the sigil for death, could not be any clearer. Originally, he thought the card portrayed the Dark Man. Now he understood it referred directly to himself. He no longer needed an agent, an understudy, to commit his crimes. Death walked alongside of him now.

He reached across the desk, over the tarot deck, and grasped the butcher's cleaver. The wood handle felt warm beneath his fingers. As if it had just been passed on to him from another.

40

Janet woke up with a start, her body drenched in a cold sweat. Groggily, she shook her head, trying to clear out the nightmares. Her eyes still heavy with sleep, she looked around the room for a clock. She gasped when she saw it was nearly eleven. Time for her to get moving.

Taine was not the type to have a supply of women's clothes on hand. With a shrug of disgust, she put on her clothes from last night. She could change as soon as she got back to Brentwood. The cocktail dress looked like a wartime casualty. She couldn't help grinning as she combed out the tangles from her hair. She felt like a combat veteran herself.

Wandering into the kitchen, she found a note from Taine propped up against a basket of croissants. "I let you sleep. You needed the rest. Besides, resisting temptation is good for my willpower. Fresh juice in the fridge. I've gone to warn Angel about Arelim. Call my office when you can. Lots of love."

She smiled as she bit into one of the fluffy rolls. By the time Papa Benjamin and Ape Largo left last night, the last thing on her mind was sex. All she wanted to do was take a quick shower and go to bed. Taine never even raised the possibility of anything more. By the time she emerged from the bathroom, dripping wet and feeling a bit more frisky, Taine was already fast asleep. Properly chagrined, she had crawled under the covers next to him and snuggled up close. It only took a few minutes for her to drift off as well.

Thinking of sleep focused Janet's attention on the nightmare that woke her up. She still remembered most of the details. Surprisingly, the dream dealt not with her experiences with the Dark Man, but with the tragic death of her brother many years before. Something about that night bothered her. Janet shook her head in annoyance. She disliked coincidences, especially when they concerned her son. For the first time in nineteen long years, she found herself questioning the circumstances surrounding her brother's accident.

She finished her croissant and a glass of orange juice before admitting defeat. After nearly two decades, even the most vivid of memories faded into dim recollections. Licking the last few crumbs off her fingers, Janet headed for the living room.

It was time for her to head home, but she didn't feel like leaving. For all of the violence of the night before, she felt at peace in this apartment. Taine lived here and she loved Taine. That alone made it a haven from the doubts that continually nagged at her subconscious. Stalling, Janet studied the hardcovers crowding the solitary wood bookcase in the corner.

To her amusement, more than half of them were mystery novels. Taine evidently liked hard-boiled private eye stories. She quickly scanned the titles. Books by Hammett and Chandler jammed the shelves next to more recent work by Parker, Leonard and Estelman.

The rest of the shelves were filled up with an eclectic mix of nonfiction works. As far as Janet could tell, there was no sense or order to the collection. Taine impressed her as a man with a wide range of interests. His taste in books reflected that trait.

One small group of books dealt with the occult. Most of them were trade paperbound volumes of commentary on *The Kabbalah*. Janet recognized the name from earlier remarks made by Taine. She knew nothing about the book other than it dealt with mystic beliefs. Curious, she took the thinnest volume off the shelf. She was a natural speed reader. It wouldn't take long to finish this one text. She could leave for home after that. Settling down on the battered couch, Janet started reading.

An hour later, she closed the book in dismay. She had barely made it through two chapters. The material was incredibly dense. It dealt with all sorts of occult traditions. What little she understood made no sense. It forwarded concepts she found impossible to comprehend.

According to mystic tradition, God existed in a perfect state of being known as Azilut before creating our universe. To give form and substance to our world, Elohim inscribed his perfect name on the void. He extended his identity to all things. Thus, in a sense, the true name of God became the universe.

From that belief came the concept that the true name of any entity contained the essence of that being. She was vaguely familiar with that idea from her religion courses in college. Knowledge of your enemy's tr' name gave you power over him. The same r extended to both human and supernatural bein' one of the basic principles of magic.

At least now she understood the importance of words in magic rituals. Or at least she thought she did. Arelim used certain words to summon the Dark Man. And the magician controlled the Sheddim by those same words. Or so the book implied.

Using that same reasoning, it then followed that knowing the true name of God gave you power over all things. That was because the entire universe was an extension of God's identity. The exact nature of that power was not discussed in either of the chapters she managed to finish. Janet got the impression that the author was not sure of that himself.

It was a secret sought after by all the great magicians of history. For the actual name was already known. It appeared a number of times in the Old Testament. Occult scholars called the sacred name, a group of four Hebrew letters, the tetragrammaton. Those symbols, Yod He Vau He, formed the phrase, "He is," the basic foundation of all Jewish belief.

However, as that name was held in such awe by the early Hebrews, it was rarely spoken and never above a whisper. Only an inner circle of priests knew the true pronunciation of the name. Over the centuries, the number of those privy to the secret shrank and shrank until finally, no one was sure of the correct articulation.

The secret was lost. Knowing the name was not enough. Only the correct way of saying it could unlock the power it contained. And that was the greatest mystery of *The Kabbalah*.

Yawning, she replaced the volume in the bookcase. Time enough to finish it another day. She had been hoping Taine might return to the apartment, but no such luck. It was nearly one o'clock. She had just enough time to stop off at Brentwood and change before picking Tim at school. That nightmare still haunted her She wanted to personally keep an eye on her of the day.

41

Martha answered the bell at Brentwood. Her eyes widened in dismay when she saw the condition of Janet's clothes. "What happened to you, Miss Janet?" she asked, obviously trying to mask her shock.

Keeping her eyes firmly fixed to the floor, Janet rushed by the housekeeper without a word. Sometimes, no explanation worked. Reaching the stairs, she hesitated for a moment. "Where's Leo?"

"He left early this morning," said Martha. "Mr. Packard didn't say when he would be back. You know why. He never likes to stay around Brentwood on *this* day."

Janet shuddered. After all these years, her brother Ralph's ghost still haunted her father. Leo never adjusted to the death of his only son. In a way, he seemed to blame himself for the accident. The thought started Janet shivering.

"You're cold, Miss Janet," said Martha. "A dress like that isn't made for springtime in Chicago. Go upstairs and change into something warm. I'll make you a nice hot cup of tea."

"That sounds wonderful," said Janet, heading up the stairs. "Did Bruno go with Dad?"

"No, ma'am. Bruno took the car in for a tune-up. He planned to pick up Master Tim right afterward."

"Okay. Though I might go for Tim myself today. He probably misses his mom. And I miss him."

A hot shower and a change of clothes brought her back to life. Sitting on the edge of her bed, she toyed with the idea of calling Taine. Reluctantly, she decided against it. No reason to bother him now. Once she got Tim, the two of them could stop in to see the detective.

Janet shook her head. In spite of all her mental precautions and warnings, she never changed. Here she was, head over heels in love with a man she knew nothing about. Taine might be married to five different women and have fourteen children. Or be on the run from the law for obsessive kleptomania. Not that it mattered very much. Her heart still ruled her mind. She trusted her emotions, however foolish that might be. She loved Taine and he loved her. That was enough.

The doorbell rang, breaking into her thoughts. Wondering who it was, she left her room and hurried over to the stairs. Looking down, she saw Martha had already answered the door. It was only the mailman.

Standing there, staring at the two figures, a weird sense of deja vu swept over her. It was her dream all over again. She was ten years old, listening to her father speak with the policeman. The same agony twisted his face as he repeated those terrible words, "A hundred daggers."

He stood there frozen for a second, unable to move. She remembered him slowly raising one hand to his face, brushing away the tears. As he did so, she caught a glimpse of an odd ring on one of his fingers. The hall light bounced off the metal, causing it to shine. Ten-year-old Janet saw the design, but it was Janet nineteen years later who recognized the pattern. It was the seal of the Black Lodge.

She reeled in shock and surprise. All of the blood in her body rushed to her head. She felt terribly weak, terribly afraid. Her legs collapsed beneath her like rubber bands. With a low moan, she desperately clutched the stairway railing for support. Below, Martha turned from the mailman. "Are you all right, miss?" she called up to the second floor, as if sensing Janet's distress.

Unable to speak, Janet managed a mute nod. After all these years, she knew the truth. That was why the symbol of the Order looked so familiar. She had never seen it in a textbook. Instead, her father had once worn a ring identical to the one sported by Roger. Leo Packard belonged to the Black Lodge.

Now she understood why Taine hesitated telling her

any secrets about the Lodge. He obviously suspected her father of belonging to the Order. It made perfect sense. Only naive little Janet never guessed the truth.

The Black Lodge recruited its members from the rich and powerful. Not many men were wealthier than Leo. Every bit of information fit together in a damnable pattern. Even his business dealings with Harmon Sangmeister took on a new, more sinister significance.

Shaking off the effects of her near collapse, Janet rushed back to her room. She couldn't afford any weakness now. All of her life she had trusted her father, relied on him, depended on him. What took place nearly twenty years ago might not have any bearing on the events this week. However, she dared not depend on it.

Martha and Bruno worked for Leo. That fact alone branded them in her eyes. She could no longer trust either of them. Desperately, she wondered what their relationship was with the Mystic Order of Antioch? Janet remembered how much Mrs. Kearny feared Bruno. Could the teacher have sensed something that Janet never realized? It seemed impossible. The chauffeur treated Timmy like his own son. Yet Bruno also served her father. She feared the worst.

School let out in twenty minutes. That gave her just enough time to get there and take Tim with her. This latest revelation called for extreme action. Better to anticipate the worst than hope for the best.

Grabbing her purse, she hurried out into the hallway. She could hear Martha puttering about in the parlor. Trying to make as little noise as possible, Janet quickly descended the stairs to the front foyer. Once through the main door, she ran for her car. Every second counted. Gunning the motor, she sent the BMW roaring into the street.

Friday afternoon traffic crawled along at its usual intolerable pace. From time to time, Janet glanced nervously at the clock on the dashboard. Today, she would make it just in time. With a little luck, she might even arrive a few minutes early.

Driving, she mentally reviewed Leo's actions of the

past few days. Nothing he said or did indicated he maintained any ties with the Black Lodge. If anything, his obsessive hatred of Roger placed him squarely against the Order. She shook her head in bewilderment. This whole thing bordered on lunacy. Did she really suspect her own father of secretly plotting with her psychopathic ex-husband against her son?

A few hours ago, she would have dismissed the entire notion as absolute madness. Now she wavered between the two possibilities. Leo always disappeared on the anniversary of Ralph's death. He never returned until the next morning. Not once in all those years had he ever offered any explanation of where he spent those hours.

Her conversation with Taine made it quite clear that the Black Lodge met this evening. Was Leo planning to attend that gathering? Was Roger? And where did Tim fit in? A vague reference to the Black Mass flickered through her thoughts. Unmentionable horrors suddenly seemed all too real. Janet jammed her foot down on the gas pedal. She had to get to the school before Bruno.

She arrived at Sullivan Preparatory School at four minutes before the hour. As usual the school parking lot was already filled. However, there were a number of spots on the street. Janet steered her car into one less than a hundred feet from the entrance. Looking around, she spotted her father's Rolls Royce in the middle of the lot. Bruno rested against one door, carefully cleaning his nails. No matter. Timmy was going with her.

Totally without warning, a man's hand reached through the open car window and grabbed her by the back of the neck. Pain arched down her spine as bony fingers dug deep into her skin. Something cold and metallic pressed hard against her windpipe.

"It's a knife, Janet dear," whispered a voice in her ear. "Make one move and I'll cut your throat."

Waves of panic swept through her. "Roger," she managed to choke out. The steel blade served as a frighteningly efficient gag.

"You remember me," her ex-husband said sarcastically. "What a surprise. Keep both hands on the steering wheel where I can see them. Try something and things will get real messy. I'd hate to get blood all over this nice leather interior."

The grip on her neck never slackened. "How nice to see you again," Roger continued, almost cheerfully. "I suspected you might show up today. So I kept a close eye on the street. My friends will take care of Bruno. He won't cause any trouble. We can watch all the action from right here."

Out of the corner of her eyes, she could see him resting casually against the side of her car. To anyone else, Roger must appear to be a friend holding a casual conversation with the person inside the auto. She was totally helpless.

He shifted the knife slightly, nicking her soft skin. Warm drops of blood trickled across her neck. "Don't make me kill you, Janet," he said, sounding slightly nervous. "I will if I have to. Be a good girl and I'll let you go free."

His voice cracked with emotion. "I want to destroy you. I want to hurt you the way you hurt me. This way, you'll suffer for a long time. I know how much you love that little brat. Killing you wouldn't be half as much fun as knowing you're alive and suffering."

"Tim's your son, too," she gasped out, feeling the bite of the knife. "Please don't harm him."

"Sorry, dear, but I have no choice in the matter. My Master requires our son for a certain ritual tonight. My whole future depends on me delivering Tim to that ceremony. Ah, isn't that the school bell?" He laughed. "Watch closely now. Lights, camera, action."

Janet saw it all happen. Dozens of children came running out the side door of the school. Bruno started forward, scanning the crowd for Tim. As if by accident, a young man crossed his path, stumbling as he did so. Instinctively, the bodyguard reached out to help steady the stranger. He never even saw the two other young men who circled in from behind.

For the barest instant, bright metal flashed in the sun-

light. Bruno died without a struggle. Unnoticed by anyone, he sagged lifelessly into the arms of his two
attackers. Grabbing the body under the arms, the killers
hustled the corpse back to the Rolls. He disappeared
into the backseat of the car. Tears filled Janet's eyes.
Poor Bruno deserved better.

Meanwhile, the man who stumbled was busily talking
to Tim. He showed the boy a piece of paper and pointed
to a car parked close by. Janet wanted to scream. She
could see her son nodding in agreement. Smiling, holding hands, Tim accompanied the killer to the auto. Seconds later, the kidnappers were gone.

"Amazing how easy it is to fool little kids," said
Roger, as she watched the other car drive off. "Especially innocent ones like Tim. They believe all sorts of
notes from their parents. Even ones written by somebody else. Don't worry, my love. He's perfectly safe
with my friends. They actually like children. They'll
keep Tim amused till tonight."

"Then what?" she demanded, ignoring the steel at
her throat.

"Why not ask your new boyfriend?" said Roger. Pulling the knife away, he viciously shoved her face-first
across the seat of the car. By the time she sat up, he
had disappeared into the crowd.

It would have been easy then to just give up, to abandon herself to despair. But Janet refused to let that happen. Instead, she drew in several deep breaths to steady
her nerves. Turning the key in the ignition, she steered
her car into the traffic. Roger and his friends had too
much of a head start. There was no way she could track
them down. And if she found them, there was nothing
she could do on her own. She needed help. The police
would ask too many questions she couldn't answer. Her
only hope was Taine.

Roger thought she was beaten. He always underestimated her nerve. She never gave up. No matter what
the odds, she would rescue her son. Or die trying.

42

Hungrily, Felice bit into the custard-filled donut. The action sent a thin stream of yellow goo spurting across her chin and upper lip. Slowly, sensuously, she licked her features clean. Felice trembled in ecstasy. Cream donuts turned her on. Eating them reminded her of sex. She giggled. These days, nearly everything reminded her of sex.

It was a little after four in the afternoon. She was fully recovered from her encounter with the Dark Man the night before last. She couldn't afford not to be. The rent had to be paid. As did the crack dealers. Her encounter with the Dark Man had not cured Felice of her taste for dope. But she was careful not to buy any from the Children of Danballah.

"Enjoying yourself, Felice?" someone asked from behind her back. A heavy hand fell on her shoulder.

Felice froze. It was the Dark Man, she thought, panic-stricken. He had come back to get her. Then common sense took over. She was sitting at the counter of a donut shop in the Loop. This wasn't the Dark Man's time or territory.

Felice swung around and found herself facing two grinning detectives. "She's the only hooker I know who sucks off donuts," said Calvin Lane.

"She's hot," said Moe Kaufman, nodding. "She'll burn the jelly right out of them poor pastries."

"My, my," said Felice, looking the two men up and down. "What do we have here? The Sylvester and Tweetie Bird of the Chicago Police Department. What a surprise, seeing two officers of the law in a donut shop."

Felice laughed at the sour expressions on the detective's faces. Chicago cops were notorious for wasting time in fast-food joints. "We're here on business," said Kaufman.

"Not with me you ain't," said Felice, swinging one leg casually back and forth as she spoke. Wearing her usual micromini leather skirt, the move showed off a lot of thigh. She got a kick out of flashing the cops. Especially when she knew they had no thoughts of arresting her.

Kaufman and Lane were detectives, not street cops. They didn't spend their time cruising the streets busting hookers. Instead, from time to time, they came to her looking for news. It was an easy way to make a few bucks when times were slow. Not that it mattered much at the moment. Business was booming. "I don't got nothing to sell today."

"Maybe, maybe not," said Calvin Lane, sliding onto the chair next to her. Kaufman eased into the one on her other side. "We just want to ask you a few questions."

Kaufman signaled for coffee. Smiling, he asked, "Run into Crack Annie lately?"

"Crack Annie?" repeated Felice, trying to think of something to say. "Haven't seen her in a few weeks. I've been busy."

"Word on the street is that you're one of the regulars at her crack parties each week," said Lane. He took a sip from his coffee cup. "There was a get-together on Wednesday night."

"I missed it," said Felice hurriedly. "I was busy." She smiled. "I was entertaining some college dudes. I got witnesses, two of them."

"Stay cool," said Kaufman, shrugging his shoulders. "We're not looking to take you in. All we want is some information."

"That's right," said Lane. The two detectives alternated speaking, keeping her off balance trying to follow the conversation. "Tell us about the Dark Man."

"Don't know nothing 'bout no Dark Man," muttered Felice.

"I think you do," said Kaufman. "He's a big dude who wears a black overcoat and carries a butcher's cleaver. We think he visited Crack Annie's party the other night."

"He killed all your friends, Felice," said Lane. "Don't you want us to catch this maniac?"

"He'll kill me next," said Felice softly.

"No way," said Lane, shaking his head. "The Dark Man isn't going to waste time tracking down people like you. We already interviewed another girl who escaped him earlier. She's doin' fine."

"Yeah," said Kaufman, grimacing. "Making crack and dreaming of a pink Cadillac."

"Let's hear it," said Lane. "What happened at Crack Annie's?"

Felice spent the next fifteen minutes describing the events of Wednesday evening. The officers sat silently through her entire recital, not interrupting once. When she was finished, Calvin Lane was the first to speak.

"Jibes pretty much with what Lisa Ray told us." He stared at Felice. "You sure this Dark Man was that tall? Maybe he was so big and bulky, you imagined he was a six-footer."

"I knows what I saw," said Felice. "He was a big mother."

Lane looked at his partner and shrugged. "Lisa wouldn't budge from her description, either."

"I don't care," said Kaufman. "Our buddy has the motive, strength and opportunity. He's my choice until someone else better comes along."

"Hey," said Felice. "Didn't you fools pay no attention? The dude had no face. And Annie stabbed him good. How you explain that?"

"He wore a mask to hide his features," said Kaufman. "As to the knife, you were high on crack. The stuff played tricks with your mind. You *thought* you saw Annie stab him. A steel blade can't cut through mesh body-armor."

239

"Nothing supernatural about the Dark Man," said Lane. "He's a hustler trying to take over the Children of Danballah."

"Doin' a pretty good job, the way I sees it," said Felice. "When you boys gonna take him down?"

"Soon," answered Moe Kaufman. "Real soon."

43

The police consider Ape their prime suspect in the killings," said Papa Benjamin. The voodoo priest looked anything but pleased. Sitting next to him, Ape shrugged his shoulders as if to say, "What else is new?"

Taine nodded in silent agreement. Looking at the case from the police point of view, Ape made a wonderful choice for the Dark Man. His involvement with Willis Royce placed him right in the thick of the speculation about a drug war in the streets. Only a few men possessed the strength to wield a butcher's cleaver with such deadly efficiency. Ape was one of those few. And his reputation labeled him a ruthless, maniacal killer.

"They found the mess at the Temple," said Ape, as if reading Taine's mind. "According to the news, there were chopped up bodies all over. Right away, a couple of hotshot detectives noticed mine was missing. Putting two and two together, they decided I murdered all the others. Nice to know the cops think so highly of me."

"Can you blame them?" asked Taine.

"Nah. Sometimes I scare myself looking in the mirror. But it still doesn't make me a mass murderer. Usually guys like that dress in business suits and sound real normal. I look too much like a maniac to be one."

"Try telling the police that," said Taine. "We destroyed the Dark Man. I never realized we needed his body."

"They won't close the case until they pin the murders

on somebody," said Ape. "Unless we come up with a likely suspect, I'll be on the run for the rest of my life."

"Arelim . . ." began Taine. The rest of his sentence was lost as a frantic Janet Packard burst into the room.

"They got Timmy," she said, in a voice so calm it was frightening. "Bruno's dead. And I know the truth about my father."

Taine was up and out of his chair in an instant. Ignoring the others, he hugged Janet close, holding her tight against him. At first she remained unmoving, stiff and unyielding. Then gradually, he could feel the tension lessening within her. The madness that gripped her retreated before his concern. Her body softened, relaxed beneath his touch. Her head rested on his shoulder. Softly, she began to cry.

The tears started slow, but within seconds were falling uncontrollably. Great wracking sobs shook Janet's body. Taine felt incredibly helpless. Gently, he stroked her hair and kept her close. There was nothing much else he could do. All the words in the world, all the reassurances, meant nothing.

Finally the tears came to an end. Straightening, Janet brushed her hair back away from her eyes. Taking a tissue from a distraught Mrs. McConnell, she dabbed her eyes dry.

"Sorry for the tears," said Janet. "I lost control for a minute. Roger did it. He planned the whole thing."

Briefly and to the point, she described everything that happened at the school.

Taine shook his head, annoyed with himself. "I underestimated, seriously underestimated, your ex-husband. When I spoke to Willis Royce, he indicated that he never heard of Roger. From that I assumed he had no actual connections with the Black Lodge. I dismissed him as an annoying nuisance with delusions of grandeur. Your father's precautions seemed adequate."

"Forget my father," said Janet bitterly. "I know all about him, too. It just took me a long time to realize his connection with the Order. He must have joined right around the time Ralph died."

She paused, a strange look on her face. Taine sighed deeply. Despite Janet's suspicions, he trusted her father. Leo seemed genuinely devoted to his grandson. And to a lesser extent, his daughter. Not that she would ever believe that now. The truth hit Janet like a brick in the face. A slowly dawning comprehension filled her eyes with a blind, all-consuming horror.

"That accident never took place," she said, haltingly. "They fixed the whole thing." Angrily, she grabbed Taine's shirt with both her hands. "They faked the crash. Didn't they? Didn't they!"

Taine nodded, unable and unwilling to deny the truth. "Just like they did for the Sangmeister's boating accident," he said somberly. "Not to mention the gangland slaying of Royce's son. And god knows how many others. Like I explained to Jack Korshak, given enough money you can always manufacture the necessary evidence."

"Hey," said Ape, a slight edge to his voice. "You want to clue us in on what you're talking about? After all, Papa Benjamin and I want to help. We can't do much if you keep ignoring us."

"The greatest strength of the Black Lodge is the secrecy that surrounds it," said Taine. "For all of their bluster, Caldwell and Royce refused to discuss the basic workings of the Order. They were bound by an oath stronger than even their fear. Membership in the Black Lodge requires a payment in blood."

"I don't like the sound of that," said Ape, shaking his massive head from side to side. He looked from Taine to Janet and then back to Taine again. "I don't like it one bit. Not after the way you've been talking about kids dying."

"Their children?" said Papa Benjamin, his voice shocked. "Their sons and daughters?"

"There is only one way to gain admission to the inner circle of Initiates of the Order of Antioch," said Taine grimly. "That method has remained unchanged for centuries. To join that select group, the candidate must sacrifice his eldest child at a Black Mass, as held by the Lodge each year on the eve of Walpurgis Nacht.''

"May first," said Janet. "Tonight. Roger plans to use the life of my son, his child, as his admission ticket to this band of inhuman monsters."

"Unfortunately, they are all too human," said Papa Benjamin. "Such greed comes only from within. No devils or demons force these men to act this way. Their lust for power makes them mad."

Rising from his chair, Papa Benjamin hobbled over to Janet. The events of the past twenty-four hours had weakened his body but not his spirit. Reaching out, he clutched one of her hands with both of his.

"All of my days I have served the voodoo Mysteres. As did my father, and his father before him, and so on back to the time when my ancestors first came to Haiti from Africa. Only once during my entire life have I let my personal desires interfere with my duties as a houn'gan.

"That was when two arrogant killers murdered my only son. In a fit of black rage, I asked the Great Serpent to strike at them for me. They paid the price, but their deaths did not bring my child back to life. My revenge meant nothing to him."

There was no hesitation in Papa Benjamin's voice. *"I refuse to let another child die.* No matter what the price, I will not let this sacrifice take place tonight."

"Yeah, me neither," said Ape. "I've taken about all the crap I can handle from this Black Lodge. I may look like a freak, but I try not to act like one. Nobody ever accused me of hurting a kid, much less sacrificing one to the devil. Time for somebody to teach these bastards a lesson."

Taine shook his head, feeling only a twinge of remorse. He had hoped not to involve Janet in his rescue attempt. He realized now that he needed her help. He needed all of their help. They were all involved in this madness. Together, they had defeated the Dark Man. Perhaps pooling their strength they stood a chance against the final scheme of his master, Arelim.

"The police can't help us. They would never believe our story and I'm not sure we can trust them. Like I said, the all-powerful dollar works wonders with the truth. We're on our own.

"Fortunately, I had Mrs. McConnell do some checking for me the past few days. She located where and when the Lodge meets tonight. Originally I planned to attend the Mass on my own. I owed that much to Angel Caldwell. However, I made my rescue plans before Roger kidnapped Tim. That changed everything."

Grimacing, Taine clenched his fists in anger. "Both of their lives are in jeopardy. There's only one way to save them. Some how, some way, we've got to infiltrate and then destroy the Black Lodge."

44

Taine put down the phone, his features grim. "Still no answer. Either Angel got out of town, or she's at the ceremony. I suspect the latter."

Biting her lower lip, Janet nodded. She had expected nothing less. It was nearly nine o'clock. There was no time left to try any more calls. The Black Mass started within the hour.

During the past sixty minutes, her spirits had been sinking lower and lower. All of the outrage she had felt earlier was gone, replaced only with emptiness. Deep within her heart, she knew it was too late. Too late for plans, too late for rescue, too late for hope.

They had eaten a light dinner in Taine's office. There had been no mention of Bruno's murder on the evening news. Either his body had not yet been discovered or the police were keeping the killing under wraps. Sooner or later, the story would make headlines. Tim was the grandson of one of the richest men in the United States.

Link the Packard name with a mysterious death and a possible kidnaping and you had front page news. Especially when neither the boy's mother nor grandfather could be found. Janet prayed the story would end happily. Despite all of Taine's assurances, she felt Tim was doomed. And, without him, her life meant nothing.

As if reading her mind, Taine came over and squeezed her tightly around the shoulders. "Don't give up without a fight," he said. "I have a few tricks up my sleeve. The bad guys don't always get the last laugh."

"I gave you my word," said Papa Benjamin, sounding slightly peeved. He looked a bit indignant. "Do not take such a promise lightly. All of the powers of the voodoo Mysteres stand behind me."

"You heard him," said Ape, grinning. "And whatever Papa Benjamin says goes double for me."

The big man's face took on a more serious expression. "Most of my life, I've been on my own. None of the breaks ever went my way. Life pushed me around and when I could, I pushed back. With an attitude like that, I had more than my share of troubles. Now for the first time ever, I feel that I'm doing the right thing. To a loner like me, it's nice to be on the side with the angels. Papa Benjamin speaks for the both of us. Arelim and the Black Lodge are gonna take a beating tonight." Ape slammed one big fist into the palm of his other hand. The sound of flesh hitting flesh resounded like a bomb in the small room. "Ape Largo takes no prisoners."

Janet shook her head in bewilderment. "You're all gambling your lives in a fight we can't possibly win. It just doesn't make any sense."

"It makes all the sense in the world," said Taine, pulling on his overcoat, then helping her with hers. "Remember what I told Angel Caldwell when she first came to see me? Magic has no orientation. It is neither black nor white. Only the user's intent gives it direction."

He turned her around so that they stood face-to-face. "The members of the Black Lodge think only of themselves. They care for nothing other than their own profit.

That is the real purpose behind these sacrifices. It proves to all those assembled that the candidate is willing to perform any act, any abomination, for the sake of his personal success."

"It also explains that strict code of silence you mentioned earlier," interjected Ape. "What a perfect way of maintaining absolute loyalty to the Lodge. The Grand Master probably keeps nice detailed files on all of his acolytes. One wrong word and a few photos get sent to the police. The threat of exposure keeps everybody in line."

"Exactly," said Taine, still looking Janet directly in the eye. "This Order lives on hatred and greed. It thrives on the basest emotions imaginable. Unfortunately, in this imperfect world of ours, too many people have stopped fighting back. They accept evil as inevitable and uncontrollable. Calling themselves 'realists,' they condone the most horrible crimes as the result of an unjust society. They think of the universe in terms of gray, never once considering that black and white actually exist.

"Not Sidney Taine. I refuse to compromise with evil. The same holds true with Ape and Papa Benjamin. Tonight we work together for one reason. It's the right thing to do. And that places us in absolute and total opposition to the principles and aims of the Black Lodge. To me, that makes perfect sense."

"You're crazy," said Janet, tears filling her eyes. "All three of you are crazy." Then she shook her head defiantly. "Make that, all four *of us* are crazy. What are we doing standing around here? Let's get going. We're wasting too much time talking. Timmy needs me. I can't let him down."

"Now," said Taine, releasing her, "that sounds like the real Janet speaking. Not the pale imitation that stood here a few minutes ago."

"You ain't kidding," said Ape. "Let's go kick some butt."

45

According to Mrs. McConnell's information, Harmon Sangmeister owned a huge country retreat in the far southwest suburbs. It hadn't surprised Janet one bit when she recognized the location as being within a few miles of the scene of her brother's "accident." Finally after all these years, she knew the terrible truth about Ralph's murder.

Taine drove, with Ape Largo beside him. Janet and Papa Benjamin sat in the back. Only Ape was armed. In a belt holster nestled in the small of his back, he carried a snub-nosed .44 automatic. He had admitted to her earlier that he wore it more for self-confidence than any real purpose. Outnumbered twenty to one, they were counting on guile, not firepower, to save Tim's life.

They rode in silence, each of them sunk deep in their own thoughts. Covertly, Janet studied the faces of her companions. She wondered what each of them was thinking.

For what seemed like the hundredth time in the past few days, Janet found herself pondering Taine's background. He knew much too much about the occult for mere idle curiosity. That "New Age" detective nonsense didn't fool her either. Taine was no Yuppie involved in channeling or crystals. His beliefs were anchored in ancient, essential truths. Who was Sidney Taine, really? It was a question that would not go away.

The night sky was clear and full of stars. Once outside Chicago city limits, they made good time. A few turns off the main highways brought them onto a deserted country road. No other car disturbed the silence as they swiftly closed in on their destination.

Twenty minutes before ten, Taine steered their auto onto an isolated, unlit road in the midst of a heavily wooded area. It was little more than a blacktopped strip disappearing into the forest. Shutting off the headlights, he slowed the car down to a crawl. A hundred yards ahead on the trail, barbed wire gleamed in the moonlight.

"Welcome to Harmon Sangmeister's estate," said Taine, tersely. From the sound of his voice, Janet guessed he was annoyed about something. "I never once considered the possibility there might be guards at the entrance. We'll have to bluff our way inside."

"Hold on," said Ape, gently opening his door. "Not so fast. You're a city boy, Taine. Just the opposite with me. I spent most of my youth playing in woods like these. The circus traveled throughout the Midwest touring farm towns. I was born for this type of terrain."

As if to emphasize his point, Ape clenched his hand into a huge fist. Powerful muscles rippled in his arms and chest. "Strategy works most of the time. But brute strength has its place, too. Give me fifteen minutes and then roll up to the fence nice and slow. I'll be waiting."

The big bodyguard vanished into the forest. Taine turned around to the two of them, an astonished look on his face. He started to say something, then just shook his head. Janet giggled. Beside her, Papa Benjamin chuckled softly. "That one will make an effective houn'gan someday. He is a man of many talents."

"You can say that again," whispered Taine. "I'm glad he's on our side."

Exactly a quarter hour after Ape left, Taine eased their car along the road to the gate. No one hailed them as they approached the stockade fence. Two nearby wood sentry boxes stood empty. The place appeared deserted.

As they drove through the entranceway, a shadow darker than the darkness detached itself from the nearer guardhouse. "Keep the lights off," said Ape as he slid back onto the seat next to Taine. "There's a parking lot around the next bend. Looks like we're last to arrive."

"Any problems with the sentries?" asked Taine.

"Nope," said Ape, grinning. "There were two men at the gate, another two patrolling the perimeter. None of them expected any trouble. It was easy."

"Too easy," said Taine, as he steered their car into the parking lot. "Security should have been a lot tighter."

"It's a trap," said Ape, nodding his head in agreement. "Someone important expected us to show up. They must have pulled the rest of the guards. So, what else is new. I don't see that we had any choice in the matter.

"Stop here," he commanded abruptly, as they pulled alongside of a long, narrow cabana.

"I scouted around for a few minutes after I neutralized the opposition. This place right here evidently served as the changing room for all the visitors tonight. When I checked it out, there were still lots of robes and stuff like that inside. On the other side of the building, a path leads through the woods to some sort of outdoor arena. It reminded me a lot of one of those Greek amphitheaters. There were too many people milling around, drinking and talking, for me to do much snooping. And I had to get back and meet you."

"Mrs. McConnell got a copy of the contractor's blueprints for the entire estate," said Taine. "In the plans, the arena is described as an entertainment center. The architect designed the place according to exact specifications provided by Sangmeister. There's even a raised stage that connects directly to the back of his mansion."

"How convenient," said Ape. "Great place to throw a rock concert for a few hundred friends. Or sacrifice an innocent kid to the devil."

Hastily, they entered the cabana. The place was deserted. A stack of monk's robes covered a center table. "Put one of these on," said Taine, pulling a cassock over his head. "They'll serve as perfect disguises. We'll blend right in with the Lodge members."

"Shouldn't we hurry up?" asked Janet, as she struggled into the black robe. "You said the ceremony started at ten o'clock. It's already five minutes past the hour.''

"Like any big group, I doubt if the Lodge will start exactly on time,'' answered Taine. "But you're right. It's time for action. However, I have to warn you about one more thing before we go.''

Taine looked around at all of them. "Magic always follows one of two paths. From his use of blood sacrifice and a doppleganger, it seems pretty obvious that Arelim is a believer in *Tiferet,* the way of the Physical. None of us possesses the knowledge or skill necessary to match his power. To defeat him, we must counter with *Yesod,* the way of the Spirit.''

Starting to feel uneasy, Janet said nothing. There was something in Taine's tone of voice that frightened her. He sounded much too intense. She suspected she was not going to like what was coming next.

"The only way I can use this magic is with your complete and absolute cooperation. No matter what happens, no matter what occurs, you must *remain silent.* Our only hope of saving Tim rests with Arelim's colossal overconfidence. We can't interfere with his other plans for tonight. The minute we threaten his schemes, our own rescue attempt is doomed. I know none of this makes much sense yet, but it will. Believe me, it will.''

"That it?'' asked Ape. "Nothing else you want us to do?''

"I feel so . . . useless,'' said Janet. "Shouldn't we just dash in there, find Tim, and get away?''

"Sounds good to me,'' said Ape.

Taine shook his head. "Tim's probably hidden away somewhere in Sangmeister's mansion, hypnotized or sedated. We'd never find him before the ceremony. And remember, there are nearly a hundred hostile members of the Black Lodge out there. We can't fight them all.''

"What other choice is there?'' asked Ape, starting to sound angry. "They ain't gonna just give us the kid.''

"Perhaps they will,'' said Taine evenly. "Perhaps they will. Remember, don't give up hope no matter what happens. The Way of the Spirit doesn't always require active participation by all those involved. Your presence here is enough."

"Our strength is your strength," said Papa Benjamin, cryptically. "We will not fail."

Janet wished she shared the voodoo priest's confidence. Despite all of his assurances, all of his promises, Taine had revealed absolutely nothing of his plan. They were depending on him for guidance. It all came down to trust. Despite all of her misgivings, her fears, Tim's life as well as all of their own rested in Taine's hands. Silently, she prayed that it was not the greatest mistake she ever made.

46

Taine snorted in amusement as he checked out his companions. They looked like four refugees from *Ivanhoe*. All of them wore heavy wool monk's cassocks, grim and black and reaching to the floor. The deep hoods effectively served to shroud their features in shadow. Draped over each robe was a white surtout emblazoned with a bold red passion cross. However, unlike the emblem of the Crusaders, the symbol was reversed, with the long arm up, its transverse arm lowered.

"Please take your places," said a sharp voice from behind them. They froze motionless, caught completely by surprise. "The ceremony will begin shortly."

Raising a hand, Papa Benjamin pointed to a loudspeaker hidden in the rafter of the cabana. Taine breathed a sigh of relief. He should have guessed that the whole estate would be wired for sound. Waving an arm, he gestured to the door leading to the amphitheater.

A thin bead of sweat trickled between Taine's shoulder blades as he led the way to the outdoor arena. Janet followed close behind, with Papa Benjamin third, and Ape bringing up the rear.

The cool, crisp night air sent chills running up and down his spine. Tight muscles bunched in knots beneath his skin. Hidden in the folds of his cassock, his hands clenched into fists. A man could only stand so much. The events of the past few days had stretched his temper to the limits. His patience was nearly exhausted.

The burden of four lives weighed heavily on his soul. Tim and his mother, Ape Largo and Papa Benjamin, all depended on him for their rescue. Originally, his plans dealt entirely with the destruction of the Black Lodge. Nothing else mattered. Used to working alone, he never worried about his own safety. In the past, he always relied on his own special skills for protection. That all changed when he met Janet Packard.

Taine couldn't help feeling a bit chagrined. Romance complicated everything. Up to this week, he carefully managed to avoid entangling situations. It kept life much simpler. Now, engaged in the most dangerous case of his entire career, he fell in love. So much for timing. *Man plans and God laughs,* he decided wryly.

The amphitheater formed a giant horseshoe, with the open end facing Harmon Sangmeister's mansion. Built to resemble an outdoor concert arena, there were well over two hundred seats built into the concrete. Approximately a third of them were filled tonight. All present wore the monk's robes and white surtouts of the Black Lodge. Taine's group blended in perfectly with the rest.

Carefully avoiding any eye contact with curious Initiates, Taine led his small party up the stairs to the top row of the theater. Here, free from any restraining walls, the night wind swirled wildly. Fortunately for them, no one else dared the cold. They had the upper levels all to themselves. Ignored by the other Lodge brothers, they made their way across the top of the arena until they were directly opposite the stage. Taine motioned for everyone to sit.

The large number of seats in the arena puzzled Taine for a minute. The Lodge never totaled more than a hundred people, yet there was room for nearly triple that number in this stadium. Then he mentally noted that the apparent random seating arrangement favored by most of the members was decidedly not random at all. Only a small handful of Initiates sat next to anyone else. Most of them were isolated from their fellows by one or more empty chairs. Even among their own kind, the brothers of the Black Lodge trusted no one.

Taine shifted his attention to the center of the arena. Filling most of the open end of the amphitheater was a huge raised stage. Five feet high, fifteen feet wide, it extended all the way back to Sangmeister's huge home. A series of recessed lights provided just enough illumination to brightly light the front section of the platform, while leaving the rest of the amphitheater and the back of the stage in semidarkness. In the center of the floor rested a speaker's podium, complete with microphone. At the foot of the lectern, Taine spotted a large silver bowl.

A few feet away from the lectern stood a massive, ten-foot-long, inverted wooden cross. It was secured to the stage at a forty-five degree angle, so that the base of the cross pointed out at the audience like a medieval catapult. Taine shook his head in disgust as he noticed the leather thongs high up on the base as well as on each arm of the transverse bar. All of the necessary ingredients for the Black Mass were present.

Clustered in a semicircle around the base of the structure were a dozen plush hardwood chairs. Eleven of the twelve were occupied. Wearing red instead of black cassocks, these were the Masters of the Lodge. Only Willis Royce was not in attendance.

"Welcome now the Grand Master of the Order of the Mystic Knights of Antioch," came the same voice as before over the loudspeaker. "All rise."

Standing along with everyone else in the arena, Taine drew in a deep breath. After all the waiting, the actual start of the ceremony was almost anticlimactic. He felt sure things would not stay placid very long.

Two robed figures emerged from the darkness cloaking the rear portion of the platform. Dressed in robes the color of purest gold came the Grand Master of the Black Lodge, Harmon Sangmeister. Even the heavy cassock could not hide the millionaire's emaciated condition. His body was so twisted with pain that he walked only with the help of his companion, a tall slender individual wearing the robes of an ordinary Initiate. A muffled groan of pain accompanied his every step. An audible ripple of surprise ran through the arena as the crippled Grand Master made his way forward. Evidently, no one in the crowd realized before the apparent seriousness of Sangmeister's condition.

Finally after several long, agonizing minutes spent shuffling across the floor, the oddly matched pair reached the podium. With a shrug of his head, Sangmeister gestured for the other man to back off. Gaunt, gnarled, trembling hands emerged from the voluminous sleeves of the cassock and gripped the edges of the stand with deathlike intensity.

Slowly, Sangmeister leaned forward until his head nearly touched the stationary microphone. "By all the powers of darkness," came his harsh whisper, "I call this meeting of the Mystic Knights of Antioch to order."

Still buzzing, the audience regained their seats. Even Taine had to admit that the elderly millionaire looked like he was ready to collapse on stage. Perhaps that report on AIDS had not been faked after all.

The reaction from the other Lodge members was not lost on Sangmeister. "Silence!" he whispered defiantly, the microphone amplifying his voice a thousandfold. "I'm not dead yet."

"It won't be long," shouted someone from the stands. Shielded by the darkness, other Lodge members roared their approval.

"Bastards," said Sangmeister weakly, his voice barely audible over the din. "I hope you all rot like me."

With a shake of his head, the Grand Master sent the gold cowl of his cassock tumbling back to his shoulders.

The sight of his hideous features shocked the crowd into silence.

A bleached white skeleton of a man chuckled in mad triumph at the dismay caused by his unveiling. Sangmeister's face, skin taut right to the bone, was a red mask of burst blood vessels and dying flesh. All of his hair was gone. Even his eyebrows were missing. Dark black lines circled his mouth and eyes, emphasizing the hollow emptiness of his sunken features.

"Welcome to my personal hell," he whispered to the startled Lodge members. A thin line of blood dribbled out of the side of his mouth and ran down his chin. Red drops stained gold cloth.

"Remember my delightful smile the next time you screw some cheap slut," he said, laughing insanely at the silent throng. "Or maybe your wife or girlfriend has already infected you. Wouldn't that be a wonderful surprise."

Raising one clawlike hand up to shoulder height, Sangmeister beckoned to his assistant. "Bring forth our reluctant altar girl."

The Initiate disappeared into the darkness at the far end of the stage. He emerged seconds later brutally shoving a naked young woman ahead of him. Savagely, he herded her toward the huge cross. Her cries of despair rang through the arena. "Help me, help me," she begged the crowd desperately, to be greeted only by silence. No one dared help Angel Caldwell.

"Welcome, daughter," said Sangmeister, his monstrous face twisting in a sneer of hate. "Thank you for sharing your charms with our group. Please, mount our Holy of Holies and prepare yourself for our offerings."

Cursing softly, Taine risked a quick look around at his companions. Ape Largo was half out of his seat, ready to charge the stage. Only the restraining touch of Papa Benjamin's hand on his sleeve held him in place. "Not now," said Taine, in a low voice. "Not *yet*."

With a muffled oath, Ape dropped back into his chair. Taine understood the bodyguard's frustration, but it was too early to act.

On his other side, Janet sat stiff and unmoving. He knew there was nothing he could say now that would calm her fears. There was much worse yet to come.

By the time he turned back to the stage, Angel had already been strapped onto the cross. Bound face-first, she was spread-eagle against the rough wood, completely exposed to the Lodge members. Her hands were bound together and pulled high over her head, held tight by a leather thong to the inverted base. Her feet were strapped to the ends of the transverse bar, spreading her legs wide apart. Droplets of sweat glistened on her white skin. Eyes blazing at her tormentors, Angel was silent now, obviously realizing the futility of pleading with her father and his colleagues.

"The altar is prepared," said the Initiate solemnly to Sangmeister.

"Good. The time is right. Let us begin."

"All rise," said the Initiate loudly to the crowd. Many of them were already on their feet, anticipating his announcement. Most of them had participated in these ceremonies before.

Reversing the sign of the cross on his chest, the Initiate solemnly chanted, "Aquerra Goity, Aquerra Beyty."

To which the Lodge brothers responded, "The Goat above, the Goat below."

"In the unholy name of Satan, our Lord and Savior, be seated," commanded Sangmeister.

As they both sat down, Janet nudged Taine. "That's Roger," she whispered, nodding in the general direction of Sangmeister's assistant. "I recognize his voice."

"I suspected as much," replied Taine. All of the players in this grisly drama were present. One of them was Arelim. The final confrontation was about to take place. The Black Mass had begun.

47

O ur Father," recited Harmon Sangmeister in surprisingly strong tones. "Who art in Hell."

The Grand Master paused after every few seconds to let the membership repeat his benediction.

"Cursed be thy Name."

Janet squeezed her eyes shut, blotting out the sight of the obscene ceremony on the stage below. But there was no way she could close her ears to the twisted prayers of Harmon Sangmeister.

"Thy kingdom come. Thy evil will be done. On Earth, as it is . . ."

Without warning, the chanting stopped. Beside her, Taine jerked upright in his seat, caught by surprise by the turn of events. Quickly opening her eyes, she scanned the floor of the arena for the cause of the disturbance. It took only seconds to discover the problem. One of the red-robed Masters of the Lodge was on his feet and shouting something at Sangmeister.

With the man facing away from them, it was hard to make out what he was saying. The wind carried away most of his remarks. But it was abundantly clear from the rage evidenced on Sangmeister's face that he did not take kindly to the other's remarks.

"It's Victor Caldwell," said Taine quietly. "He's challenging Sangmeister's authority to conduct the service. He says Harmon is too weak and sick to serve the Lodge any longer as Grand Master. He wants to be the one who replaces the old man."

"You can't be serious, Victor," said Sangmeister, his voice trembling with anger. Oddly enough, he sounded a bit stronger than before. "I've served the Lodge for nearly twenty-five years. You can't just push me out because I'm getting old. The Order owes me better than that."

Caldwell turned and faced his fellow Lodge brothers. "I've put up with your crap long enough, Sangmeister," he shouted to roars of approval from the crowd. "Either step down voluntarily or submit to Trial By Combat."

"Trial!" screamed a man a few rows down from Janet. Then another, and then another. Soon, the entire Lodge membership had picked up the cry. "Trial, Trial, *Trial!*"

Sangmeister's face flushed bright red, as if shocked by the reaction of the crowd. Trembling, he swung his head back and forth, surveying the arena for some sign of support. He found none. By now most of the membership were back on their feet, shouting their approval of Caldwell's challenge.

"So be it," said Sangmeister softly. "Let those Masters who dispute my rule come forth in judgment."

With a roar of triumph, Victor Caldwell mounted the steps leading to the stage. Behind him came two other red-robed Lodge members. From beneath their robes, all three men pulled ornately carved daggers.

"Ceremonial knives," said Taine. "Normally they are used only in certain magical rituals. But they also come in handy solving arguments."

"Draw your weapon, old man," said Caldwell to Sangmeister. He was close enough to the microphone that it projected his words to the entire arena. "Or die without a fight."

Sangmeister made no move to comply. Instead, he appeared almost complacent as the trio approached. "I've known of your ambition for years, Victor," he said tranquilly. "But I never expected treachery from Nagle or Pierce. How good it is to finally learn the truth."

Janet bit her her lower lip. Somehow, Sangmeister seemed bigger than before. During the past few minutes, his body had fleshed out, gaining both height and weight. The slackness was gone from his features. There was a strength in his voice that had been missing earlier. He looked and sounded years younger.

There was a familiar ring to his voice. Janet cringed, suddenly very afraid. Next to her, Taine nodded to himself, as if in confirmation of her worst nightmare. Huge dark shadows gathered behind Harmon Sangmeister. Shadows that seemed to possess a life of their own.

"Get him," Caldwell yelled to his allies. "Get him, quick!"

All three men rushed forward, slashing wildly with their knives. But they acted a few seconds too late. Without warning, all the lights in the amphitheater went out. The entire arena was plunged into darkness.

On stage, a man shrieked in pain. A wordless, intense scream of pure agony, it rose to shrill heights before coming to an abrupt end. Somehow, though all the lights were out, the microphone was still working.

A low moan of fear swept through the crowd. No one had anticipated this turn of events. Something monstrous was taking place on stage and they could hear every word of it.

"No, please god, *no!*" screamed a different man.

"Too late to call on him," came the reply, in a voice smooth as silk.

Thunk. The amphitheater quivered with the force of the blow. *Thunk. Thunk.*

The audience was in an uproar now. Above it all rose the grisly sound of steady chopping. A deep, powerful laugh filled the night. Terrified, Janet reached out and gripped Taine by the arm. She recognized that voice.

The lights flashed back on as unexpectedly as they had gone out. Even expecting the worse, Janet was shocked by the scene they revealed.

Three smashed and bloody bodies lay in huge pools of blood on the wood floor. The men had been hacked to pieces. Their tattered robes clung to their mangled forms. The entire stage dripped with blood. Splashes of bright red even dotted Angel Caldwell's nude white body. The young woman's eyes were closed, but whether she had fainted or was just frightened beyond belief, Janet couldn't tell.

Janet choked down a scream. A trio of grisly ornaments decorated the lectern. The heads of the three rebels looked out at the audience, their final expressions twisted in mindless, overwhelming horror. Behind them, gripping a butcher's cleaver dripping with gore, stood their intended victim. Chuckling softly, he surveyed his horrified audience.

The Grand Master of the Black Lodge had undergone an incredible transformation. The disease-ridden, elderly man of a few minutes before had disappeared. In his place stood the real Harmon Sangmeister. Still clad in the gold cassock and white surtout of the Order, he was a powerfully built, tall man with hawklike features and burning black eyes. Ageless and evil, he could have been thirty—or a hundred. At his feet, darkness swirled in eddies like some living thing.

Sangmeister's thin gash of a mouth twisted in a grim smile of satisfaction. Shadows clung to him as he spoke.

"Anyone else unhappy with the way I run this organization? I thought not." He laughed. "Remember, dissent is an integral part of our Order. Anyone attending is welcome to disagree with my policies. However," and he laughed again, harshly, "all arguments are resolved through Trial By Combat."

With a flourish, he raised the bloody butcher's cleaver into the night air. "There is only one law. The strong take what they want. Nothing else matters."

Janet turned to Taine. There was no mistaking that voice. Though she had only heard it one time, it would live in her memory forever.

As if sensing her questions, Taine nodded slightly. Keeping his face fixed forward, he leaned his head close to hers. "Poor Victor Caldwell never realized the truth until it killed him. His most powerful ally was actually his worst enemy. Victor and his friends, including Willis Royce, never had a chance. No wonder the Dark Man was so effective in his attacks on the crack market. As Sangmeister's doppleganger, he possessed all of the

Grand Master's memories. He knew every secret of the Children of Danballah."

Taine paused. "Harmon Sangmeister is Arelim. And by all indications, Arelim is the Dark Man reborn. To save Tim, we'll have to defeat that monster again. This time, unfortunately, mirrors won't work."

48

Get this garbage off the stage," said Sangmeister brusquely, waving one hand in the general direction of the three corpses. "The ceremony must continue."

As if waiting for his commands, a half-dozen men came running out from the shadows leading back to the mansion. They worked with smooth, silent efficiency, clearing the stage of bodies while scrubbing the floor clean of blood. Experts at their craft, they had evidently done such work before. Violent death, Janet guessed, was no stranger at these meetings.

"Leave the heads," said Sangmeister. "Let them remain here as reminders of the price of treachery."

Almost fondly, he patted Victor Caldwell's blood-stained forehead. "This traitor deserved to die. He committed the one unforgivable crime of this Lodge. He cheated us.

"Given total control of one of our most important money-making enterprises, the crack cocaine network, Caldwell was still not satisfied. He wanted a larger cut of the action. Working hand in hand with Willis Royce, another traitor to our Order, he cunningly siphoned off large amounts of cash from the take each week. He blamed the continual shortfall on the rapidly declining price of drugs in a boom market. Meanwhile, the two renegades and their silent partners, Nagle and Pierce, deposited millions of dollars of *our* money in numbered

Swiss bank accounts. Now do you understand why I had to act in secret?"

Listening to Sangmeister's explanation, Janet sensed a subtle shift in the temper of the audience. The mood changed, from overwhelming, mindless fear to annoyance and then to anger. Money obsessed these people. They were willing to forgive any excess, any crime, if it paid enough.

"I grew aware of Caldwell's perfidy many months ago. It was obvious from the first that he was working closely with Willis Royce. However, I suspected that other members of the inner council of our Order were involved as well. Determined to expose them all, I decided to create an outside menace threatening the entire drug operation. Thus I called up the Dark Man, the supposed agent of a mythical White Lodge.

"My ruse worked perfectly. Caldwell found himself unable to handle the Dark Man on his own. He turned to me for aid. My feigned weakness drove him to desperate measures. Royce's death compounded his problems. An abject coward, he dared not face me alone, even in my supposed critical condition. He was thus forced to call on his veiled confederates. Tonight, the trap sprung shut. Three traitors perished."

"Great," someone called sarcastically from the audience. "You virtually wiped out the most profitable branch of our activities catching these renegades. What do we do now about the crack market? Abandon it?"

Sangmeister smiled, as if waiting for that question. Janet wondered if perhaps the Grand Master had agents planted in the audience, prompting the crowd just at the right moments. Too many of the happenings tonight seemed the result of cold and calculated orchestration. The more she considered the idea, the more positive she became of its truth. This whole evening was a puppet show run by Sangmeister for his own amusement. All of them present were mere pawns in his demented game.

"The Dark Man destroyed the Children of Danballah," said Sangmeister, "but the drug trade continues to flourish. We can easily recapture what was ours, and even expand into fresh, untapped markets. New addictive drugs are constantly finding their way into the American mainstream. Why should we concentrate solely on crack when we can branch out into crank, a powerful narcotic not dependent on cocaine for its base? Cheap, deadly and easy to make, it is the leader in the coming wave of addictive drugs for the 1990s. The possibilities are staggering. What we need is the will to compete in a cutthroat market and a man with the necessary ruthlessness to eliminate our enemies. I think we have both.''

It sounded like a pep talk for a group of dedicated businessmen looking for investment opportunities. In a way, it was. Only the potential investors were members of the Black Lodge. And the product under consideration was death.

"In the course of my work, I recently encountered a young man possessing all the skill, determination and sheer viciousness to insure our success. Ambitious and utterly without morals, he is the perfect choice to head our new drug operation. His name is Roger Fremont.''

With the hood of his cassock pushed back to reveal his drawn features, Sangmeister's assistant stepped forward. No one in the audience said a word in protest. They seemed willing to go along with anything the Grand Master wished.

If anything, Roger looked worse than the last two times Janet had seen him. She found it inconceivable Sangmeister wanted this burned-out wreck in charge of a multimillion dollar narcotics network.

In his hands he carried the widemouthed silver bowl, retrieved from the side of the podium. Carefully, he placed it directly beneath Angel Caldwell's shapely buttocks. "The altar stands prepared,'' he announced, his voice trembling with anticipation.

"Bring forth the Lamb,'' said Sangmeister.

Janet wanted to scream. Another Initiate came striding out of the darkness into the circle of light on stage. In his arms, he carried an unconscious child dressed entirely in white. Tim. Gently, the man laid the boy across Angel's nude body.

"Steady," said Taine, his hand clutching her as if trying to give her some of his strength. "The time isn't right yet. Trust me. Please. Give him that second chance."

She had no idea what Taine was talking about. All she knew was that her son, her baby, was about to be killed by those maniacs, and there was nothing they could do. Nothing at all. She felt her world crumbling to pieces around her.

"As is the custom, to join the Inner Circle of the Lodge, an Initiate must signal his obedience to the Order by sacrificing that which is most dear to him. Are you willing to drink the blood of your firstborn child, Roger Fremont, to become a Master of this Lodge?"

"Yes," said Roger, without hesitation.

"Then so be it," said Sangmeister.

Trembling with emotion, Roger stepped up to the human altar. From beneath his robe, he pulled a silver dagger. "Aquerra Goity, Aquerra—"

"No!" shouted someone from the audience. A red-robed master dashed up the steps and onto the stage. "You can't do this. I forbid it. I forbid it."

Janet felt her senses reeling. It was her father.

"Sorry, Leo," said Sangmeister, looking anything but. "You know the rules. No one interferes with the sacrifice. The penalties are," and he hesitated, smiling, *"quite severe."*

"Screw the rules," said Leo. He raised a snub-nosed automatic into the air. "I gave the life of one of my children to this damnable Lodge. It was the biggest mistake I ever made. For twenty years, I've suffered for that one insane moment. Now you want the soul of my only grandson. I won't permit it. You can't do this to me again."

Hot tears filled Janet's eyes, blurring her vision for a second. She remembered a cryptic conversation between her father and Taine from the night before. Now she understood the significance of those remarks about sin and redemption. Taine had known the truth about Leo all along. Her father was the one who deserved that second chance.

"I thought you knew better, Leo," said Sangmeister, shaking his head in mock despair. "My warding spells protect me from bullets."

"They shield you," replied Leo, nodding his head in agreement. He turned and pointed his gun at Roger. "But not that scum."

Serenely, he squeezed the trigger. The gun in his hand barked once, then again. Roger's mouth dropped open in a look of incredible surprise. Two small black holes appeared side by side in the center of his forehead. The silver dagger dropped from his lifeless hand. Without a word, he slumped to the floor, dead.

"A life for a life, Leo," said Sangmeister, stepping from behind the altar. The butcher's cleaver gleamed brightly in the footlights.

"I realized that," said Leo, letting go of the gun. "No reason anymore to sacrifice the child, though."

Sangmeister shrugged, as if in agreement. He raised his blade for the killing blow. But before he could strike, Leo collapsed in a crumpled heap at his feet.

Bending over, Sangmeister examined the motionless figure. "Poison," he announced, with a grim chuckle of amusement as he stood up. "Even in the end, he refused to play by the rules. Of all those who opposed me, he was the only one with real style."

With a wave of his hand, Sangmeister summoned his help. "Clear these bodies off the floor. This place is starting to resemble the last act of *Hamlet*. Remove the child also. I owe the old man that much. After all, the boy served me well. His presence forced Packard into his confrontation. He's been a thorn in my side for years. No more. I alone rule this Lodge. And once again we are at peace among ourselves."

"Not yet," came the sharp retort from right next to Janet. Taine was on his feet, his grim features exposed to the night winds. "By the rules of this Order, I claim the right of Trial By Combat."

"Mr. Taine," said Sangmeister, pleasantly. "How nice of you to show up. I was hoping you would attend our meeting. And I see you brought your friends with you. Wonderful."

Sangmeister paused, as if lost in thought. "I am at a loss regarding your demands, however. Are you a member of the Black Lodge?"

"I don't have to be. You said it yourself only a few minutes ago. Remember? The rules of the Order are quite explicit on that topic. Anyone attending the ceremony is welcome to disagree with you. *Anyone.*"

Frowning, Sangmeister reluctantly nodded in agreement. "You seem to know quite a bit about our Lodge. Too much, in my opinion. In any case, I accept your argument. Who do you wish to challenge? One of the Initiates, perhaps even one of the few remaining Masters?"

"None of them," said Taine. Raising one hand, he pointed a finger directly at the Grand Master. "You hold the only true position of power in this Order, Sangmeister. That's what I want. I challenge you to Trial By Combat for control of the Black Lodge."

49

By the time they reached the stage, Sangmeister had regained control of his temper. For a few seconds after hearing Taine's purpose, the Grand Master appeared ready to explode. Rage contorted his features as they turned a deep shade of crimson. Obviously he had been caught off guard.

Now, however, he was in complete command of his faculties. A sardonic smile crossed his face as they lined up before him. "We finally meet. What a pleasure it is to be face-to-face with my most troublesome foes."

Sarcasm laced every word. "Here you all are, the New Age detective and his faithful friends—four fools looking for death."

Taine shuddered. More and more, the Grand Master was taking on the shape and characteristics of his supernatural double. The old man seemed to grow taller, more massive, with each parting second. Black shadows swirled about, cloaking him in darkness. He spoke in smooth, honey-sweet tones not his own. Without any conscious thought or effort, Sangmeister was transforming into the Dark Man.

"You're being overwhelmed, Sangmeister," said Taine, knowing he was wasting his breath. Still, he wanted to give the old man one last chance. "Your creation is taking you over, body and soul. Soon nothing human will remain—only darkness."

Sangmeister laughed harshly. "Stop whining, Taine. You don't understand what is taking place. I'm in complete control of the situation. *I initiated the change.* Soon all of the powers of the Dark Man will be mine. Already I can feel his strength flowing in my veins. He doesn't require much. A few more blood sacrifices should complete the process. Then Harmon Sangmeister and the Dark Man will cease to exist as separate entities. Instead, there will be only one—Arelim."

"You are the fool, not us," said Papa Benjamin unexpectedly. The voodoo priest's voice rang clear and true as a bell in the night air. "Hiding behind a new name will not save you from the fires of Hell."

"Yeah," added Ape Largo. "You can call a pile of shit a rose, but it still smells like shit. Just like you, buddy."

"How poetic," replied Sangmeister. He sneered at Ape. "It will be a pleasure chopping you to pieces, Mr. Largo. I'll try to make the pain last a long time."

Smiling, he took a giant step closer. He raised the blood-stained cleaver. "Why you threw your life away I'll never understand. You actually escaped the Dark Man. You cheated certain death. Yet you came here tonight, risking your life for people you hardly know. It makes no sense."

"Altruism means nothing to a self-centered maniac like you, Sangmeister," said Taine, measuring his words carefully. "Ape wants to know his place in the universe. He's a man searching for his destiny."

Sangmeister stopped short, as if unexpectedly hit in the face. "What do you mean by that?" he asked, his voice no longer so confident.

"Exactly what I said," replied Taine. The Grand Master looked stricken. "The Wheel of Fortune stands for Ape Largo, a man seeking his destiny.

"Pope Joan is Janet Packard, the mysterious woman.

"The Hermit represents Papa Benjamin, whose hidden wisdom matches your own."

"One person left," said Sangmeister, shifting back toward the lectern. The Lodge Master's voice trembled with fear. "What card do you represent, Taine?"

"The thirteenth trump, of course," he answered with a nod. "La Mort, the skeleton."

"Death," whispered Sangmeister. His features were the color of cold ashes. "Who are you, Sidney Taine?"

"I revealed the truth to Victor Caldwell," answered Taine. "Not that it mattered very much. He immediately jumped to the wrong conclusion. You've known all along who I represent, Sangmeister. Does it really matter?"

The Grand Master shook his head in bewilderment. "I don't know what the hell you mean," he said angrily. "Nor do I care."

Desperately, he swung the butcher's cleaver up over his head. "The solution to all my problems rests in this blade."

On his right, Taine saw Ape Largo clench his huge hands into fists. The big man intended to die fighting. Next to the bodyguard was Papa Benjamin. The little priest stood straight and unafraid, his arms folded across his chest.

Janet was on his left, her shaking hands clutching his

arm for support. She obviously expected to die in the next few seconds. Yet she remained by his side.

Their strength, their courage, their love enabled him to reach the necessary state of grace. "Four words of power gave your creation unnatural life," said Taine loudly. The microphone on the podium sent his words hurtling out into the crowd. As if sensing something terribly wrong, they began to rise. "It ends with one other."

"*No-o-o!*" shouted Sangmeister, leaping forward to hack and tear. He never reached them. Calmly, deliberately, Taine correctly pronounced the tetragrammaton, the true name of God. "*YHVH.*"

50

In a single heartbeat . . .

Janet's sense of identity exploded in an exponential curve that defied all limits. She was one, then a hundred, then a thousand, then a million, then a billion, then all mankind. Then, all life, human or otherwise. Her personality fragmented into trillions of pieces, experiencing life in every possible stage of existence, from the barest spark of self-awareness to the most complex organisms on Earth. And everywhere, she found love to be the universal principle that governed all things.

In a true state of grace, Janet beheld the Divinity of Life itself. By inscribing his name on the cosmos, God endowed each and every living being some small part of the Creator's will. Everything in the universe was a piece of a gigantic pattern whose ultimate purpose was beyond human understanding.

To Janet, gazing upon the ever-increasing depths of the landscape of Creation, it was a confirmation and renewal of her love for her son, her family, her friends. She perceived the complexity and unity of all life. For one sublime moment, she experienced the totality of the physical universe and God's supreme presence.

. . . it came to an end.

Taine was shaking her gently by the shoulder. "Are you all right?" he asked.

"I've never felt better in all my life," she replied. Still glowing from her one moment of spiritual lucidity, she looked up at Taine. "You've experienced this before?"

"Only once," he said, with a smile. "Unfortunately, the effect wears off quickly. Humanity isn't ready yet for a perpetual state of grace."

"I saw love," said Janet.

"Brotherhood," said Taine, simply.

Ape Largo, a look of awe on his face, came up to them. "I'm taking Mrs. Caldwell off that cross." He glanced over his shoulder at a motionless Harmon Sangmeister. The Grand Master appeared frozen in his tracks. "He ain't gonna be objecting to what we do, anymore. Nor is anybody else. Whatever you did, Taine, it sure put this crowd on ice."

Janet looked around the amphitheater. Except for the four of them on stage, no one else was moving. All of the Lodge members were sprawled in their seats, unconscious or dead. Janet wasn't sure which. Nor did she care.

"What did you see, Ape?" she asked, curiously.

"Truth," he replied. "Peace. Forgiveness. During that one instant, I experienced the sufferings of a million others. The pain they felt burned out the bitterness in my soul. Through that, I realized the insignificance of my own physical limitations. The only limits on my success were ones of my own making."

He grinned. "No more diminished expectations for me. I'm gonna be the best damned houn'gan imaginable. Excluding Papa Benjamin that is."

"Of course," said the voodoo priest, solemnly. "As should always be the case between teacher and student."

Then he, too, smiled. "Affirmation. I spent most of my life teaching that all life is one in the glory of God.

I must admit it was refreshing to finally experience the revelations I preached.

"I can die happy now." He laughed when he saw the shocked look on Ape's face. "Not that I intend to do so for another twenty years or more. Life still holds too many pleasures for me to abandon it so early."

Turning to Janet, his features grew stern. "I kept my word, did I not? Your son survived this madness. Perhaps next time you will have more faith in your friends."

Janet saw no reason to mention that Taine had done most of their rescuing. Besides, she wasn't exactly sure whose power had saved them all. Or how.

"I apologize," she said, trying to sound properly humble.

"Good," said Papa Benjamin. "Now, should we not try to find your little boy? He must be somewhere inside the mansion."

It took the two of them fifteen minutes to find Tim asleep in a bedroom on the second floor of the huge building. Tears of relief trickled down Janet's cheeks as she knelt down and gently hugged him. Tim stirred but did not waken.

"He is in a light trance," said Papa Benjamin. "I use much the same technique in many of my own ceremonies. There is no cause to worry. I will take care of his recovery. Tomorrow he will awaken without any memory of what happened during the past twenty-four hours. Go now. I need to be alone with him for a little while for the spell to work."

Reluctantly, Janet departed. She wanted to be with her son, but there was no arguing with Papa Benjamin. And Tim's safety and well-being came first.

She returned to the stage to find Taine examining Harmon Sangmeister. The big detective was gently trying to pry open Sangmeister's fingers gripping the butcher's cleaver.

"What happened to him?" she asked, shuddering.

The Grand Master was still alive. His chest rose and fell with his steady breathing. Physically, he looked exactly the same as before. All except his eyes. There was no sign of intelligence in his gaze. Dead, empty pupils stared out into infinity.

"The tetragrammaton affects each individual in a different manner. Basically good people, such as the four of us, merged with the positive aspect of God's name. Though all of our experiences were unique, they all reflected the wonder and joy of the Divine Presence."

"That didn't happen with Sangmeister," said Janet, reaching for the truth. "Nor the rest of the Black Lodge."

"Their minds combined with the *negative* aspects of God's will," said Taine. "For that one instant, they experienced all of the despair and hatred in our world. A thousand lifetimes of lust and degradation flooded their minds. The more innocent ones collapsed immediately. They were the lucky ones.

"Others, like Sangmeister, absorbed the full impact of that anguish. No man living could endure that torment. A few are dead. Most of the rest went insane. Ape is going through the audience now, trying to get some sort of casualty count."

Cautiously, Janet touched Sangmeister's arm. It felt hard as steel. Muscles stretched to the breaking point, he was frozen in place.

"Linked by the Dark Man to the outer darkness, Sangmeister suffered through the tortures of the damned. I feel sorry for him. He lived through agonies a million times greater than any he inflicted. It destroyed his intellect. Physically, he's still alive. But his mind is gone, wiped clean."

"You can feel sorry for that son-of-a-bitch," said Janet, "but I can't. He got what he deserved."

"Being Grand Master of the Black Lodge wasn't enough for him. He wanted complete control over the organization and its lucrative drug operation. So he came up with a complicated plan to eliminate all of his rivals in the Order. You and Tim and even Roger were merely pawns he used to strike at your father. Just as he tried using Angel to upset Victor Caldwell. That failed because that fat slug didn't give a damn about his wife."

"How is Angel?" asked Janet, suddenly aware the woman was nowhere to be seen.

"Ape helped her into the house. Being tied to the cross that way exhausted her. She passed out well before the gruesome stuff started. After a few days rest, she'll be fine."

"And with her father and husband both dead, a very rich lady as well." Janet latched onto one of Taine's arms. "You stay away from her. I didn't suffer through all this to lose you to that blonde."

Taine laughed but made no effort to pull free. She took that to mean he agreed with her assessment of the situation. Then the full import of her words sunk in.

"It never occurred to me, but with Leo dead, I stand to inherit quite a bundle as well."

Thinking about her father brought tears to her eyes. She looked up at Taine. "He saved Tim's life."

"At the cost of his own," said Taine. "I think Leo considered it a fair bargain. You should remember him for that, not for a terrible mistake he made twenty years ago."

Janet nodded. "If sin exists, then so must redemption," she said, echoing his words of the night before.

"Otherwise only evil triumphs," he concluded, somberly. "And that happens all too often."

Taine gently separated his arm from hers. "No more romance till we get home. We should be leaving."

"It all worked out in the end," said Janet. "Just like you said it would. All we have to do is call the police after we're gone. There's nothing here to link us with this place."

"Victor Caldwell bragged that even death could not destroy the Black Lodge. Whenever one Master perished, another rose from their ranks to take his place. He was right. However, he conveniently ignored one equally important fact.

"The Lodge exists only through absolute secrecy. Destroy that and the Order disintegrates. Once the newspapers get a hold of this story, think of the scandal. The wealthiest and most powerful men in Chicago linked with a satanic cult. Publicity will destroy the Black Lodge. Whatever records Sangmeister kept will serve as nails in its coffin.

"We'll make an anonymous call to the two detectives who are after Ape. They sound pretty sharp. It won't take them long to link the order with the Dark Man's murder spree. Especially when they find Sangmeister standing there clutching a blood-stained butcher's cleaver. That will clear Ape's name as well as provide a solid explanation for the killings."

"How will they untangle what happened here tonight?" she asked.

"Who knows? Who cares?"

"Sangmeister thought of himself as the master schemer," she said quietly. "He manipulated people like pawns. You said it yourself. This all took place because of his mad lust for complete control of the Lodge. Yet you outguessed him at every turn. Who are you, Sidney Taine?"

"Yeah, I was wondering that, too," said Ape Largo, coming up silently behind them. "I thought Sangmeister was gonna have a stroke when you started talking about the tarot cards. What's your secret?"

Taine grinned. "I can't argue with such persistence. In his office, I revealed to Victor Caldwell that I belonged to an organization concerned about the future of the Black Lodge. He immediately leapt to the conclusion that I came from another group of black magicians. I saw no reason to correct his mistake."

"Then a White Lodge exists as well?" asked Janet.

"Of course. I was given the long-term mission of infiltrating and destroying this order. Coincidence and luck thrust me into the center of things long before I expected. In the end, it worked out fine. My job here is finished."

"Now what?" asked Janet, with a sinking feeling deep inside.

"I go back to being a detective full-time," he replied.

"Maybe I'll even settle down and get married. If the right young woman agrees."

"I think she will," said Janet and threw her arms around his neck.

"Hey, cut it out," said Ape after a few seconds. "Don't you guys have any shame? You can do that stuff when you're alone."

He waved an arm in the general direction of the still senseless audience. "What are we gonna do about these jerks?"

"The police will take care of them," said Taine. "Let's find Papa Benjamin, Tim and Angel and get going."

"I guess we won," said Ape as they walked back to the mansion.

"Just a skirmish," said Taine. "The war continues. But for now, for here, the Black Lodge has met for the last time."